WISCONSIN
Brides

Three Old–Fashioned Love Stories

from the Great Northwood

JILL STENGL

BARBOUR
PUBLISHING

Time for a Miracle © 1999 by Jill Stengl
Myles from Anywhere © 2001 by Jill Stengl
Lonely in Longtree © 2007 by Jill Stengl

ISBN 978-1-59789-991-8

Published by Barbour Publishing, Inc., P.O. Box 719, Uhrichsville, Ohio 44683, www.barbourbooks.com

Our mission is to publish and distribute inspirational products offering exceptional value and biblical encouragement to the masses.

 Member of the
Evangelical Christian
Publishers Association

Printed in the United States of America.

Award-winning author Jill Stengl lives in a log home beside a lake in northern Wisconsin with her husband, Dean, two of their four children (the other two are grown), and three very spoiled cats. Along with writing and reading, Jill enjoys singing with her church's worship team, home schooling her youngest son, quilting, and scrapbooking. She thoroughly enjoyed researching nineteenth-century Wisconsin for these books—and there is so much yet to discover!

You're welcome to contact Jill at jpopcorn@charter.net.

Time for a Miracle

Dedication

With love to my second set of parents, Dick and Donajean Stengl.
Your love and support for me are one of God's special gifts.
Thanks for raising such a wonderful son, too!

Thank you to Paula Pruden-Macha, Virginia Macha,
and Peggy Arensmeyer for your criticisms and great advice.
I couldn't have written this book without you,
my dear friends. God is very good.

Prologue

Wisconsin, 1880

Wind soughed through pine boughs and clattered through oak branches. Although the predawn sky was clear and starry, snow flurried, blown from scattered drifts. A lone horse and rider slogged along a path beneath the trees. Massive shoulders hunched against the cold, hat pulled over his ears, the man repeatedly glanced backward. His horse jerked its head and jigged.

With a yank on the reins, the man grumbled aloud, "Things was going so good. Now I'm back to running, always running. It ain't a fittin' life for a decent man. I never hurt nobody. I don't deserve this."

Tensing, he reined in his horse, but the sound of hoofbeats continued. Panicked, he dug in his heels, but the gelding refused to give him even a short burst of speed. Dropping its head, it took the bit between its teeth and settled into a jolting trot. The large rider berated it in obscene terms; the horse only pinned back its ears.

A cry drifted between the trees, "Hey, wait!"

Instead of pausing, the rider removed his hat and began slapping his mount's hindquarters. The horse hunched its back and threatened to buck.

Out of the shadows behind appeared a horse and rider. The stranger's horse whinnied a greeting as it slowed to a walk, and the obstinate gelding answered cheerily.

"Where are you off to at this hour, Fairfield? Why use this old Indian trail when there are good roads aplenty? A person would think you were trying to hide. . .or escape."

Recognizing the jocular voice, the first rider sighed in relief. "Don't scare me like that! I thought nobody else knew about this trail."

"So, where are you going?" The newcomer reined his horse alongside.

"Far away as I can get. It's a long story."

"You're surely not leaving town for good?" Sarcasm tinted the query.

"There's nothing else I can do. Say, Nick, would you meet someone for me at the train today?"

"Let me guess—Mrs. Fairfield."

"How'd you know? She's the whole problem. . .or most of it."

"I should think a lonely husband would be happy to see his little woman

7

after all these years of solitary bachelorhood. Is she a hag or only a nag?" Derision fairly dripped from Nick's words.

The runaway swore roundly. "None of your business. Just meet her for me, would you? Tell her. . .tell her I was called away on business. Tell her it was a case of mistaken identity—I'm the wrong Jerry Fairfield. It could happen."

"Sorry, but I'm not interested, Charles."

The fat man blanched and hauled his horse to a stop. "What did you say?"

"I know who you are, Charles Rufus Bolton."

"How do you. . . ? Who are you?"

"Don't know me, do you? I didn't know you either at first, but time narrowed the possibilities. Who but you would be stupid enough to build a luxurious mansion in the middle of nowhere? Think, Charles. Who would have reason to track you all over the country these twenty years?"

"Patrick," Charles whispered, aghast.

Chapter 1

How much more shall your Father which is in heaven
give good things to them that ask him?
MATTHEW 7:11

Picking his teeth with a clean straw, Obadiah Watson leaned against the doorframe of the blacksmith's shop and watched the outside world. There was little to be seen in the sleepy town: a wagon full of children waiting before the dry goods store, two horses tethered in front of the saloon having a squealing disagreement, a pair of elderly ladies intent upon the latest gossip, a few other men lounging in doorways. Sheriff Martin sat before his office, cleaning his rifle, his chair balanced precariously on two legs. Spotting Obie, he nodded and waved.

Behind Obie, inside the smithy, a cross-looking paint mustang stood on three legs while the burly smith rasped his left hind hoof and fitted the second of his four shoes. Tossing his head, the horse cast resentful glances at Obie, first with a blue eye, then with a brown eye.

Obie ignored his horse's indignation. "Snow's melting off quick," he observed. "Spring's here to stay, I think." Tossing the straw down, he took off his woolen jacket and laid it over a stall door, then stretched his arms over his head and swung them around to work out the kinks. Suspenders strapped his baggy shirt against his body, and dungarees tucked into his high boots at the knee.

The dour blacksmith countered, "Never depend on an early spring. Almanac predicts more snow."

A high-pitched voice drifted from across the street. "Hey, Uncle Obie!"

The children in the wagon had spotted him. Obie sauntered across the empty street to chat. "Howdy, Amos. Howdy, Benny. Good mornin', Fern. How's the little un today?" He touched Baby Daniel's dimpled arm.

Fern shifted the baby higher on her skinny knee and answered in a lofty imitation of her mother, "Well enough. He's cuttin' teeth and drools like anything."

Daniel grinned at Obie and proved his sister correct. His chubby chins glistened in the sunlight.

"He's a cheerful chap, that's certain."

"Uncle Obie, you gotta hear what I caught last Friday: two crappies, a smallmouth bass, and a trout! I cleaned 'em just the way you showed me, and Ma cooked 'em up fer us. She says I'm an expert," Amos boasted.

"Amos, Ma says you're not to call Mr. Watson 'uncle.' He's no real relation," Bennie reminded his big brother.

"Everybody calls 'im that. It don't mean nothin'." Amos shrugged off the caution.

"You'd best obey your ma." Obie's smile faded. "I don't mind what you call me as long as we're pals."

"You'd best get on afore Ma sees us talkin' with you," Fern whispered. "Pa says we can talk to you, but Ma doesn't like it, and she makes a fuss."

A shadow crossed Obie's face; then he briskly slapped the wagon's side and backed away. "Right. You take care now. I'll see ya at the fishin' hole, Amos. You're a fine baby watcher, Miss Fern. Good morning."

When he returned, the smith was still laboring over the same hoof. Obie avoided his horse's accusing gaze. "Hiram, I'll be at the sheriff's if you need me."

"Go on ahead," Hiram huffed, glancing over one sweaty shoulder. "Jughead's always good for me. Aren't you, boy?" The mustang swung his head around and gave the blacksmith a sour look. "He'll be here waitin' for ya."

When Obie approached, Sheriff Boz Martin set his chair legs down and collected his gun and cleaning rags. "C'mon in for coffee. How you been?"

"Well enough. We got a heifer calf yesterday morning and another due anytime. How's things with you?" Obie accepted a cup of Martin's thick, noxious brew and took a chair.

Boz lowered his considerable bulk into his armchair and sighed, sounding something like a deflating bagpipe. "Slow, mighty slow. Don't know why I took this here job, anyway. Things are popping out West, and here we sit, rubbin' elbows with sodbusters." He spat toward the brass cuspidor in the corner.

"Sorry you feel that way, Boz. Don't let me hold you back if you're wanting to leave. I'm a sodbuster now, and I like it fine. My wranglin' days are past. Feel like settling in hereabouts and putting down roots. Clearing my name just doesn't seem so important anymore. I have friends here who value me for who I am, not for what I've been. That's what counts most."

Boz chuckled. "Find a little woman to feather your nest?"

Obie looked sheepish. "Not yet, but I'm lookin'."

"Best not be too particular, at your age." Boz gulped his coffee and wiped his drooping moustache on his sleeve. This moustache was the sheriff's pride—the waxed ends curled far below his jowls, and the thickness of it obscured his mouth.

Obie thoughtfully stroked his own modest moustache with one finger. "If God wants me to marry, He'll send the right woman. There must be one somewhere who'll overlook my past."

Boz gave a derisive sniff. "As though God has answered any of your prayers. You sure are slow on the uptake. Haven't you figgered out by now that He just ain't interested in over-the-hill cowpokes like us? If there even is a God, which you couldn't prove by me."

"You ready to give up our search, Boz?" Obie's gray eyes were sober, but held no blame.

"Wish I had the guts to tell you 'yes,' but I jist cain't let an ol' pard down. I'll stay on as long as you think there's hope."

"God does answer prayer. Sometimes His answer is 'wait.' I have a feeling that my waiting time is nearly over. Can't tell you why I feel that way, but I do. Maybe while God is handing blessings my way, He'll throw in a good woman and some little ones. You never know."

Boz snorted.

Obie sipped at his coffee and wondered whether his throat and stomach retained their linings—Boz's coffee made arsenic seem like a soothing balm.

A train whistle brought his eyes up to the wall clock. The train was late again.

"Gonna meet the train?"

"Might. Have nothing better to do. You coming?"

"You go on. I got paperwork to sort out."

"Thanks for the coffee." He left the cup half full.

Obie ambled toward the station, his boots squishing through mud in the road, then clopping on the boardwalks. Lifting his hat, he rubbed at his short, thinning hair, enjoying the breeze against his scalp. On a day like this, how could a man doubt the goodness of the Lord, let alone doubt His existence?

He smiled at everyone in passing. Some people returned his smile; others ignored him or gave him chilly stares. He was used to the mixed bag of reactions.

The train had already pulled in and lay waiting, spurting steam at odd intervals. On the platform, Obie purchased a *Longtree Enquirer* from a youthful hawker, tucked the paper under his arm, and leaned against a post. As he watched people climb into and out of the passenger cars, his impassive face hid a multitude of thoughts and dreams. He watched a reunited family exchanging hugs amid joyous laughter and a pair of lovers clinging together after a long separation. His moustache twitched, and a flicker of envy touched his soul.

Lord, I know that You need single men in your service, but I grow weary of working alone for You. I ask only for someone to love—someone who will love me in return. Other men find wives; why can't I?

His sad eyes scanned the female faces in the crowd. There were sweet faces, cross faces, attractive faces, homely faces, old or young faces—not one face that captured him, not one face that—

He froze. Not five feet away she stood. Her silvery blue eyes knocked him for a loop—yet it was not their beauty alone that stunned him. He felt as though he knew her, and she also seemed to recognize him.

She smiled slightly before looking away. She was searching for someone in the crowd. Evidently his had not been the face she sought. He swallowed hard and blinked.

She was the loveliest woman he had ever beheld. Clad in a blue plaid traveling suit and a plumed hat, dark hair modestly coiled at the nape of her neck, she held a bandbox in one hand and a reticule in the other. She was not slender, but neither was she plump. In Obie's opinion, her shape and size were perfect. She was not too young; he judged her age at midthirties.

Lord. . . ? but he dared not complete the question even in his thoughts. Could this woman be the immediate answer to his prayer?

Then he realized that she was not alone. A young boy and two tall girls had descended the steps behind her and now clustered near her skirts. They, too, searched the station, but did not seem to find the face they expected to see.

Though not a soul could have guessed his thoughts, Obie Watson felt his face burn. He tipped his hat down and tried to look bored. Of course, such a prize would have been snapped up long ago. Not only was she married, but she also possessed three fine children. Their father must be the happiest and proudest of men.

The family looked worried. Irritation wrinkled the lady's brow, but she sounded resigned. "It looks as though he is late, my dears. We must wait inside the station for him."

"Mama, I'm so tired," the younger of the girls complained.

"We're all tired, Eunice."

"I bet he'll never come," the older girl stated sharply. She was taller than her mother, with olive skin and great dark eyes. "I bet it was just a cruel trick."

"Beulah, that will be enough," the mother said firmly, and the girl closed her lips.

The little boy looked pale and sad, but he manfully picked up his valise and walked behind the others into the station. Since Obie could not follow them inside without being obvious, he returned to the smithy with a heavy heart.

Lord, I know You don't play cruel jokes, so what is Your purpose here? I ask for a wife and You show me the woman of my dreams. . .but she's already married. Does this mean that I should give up my dream of a woman's love? If this is Your will, Lord, I will accept it. . .under protest.

Jughead waited at the smithy's hitching rail. At sight of Obie, he nickered with fluttering nostrils. "Howdy, ol' pard." Obie rubbed the mustang's forehead, mussing his long forelock. Then he entered the shop to pay for Hiram's service.

Minutes later, the paint trotted along the road with Obie lounging in the saddle. The horse started heading toward home, but Obie directed him to the train station. Jughead argued for a moment, then gave in with a testy snort.

Obie tethered Jughead to the rail and hurried inside. Surely the tardy husband had collected his family by now, but he would check, just in case. To his surprise and undeniable pleasure, the family still occupied the row of benches near the ticket window. He was nearly on top of them when he entered the tiny room. The ladies had been nodding off, but all three popped awake at his sudden appearance. The boy slept with his head in his mother's lap.

Obie sucked in an audible breath. Blue Eyes was even more exquisite from close range.

Three pairs of eyes regarded him expectantly, and he realized that he needed to say something. . .anything. He opened his mouth, but nothing came out. Stopping to clear his throat, he hauled off his hat and said, "I was wondering if you were still here."

The lady blinked. Her lips parted, but she seemed at a loss for words.

"I mean, I wondered if you might need help. Who's supposed to pick you up?"

"I am Violet Fairfield. Do you know my husband, Jeremiah Fairfield?" An odd intensity colored the question.

Obie barely kept his jaw from dropping. This charming family belonged to Jerry Fairfield? Jerry had never given any indication, any hint that he possessed a wife and family. *Lord, tell me it isn't true!*

She was waiting for an answer. Obie nodded, unable to speak.

Her voice sounded choked. "You do?"

"He owns the farm next to mine."

"I see." He saw her lower lip quiver. A desire to punch Fairfield on his flabby jaw flashed through Obie's mind. What had the man done to deserve a wife like this?

"We thought Father was dead, but we learned just two weeks ago that he's alive," the younger girl proclaimed.

"Eunice, hush!"

Mrs. Fairfield turned back to Obie with a touch of color in her pale cheeks.

Just then another man stepped into the station, started with surprise, and cried, "Aren't you Violet Fairfield?"

"Yes, sir, how did you—?"

He nearly pulled her off the seat with the vigor of his handshake, waking the little boy. "What an unexpected surprise! Jerry asked me to come pick up a package for him today; I had no idea he meant you. What a jokester!"

"Excuse me, sir—" she began, but he interrupted.

"Pardon me, I'm Nicholas Houghton, your husband's friend." He gave Obie a glance. "Move on, pal, you aren't need—" Then he did a double take, and a look of startled guilt flashed across his features. Instantly he broke into a broad smile and proclaimed, "Thanks for trying to help, Watson. I can take it from here." Turning back to Violet, he blocked Obie's view of her with his broad shoulders.

Obie sidled to one side, feeling shorter than ever. He recognized Houghton as a handsome rogue who drifted in and out of local towns, working at various jobs and keeping the saloons in business.

Violet looked bewildered. "But where is Jeremiah?"

"He only told me that he had to go out of town. It must have been important for him to miss meeting you, Mrs. Fairfield. Jerry is one lucky man!" He laughed, showing straight white teeth that contrasted handsomely with his thick side-whiskers.

Violet Fairfield's reply was chilly. "I'm sure we are pleased to meet you." She squirmed her hand out of his grip and placed both hands behind her back. "These are my children, Beulah, Eunice, and Samuel."

Since the introduction seemed to be directed toward both men, Obie smiled at the children. Samuel caught his eye, hesitated, and smiled timidly. Eunice nodded, flashing a hint of a dimple. Beulah closed her eyes and leaned against the wall.

Mr. Houghton barely acknowledged the children. "Fine family. Since Jerry wasn't sure how late he'd be, it'd be best for you to stay overnight in town. I recommend Amelia Sidwell's boardinghouse as the finest in Longtree; I've stayed there myself on occasion. Leave your luggage, please; I'll have it delivered for you. This way, ladies, and. . .boy."

Mrs. Fairfield sent Obie an entreating look. "Is this boardinghouse one *you* would recommend?"

Houghton took the lady's elbow as if affronted. "Madam, do you not trust my advice?"

"I seek only his corroboration," she said firmly, jerking her arm out of his grasp.

"You'll be comfortable at Amelia's," Obie affirmed quietly. "I'll check on you later." Though he spoke to Mrs. Fairfield, the words carried a hint of warning to Houghton.

The tall man glowered. "This way, Mrs. Fairfield," he said stiffly. "I have a hired rig out front." She laid her gloved hand on his offered arm, but cast one last glance at Obie before exiting the room.

The children followed reluctantly. "Good-bye," Eunice said. "Hope to see you again soon."

Obie returned her wave and a moment later was alone in the station. He slowly sat on the bench and leaned against the wall. Fairfield luggage surrounded his feet.

Had Jerry Fairfield deserted his family, leaving them to believe him dead? If so, the man was a bigger fool than Obie had thought.

"Hey, cowboy!"

Obie looked up. The ticket master stood in the doorway, fists on hips. "That fancy fellow told me to have all this baggage delivered to Amelia's. What does he think this is, the post office? You can turn a penny if you'll deliver it for me. Team and wagon are in the stable beside the station."

Obie accepted the job, though he had no need of money. While it wouldn't be wise to dream about Violet Fairfield, there was nothing wrong with helping a woman in need. Until Jerry arrived to take over his responsibility, Obie determined to help the Fairfield family as he believed Jesus would under the same circumstances.

Houghton's hired surrey still waited in front of Amelia Sidwell's white-washed clapboard house when Obie arrived. He tethered the ticket master's team and began to unload luggage. Holding a bundle under each arm and a valise in each hand, he strode up the flower-bordered walkway. The front door opened magically before him, and Eunice peeked around it. "Hello!"

"Where shall I take them?" he asked, returning her smile. She was a rather plump girl, but her smile was pure sunshine.

"I'll show you. Mr. Houghton is still talking with Mama in the parlor." She led the way upstairs and opened the first door on the left. "Right in here, sir."

Beulah perched on the guest room window seat, resting her chin on one fist and staring blankly down at the flower garden beneath her window. She gave Obie a solemn nod and turned back to the window. Samuel was asleep on the biggest bed. His thin cheeks looked too pale. Obie placed the bags on the floor and sneaked out of the room. He heard no voices from the parlor although the door stood slightly ajar.

His arms loaded again, this time with a satchel, a heavy leather grip, and two hatboxes, he shoved the front door open with his foot. A deep voice stopped him in the entryway.

"Obadiah Watson, what are you doing, carryin' bags into my house?" Amelia Sidwell looked like someone's maiden aunt, all sharp angles and flat planes, and her voice could easily have belonged to a man.

"Delivering luggage," he explained, feeling sheepish. Amelia was a good sort of woman, but she invariably triggered his "flight instinct." He sidled toward the stairway.

"That Fairfield woman ain't been in town one hour, and she's already got men fallin' over themselves to he'p her out. It figures!" Amelia chuckled. "You ain't never set foot in my house afore, and look at you now! Fool man. The woman's married, you know."

Obie made his escape, and thankfully Amelia had vanished when he returned downstairs. After a third load of bags, he brought in the massive trunk. Judging by the volume of luggage, the Fairfield family intended to stay indefinitely.

Eunice met him at the door again. "Are you sure your mother wants this upstairs?" he panted, setting the brassbound trunk on the entryway rug. "You'll likely be moving to your house as soon as your father returns to town."

Eunice looked uncertain. "Shall I ask her?"

The parlor door flew open. Violet rushed out and nearly collided with Obie. "Pardon me—oh, it's you!" Relief swept over her face. She stepped quickly around him, clutching at his sleeve. "Did...did you deliver our things? I didn't realize that you worked for the railroad..." She glanced apprehensively over Obie's shoulder as Houghton appeared in the parlor doorway.

Obie straightened to his full height, at least a head shorter than

Houghton's. "I don't, ma'am, but they asked me to deliver your things. They don't generally deliver baggage." As he spoke, he glared at Houghton, communicating a silent threat.

"I'm sorry! I was under the impression that they. . . Oh, well, what do I owe you?" Violet opened her reticule with shaking fingers.

"Not a cent, ma'am. I was happy to help out. Do you want this trunk upstairs?" Obie never took his eyes off the other man. Almost imperceptibly he inclined his head toward the front door.

Houghton's eyes narrowed and his fists clenched, but he edged toward the door.

Mrs. Fairfield looked flustered. "But I can't let you. . .I mean, this is too kind. . ."

"Consider it a service rendered as to the Lord, ma'am, and don't let it worry you."

"Yeah, little ol' Pops Watson is always doing 'good deeds.' He's kind of an institution around town." Houghton sounded as if he thought Obie belonged in an institution. He reminded Obie of a cornered stray dog, snarling, yet with its tail between its legs.

"Mr. Watson, is it? Well, perhaps I can do something for you in return someday," Mrs. Fairfield said. "It's good to know that some people are kind without expecting payment."

Nick Houghton sent her a venomous glare. Obie moved to intercept it. His hands clenched into fists. Houghton noticed, and his sneer faded.

Oblivious to the silent confrontation, Violet continued, "Oh, and please leave the trunk down here. I will ask Mrs. Sidwell to store it until someone. . . until my husband comes for us."

His broad forehead glistening, Houghton reached behind his back for the doorknob. "I've. . .uh. . .got to return that rig. I'll see you again, Mrs. Fairfield. If you need anything, send for me. I'll likely be at the Grand Hotel."

After Houghton had slithered outside, Obie excused himself. "I'll see you around, ma'am."

"Will you be at church on Sunday?" she asked, looking as though she really cared.

"I'm generally there every week." He tipped his hat to her and winked at Eunice.

Violet followed him to the door. Before he stepped outside, she touched his sleeve. "Thank you. . .for everything."

Maybe she hadn't been oblivious after all. He swallowed hard. "Anytime, ma'am." His voice sounded like a bullfrog's croak. Violet was scarcely touching his arm, but he felt as though he had to tear himself from her in order to walk out the door. His heart filled his chest, throbbing painfully.

Later that day, riding home on Jughead, he slouched in the saddle and dreamed. Blue eyes weren't supposed to be warm and melting; not even Obie's collie dog Treat had eyes to match Violet Fairfield's in pure eloquence. The man's lips twitched as he considered his own thoughts. The lady probably wouldn't be flattered by a comparison with a dog, but it was the best he could do.

The more he tried not to think about that woman, the more she filled his mind. Every detail of her appearance, her voice, her scent, and her touch on his arm seemed branded upon his memory. Obie had never touched a woman or held one in his arms since he was a small boy being cradled by his mother. This innocent encounter with a married woman loomed large in his mind. . .and bothered his tender conscience.

Lord, why would she look at me that way? I'm no handsome gent, and I'd stake my life she's not the type of woman to flirt with a man who isn't her husband. My best guess is that she desperately needs a friend. Is that my role in Your plan? I liked my idea better, but You know best.

Chapter 2

For I know the thoughts that I think toward you, saith the LORD,
thoughts of peace, and not of evil, to give you an expected end.
JEREMIAH 29:11

Violet stepped to the window and pulled back the curtain. The trotting horse she had heard continued on past the gate. Would Jeremiah come? This waiting frayed her nerves. Gnawing the side of one finger, she closed her eyes and sighed. The day had already been eternally long.

Beulah rolled over in her sleep and let out a snort. Eunice snored quietly. Samuel murmured in his sleep. Violet envied their peaceful slumber. Whether Jeremiah showed up tonight or not, Violet knew she would sleep very little.

Lord, I don't have the strength for this! I'm frightened.

Moving to the side of her bed, she slowly sat down, then lay back and closed her eyes. Even though sleep was far from her, she would rest her body and her eyes. She continued to pray, *Please give me wisdom. I feel so alone. If Jeremiah is alive, it is obvious that he no longer wants me, for he has not attempted to contact me in nearly five years. If this is simply another man with the same name, I have traveled all the way from Maryland for nothing.*

Lord, despite evidence to the contrary, I cannot believe that Jeremiah is alive. My heart tells me that he is dead...and yet these people claim to know him. Perhaps he was injured and has lost his memory of me. Otherwise I cannot believe that he would cease to love me—not Jeremiah. I'm sure I could teach him to love me again, perhaps revive his memory.

She shook her head abruptly. *This all seems foolish. I have mourned Jeremiah and all but forgotten my love for him. There must be some mistake. No matter what comes, I stand to look foolish in the eyes of this community.*

This community...Violet started a new line of thought. What manner of community was this, anyway? She had scarcely noticed the town during the ride from the station.

Nicholas Houghton frightened her. In the parlor that day, he had grabbed her wrist and pulled her against him before she knew what he was about. Only by shoving him off balance had she managed to escape his powerful grasp, and even then he would surely have caught her again if that kind man...what was his name? Watson...if Mr. Watson had not rescued her. Perhaps Amelia Sidwell would know Mr. Watson's first name.

Violet's lips twitched when she recalled the way he had faced down Houghton. In retrospect, the scene was rather amusing, though she did not altogether understand what had happened. For some reason, Nick Houghton feared that living portrait of a Wild West cowboy.

Violet didn't fear Mr. Watson. She had found him charming, in a rough-cut manner. Despite his diminutive size, he was altogether masculine, and she was well aware that he found her attractive. *Would I be having such thoughts if Jeremiah were really still alive?* she wondered.

∽৩∾

"Come 'ere and let me give you a kiss," Hattie Thwaite commanded, and Obie dared not refuse. Bending over her bed, he let her plant a kiss on his stubbly cheek. She patted his face with age-spotted hands, and love for him glistened in her faded blue eyes. "You're an angel straight from heaven, Obie Watson, and the Lord sent ya here just for me. Now you come back and see me soon, whether you think I'm dyin' or not, you hear?"

"I'll be back, Hattie. You take care now, and try to get some sleep." Obie tenderly patted her thin arm and walked quietly from the room.

"Obie, we cain't thank you enough for coming to us. I hated to wake ya so late at night, but Doc said she mightn't last till dawn. Now Hattie looks right hearty this morning, but you're lookin' a mite peaked," Cyrus Thwaite said, escorting his guest to the door. "Go home and get some sleep, son. I fed your horse; he shoulda finished eatin' by now."

The old man looked so frail, as though a puff of wind could have knocked him down, but Obie knew better. Cyrus was a tough old codger, likely to out-live half the town. His wife, however. . .Obie feared for the feisty, cranky little lady. She suffered from chronic digestive problems, but the doctor had told him that last night's illness had involved her heart.

"I was happy to come, Cy," he smiled, squeezing a shriveled shoulder. The Thwaites had settled in Longtree back when it was a frontier town, sixty years ago. Obie could not imagine the town or the church without them. "I'm sorry Rev. Schoengard couldn't be found, but I'm always glad to sit with a pretty lady like Hattie."

"Aw, you're a minister in all but name," Cyrus scoffed. "Your scripture reading is as fine as any in church. The minister's reading irritates her sometimes—he pauses in all the wrong places, she says. Hattie likes your deep voice—makes her feel young, she says. You're one of the few people she really likes, you know."

Obie rolled his eyes and grinned shyly. "Well, I say you'd better watch that one; she's likely to run off with me sometime."

Cyrus chuckled. "You ever need anything from us, you let me know, Obie. And thanks for the milk and butter—Hattie says your cows give pure cream, that they do."

Out at the Thwaite's barn, Obie noticed that some fence rails had splintered, so he took a few extra minutes to repair the corral. The only nails he could find were bent and rusty, but he straightened them with a few blows of the hammer and put them to use. "That oughta hold you for a while," he told Cyrus's bony old mule.

Jughead was just finishing the last wisps of hay in his manger when Obie rousted him out. The little mustang never needed to be tied up; he stood quietly while Obie bridled and saddled him. "Wish I could do more to help around here," Obie told him, "but Cyrus always wants to return the favor, and he has nothing left to give. Maybe I'll sneak over some night and tinker with that pump."

Jughead yawned as Obie mounted up and headed him toward home. It was contagious. Obie also yawned widely, then let go of the reins to stretch his arms over his head. "Didn't expect this to turn into an all-nighter. Al and Myles will think I did it just to get out of my chores." He smiled sleepily and picked up the reins.

A cluck and a whoop brought Jughead to life, and the paint broke into his ground-eating lope. "Let's get home, buddy."

⌘

"Honey, you've been staring out windows since dawn. Why don't you and the children go to church with me this morning? If Jerry got in late last night, he mighta figured it was too late to wake you and went on home." Amelia stood in the dining room doorway holding a stack of clean china plates.

"Maybe so," Violet sighed, restraining a yawn. "I would like to attend church. I'll hurry the children up. When will you leave?"

"In about twenty minutes."

"We'll be ready." Violet desperately needed some spiritual support.

⌘

"Are you sure you want to go to church, cousin? Thought you'd want some sleep after sitting up all night. Go ahead, if that's what you want. Myles and I can take care of things here. Marigold delivered this little fellow at the crack of dawn with no trouble. She didn't miss you, far as I could tell." Al grinned at Obie while rubbing the Jersey cow at the base of her horns. The gentle animal leaned into the boy's caresses.

Albert Moore, Obie's young cousin, had traveled east from California with him four years earlier. Along with Myles Trent, their hired man, the two had turned their farm into a prosperous operation through hard work and sensible investments. They had differences of opinion about how the farm should be run, but usually resolved these without any hard feelings.

Obie hovered uncertainly in the barn doorway. "It's a fine calf, Al—every bit the Jersey bull we'd hoped for. But. . .are you sure you don't mind me running off?"

"Not now that the milking's done. You go on. I'll have a private time with the Lord later today. He won't mind me missing church this once. Get going, or you'll be late."

Obie headed outside, picking his way between mud puddles. It was a brilliant morning, though the air was still chilly. Jughead waited at the hitching rail, his long ears pricked. Spotting Obie, he gave a cheerful nicker.

"You're a pal, Jughead," Obie answered. "Ready for church?" He swung into the saddle and turned the horse toward town.

Obie had changed into a blue-gray wool shirt and black wool trousers that bagged around his hips. The clothes were hot and itchy, but he wanted to look his best. His boots were polished, and his string tie sported a silver concho. He smelled clean after a quick morning sponge bath.

He pushed Jughead into a lope, enjoying the breeze on his face. Soon, town buildings appeared on the horizon and the church steeple came into sight. Horses and assorted vehicles already crowded the yard, and the church building bustled with people.

Reverend David Schoengard delivered a stirring sermon about the building of Solomon's temple, but Obie heard little of the message. He sat in the back of the church, arms folded across his chest, and studied the back of Violet's hat. She sat at one end of a row with Amelia Sidwell on the far end and the three children in between.

After the service, a few people clustered at the end of Violet's pew to introduce themselves and welcome her. When she lifted her face to greet them, Obie noted the pallor of her smooth cheeks and the dark circles beneath her eyes. Then Obie saw Caroline Schoengard, the pastor's wife, greet Violet in her friendly way, and he relaxed his vigil. Perhaps Violet would not need his friendship after all.

Samuel caught sight of Obie, tugged Eunice's sleeve, and pointed him out to her. Obie winked and waved, and the two children brightened. As Beulah talked with another girl her age, her moody look faded away. She was rather handsome when she smiled.

The congregation gradually moved outside, and Obie drifted with the flow, keeping the Fairfields in sight. His distracted air puzzled friends who spoke to him, for Obie was usually an attentive listener. The Fairfield family moved toward Amelia's surrey as though preparing to leave. Obie wavered. He wanted to speak with Violet, yet he had no good reason to detain her.

"Uncle Obie, sir, my brothers want to ask you for a ride."

Glancing down and back, Obie smiled at a six-year-old with serious blue eyes and wild yellow hair. "They do, eh?"

Four-year-old twins held hands and nodded in unison. One popped a finger into his mouth. "Good morning, Scott, Bernie, Ernie. Does your mother know where you are?"

All three boys nodded again. Unable to resist their pleading eyes, Obie followed them to a grassy place alongside the church. It was just as well. For his own sake, he needed to forget about Violet Fairfield. As soon as Obie bent down, Reverend Schoengard's three sons tackled him, and he rolled over, laughing. Other children came running from all directions to join in the fun.

An elderly gentleman with a ring of silvery hair around the back of his head was just pulling the door shut, preparing to lock it, when Violet clattered up the church steps.

"Excuse me, sir! I left my Bible inside."

"Now that be one possession a body cain't do without fer a week," the kindly man said, opening the door for her. "We're almighty glad you joined us today, Miz Fairfield."

Violet walked quickly to the correct row, picked up her worn Bible, and hurried back outside. "Thank you, sir. I'm afraid I don't recall your name. . . ?"

"Jes' call me Cyrus, ma'am. I'm sort of the trustee of this here church building. My wife isn't well today—"

A female voice spoke at Violet's elbow. "It's good to finally have you here, Mrs. Fairfield. Most of us were unaware until recently that Mr. Fairfield was married. Since he never attends church, it's a pleasure to find that you, at least, seek fellowship with God's people."

Cyrus murmured a farewell and slipped quietly down the steps.

My Jeremiah always attended church. Violet's doubts waxed stronger. She mustered a polite smile. "We are pleased to be here, Mrs. . . ?"

"Leila Blackthorn." The plump woman bounced a smiling baby on her hip. Her own face looked as though it would crack if she were to venture a smile.

"Mrs. Blackthorn. Thank you for your gracious welcome. You have a sweet boy there," she indicated the baby.

"He's my fourth."

Hoping to cut the conversation short, Violet descended the steep church stairs while shading her eyes with one hand. "This sunshine is amazingly bright."

"The mud will vanish soon; that's a mercy," Mrs. Blackthorn concurred. "It was an early spring this year. I must say, Mrs. Fairfield, you seem a genteel woman, though I disapprove of lip rouge. A virtuous woman shouldn't paint her face, in my opinion. It gives the wrong impression to men."

"I beg your pardon. I do not paint my face."

"Indeed!" Mrs. Blackthorn lifted a doubtful brow. "Isn't that gown rather thin and flimsy for a married woman of your age? Puffed sleeves and no bustle or train? Hmpf!"

"Bustles are not presently in style back East. This gown is fashioned in the aesthetic style, which is known to be good for the health." Violet resisted the urge to stick her nose in the air, but it wasn't easy.

Mrs. Blackthorn seemed to be searching for a scathing put-down, but just as the two women reached the bottom step, a scream of childish laughter pierced their ears, and a man crawled past on all fours with a little boy perched upon his back. "Faster, faster, mustang!" the small wrangler commanded, wriggling to spur his mount on to greater speed. A cluster of laughing children scampered behind, shouting encouragement. A deep chuckle occasionally joined the shrill giggles and squeals.

Violet recognized that voice, and a smile softened her lips. Obie Watson reared up and pawed the air like an outlaw horse, carefully placing one hand behind the child to keep him secure.

"Amos! Fern! Get to the wagon at once," Mrs. Blackthorn screeched. Two of the children stopped, sent their mother horrified glances, and ran like rabbits toward the parking area.

"Disgraceful behavior," the woman whispered to Violet, enraged. "On the Lord's Day, and at the Lord's house! I must speak with the pastor. His wife allows his children to associate with absolutely *anyone*. They are leading my own children down the path of iniquity, playing with that. . .that felon! All I can say is, Reverend Schoengard shall rue the day."

"I enjoy watching children play any day of the week. I don't believe the Lord disapproves of his people having fun," Violet defended both Obie and the pastor's wife. Caroline Schoengard had given her a warm welcome—she did not care to hear the woman maligned. And what did Mrs. Blackthorn mean by calling Mr. Watson a felon?

"Well, I never!" After raking Violet with a scathing glare, Leila Blackthorn hitched up the baby and stalked away.

Although Violet knew Amelia and the children were waiting, she could not resist pausing to watch the horseplay for a moment. Her tension seemed to melt away as she watched the man romp with the little children. What an endearing sight! She strolled closer.

The little rider's clutching hands covered his "horse's" eyes, directing Obie with voice commands. "Faster! Turn left! Rear up!" Obie crawled on, waggling his head like a real horse. The other children laughed at the sight and shouted their own commands. Violet was pleased when they moved closer until, amid all the noise, Obie turned abruptly and charged into her skirts. The top of his head bumped into the side of her knee, and the little rider nearly disappeared amid blue bombazine ruffles.

"Oh!" she cried, taking two quick steps back. Embarrassed, she didn't immediately see the humor in the situation.

Little Ernie Schoengard stared up at her, and the other children backed hastily away, then turned and ran for their mothers. Too late, Ernie uncovered Obie's eyes, scrambled down, and followed his brothers.

Violet watched Obie's eyes slowly move up her figure until they met her gaze. "Good day, Mr. Watson." She resisted the urge to rub her aching knee.

"Mrs. Fairfield, I'm so sorry!" Hastily he rose, beating at his woolen trousers. It was a hopeless endeavor. Grass stains darkened the knees. His long boots, shirt, and suspenders were damp. He reached up for his hat, but he wasn't wearing one. "How are you this morning?"

"You're forgiven, and I'm well enough, thank you. It was my fault for standing too close to your riding arena, anyway." She extended her gloved hand. "It's good to see you again."

For a moment he stared at her hand; then his own hand lifted to touch it. His heavy leather glove was caked with drying mud. She saw him notice the dirt, then whip off the glove and grip her hand firmly in his bare hand. It felt hot and rough with calluses that snagged her delicate gloves.

"Yes, it is good." His voice was soft, yet so deep that it seemed to reverberate somewhere within her soul. When he released her hand, she felt bereft. These unfamiliar emotions disturbed her.

"I suppose you've heard that Mr. Fairfield has not yet come home. I don't know what to do. . . . No one can possibly understand this. . .situation, and I feel so alone. . . ."

Intense gray eyes flashed up to search hers. Startled, she lifted a hand to still her suddenly pounding heart. Blood rushed to her cheeks.

"I. . .oh! I'm sorry to babble on so. . ."

His moustache lifted ever so slightly at the corners, and he said, "If you need help, ma'am, I'll be around."

"I appreciate your offer, Mr. Watson." Violet heard her voice quiver. She sounded like a lovesick girl!

He walked her back to Amelia's surrey and supported her elbow while she climbed up. When seated, she turned to thank him. He nodded to her and Amelia, then strode away. Although he had a slightly rolling gait, his legs were straight, not bowed. He walked with head high and shoulders square, a man of confidence.

Violet realized that she was holding her breath. Glancing at Amelia, she intercepted a speculative stare.

"Amelia, what do you think of Mr. Watson?" she asked.

"Obadiah is a good man. He and his cousin work a farm next to your husband's place."

"Obadiah." Violet considered the name. "He has the kindest eyes I've ever seen."

Amelia gave her a sober glance. "How long you been married, Miz Fairfield?"

"I married Jeremiah nineteen years ago—just before he left for war. He was several years my senior, but always seemed younger somehow. You. . .you know him, don't you?"

"I've seen him about."

"Beulah has his eyes and coloring, and Eunice has his dimples. Samuel looks more like my family, especially my father."

Amelia glanced back at the children, then gave Violet another odd look. "Do tell."

"What do you think of Mr. Houghton?"

Amelia snorted. "Now there's a feller I'd keep my gals away from, iffen I was you."

"My opinion exactly. He's very good-looking, but I don't trust him an inch. Now Obadiah Watson strikes me as an honest, trustworthy man. You say he's a farmer? He looks like a cowboy to me. Maybe it's the boots or the hat."

Amelia studied her guest with sympathetic eyes. "Honey, I do my best to mind my own business and not hand out unwanted advice, but I'd say you need to borrow this rig of mine and drive out to your house today."

"On Sunday?"

"Why ever not? Lots of people take a drive on Sunday afternoon. It don't seem to bother the Lord none. Iffen your husband is at the house, he may be wondering why you haven't come a-lookin' for him."

Violet nodded. "Perhaps you're right. We'll eat dinner first, then drive out. . . if you'll draw me a map. I'm dreadful with directions."

As they turned the corner to her street, Amelia snapped, "Well, look who's a-waitin' for us. Don't be too uppity right off; maybe he's got news about your man."

Nicholas Houghton waited on the boardinghouse porch. He grinned and waved as the surrey pulled into the drive. "Good day, Violet!"

Violet returned his wave. "Please don't leave us alone together, Mrs. Sidwell!" she pleaded, awkwardly climbing down over the surrey's wheel before Houghton could reach her. Her dress caught on a protruding bolt, but she released it undamaged. The children easily jumped down from the rear seat.

Amelia nodded. "Let me turn the team over to the stable boy, and I'll be right in to join you."

Nick hurried up the path with an outstretched hand, chiding, "Violet, next time wait for me to assist you down. You might have fallen. Ah, my dear, you are well named, for your face is truly like a flower—refreshing to my eyes. Has Jerry not yet come to claim his bride?" As they stepped inside, he glanced around the entryway as though expecting Violet's husband to pop out of a corner.

"I hoped you had come with news of him."

Violet turned to the children. "Go on and change into play clothes. We'll be leaving after dinner."

"I haven't seen Jerry since yesterday. Perhaps he was delayed. May I treat you to supper at the hotel tonight? Amelia is an excellent cook, but I think you would appreciate our hotel's fine cuisine." Taking her arm, Houghton drew

Violet into the parlor, leaving the door slightly ajar.

"I don't believe Jeremiah would like that, sir. What if he were to come while I was away?"

"Ah, Violet, let us speak honestly, as adult man to adult woman. We both know that Jeremiah Fairfield has not been the husband a woman like you deserves," Nick murmured, letting his blue eyes drift over her face and body. "I cannot believe that he would leave you alone for so many years. The man must be blind as well as. . . Surely you have learned, during that time, to find solace in the company of other men."

"You are mistaken, sir!" Violet cried, aghast. "You know nothing of me if you believe such rubbish—and my husband was very good to me."

"I hope you don't believe that he has pined for you all these years," Houghton scoffed. "If so, you're a bigger fool than—"

Amelia entered the room, wielding a feather duster. "Don't mind me," she assured them. "Just touchin' up a bit before Mr. Fairfield arrives."

Muscles worked in Houghton's jaw, making his whiskers twitch, but he forced a smile and changed the subject. His intensely blue eyes studied Violet even as he spoke of trivial town gossip. She disliked him more with each passing minute. Oddly enough, he seemed confident that she found him attractive.

When he finally rose to take his leave, he pulled Violet aside and whispered fiercely, "Where can we meet to speak privately? Somewhere *she* won't be." He jerked a thumb in Amelia's direction. "It's important for your future, Violet."

Violet was skeptical about the importance of his message, but she replied, "I don't know at present. Ask me another time."

As soon as they had eaten, Violet loaded up her children and headed into the countryside, armed with a scrawled map. Amelia had scoffed at the idea of getting lost. "Jist look for a house the size of a castle, and you'll find it soon enough. Iffen ya do get lost, ask directions at any house along the road. Everyone knows Fairfield's Folly."

Last night's snow had vanished. The road was muddy and rutted, but someone had filled in the worst of the ruts with gravel. Nervous though she was, Violet enjoyed the delightful scenery. Feathery clouds drifted across a sky bluer than Nick Houghton's eyes. Trees rustled tiny new leaves in a cool breeze.

Samuel exclaimed, "Look, there's a fox!" and "I just saw a cardinal! Did you see it?"

The girls seemed indifferent at first, but soon their interest was caught. "There is a vireo, I'm absolutely certain," Beulah stated, trying to hide her excitement. "And that yellow bird was a warbler."

"I think it was a goldfinch," Eunice disagreed.

"It was beautiful, whatever it was." Violet tried to avert an argument. "Isn't this lovely country?"

"Oh, Mama, I had no idea!" Eunice raved. "When Father talked about going west to farm, I somehow imagined flat grassland or desert."

"We're not that far west," Violet explained. "This is west of Maryland, for certain, but we are a long way from the Wild West. They call this region the Midwest, I believe."

"Mama, this must be our turn. There's the white barn Miss Sidwell mentioned." Beulah pointed out the landmark.

Her heart thumping with apprehension, Violet obediently directed the horses up a neat driveway. The drive led to a farm with a low-slung log house and a large red barn. Several golden-brown cows stopped grazing to watch the buggy pass their pasture.

"This can't be right," Violet groaned. "But I guess we can ask for directions, like Amelia said."

Obadiah Watson emerged from an outbuilding, brushing his hands on a huge leather apron. Violet's heart thudded in startled recognition. "May I help you, Mrs. Fairfield?"

"I believe we are lost, Mr. Watson. Can you direct us to our farm? Amelia Sidwell told me to turn right when I saw a white barn on my left."

"Yes, but your drive is about a hundred yards beyond ours. Head west on the main road and look for a path through the trees. It's easy to miss, even when you know what you're looking for."

Violet didn't intend to look helpless and pleading—at least not consciously. But she was relieved when Watson abruptly said, "I'll ride with you a ways and make sure you find it. Wait a moment, please."

"What will Father say?" Eunice murmured as Obie emerged from the barn. He wore a flat-brimmed hat and had removed the leather coverall.

Violet tried to shrug off her concern. "I'm sure he would understand. Besides, if your father had come for us, this wouldn't be necessary."

She scooted over to make room, but Obie did not immediately climb up. "We delivered a calf this morning before church. Perhaps the children would like to see it?"

"Oh, could we?" Eunice said eagerly, and Samuel laid a beseeching hand on his mother's shoulder.

"Very well. If you don't mind waiting, Mr. Watson, I certainly don't."

Samuel scrambled down over the surrey's tall wheel. This time Violet was willing to accept help. To her surprise, Obie grasped her by the waist and lifted her bodily down. Hands upon his shoulders, she met his eyes, and color tinged her pale cheeks. "Thank you, Mr. Watson."

Inside the barn, Obie called, "Al? Myles? We have visitors to see the calves."

Two men came to meet the unexpected company. The younger man had straight black hair and dark eyes. The older man was ruddy of hair, beard, and skin.

"I'm sorry to disturb you. We lost our way, and Mr. Watson has offered to show us the new calf before he puts us back on the right track. I am Violet Fairfield, and these are my children, Beulah, Eunice, and Samuel."

Both men bowed politely, murmuring greetings. Al was a handsome boy with smiling eyes. "Ma'am, I've heard so much about you."

"Have you?" Violet asked, not knowing what else to say. Had Obie told him about her? Or perhaps Jeremiah?

"Where's the calf?" Samuel blurted impatiently.

"Right this way," Al directed, leading them to a stall. A cow stood in the roomy box stall with her head half-buried in a manger full of fresh hay. A small bundle lay beside her, knobby legs folded haphazardly.

Violet took one look at the calf's liquid eyes and melted. "Oh, isn't she sweet? Like a tiny fawn."

"He," Al corrected with another grin. "It's a bull calf."

"What's his name?" Samuel asked.

The calf gave an abrupt "Moo" and struggled to its feet.

"He doesn't have one yet."

"I would call him 'Moo-Moo.'"

Obie and Al exchanged an amused smile.

Since the calf was so new, they took only a quick look at him; but the heifer calf in the next stall was active and curious about the visitors. Although the mother cow looked grouchy, she only lowed and shook her head.

"Hollyhock calved the day before yesterday. We leave the calves with their mothers for a few days before weaning them to a pail." Al seemed to have taken over their tour. Myles had disappeared, and Obie hovered in the background.

Leaning over the Dutch door, Beulah crooned at the dainty calf, rubbing its bristly forehead. "Does she have a name?"

Obie suddenly coughed, and Violet turned just in time to see him shake his head, eyes intent upon Al. Al coughed in return, and Violet suspected him of hiding a smile. "All of our cows are named for flowers. What would *you* call her?" Al parried the question.

"Rosebud," Beulah answered without hesitation.

"We already have a Rosie," Al said apologetically. "But it is a pretty name, you're right. She's a fine calf."

Next he led them to a box stall containing a dozing red sow with a large litter of squealing piglets. Eunice and Samuel were delighted when Al escorted them into the stall and handed them each a pig, but Beulah went back to the tiny heifer. She found pigs repulsive. Violet was thankful when the mother pig paid no attention to the squalls of her offspring.

"Brunhilda trusts me," Al explained, interpreting Violet's nervous glances at the immense sow.

"Brunhilda?" Violet smiled. "Does she sing opera?"

"An aria now and then." Obie's deep voice at her side made Violet jump. He leaned his elbows on the door beside her.

She felt slightly giddy. "I'm not sure I want to hear one. Is she a soprano?"

"Brunhilda sings parts from bass to high soprano—sometimes all at once." Obie's eyes twinkled. "She's Al's project. I don't care much for hogs."

Al spoke up, "Cousin Buck wants to specialize in dairy cattle. He wants to build a silo so we can keep more cows over the winter. I like a variety of animals and crops."

"And since you do most of the work around here, that's what we've got," Obie added.

Violet glanced at Obie, intending to ask the identity of "Buck"; but when she discovered that Obie was looking at her children and not at her, she took the opportunity to examine him.

Obadiah Watson was only three or four inches taller than Violet's five-foot-two, so she didn't have to tip her head back to look at his face—a pleasant change for her. His top several shirt buttons were undone, displaying the neckline of his red woolen combinations. His jaw and neck were neatly shaven, and he looked and smelled clean. His moustache and hair were salt-and-pepper gray, though his eyebrows were black. Smile lines creased his tanned face.

"How often must you milk the cows?" she asked, picturing him at the chore.

"Twice a day."

"I've never milked a cow. I would like to learn how. Does. . .my husband raise cattle?"

"No, ma'am." Obie opened one of his hands, turning it over. The back of it was leathery and hairy; two of the knuckles had abrasions and the palm was calloused. It was the hand of a man who worked hard for a living. "Milking takes strong hands and a strong back."

"Do you think I'm too weak to do it?" Violet asked. For some reason, she felt concerned about the possibility of failure in his eyes.

"Lots of women milk cows."

Violet met his smiling eyes and felt her heart grow warm. Obadiah Watson was not flirting with her, she knew. With him she felt. . .safe.

Al took the piglets from the children and returned them to their mother. Obie unlatched the stall door, and Samuel and Eunice exited, dirty but happy. Al stayed behind to care for Brunhilda and her progeny.

There was a tug at Obie's sleeve. "Do you own any dogs, Mr. Watson?"

Samuel's quiet inquiry captured Obie's attention. He smiled at the boy, deepening every one of those creases on his face. "Not only do we own a dog, she just had pups. This farm is overrun with babies."

"May I see them?"

Obie glanced at Violet, seeking her approval. Though Violet had a premonition that she would be hearing more about these pups in the near future, she nodded. Obie led the boy to a storage room, and Violet trailed along behind. For a short man, Obie had a long, rapid stride.

"Treat?" he called softly at the open doorway. "Visitors to see your family." He explained as they entered, "Usually Treat woulda been first to greet you, but today she's busy. Her pups were born a week ago."

Sliding into the limited space, Obie closed the door behind Violet. A small window lighted the room, revealing neat wooden bins along the back wall. A wooden crate filled with wood shavings took up much of the floor space. Inside it, a black collie-type dog lay curled protectively around four pups. She growled softly as they entered, although her white-tipped tail wagged.

"Easy, girl," Obie soothed. "These are friends."

Crowded in the small space near the door, Obie and Violet watched Samuel kneel beside the box and admire the nursing pups. "Your children are beautiful, Treat," he assured the watchful mother. "I would never harm them. I'm your friend Samuel."

Treat's ears lifted for a moment, and her almond eyes studied the boy. Then she yawned widely and lay back, lifting a white foreleg to offer more of her furry belly to the pups. She had accepted Samuel in a matter of moments.

Violet looked at Obie and met his meaningful gaze. She gave a little nod, then a rueful shrug. A puppy would be a wonderful companion while Samuel adjusted to his new home, but Violet would have to speak with Jeremiah before allowing the boy a pet. Obie nodded agreement, as if he'd understood her thoughts.

Perhaps her special feeling for this man was the beginning of a wonderful friendship. On that thought, she smiled at Obie, and his face lit up in response.

Yes, this would be a special friendship indeed.

Chapter 3

So are the ways of every one that is greedy of gain;
which taketh away the life of the owners thereof.
PROVERBS 1:19

Thank you for taking time to show us your animals." Violet extended her hand to Al, and he shook it bashfully.

"You're surely welcome, ma'am. Drop by anytime you like."

While Al assisted the girls and Samuel into the surrey's rear seat, Obie helped Violet up and over the front wheel. She liked his touch, but she felt uneasy about her reaction. It felt strangely right when he climbed up beside her and took the reins, which she was happy to relinquish. Old Brownie and Ted were not difficult to handle, but Violet had never liked to drive.

"I learned a lot about farming today. Your cattle are pretty animals. I had never seen a pretty cow before. My father kept one, but she was ugly. I always liked her, though," she amended, hoping Obie would not be offended by her criticism of a long-dead milk cow.

Slowly he turned to look at her, and she saw amusement in his eyes—not mockery, but a twinkle that brought a responsive smile to her lips. "I'm so glad to hear that you liked a cow."

Before Violet could think of an answer, Obie made a right turn into a shady vale and slowed the team to a walk. Wagon tracks seemed to run directly into a stand of trees, but as they approached, the trees gave way. Tall weeds brushed against the surrey's undercarriage as it jounced over ruts and splashed through potholes. Violet held on with both hands, but she bumped against Obie more than once. Branches reached to scratch and claw at the surrey's fringed top, even snatching at Violet's hat.

Obie apologized, "I'm sorry. I didn't expect the drive to be so rough." Hauling the horses to a stop, he indicated, "Here's your house."

"Oh!" Violet gasped, unconsciously clutching Obie's arm. He looked down at her hands, then up at her startled face.

There was a chorus of gasps and sighs from the children.

It was a tall house, framed by several flowering fruit trees. Ornate grillwork and moldings decorated each gable, and many glass windows sparkled in the bright sunlight. A wide veranda wrapped around the front; Violet immediately imagined it replete with rocking chairs and dozing cats.

"Mama, is this really our house?" Beulah cried from the rear seat. "It's magnificent!"

"It's enormous!" Eunice exclaimed.

"Is that a crick over there?" Samuel blurted.

"Sure enough," Obie assured him, and clucked the team back into motion. "Mr. Fairfield had the house designed and built by a fellow from Madison. I imagine he had it built with you all in mind."

Violet looked puzzled. "I had no idea that farming was such a. . .a lucrative career." Absently she released Obie's arm and retied the ribbons of her bonnet. The house looked empty, but perhaps Jeremiah was sleeping inside after a long night on the road. The very thought of it shook her up. She felt jumpy and irritable.

Now Obie looked puzzled. "Lucrative? Farming? I should say not. Not around here, anyway. I thought your husband was independently wealthy. He purchased the farm, but never bothered to work it much."

Violet turned on her seat to stare at Obie. "Jeremiah went west to try farming, but he had little money. I assumed that he homesteaded land here, you know, lived on it and worked it for a certain amount of time until it became his. Isn't that how it's done?"

"Not around here," he repeated.

They stared at each other, pondering the situation. "I imagine your husband will answer your questions when you see him," Obie finally concluded.

Violet shook her head doubtfully. She tried to be calm, but her heart raced and her knees quaked beneath her gown. When they stopped at the hitching rail and Obie lifted her down, she had a sudden desire to bury her face in his shoulder and hide from the future. A fog seemed to envelop her, a dread of. . .something she could not place. Not of Jeremiah, certainly. Never could she have dreaded her dear husband, but her heart told her clearly that Jeremiah was nowhere near. Only pride enabled her to release her hold on Obie's supportive arm and stand alone.

The children hopped down without help, and Samuel set out to explore. "Don't go into the woods, dear," Violet called before he disappeared around the back of the house.

"I won't" floated back to her ears.

Resolutely, Violet lifted her skirts, climbed the steps, and rapped the ornate brass knocker. While waiting, she studied the veranda. In other circumstances she would have been thrilled with this house.

"Are you sure this is our father's house?" Beulah quizzed Obie. "It doesn't look like something Father would build."

"Quite sure," he stated flatly. "Guess I'll walk on home now." Heading down the short flagstone walkway, he turned back to say, "If you need anything, our farm is due east across the creek."

Violet panicked. Obie seemed like the one solid, dependable person connected with her present state of affairs. "I have no key. If he's not here, how will we get inside?" She cast another helpless look at her unlikely knight-errant.

"He might hide a key somewhere. Just a moment, I'll look around back." Obie jogged to the back of the house. Then they heard him call sharply, "Mrs. Fairfield?"

Violet and her daughters exchanged looks. In single file they trotted back down the steps and around the house.

Obie waited at a side door, his face sober. The glass panes were shattered, and the door stood ajar. "Oh, my!" Violet covered her mouth with one hand.

"Ma'am, let me check inside first," he requested.

Violet looked into his grave eyes and nodded helplessly. "Please do." She put her arms around her daughters while they waited for Obie to return. "Let's pray, girls. We need wisdom to know what to do."

"I like Mr. Watson, Mama," Eunice said quietly. "Do you?"

"Yes, dear. I like him very much. I think God sent him to help us right now." The three bowed their heads while Violet spoke a simple request for guidance.

When they lifted their heads, Beulah said, "Mama, you don't think Father is really alive. I can tell that you don't, and I don't either. I think we're entering a stranger's house uninvited. I think God lost control somehow, and our world has gone crazy—that's what I think."

"I am confused, Beulah. But I know a few things for certain: God has not lost control, God loves us, and He has a plan in all of this. We just can't see it right now."

The girls still looked worried.

Obie appeared in the doorway. "Your husband isn't here. Somebody ransacked the house."

Violet released her breath in a puff. A thief had broken in, that was all.

Obie stepped back to allow them entrance into a large kitchen with a modern cookstove and a pump at the sink. Cupboard doors hung open; cans and utensils littered the floor. The table was ugly, the chairs mismatched, but the room itself was handsome. "It's got newfangled gadgets I'd never heard of before," Obie commented, trying the pump handle. "This one seems mighty practical."

"Imagine, running water inside the house!" Eunice exulted.

Violet led the way from room to room. The hardwood flooring amplified their footsteps. "How beautiful!" Violet breathed. In spite of shredded chair cushions, fireplace ashes, and andirons scattered across the floors, the house was fine indeed. A fieldstone fireplace dominated the sitting room; a carved balustrade accented the stairway. A crystal chandelier hung in the dining room, looking lonely in the otherwise empty chamber. Plasterwork decorated the downstairs ceilings and moldings, making each room a separate work of art.

"The damage could be easily repaired," Violet remarked, picking up a shard of pottery. "Isn't this house magnificent?"

The girls agreed heartily, but Obie muttered, "Too busy by half."

While Obie opened a window to let in fresh air, the girls and their mother began to peer inside closets and cupboards. "Mama, this is the nicest house ever," Eunice proclaimed. "I love it! Have you ever seen so many closets in all your life?"

"I'll be first upstairs!" Beulah announced, and clattered up the wooden steps. "I do believe there's a closet in every room up here," she called down the stairwell. "And what a glorious view! Mama, there's a small lake not too far away. I surely do wish this house were ours."

Violet and Eunice followed, hurrying from room to room. Each of the four large bedrooms did boast a window and a commodious closet.

Entering the master bedroom, Violet stopped short, her eyes wide. A bow-tie quilt she had stitched with her own hands many years earlier lay in tatters across a shredded bolster.

Trembling, she crossed the room and lifted the window sash. Feather-tick stuffing drifted up from the slashed mattress as she gazed sightlessly out the window. *Am I wrong, Lord? Is Jeremiah alive?* Even as she prayed, she shook her head. Despite the quilt, this room felt like a stranger's bedroom.

Attempting to shrug off her apprehension, Violet hurried to find the girls. "Perhaps we can return in the morning and begin cleaning up the house. If. . . *when* your father comes, I will discuss with him the possibility of sending for our furniture—the things that belonged to your grandparents. Since we have this lovely house, we should fill it with the beautiful things we already own rather than order new ones."

"I want to stay here always, Mama," Eunice declared. Elbows on the windowsill of a back bedroom, she stared into the forest beyond the barn. "I want this bedroom, all right? This place feels like home."

Obie found Samuel squatting beside a limpid pool just above a beaver dam. He sat beside the boy, gazing into the brown depths. A sleek form swished past, leaving ripples upon the surface.

"This pond is full of trout," the man observed quietly. "Some of the local boys use it as their fishin' hole."

"I can hardly wait to drop a line in there. I wonder if Father ever fishes here."

"He might."

"Do you fish here?"

"I've caught a string or two. My farm begins on the far bank, so we share the pool and this stretch of the crick. Beavers made this pond. Their house is over there in the deepest part."

"I saw trees they had chewed."

"Didn't your mother tell you to stay out of the forest?"

"This isn't the forest, it's just a stone's throw from the springhouse." Samuel looked anxious, but Obie nodded, apparently satisfied with the explanation.

"Is Father in the house?"

"No, he isn't here."

Samuel appeared neither disappointed nor relieved. "I barely remember him. I was pretty little when he left us. I remember his dark eyes and bushy black side-whiskers, but that's about all."

Obie gave the boy a quick glance and frowned. Samuel's description did not match the Jerry Fairfield he knew. Could there be some mistake, or was the child's memory faulty?

Boy and man sat quietly for long minutes, content to watch flitting damsel-flies and listen to birdcalls. A plunk sounded across the pool, and a V-shaped ripple in the water indicated a beaver's path. Obie and Samuel exchanged glances and smiled.

Approaching from behind, Violet saw them share that smile, and her heart warmed. Samuel rarely smiled. Obie Watson was good medicine for the boy, it seemed.

"I hate to interrupt, but we need to be getting on back to town. I must return Amelia's surrey."

The man rose quickly, brushing off his backside. "Then I'll be getting on home now." He held aside branches for Violet and followed her back to the house. Samuel reluctantly trailed behind.

Brownie and Ted, waiting at the rail, suddenly lifted their heads and whinnied. An answer came from the direction of the road. Moments later a riderless horse trudged down the drive, limping painfully. It was saddled, and its reins dangled loose.

Obie approached it, talking softly to the large liver-chestnut horse. The animal was skittish at first, but he calmed under Obie's firm, gentle hands. Obie felt its shoulders and legs and checked it over thoroughly.

He turned to Violet, and she quailed at the expression in his eyes. "Mrs. Fairfield, this is Jerry's horse, Barabbas."

"Do you...do you think maybe the horse fell with Jeremiah? Is that why it limps?"

"Maybe, but I don't think so. One rein is snapped short, so I'd guess that Barabbas stepped on it and lamed himself when he was coming home alone. One way or another, it doesn't look good. I'll tell the sheriff right away, and we'll go looking for Jerry."

Violet felt weak. "If you think it's necessary...," she faltered. "Mr. Watson, you have been very kind to us. Thank you for all you've done."

He did not seem to know how to respond, but Violet thought his color heightened.

Impulsively she said, "I would like to go with you on your search."

He lifted a brow. "Why?"

"Well, because this man may be my husband."

She saw a flicker in his eyes. "You have doubts, then?" Abruptly his voice changed, grew harsher. "You watch over your young'uns and leave this to men." He took her elbow and directed her toward the surrey.

Violet bristled. "Are you implying that I would be in the way?" She glared down at him as he helped her to the seat.

Still grasping her arm, he said, "I'm not implyin' anything. I'll tell you straight out—you'd be in the way. You don't know the area, and I reckon you don't ride any better than you drive." Obie's eyes sparked with a blend of amusement and irritation as he backed away. "You'd be nothin' more than a distraction."

Violet flushed, angry, but lacking a snappy rejoinder. "I have a right to search for my own husband." Now she argued simply for the principle of the thing.

Obie loosed the team, settled the reins in her hands, and handed her the whip.

"Then you'll search alone, 'cause you aren't comin' with me." Turning on his heel, he left her gasping like a landed trout.

⚭

When Violet drove into Amelia's yard, Nicholas Houghton appeared in the stable doorway. "Where have you been? I've been looking everywhere for you, and that Sidwell witch wouldn't tell me a thing."

While the children scrambled down from the surrey, Violet had no choice but to let Nick lift her down. His grip felt intimate, disrespectful. She released herself quickly. "I've been to our house."

"Alone?"

Violet turned the team and rig over to Amelia's stable boy, telling him, "Thank you very much."

"Violet, did you drive out to that house alone?" Nick persisted.

"If you call the four of us alone, then yes." Violet marched toward the house, removing her gloves. Nick trailed after her.

"Uncle Obie Watson helped us find the house," Eunice informed him. "Mama drove up his drive by mistake, and he set us straight."

Nick's already stormy face darkened. "Stay away from that man, Violet. He's trouble."

"Whatever do you mean?" she demanded, rounding on him with narrowed eyes.

"Watson's bad through and through. He's got a prison record! I'm telling you, stay away from him!"

It was a poor choice of words. Violet refused to allow two men to dictate to her in one day. She drew herself erect. "Mr. Houghton, you have no right to tell me anything. Good day."

Nick grabbed her arm. "He's after something, Violet. Don't trust him for an instant!"

With an icy glare, Violet ordered, "Unhand me, sir. And stop calling me Violet. I am Mrs. Fairfield to you."

To her surprise, he released her. She picked up her skirts, gathered up her brood, and entered the house, thankful that he did not follow.

Sheriff Boz Martin bent over to study the chestnut gelding's right rear shoe. "Sure enough, Buck, there's a notch on the outside edge. That'll make him easier to track, and the muddy roads will help—but are you sure we can backtrack him more than a mile or two? I think we'd do better to try to trace Fairfield by asking at nearby towns. That way we'd have a general idea which direction he rode."

Obie released Barabbas's leg and straightened, patting the horse's muscular haunch. "It would be quicker to backtrack the horse. He can't have traveled fast or far. Jerry might well be in urgent need of help. I'll go alone if you want to try your way."

Boz twisted his round face into a grimace. "Stubborn cuss. All right, we'll try your way; but I'm warning you, it won't be easy."

The men watered Barabbas and turned him out to pasture before mounting up. The lonely gelding limped along the fence line, following the other horses. When he could go no farther, he craned his thick neck over the top rail and whinnied a plaintive farewell.

Obie followed the trail easily from the saddle, his narrowed eyes picking up each hoofprint in the soft mud. Even Boz could tell that Barabbas had stopped occasionally to graze by the roadside. "He might not have come far, traveling slowly like this. Else it could be that he's been traveling for a day or two."

"Been little other traffic lately. That helps."

"Fairfield was heading toward Redcliff."

"Likely."

A few hours later they came to a place where Barabbas had emerged onto the main road from the forest. Boz sat back on his saddle, wheezing slightly. His yellowed moustache blew outward with each breath he exhaled. "Now what? Why would Fairfield be traipsin' around in the forest?"

"To keep from meetin' anyone, most likely. There's a passel of Indian trails through these woods. C'mon."

"You're going in there?"

"Of course. A horse crashing through undergrowth makes an easy track to follow." Obie rode Jughead through the ditch and up into the trees. Boz's horse followed unwillingly, ears laid back and eyes rolling.

Branches slapped the men's faces, and insects rose in clouds from beneath the horses' feet. "I was hoping there wouldn't be many bugs, but this heat has brought them out," Obie observed gruffly, slapping at his cheek. Jughead lashed his tail and twitched his skin. Obie squashed a deerfly on the horse's shoulder, leaving a splotch of blood on the white hair. Boz muttered oaths under his breath.

They crashed through a shallow ravine, climbed into a thicket of hardwood saplings, and labored up a ridgeline, following Barabbas's clear track. After more than an hour of arduous trailblazing, Jughead suddenly shied and gave a weird screeching cry. A large dark mound lay ahead, sprawled across the narrow trail. Flies swarmed around it, and an acrid odor filled the air.

Within seconds Obie knelt beside the prostrate body. Boz heaved himself off his horse. "Dead?"

"Not quite. Gut shot." The front of the man's expansive waistcoat was brown, purple, and crimson with dried and fresh blood. The sight of a small hole beside his fourth waistcoat button told the trackers all they needed to know. A bullet in the belly almost inevitably meant a lingering death.

Suddenly his bleary blue eyes opened. "Water," he croaked. Obadiah took his canteen from Jughead's saddle and held it to the injured man's lips. He drank, though most of it dribbled down over his chins. "Thank God," he breathed.

Obie's surprise at the prayer must have shown, for the wounded man's cracked lips twisted into a smile. "Lyin' here, had time. . .make right with God. Buck Watson, forgive me?"

Obie gripped one hot, fleshy hand. "For what?"

"Yuma. Boz, I never killed anyone. Find Fairfield by old chimney. . .road south. Buried him there. . .years ago. Read my letter—tells all. Give all I own to Fairfield's wife, please?"

Obie and Boz exchanged glances. "You're not Jerry Fairfield?"

"Don't know me yet? Charles Bolton. Guess I was. . .a good actor. I knew you right off, Buck, even though you. . .changed your name. It was Patrick done me in. I didn't know him either until he said—" The dying man took a shuddering breath and convulsed, knocking Obie back with one flying arm. "Pain! Oh, God, help me!"

Obie was too stunned by these revelations to speak. Boz tried to question Charles again, but he would only moan, "The letter. Read the letter!"

He soon drifted into an unconscious state, each breath moaning from his lungs.

Still sitting on the ground where he had fallen, Obie stared blankly at the sheriff. "Think he'll come to again?"

"For his sake, I hope not. You still don't recognize him?"

"Twenty years ago he was a skinny kid with curly blond hair and big white teeth."

Boz considered the obese, nearly bald man whose teeth were rotting away and understood Obadiah's lack of perception.

"What letter was he talking about?"

Looking mystified, Boz shrugged. "We'll search him later."

They held solemn vigil over Charles Bolton until the man's labored breathing stopped entirely. Obie pulled off his shirt and wrapped it around the dead man's face. "I'm thankful he had time to make his soul right with the Lord."

Boz gave him a quizzical look. "If you say so. I wouldn't wish a death like that on a dog. Can you imagine killing your brother that way?"

"Not even my worst enemy. What do we do with him, Boz? Bury him here?"

"What about Mrs. Fairfield?"

Obadiah dropped his head into his hands and rested his elbows on his upraised knees. He ran his fingers through his hair, knocking his hat to the ground. "This is too complicated for me. Charles said he buried the real Jerry Fairfield. . ."

"By the old chimney. I'm thinkin' he meant that burned-out foundation alongside the road to Rockford. You know, the old Miller place?"

Obie was thinking along different lines. "If Patrick shot Charles, he must still be in the area. I wonder if he has been living around here all the time, just like Charles has, and we don't know him. Even Charles didn't know him—his own brother. Patrick was a kid when I last saw him. Twenty years would make quite a difference."

"How old would he be?"

"Thirty-three or -four—and he undoubtedly knows who I am. But if he's been living here for a while, why did he just now kill Jerry—I mean, Charles?"

Boz could only shake his head. "Maybe Charles had the gold?"

"He never mentioned it—but remember how I told you earlier that someone ransacked his house?" Replacing his hat, Obie scrambled to his feet. "C'mon, Boz, we'll grow moss a-sittin' here. Charles needs to be buried quickly, and I think it ought to be in the church graveyard. He may have been a thief and a liar, but God forgave him and so should we."

"Buck, if I was you, I'd want the varmint strung up by the ears."

"He wasn't so bad as all that—just selfish and lazy. Patrick and Edwin were the vicious Boltons, not Charles."

"He let you serve time at Yuma for their crimes. That's vicious enough for me. Wait, let me search him for that letter."

It only took a moment's search. In Charles's left hand, crumpled and filthy, was an envelope with graphite pencil scribbles on both sides. Boz puzzled over it, handed it to Obie, but neither of them could make heads or tails of it. Only a word here and there was legible. "May have to send this away to be analyzed."

"He was dying when he wrote it," Obie defended the departed man. "Can you at least read the signature?"

"Well enough. If he confessed to the robbery, your record should be cleared."

"I had thought of that."

Together the two men loaded Charles Bolton's immense body up on Boz's fidgeting gelding. Although Jughead was the more tractable horse, he was too small to carry such a heavy load. Boz Martin rode the mustang while Obie walked alongside the bay, holding the body in place. This time they followed the trail, and the going was easier.

"What say we don't tell anyone that Charles was alive when we found him?" Boz suggested after a long silence. "And not a word about the letter."

As Obie tramped along, feeling a blister rise on each heel, his mind spun in confused circles. *Lord, help me. The fact that Violet has been a widow for years doesn't excuse me from dreaming about her when I thought she was a married woman. I must be crazy—a man just died a horrible death, Violet's real husband died who knows how or when, and there is a killer loose in the area—yet I feel like shouting for joy because she's free!*

Chapter 4

The just man walketh in his integrity:
his children are blessed after him.
PROVERBS 20:7

Violet awoke to heavy pounding on the boardinghouse's front door. Curious and groggy, she slipped a dress over her chemise. Still buttoning up the front, she stepped out into the hall and listened while Amelia cautiously opened the door. "Obadiah Watson." The lady's voice held little warmth. "What are you doing here? It's too late for social calls, and. . .what has become of your shirt?"

"I need to see Mrs. Fairfield. It's important."

"You cain't barge in and demand to see a lady at this hour—and not even decently dressed! Hev you been drinking?"

"Mrs. Sidwell, the sheriff is here, too. We have information about—"

"Is. . .is that a body hanging over the saddle?" Amelia squealed. "Oh—"

Obie's voice was forceful. "Quiet, ma'am. Don't wake the town. We must speak with Mrs. Fairfield. If you won't fetch her, I'll go up myself."

"That won't be necessary." As though in a trance, Violet descended the stairs, one hand resting on the banister. On the third step she stopped and asked bluntly, "Is my husband alive?"

Looking weary and sorrowful, Obie put one boot on the bottom step. His low voice reached her ears only. "I'm afraid not, ma'am. He's been dead for years."

Violet slowly sank toward the step. "I knew it all the time. And I came all this way—" Suddenly her world went black.

The next thing she knew, Violet vaguely felt herself lifted in strong arms. It was pleasant to rest there against a man's chest. It had been many years since a man had taken care of her. Always she was the caregiver.

Then she gasped and started awake as powerful fumes cleared her head. Amelia sat back, satisfied, and corked her bottle of smelling salts. "Thought that would bring you back to us."

Violet propped herself up on her elbows. She was reclining on the parlor sofa. She and Amelia were alone in the room. "Did you carry me in here?"

" 'Course not. Obadiah did. He's out talking with the sheriff. I think they're

41

taking the body to the undertaker. I'll go check."

When Amelia was gone, Violet slowly sat up, still feeling light-headed. She closed her eyes and tried to remember Jeremiah's face, but it had faded from her memory. A tear trickled down her cheek.

"Ma'am?"

Violet looked up into Obie's compassionate eyes. Taking her totally by surprise, a sob tore from her throat. More tears followed. Obie knelt before her and offered a clean handkerchief. Violet blew her nose and wiped her eyes, but the tears would not stop. "I'm sorry!" she gasped. "It's just that. . .oh, everything!"

"I'll listen if you want to talk."

"I. . .I. . .thank you," she sputtered. His calm regard helped her regain control, and soon she poured her troubles upon his sympathetic ear.

". . .and when I received the package containing his watch, purse, and other personal effects, I knew he was dead. I had already suspected as much, for he had not written to me, and Jeremiah was a faithful correspondent. There was no letter in the package, nothing to tell me how or where he died. I didn't know what to do. I was living with my in-laws in Maryland at the time, and neither of them was well—they have since passed on. I simply mourned my husband for a year, then moved on with my life."

"Did you not have friends at church who would help you? What about your family?"

She studied the wadded handkerchief and confessed, "My parents were far away in Connecticut, and I was too proud or too shy to ask for outside advice. Our pastor never pressed me for details about Jeremiah's death; he simply accepted my word about it. Then, only a few weeks ago, I received an anonymous telegram from Longtree informing me that Jeremiah Fairfield was living here. It shocked and terrified me, you can imagine, to think that my husband might yet be living, for it implied that he had deserted me. This was beyond my imagining; Jeremiah always doted on me and adored his children. Also, he was a good and godly man. I knew that he would never voluntarily abandon us."

Obie nodded. "Of course not."

"Can you explain this mystery? I've been living under a dreadful cloud of apprehension ever since that telegram arrived. How do you know for certain that Jeremiah is. . .dead?"

Obie eased himself up to sit on the sofa beside her, and Violet sat back to listen. "Mr. Fairfield apparently died more than four years ago. While traveling here, he met a man named Charles Bolton. Since Bolton told us that he didn't kill anyone, I assume your husband died of natural causes. Bolton buried him and took his name and identity. The disguise worked for several years, but someone must've suspected him—and whoever it was sent that telegram to you. When your reply arrived, Bolton panicked, ran, and was shot. Before he died, he confessed his true identity and told us where your husband is buried.

We will hunt for the grave as soon as possible."

Violet blinked. Oddly enough, she noticed right then that only the top of Obie's red combinations covered his upper body. His suspender straps dangled around his waist. He did still have a blue neckerchief knotted around his tanned throat, but his hairy chest showed beneath it. At another time she might have been tempted to laugh.

She returned her gaze to his sober eyes. "There is more to this story, I'm sure. What do you need me to do?"

"We need you to come to the sheriff's office. He'll tell us both what to do."

"It's late to call for a buggy."

"I'll put you on Jughead. It's only a short way."

Violet regarded her delicate muslin gown. "But—" This was no time to worry about getting her dress dirty. "All right. I need to ask Amelia to keep an eye on the children."

Minutes later she was perched sideways on Jughead's saddle, her legs dangling over the horse's left shoulder. It was not a comfortable seat, and she could feel the rhythm of each hoofbeat. Sometimes her feet bumped against Obie, who walked beside his horse.

The town was dark and still, yet Violet felt safe with Obie. She looked up at the stars and sighed. *Back to being a widow—not that I ever stopped feeling like one. How will I tell the children about this? Maybe I should never have told them about the telegram.*

Jughead stopped before the sheriff's office. A light glowed in the window. Obie lifted Violet down. "Go on inside. I'll be a minute," he ordered, fiddling with Jughead's cinch and reins.

Inside the office, by the dim light of a lamp, Violet saw the sheriff draped across his chair, snoring deeply. She cleared her throat, but he never flinched. "Sheriff?" she said, then louder, "Sheriff Martin?"

One final snort and his boots hit the floorboards. "Huh? What?" He grabbed the gun on his hip. "Oh, ma'am, you're here." He rubbed his fleshy face with one hand, looking sleepy and sheepish. "Where's Buck?"

"Buck?"

"Watson. Buck Watson. I can't call him Obie. It just don't fit him."

"He'll be right in. Since it's very late, can we get to the point? Mr. Watson tells me that the man you all thought was Jeremiah was actually someone else, and now this someone else is dead."

"Bolton gave us the location of your husband's grave. We'll verify his statements as soon as possible." The sheriff looked bored. "Ma'am, I'll be brief. Bolton's murderer could be just about anyone in this town. For now, we need to keep quiet all the facts around Bolton's death, all right?"

Violet nodded, wide-eyed. "But people won't understand how I know that I am a widow."

The sheriff pursed his lips, glancing up as Obie entered. "We could just let people think that you refused to view the body, so you wouldn't know about the impersonation. That's reasonable, and it's happened before when a body is battered or decomposed. That way the murderer will think we don't know about Charles and the gold."

Violet shuddered and looked pale. Obie quickly drew up a chair for her, and she sat down. "Gold?" she inquired weakly.

"That's a story for another day. It explains why Bolton was killed, but it doesn't involve you, ma'am, so don't worry about it. By the way, one of the last things Charles said was that you were to have his house and all he owned. I think he wanted to make it up to you—make up for using your husband's name, I mean."

"The house. . .is mine?" Violet breathed in awe. "But. . .it was never Jeremiah's. How. . . ? Isn't there someone related to this man who would rightfully inherit his property?"

Obie and Boz exchanged looks. "Charles's brother shot him. If he steps forward and claims the farm, we'll nail him for murder. I don't think he'll be that stupid," Boz said. "Their father died in an Apache raid years ago, and their mother died in childbirth. The eldest brother was killed twenty years ago. There are no other relatives that we know of."

Obie's face looked grim. "The gold originally belonged to another man in New Mexico Territory, but he died in the same Apache raid."

"How horrible!"

"That entire settlement was wiped out, though I've heard that more Americans have moved in since. It's a dangerous area and likely always will be until the Apaches are subdued once and for all."

"That'll be the day," Boz scoffed.

Obie only lifted his brows. "Boz, if you're done, I'll take Mrs. Fairfield back to Amelia's. She looks exhausted."

"She's not the only one. We'll plan the funeral, ma'am. Charles will have to be buried under your husband's name until the mystery is solved. Hope you don't mind."

Rising, Violet took Obie's offered arm. "I don't mind. May I tell the children the true story?"

"I'd rather you didn't. I'm not asking you to lie; just tell them that we need to keep them in the dark for a while. They'll find out everything in the end. Good night, Mrs. Fairfield. I'm sorry ya have to be involved in all this."

"Good night, Sheriff, and thank you for all you're doing."

Obie tightened Jughead's girth again before lifting Violet to the saddle. Strange, how she enjoyed his touch while Nick Houghton's left her feeling soiled.

It was a beautiful night, starry and cool—a perfect night for romance, not for murder and mystery. It wasn't difficult to imagine slipping down from the saddle into Obadiah Watson's strong arms. She had never kissed a man with a moustache before, and she suddenly wanted to try it. Obie's moustache covered most of his upper lip. It would probably tickle, but it wouldn't get in the way of a kiss.

Buck Watson. He had once been called "Buck." She could easily imagine him as a young, lithe, virile cowboy with a gun on his hip and a wicked sparkle in his eyes. Even now, in spite of his gentle ways and silvery hair, he impressed her as a man of action and restrained passion. He made her feel womanly and desirable. She hadn't felt that way in many long years, and she liked it exceedingly.

Shocked by her own thoughts, she sat up straighter and closed her eyes. *I shouldn't be dreaming of romance at a time like this, yet. . . Lord, even though I loved Jeremiah, I have learned, during the last five years, to live without him. I can't even say that I miss him anymore, though memories of our past together will always be sweet. Am I wrong to wish to go on with life and perhaps find a new love?*

Her eyes lowered to Obie's flat hat and square shoulders. *All romance aside, this man is hardworking, kind, and, from what I've seen, he's committed fully to You. My children like him very much, and. . .so do I.*

～⌘～

"I hate to disturb you two, but the children will be downstairs in a minute or two." Amelia's voice disturbed Violet's slumber. Wincing, she tried to stretch her legs, but they were folded into a cramped position. She reached a hand up and felt the arm of the sofa. Her eyes flew open. She was lying on the parlor sofa, fully clothed but for her hat and shoes. Her hastily pinned-up braid had come loose during the night and wrapped across her face like a soft, thick, frazzled rope.

She sat up and blinked. Across the room, Obie slumped in one of Amelia's stiff chairs, arms dangling over the chair arms, booted feet extended on the hooked rug. He was fast asleep. A patch of hairy chest showed through where a button was missing from his red combinations. His jaw was dark with whiskers. To Violet he looked. . .huggable.

"Obadiah, wake up!" she called gently. "Why are we sleeping in Amelia's parlor? I don't even remember arriving."

Obie reached up to rub his forehead and yawned, starting to stretch. He groaned, reaching for the small of his back—and froze when he spotted Violet. "Mrs. Fairfield!" His voice was gruff. Violet had never before noticed the thick black lashes framing his eyes, for the piercing gray eyes themselves usually commanded her full attention.

"Mama?" It was Samuel, standing in the doorway. "What happened? Why are you down here already?"

"Oh, my dear," Violet sighed, recalling the news she had yet to tell the children. "Where are your sisters?"

"Getting dressed. Hello, Uncle Obie. Did you sleep here all night?"

"Good morning, Samuel. Yes, most of the night."

"Uncle?" Violet questioned.

"That's what all the kids call him. He said I could."

Obie turned to Violet. "With your permission, of course."

"I don't mind if you don't." She lifted a hand to smooth her hair and saw his eyes follow the motion. She had no memory of arriving home. Had he carried her inside and removed her shoes and hat? "Did I. . .did I fall asleep on your horse?"

"Yes, ma'am. Almost fell off backwards."

Her eyes widened. He must have caught her. Blood heated her face.

"You were terribly tired, ma'am. No shame in that." His voice was tender, soothing. "Want me to stay awhile? I will, if you need me."

Violet wasn't sure which of her turbulent emotions caused the lump in her throat. She nodded. "I will bring the girls down, and we can all discuss this together."

When Violet returned with her daughters, Samuel was nestled against Obie's side on the davenport, avidly listening. ". . .and that squirrel fooled Treat so completely, she looked silly for days afterward, hunting around that stump as though she expected to find him there. And all the time he was laughing at her from his back doorway."

Samuel chuckled; then he frowned at his mother and sisters. "You came too soon."

"Mama says it's important," Beulah informed him. She and Eunice looked apprehensive. They perched quietly on Amelia's fancy carved chairs, studying their mother's pale face.

Violet stood on the hearth, preparing to speak, but her knees felt rubbery. Moving to the davenport, she sat beside Samuel, drawing strength from Obie's presence. Samuel shifted to lean against her, and she hugged his small body.

"Last night I learned that your father is truly dead after all. He died and was buried more than four years ago, not long after he left us." Violet's voice broke. She squeezed her eyes shut, trying to hold back the tears. Seeking comfort, she reached out to Obadiah. He took her hand and pressed her fingers to assure her of his support.

The girls stared at the floor. Beulah sighed. "I always knew it. Father would never have deserted us. During our train trip out here, I kept thinking about the way he kissed you good-bye that last time, as though he would never let go."

"I wonder if he knew he wouldn't come back?" Eunice pondered quietly.

Violet continued, "We may keep the house. Your father would have wanted us to enjoy living in it, I'm sure."

She interrupted questioning exclamations to explain, "The man who has been using your father's name was killed yesterday. We must pretend for a while that he was really your father. I can't explain it all to you right now, but the sheriff has asked us to do this to help him catch the murderer. Do you understand?"

"Not really, Mama, but I'll try to pretend."

"Do you mean we need to cry at a funeral and stuff like that?"

"Must we go into mourning again?" Eunice groaned.

Violet sympathized. "It won't be fun, but I'm sure we can do it. Just think about your father, and don't talk to *anyone* about what happened, all right?"

"Except for Uncle Obie. He's our friend." Samuel pulled away from Violet and moved closer to Obadiah, who wrapped his arm around the father-hungry boy and hugged him close.

Violet watched them and felt a stirring of joy. "Obie, would you pray for us?" she asked suddenly.

"Yes. I've been thinking of a Bible verse that describes your family," he stated. "It's found in Proverbs: 'The just man walketh in his integrity: his children are blessed after him.' Children, from what I've heard about your father, this verse describes him well."

Holding hands, they all knelt on the floor before the sofa, and Obie prayed aloud, requesting God's healing touch upon the Fairfield family, His guidance for their future, and His blessing on all their ways. After the "Amen," Violet watched as each of her children gave Obie a fond and grateful hug—even Beulah.

"I must get home, Mrs. Fairfield. Al and Myles will be wondering about me." Obie picked his hat off a side table and brushed imaginary dirt from its brim. "I'll check on you soon."

Chapter 5

The fool hath said in his heart, There is no God.
PSALM 14:1

Here it is, Boz. Charles carved Fairfield's initials on the crossbeam." Obie lifted his lantern to examine the crude wooden cross that stood in the lee of a crumbling rock chimney.

Boz approached, threw down his cigarette, and removed his hat in respect for the dead. "Not much question now that she's a widow," he observed.

Obie gave him a sharp look. "You having thoughts about marriage, Boz?"

The sheriff's moustache puffed outward. "Mebbe some thoughts, but no expectations. She's a fine woman—too fine for the likes of us. This Jeremiah Fairfield musta been quite a man to catch a woman like her."

Obadiah said nothing, but his moustache twitched as he contemplated his friend's words.

"You're sweet on her, ain't you?" Boz observed.

Obie nodded silently.

"Thinking she's the little woman God sent your way?"

"Maybe."

Boz's wheezing laughter disturbed the quiet grave site. "I cain't believe you, Buck! Still believe that God answers your prayers? You've lost what little sense you ever had."

"God can work miracles, Boz. I know, somehow, that He's going to clear my name. Surely, you can't help but see how everything is coming together. Bolton's confession, the letter—he maybe even told on that envelope where the gold is hidden. Can't you see? God promised that His justice will prevail—and even if I don't live to see it, I know that the truth will win out eventually."

"Buck, ol' boy, let me make you a deal. If your name is cleared of this crime and you marry Violet Fairfield, I promise I'll believe that there is a God."

Obie's head snapped around. "No fooling? You'd better think hard before you strike a bargain with God. If you decide that He exists, the next logical step is to give your life to Him."

Boz lifted his right hand. "I swear it. I'm not worried; there's no chance that I'll lose. I think the world of you, Buck, but let's face it: You're no prize. What have you got to offer a woman like Violet Fairfield? Pigs'll fly from pine trees before she marries the likes of you."

"You may be right, Boz. But I do know that God has a sense of humor, and you just challenged Him to prove you wrong. I've got more hope of Violet marryin' me now than I ever did before!" Obadiah's eyes glimmered in the lamplight.

It was four days after the funeral. The children were busy with school and activities with their new friends. Violet found time weighing heavy on her hands. She was unaccustomed to idleness.

"Amelia?"

"In the scullery, ma'am. You needin' anything?" Amelia Sidwell backed out of her storage closet with a sack of cornmeal in her hands.

"I wanted to ask if you need anything at the store today. I plan to walk over to the parsonage this morning. Mrs. Schoengard keeps asking me to drop by, and I have plenty of time now."

Amelia understood the unspoken "now that the funeral is over."

"Any word on when you can move out to the house? I understand there were some legal questions to settle first, but it does seem that a woman should have clear claim to her husband's property. I hate to be takin' your money when you could be settlin' into your own place."

"I might stop by the sheriff's office and ask about that. So, do you need anything?"

"Not that I can think of at the moment. You just go on and have yourself a good time. Iffen the children come home before you're back, I'll keep watch over 'em. Don't you worry yourself none."

"Yes, ma'am."

Violet didn't bother to request a buggy. The center of town was only a few streets from Amelia's boardinghouse, and the parsonage was even closer. She wore sturdy walking shoes, a black gown, and a black straw bonnet. It was depressing to be back in mourning, but she understood the necessity...for the time being.

Without realizing it, she kept her eyes peeled for a glimpse of Obadiah Watson. She hadn't seen him since the funeral. He had acted as a pallbearer for his erstwhile neighbor—in spite of protests from a few townspeople who considered him a suspect in the murder. Violet had heard murmurs from various sources that caused her to wonder what scandal lay in his past. "Buck" Watson might have been wilder than she had imagined.

Caroline Schoengard welcomed her warmly. "Violet dear, please come in! You caught me in the midst of baking pies. My mother-in-law is watching the children for me so I can get some work done."

Violet chuckled. "I know how that goes. Put me to work, Caroline. It's always easier to talk with busy hands."

So Caroline assigned her the task of picking through and hulling strawberries. Violet laid aside her bonnet and gloves, donned a spare apron, and set to work. "It's nice to feel useful again," she confided. "I do love Amelia, but she doesn't want another woman in her kitchen. Anything I do, she does over again her way. It's enough to make me feel like a second-rate homemaker!"

Caroline smiled as she rolled out pastry. "She is an exacting person, but no one can fault her as a friend. She'll stick with you through anything, Violet, and I happen to know that she thinks highly of you and of your children. She's been concerned about you since your husband's sudden death. It must have been an awful shock, coming all the way out here only to have him murdered on the day after your arrival."

Violet felt awkward. She didn't want to lie to her friend, yet it seemed rude to say nothing. "It would have been worse, perhaps, if it hadn't been so long since we last saw him. I had a premonition that things would never be the same for us. Perhaps the Lord was preparing me for the...the strange occurrences to come."

With a sideward glance, Caroline considerately dropped the subject. What do you think of our town? People are speculating about whether or not you'll stay in Longtree now that Jerry's gone. You could sell the Folly—I hope you don't mind that name for your place?"

"Not at all."

"Good. Anyway, you could sell the house for a good price, I'm sure. It's rather fancy for the location; but the farmland is premium, and it's close to town."

Violet rinsed and sliced several berries and dropped them into the bowl before replying, "I have no plans to sell at present. The children are happy here. They have made many new friends, and all three wish to keep the Folly. It is far finer than any house we've lived in before—including my parents' home in Connecticut. This is a pleasant town, and the scenery around here is wonderful—so many trees and lakes. We have no desire to live anywhere else."

"The winters are harsh, let me warn you."

"I'm sure we will adjust. I prefer cold weather to hot, humid weather. I tend to wilt in the heat." After a long pause she continued, "Caroline, I did have a particular reason for coming to see you today."

Caroline pricked the pie shells with a fork. "I thought you might."

Violet sat back in her chair, resting her hands on the berry bucket. "In Annapolis we had a visitation ministry in which certain members of the church volunteered their time to help out those in need, such as widows, the elderly and infirm, or those with sick family members. We would clean, cook, bake, make repairs, or simply read aloud—whatever the person needed most. Is there any such ministry at this church right now?"

Caroline tried to conceal a smile. "Nothing is organized, but you're not the first person to express interest in this type of ministry."

"That's wonderful! Do you think there are enough of us to form a 'care committee,' or is that not an option?" Violet's hands flew as her excitement grew.

TIME FOR A MIRACLE

"I'll discuss it with David tonight. Don't you really know who does most of this type of work in our community?"

Violet looked closely at her new friend. "Should I know?"

Caroline grinned. "Do you have enough berries ready to fill these two shells? I'd like to get the first two pies in the oven while we fix the rest."

Violet helped fill the shells and add the top crusts, but her mind was full of questions. Once the pies were in the oven, she cornered Caroline. "Why do I feel as though I'm missing something important here?"

Caroline shook her head. "I'm sorry, honey. It's just that I can't help wondering if God has a secret plan. Your sudden arrival, the strange happenings, the feeling of mystery in town..."

"Caroline, you're not answering my question. Why did you look amused when I asked about a visitation ministry?"

Caroline rolled her blue eyes and brushed back a wisp of blond hair. "Because Obadiah Watson is practically David's assistant pastor in this community. He voluntarily takes food to the elderly, sits with the sick, works around other people's farms when they are laid up—nearly everything that you just professed interest in doing. Now do you understand why I smiled? I don't mean to be nosy, but I couldn't help thinking how ideal it would be if you and he made a match. I know you're only recently widowed and probably need time before you'll feel ready for remarriage, but, well... Do you see what I mean?"

Violet felt the tide of blood roll into her face, but she was helpless to stop it. "Oh."

"Now I've gone and made you uncomfortable." Caroline wiped her hands on her apron and placed an arm around Violet's shoulders. She was a tall woman with a sturdy frame, and Violet felt like a child beside her, although she was several years older than the pastor's wife.

"I don't mean to interfere, Violet. I hope you know that David and I only want the best for you and your family. I'm so thankful you're here in town. I've needed a friend—someone I could talk to about the Lord and about personal matters. I've seen a tender spirit in you, and I know that your walk with the Lord is genuine and sincere. You're not a gossip, and you're a fine mother. No matter what rumors circulate about you, I can judge for myself that you're the kind of person this town needs."

Violet's heart warmed. Caroline might be lacking in tact, but she was unaffected and truly kind. "Thank you, Caroline," she murmured. "I need you, too."

≈

After partaking of a generous luncheon of ham sandwiches, baked beans, and strawberry pie, Violet took leave of the parsonage. In marked contrast to her sober attire, there was a spring in her step and a light in her eyes as she headed toward town. Caroline's offer of true friendship had been exactly what she needed. It was good to know that someone, another woman, believed in her no

51

matter how odd the circumstances of her arrival had seemed.

Sheriff Martin sat in front of his office, cleaning a rifle. At Violet's approach, he set down his front chair legs and invited her inside. "I been meanin' to ride over for a talk with you, ma'am."

"I was simply wondering what progress had been made on your. . .investigation." Violet followed him into the stuffy, smelly office. Through an open door behind his desk, she saw a row of jail cells. Someone back there warbled an off-key ditty that made conversation somewhat difficult.

The sheriff yelled for the singer to "knock off" and closed the door with a bang. "Sorry, ma'am. He's supposed to be sleepin' it off; he went on a real spree last night."

"I see." Violet accepted an offered chair, though its seat was torn and springs extruded from the holes. She sat gingerly, wishing she had not come. The other night, when Obie had accompanied her, she had not noticed the condition of the office. Neither had she noticed the unsavory habits of the sheriff. He shifted a chaw into his other cheek and spat toward the corner. A glob streaked down the wall near the cuspidor, joining others of its kind.

The smells in this building nearly overpowered Violet. She unobtrusively pulled a scented handkerchief, edged in black lace, from her reticule and lifted it to her nose.

Martin settled into his creaking chair. "Mrs. Fairfield, I'm sorry to mention such a. . .an unpleasant thing, but Buck 'n' me found your real husband's grave the other night."

Violet felt thankful to be sitting down.

"There was a wooden cross marking the spot, with J.F. carved on the crossbeam. There's no doubt that it's Jeremiah Fairfield's grave. We left the body undisturbed for now."

She nodded. "Where's Mr. Watson?"

Boz gave her a close look. "At his farm, I reckon, or with Hattie Thwaite. He spends a lot of time with her. Why?"

Obie had a lady friend? Why had she not been told? "I just wondered," she said lamely, feeling small and alone. "I do appreciate all the trouble you've gone to for me."

"It's part of my job. Can't say I enjoy it, but it had to be done." Violet could hear him breathing. A heavy man with a barrel chest, he wheezed like a blacksmith's bellows. "I'm sorry you can't give your husband a Christian burial right now. He can be reburied at the church once this mystery is solved."

Violet nodded. "I'm sure he doesn't care. He's too busy enjoying heaven to worry about a headstone over his body here on earth."

Boz looked surprised and impressed. "That's one way to look at it. You're sure he's in heaven, huh?"

"Yes. Jeremiah knew the Lord well."

"Like Buck does." Without looking for a reply, the sheriff said, "You can move out to the house anytime you like. Strange that it's called Fairfield's Folly when 'twasn't a Fairfield what built it. Kinda prophetic in a way. Reckon you'll want to clean. I checked it out after Buck told me about the break-in. It's a mess."

"I will send for my furniture right away," Violet brightened. "We'll have plenty of time to clean before our things arrive. You're sure it's rightfully ours?"

"Sure as I can be. No one else claims it, and Charles himself willed it to you. Buck and me are witnesses to that, and we wrote down his last words in case your claim is ever contested. I had a lawyer check things out, and he's handling all the legal work. He'll have some papers for you to sign, no doubt, but for now you're free to move in. If you need any help, let me know." Sheriff Martin smiled, or at least his face crinkled up and his tobacco-stained moustache lifted at the corners.

"Thank you, Sheriff." Since the interview seemed at an end, she rose with a rustle of petticoats and extended her black-gloved hand. "I appreciate all you have done for us."

"I ain't done much. The Schoengards did the funeral, and Buck arranged for the coffin and the hearse and all. By the way, you did a fine imitation of a grieving widow at that service, ma'am, and I'm appreciatin' how you've gone into mourning like your husband really just passed on. You've helped us more than we've helped you."

"I don't think that is possible. By the way, Sheriff, may I ask why you call Mr. Watson 'Buck'?"

"That was his name back when I met him. He started going by Obadiah a while back, but he'll always be Buck to me."

"How long have you known him?" Violet forgot about leaving.

"Oh, we were wild young cowhands together out West many years back. Then our ways parted, and I heard about his conviction. Always figgered it was a frame job. I met up with Buck after his release. He says he 'met God' while he was in prison. Seems a strange place to meet the Almighty, but I cain't deny the change in Buck Watson. He was lucky to live through Yuma—not many could survive it."

Prison? "What was he like before?" Violet asked, trying not to sound shocked.

The sheriff gave her a penetrating look. His moustache twitched from side to side as he chewed solemnly, rather like a cow. "Back in the fifties we worked as hired guns, cow-punchers, horse breakers, or as trail guides for wagon trains. Anything to make a living. Buck always had honor, though, and he never placed value on gettin' rich. If he says he didn't rob the DeVries gold shipment, I believe him."

Violet's eyes were large. She swallowed hard. This was more information than she was prepared to assimilate at the moment.

"I may regret this, but I'll tell you somethin' else, ma'am. Buck's always been honorable where women are concerned. He'd make a fine husband, if you're thinkin' on those lines."

Violet plucked at her cuffs with nervous fingers and tucked her reticule under one arm. "I like and admire Mr. Watson, sir, but marriage is far from my mind at this time." She hoped the second part was not a total lie. She wanted to ask about Hattie Thwaite, but did not have the courage. Prison sentence? So Houghton had not lied about Obie after all.

The afternoon was waning into evening shadows when Violet stepped out upon the boardwalk. Not many people were on the street at this hour. Sighing, Violet started back toward Amelia's. Another day without a glimpse of Obadiah Watson. Was he working at his farm or helping a needy family. . .or entertaining another woman?

"Violet!" a masculine voice hailed from across the street. Violet tried not to grimace. She did her best to avoid Nick Houghton, but he had a way of popping up anywhere and everywhere. The man was impossible to discourage, it seemed. He hurried across the street, holding his hat in place. The sunset lit his bright eyes and dazzling smile. A mane of golden brown hair flowed to his shoulders, and thick side-whiskers emphasized his square chin.

"Hello, Mr. Houghton. How are you this evening?" Violet did not offer her hand.

"Fine, now that I've seen you. Violet, I've seen few women who look ravishing in mourning, but you top my list of lovely widows. What were you doing in the sheriff's office?"

"He had a few questions to clear up. He's investigating my husband's death, you see. Now I must be going, sir, as I have not yet supped this evening."

"Hurrah! I've been longing to take you to dinner, my dear. This is my lucky night."

"I don't believe that would be proper, Mr. Houghton. I am in mourning, you know."

"Fiddlesticks! As though anyone in Longtree cares about such niceties. What could be more public and innocent than supper in the hotel dining room?"

"I thank you, but no. Amelia will have saved supper for me, and I must be getting on home." Violet increased her pace, but Nick's long legs had no trouble matching it.

"How are you, Violet? I haven't really had a chance to ask since the funeral. Such a shocking thing, Jerry's death! A robbery, I suppose they've decided."

"I am as well as can be expected," she answered honestly. "The children keep me occupied. They are making many friends here. Although school will be out for the summer in a few weeks, I have encouraged them to attend. It has helped them adjust to our altered circumstances."

"So you intend to stay here? Why don't you sell out and move back East?"

"I like it here." For the first time she questioned her own motives. Why did she like it here so much? It was a beautiful setting, but scenery was not the reason for her determination to stay.

Nick blurted, "Violet, my dear, you must be reasonable. This is no place for a lady like you."

"I am being reasonable. The people here are kind and helpful, and I love the trees and the lakes—"

"You won't be so enthusiastic come January. This place is an icebox for months on end, and there is little to do for entertainment. I can't bear to think of you alone in that house—"

"Hardly alone with three children."

"—alone in the wilderness. Helpless. You cannot begin to conceive of the difficulties you would encounter. You could never manage that farm alone. You must marry if you plan to stay."

Marry! Violet stopped in her tracks and stared at him. She noted the slight puffiness under his eyes, the broken blood vessels in his nose, and the red wetness of his lips beneath a heavy moustache.

"Mr. Houghton—"

"Nicholas."

"—Nicholas, I feel more at home here in Longtree than I ever did in Annapolis. I don't mind the cold, and I don't mind the lack of big-city entertainment. If I marry again, it will be for love, not out of necessity. The children and I have managed to survive for several years while my husband was away, and we will manage equally well here. We are not afraid of hard work."

"My dear lady, you may need protection. Your husband was murdered, after all. Who's to say the killer would not harm you? I don't mean to alarm you, but I am concerned for your safety, Violet. I would protect and shield you from harm if you would allow me to."

Violet crossed the street and resumed her rapid pace. "I appreciate your offer, but I don't believe I'm in any danger."

Houghton grabbed her arm and pinned her with his blue stare. "I think you ought to know that a convicted murderer lives on the farm next to the Folly. It's only a matter of time before he's brought in for questioning about Jerry's death. Violet, listen to me—you must not move out there without a man for protection! Anything could happen."

"What are you talking about? Convicted murderer?" Violet hoped her confusion looked genuine.

"Everyone knows that Buck Watson killed several men and robbed a private gold shipment twenty years ago in New Mexico. He was a legendary gunman, but somehow he managed to slip the noose."

Violet recalled Boz's certainty of Obie's innocence, but she still felt slightly ill. "I cannot believe it. Obadiah Watson is no murderer. He can't be!" She remembered the bashful way he lifted her down from his horse, the grip of his strong hand when she reached out for his support, his loving hugs for the children, his deep voice lifted in prayer. . . Yet he *had* served a prison sentence. Could this horrible accusation be true?

She pulled her arm out of Houghton's grasp and hurried along the dirt walkway that led to Amelia's boardinghouse.

"You seem eager to defend the fellow. What's he to you?"

Violet tried to speak boldly, but her voice trembled. "A friend and brother in the Lord."

Houghton's jaw worked as though he gritted his teeth, but almost immediately his smile reappeared. "Research the crime for yourself then. The facts in the case will be hard to ignore. The man is a killer beyond all doubt. The jury found him guilty. His death sentence was hung up on a mere triviality."

"How do you know so much about it?"

For an instant he looked startled. "When a man with a shady past moves into a community, concerned citizens make sure they know what they're up against. I'm not the only one who has investigated the case."

"Doesn't the sheriff know about it?"

"That dolt! He's the poorest excuse for a sheriff I've ever encountered. All he ever does is clean his guns and lounge around his office. He sends his deputy out to do all the legwork. Someday he'll break his fat neck when his easy chair slips, and the town will hold a celebration."

Violet was grateful to see the picket fence around Amelia's yard not far ahead. Soon she could escape from this annoying man. "If the sheriff is that incompetent, I wonder why he keeps being reappointed."

"This is off the subject, Violet. No matter what you choose to believe about Watson, your life could be in grave danger."

"I'll take my chances. I don't believe he would harm me."

"If you had seen him pick a man off a running horse with one rifle shot while lying flat on his back, maybe you wouldn't be so pert. He's deadly."

"Have you seen Obadiah Watson do that? I don't believe it." Violet tried to keep her voice calm. "He doesn't even carry a gun."

At Amelia's gate, Nick grabbed Violet again and spun her about. "The point here is that I want you to trust me! It hurts that you don't trust my assessment of the situation. I want to be part of your life and your decisions."

He raised a hand to forestall her protest. "I realize that we met only a few days ago and that you are but newly widowed, but I knew the moment I laid eyes on you that our destinies were to be intertwined. Long hours have I listened to Jerry praise your beauty and warmth; little did I know that one day I would be able to appreciate your assets for myself." His eyes lowered to her body in a way Violet found insulting.

She flung off his hands. "Mr. Houghton, I have reason neither to trust you nor to believe a word that you say. I know nothing good of you, and you manage to insult me in some way at our every meeting. Now I must bid you good evening."

Nick watched her rush up the path. This Fairfield woman was proving more difficult than he had anticipated. She seemed to have developed an aversion to his company, and Nick was unaccustomed to having women find him distasteful. The novelty did not improve his temper. "I'll have her yet," he determined. "She is one handsome woman worth having."

Chapter 6

Behold the fowls of the air: for they sow not,
neither do they reap, nor gather into barns;
yet your heavenly Father feedeth them.
Are ye not much better than they?
MATTHEW 6:26

Al watched his cousin scrape whiskers and soap from his face with the long razor. "I don't blame you, Cousin Buck. She's a handsome woman—and for that matter, her daughters are no hardship to the eyes. I wouldn't mind paying a call on Beulah. Never did see prettier eyes on a girl."

"I have. Her mother's eyes." Obie splashed water on his smooth face and toweled off. "Thought I liked brown eyes best until I saw Violet's blue ones." He combed back his damp hair, peering into the bleary mirror.

"She can't be much younger than you, since Beulah is at least sixteen. Course, maybe she married young. She doesn't look very old—the mother, I mean. I saw the way you two hit it off that first day when she was here. No, don't say it—I know you weren't trying to flirt with a married woman, but the understanding, the. . .the. . .what's the word I'm looking for?"

"Esteem? Affinity?" Obie hauled on a chambray shirt, buttoned it, and snapped his suspenders in place. Digging a clean neckerchief from his bureau drawer, he tied it haphazardly about his neck.

"Affinity, that's it. The affinity between you two was obvious even to me. And now she's a widow! Maybe God sent her here so you two could meet and fall in love." Al tagged along behind his cousin as Obie clapped his hat on and headed toward the barn.

"Al—"

"There's nothing wrong with that. I know you wouldn't have tried to steal her from Fairfield if he had lived."

Obie stopped in his tracks, propped fists on his hips, and glared up at the tall boy. "I envied him, Al, and I coveted her. I can't deny it."

"But you repented, put your desires aside, and acted honorably. God will forgive your human failings, Cousin Buck."

Staring at the ground, Obie considered the boy's words. "How'd you get to be so smart, kid?"

"Walk with the wise, and you will be wise," Al responded with a grin. "I haven't lived with you all these years for nothing!"

Inside the barn, Al hopped up and sat upon Brunhilda's stall door. A chorus of piggy squeals rose from behind him. "You're taking Barabbas to her? I doubt she'll care for him. Maybe you'd better help her find a milder horse."

"I'll let her make that decision; she has a good mind of her own. I hear she's talking about buying a horse, but she already owns this one." Obie's dark brows drew together in concern. "Look, I've got to be careful, Al. As soon as I start thinking maybe I could have a chance with her, my common sense rears its head and I know better. When I start putting my wants ahead of God's perfect plan, I'm in trouble."

"How do you know that your wants aren't in God's plan?"

Obie clenched his fists and slammed one into the seat of a saddle on its rack. "I don't know. But I've got to be careful. I want to help her, Al. All the time I want to be with her. . .but I'm afraid. That's the honest truth. I'm afraid of what she'll say when she hears about my criminal record. Maybe she's already heard and she'll cut me dead today. I don't know. I'm afraid she'd laugh in my face if I ever told her how I feel about her."

"From what I saw, I don't think so. She seems to respect and admire you, Cousin. I think you might have a chance with her. It's about time you settled down and had a family."

Obie snorted and shook his head. His former hope now seemed like striving after the wind.

Al wasn't finished. "I think God sent her in answer to prayer: one woman, made to order."

"What makes you think I've been praying for a wife?" Obie growled, hauling Jughead's saddle from the rack.

"Maybe you haven't, but I've been praying on your behalf. If any man ever deserved a good woman, it's you. Ma always said. . ."

Obie hurried outside. Al's voice faded away.

❧

Violet entered Amelia's kitchen. "Amelia, do you know where I could find some gentle horses like yours? I've put off purchasing horses and a rig because I haven't the first idea how to go about it. I suppose I could pay to have my dry goods and groceries delivered to the house, but we still have to own some means of transportation. Nick Houghton is right about that, at any rate."

"Won't he help you find a horse?" Amelia stopped peeling potatoes to examine her boarder's face.

"I'm sure he would if I were to ask, but I do not desire his help."

Amelia's long fingers wielded a knife with such speed that the peeling seemed to fall from a potato of its own volition. "Nick's not used to a woman running the other way; most of 'em swarm him like flies."

"Indeed?" Violet picked up a knife and started peeling.

"Ya don't need to do that, honey."

"I know, but I might as well work while I chat. We've been in Longtree for nearly a month now, and I want so much to move into our house, yet it could be weeks before our furniture arrives. Do you think I would be crazy to move out there with no beds, just blankets to sleep on?"

"It's been done before. Do whatever you like, honey. You're in charge of your own life, you know."

Just then Beulah called, "Mama, Mr. Watson is out front and he wants to see you."

"Oh!" Violet hopped up, dropped her half-peeled potato back into the bowl, and smoothed her dress.

Amelia stopped to watch her with an amused smirk. "Miz Fairfield, and your first man hardly cold in his grave! You'll set tongues to waggin', though not many would blame you. A woman with young'uns needs a man about the house. Obie ain't so grand to look at, but he'll provide well for ya. Used to figger on snatchin' him up for myself, but he's too partic'lar to settle for a skinny ol' biddy like me."

She picked up the abandoned potato and finished peeling it. "You may not be too handy about the house, but he'll likely be happy jest to sit and stare at yer pretty face. Some men got that romantic streak, and nothing seems to cure 'em of it."

Violet fled the kitchen, feeling much warmer than the weather justified. She peeked through the front window. Sure enough, Obie waited at the gate. The sight of his trim figure made her chest feel constricted, as though her corset were laced too tightly. Since the funeral she had seen him only at church, where they had simply exchanged polite pleasantries. Maybe he was aware of her interest and, in his kind way, was trying to discourage her ardor by avoiding her. Maybe he was just shy.

Checking her reflection in the hall mirror, Violet tucked stray hairs back into her bun, straightened the string tie at her throat, and bit her already rosy lips. Though she hated wearing black, this shirtwaist and skirt did accent her figure and the pearly sheen of her skin. Her hair was freshly washed. She had slept well the night before. On the whole she felt pretty, and this gave her self-confidence. *Hattie Thwaite, I intend to give you competition.*

She walked gracefully through the front doorway and down the steps.

Obie opened the garden gate. "Mornin', Mrs. Fairfield."

Violet smiled her brightest at him as she stepped through. "The same to you, Mr. Watson. It's a pleasure to see you again. Did you wish to speak with me?"

He suddenly pulled off his hat and fiddled with it, looking as shy and awkward as a boy. "I brought your horse. Heard you might be needing him."

Violet then noticed two horses waiting at the hitching rail, Obie's homely paint and a strapping chestnut with a white snip on its nose.

"You brought me a. . . How did you know? Oh, you heard that I wanted a horse? My, but news travels quickly in this town. Um, thank you. I do appreciate it, honestly."

He just looked at her.

Flustered, she rattled on, "Well, I do need a horse—two, really. I guess it's obvious. . . How did you know I was planning to buy a team today?"

"I didn't know."

His unblinking regard began to irritate her. "Mr. Watson, would you please state your business and stop staring at me?"

He took a step back and donned his hat. "I didn't intend to be rude, ma'am. This is your horse, Barabbas." He indicated the chestnut. The animal took the opportunity to rub its sweaty ears against Obie's shoulder, but he shoved it away. "Remember? He belonged to. . .to Charles. You saw him at the house that day, when he came limping home. He's sound now."

"Oh!" she blurted, feeling gauche. "I. . .I forgot all about it. Is he gentle?" She reached out to touch the horse's face, but it jerked its head away, ears flattened, and snapped at the air with yellow teeth. Violet gasped, stepped back on her skirt's hem, and would have fallen if Obie had not caught her arm and hauled her back to her feet.

"Are you all right?"

Although he looked and sounded sincerely concerned, she yanked her arm out of his grasp and flashed, "I need a gentle animal, not a. . .a vicious beast!"

He blinked. "You can certainly trade him for a gentler horse, but I thought you'd want to make that decision."

She hung her head. "I'm sorry. I lost my temper at you again for no reason. You must think I'm an awful shrew."

He brushed the matter aside. "Do you know how to harness and hitch a horse?"

"I've done it before. If you think I can manage this one, I guess I'll keep him for now, but I would appreciate your. . .your advice while purchasing a vehicle. I've never bought one before. I don't know where to begin."

"What time?"

"I will leave in about half an hour. I need to arrange things with Amelia and the children."

"I'll wait, if you like, and you could ride with me to the livery stable. Irving should have some rigs to sell."

Violet glanced ruefully at the man's saddle atop Barabbas. "I'll walk. You were right about me not being a very good rider."

He looked abashed. "Forget I said that, ma'am."

"Perhaps I'll learn to be a better horsewoman under your tutelage."

"Mrs. Fairfield?" Obie doffed his hat again and fiddled with it, as if struggling for words.

"Please, after all we've been through together, I wish you would call me Violet."

He could not meet her eyes. "Violet, you look. . .mighty fine today," he stated. He then stalked to the hitching rail, released the horses, swung into Jughead's saddle, and rode away without a backward glance, shaking his bowed head.

Instead of hurrying inside, Violet stood in the open gateway and watched him out of sight. She liked Obie's square shoulders and small hips. He looked lithe and graceful on his horse. She liked his flat stomach and strong arms, and his beautiful gray eyes. . . Quickly she snapped the gate shut and hurried into the boardinghouse, hoping no one had seen her admiring the cowboy.

Later, at Irving's Livery, Violet listened and watched while the men tried a harness on Barabbas and haggled over the price. The horse objected to being harnessed. Violet's heart pounded when it kicked viciously at Obie, but he had seen the kick coming and moved out of range. Violet gasped when he calmly whacked the horse on the rump, but it subsequently allowed him to place the crupper under its tail. She had severe doubts about her ability to control this contrary beast even for a day or two.

When it came to choosing a vehicle, Violet was bewildered. Irving showed her several conveyances, pointing out their high quality and good condition, but Violet had no idea which one would best meet her needs. She looked at Obie, and he quietly stepped in and chose a modest surrey for her, much like Amelia's but with a top that folded down. Its paint was faded and chipped, but the wheels and seats were good. "You need a surrey or rockaway for the extra seating. A buggy wouldn't hold your whole family."

"Will one horse be enough?"

"Barabbas is a powerful animal. He'll manage alone until we can find him a partner or trade him for a team."

To Violet's relief, Obadiah dickered the price down. She paid twenty-three dollars cash for surrey and harness. Obie shook his head over the exorbitant price, but Bill Irving acted as if he'd practically given the rig away.

Soon the surrey was hitched to her horse, and Obie lifted her to the seat. He tied Jughead behind and hopped up beside Violet, ready to drive. "You're coming with me?" she asked, unable to hide her relief.

"I don't know how well Barabbas drives." He picked up the buggy whip Irving had thrown into the deal and clucked up the horse. Barabbas tried to rear, but Obie quickly brought him under control. The surrey rolled into the main street at a reasonable pace. Violet held the seat with white-knuckled hands.

"What are your plans for the rest of the day?" Obie asked, maneuvering through traffic.

The horse's antics had crumbled her confidence. "I wanted to go to the house and start cleaning—maybe even move into it today. This morning I ordered supplies at Russell's, but they won't fit into this surrey along with the children. I guess I should have them delivered to my house. . . Oh, I don't know what to do next! Should I have purchased that wagon instead of a surrey? I don't know what I'm doing. Nick Houghton was right—I should just sell this house and go back where I came from."

"Why?"

Violet felt tears threatening, and this made her angry all over again. "Why? I don't know when to plant things or when to harvest them. I don't know the first thing about machinery or animals. I can't drive or ride well or even saddle a horse. I don't know how to repair anything except clothing. I. . .I only know that I love this place, and I want to belong here!"

"Is this where God wants you?"

"Do you mean, am I following His guidance? I don't know where else to go. I have no family still living. But what if I lose this house? What if we have to give it up because Charles Bolton's family comes to claim it? Then we would have to go back to Annapolis, and I don't like it there." She sounded slightly hysterical, even to her own ears.

"Violet, is Jesus Christ your friend?"

Violet calmed and looked at Obie. His hat was tipped back, and sunlight sparkled on the silver in his hair. His hair was thinning on top and she could see his scalp.

He glanced over, catching her in the act of staring. "Is He?"

She had almost forgotten the question. "Yes," she said quietly.

"He loves you the same as He ever did. You need to trust Him. He doesn't allow hardships or uncertainties without good reason."

Violet sighed. "I guess I've given Him lots of good reasons."

Undeterred, Obie continued, "When God sends a blessing, He expects His children to enjoy it, not worry that He will snatch it away again. He is our loving Father, not an erratic tyrant. Do you believe that He loves you?"

"Yes."

"Then you must know that He will care for you as He promised. He wouldn't take Jerry from you without providing for your future in another way. Remember the story of the lilies of the field and the birds of the air."

"He did provide an inheritance from my parents and the house from Jeremiah's parents, which is being leased and provides us with another source of income. But if we should lose this house and farm, I'm not sure my inheritance would last until the children are grown—and I have no trade, no means of earning a living. If I simply sit back and expect God to provide our needs. . ." Her voice trailed away. "The Proverbs revile a lazy and improvident parent."

"Are you lazy and improvident?"

She frowned. "I don't believe so, but it seemed to me that you recommended me to be so."

"Trusting in God is, therefore, lazy and improvident?" Obie halted Barabbas in front of Amelia's boardinghouse, but Violet was too absorbed in their conversation to notice.

"You insist upon twisting my words into things that I do not mean!" she snapped, turning to confront him face-to-face. "I am a good mother, and I try to put my children's welfare before my own. You are a bachelor, but surely you can understand my position. Jeremiah left us nearly five years ago, and I assumed leadership of the family, though I did not crave that role. I am now responsible to provide for my children."

"I disagree." Obie secured the reins and met Violet's glare.

"What possible grounds can you have for disagreement?"

"The book of James, chapter one, verse twenty-seven. Also, many other references that refer to the church caring for widows and orphans, as they cannot provide for themselves. As a believer in Christ, your brother in God's family, I am responsible to provide for your livelihood, as is every other Christian in this town."

Violet's pride was stung. All the while she had been daydreaming about him, he had considered her a charity project! She tried to sound nonchalant, but her voice revealed her hurt feelings. "And this is why you are helping me?"

"It's one reason."

Apparently considering the discussion at an end, Obie climbed down, tethered the horse, and came to assist Violet. She tried not to notice how his grasp on her waist increased her heart rate. Once on the ground, she brushed at her dusty skirts. "I thank you for your assistance. Good day, Mr. Watson."

He said nothing but followed her inside. In the hallway, Violet stopped on the second stair and turned. Standing above him gave her the illusion of control. "I said 'Good day,' sir."

He nodded. "Yes, ma'am, you did." He tapped his hat against his leg.

"Is there something you need?" Violet tried to stare him down, but her eyes began to water. He was impossible to intimidate.

"Pack up and bring your children. I'll drive you out to the house; then I'll bring my wagon back to town for your supplies. Hurry." This said, he walked toward Amelia's kitchen.

Violet stared after him. His assumption of control irritated her, but she had to admit that his plan sounded ideal; she could potentially settle into her house this very night. A flicker of excitement banished her anger. Turning, she hurried upstairs in a hustle and bustle of skirts. "Beulah!"

Chapter 7

Pure religion and undefiled before God and the Father is this,
To visit the fatherless and widows in their affliction,
and to keep himself unspotted from the world.
JAMES 1:27

S amuel perched beside Obie, staring up at the man with evident adoration, listening and talking for all he was worth. Beulah and Eunice, on either side of their mother in the surrey's backseat, were also talking full speed, so Violet could hear little of the "man talk."

Satchels and valises were crammed in around their feet, and Obie had promised to bring their trunk and other bags when he brought the supplies. Violet was still embarrassed by her dependence on his Christian charity, but at the same time she was thankful for his help.

Violet allowed herself to revel in the beauty surrounding her and promptly forgot her gripes and worries. *Lord,* she prayed silently, trying to block out the conversations around her, *I thank You for this beautiful place and for our beautiful house. You do bring good out of every situation, don't You?*

The surrey turned, and Violet recognized the overgrown lane. Her heart responded, pounding with anticipation. Was the house as wonderful as she remembered it?

Their ride was much smoother today. Someone must have filled in the potholes. Suddenly, the surrey lurched as the horse bounded forward. Their heads snapped backwards, and Eunice let out a terrified squeal.

"Whoa, boy. Whoa, Barabbas," Obie's deep voice soothed. He hauled the big horse down to an erratic trot, though the animal was evidently itching to run wild. Violet could see Barabbas's brown mane tossing and could hear his frenzied snorts. "Steady now. It was nothing to make you fly into a panic, boy."

"What happened, Uncle Obie?" Samuel asked, clutching his seat.

"A bird flew past his nose." Once the horse was under control, Obie turned his head. "You all right back there?"

"We're fine." Violet realized that had she been driving just then, they might all have been killed, for she could never have stopped the horse from bolting. Her arms were too weak. "Thank you."

At the house they all piled out of the surrey, grateful for solid ground under their feet. The girls looked pale and shaken, and Samuel blurted, "Mama, how are you going to drive this horse? He isn't quiet and gentle like you said you wanted."

Violet lifted a trembling hand to straighten her bonnet. Her eyes involuntarily flew to Obie's face. He looked serious, almost angry, as he said, "I'll look for a gentle team for you. In the meantime, don't try driving Barabbas anywhere."

Obie lifted two bags from the surrey and carried them up the steps. Violet and the children each claimed a bag and followed him into the house. "Let's just pile our things in the sitting room for the present," Violet suggested. To her amazement, the house was immaculately clean. All the clutter and destruction had been cleared away. The windows sparkled, the floors gleamed with wax, and the cobwebs had vanished.

"Oh, Mama, look!" Eunice pointed.

A pewter pitcher filled with flowers brightened the mantel. Violet reached high and lifted it down. She touched her face to a perfumed spray of lilacs. "This is lovely."

"Mama, it's clean in here, too, and someone left two pies on the table," Beulah called from the kitchen doorway. "They look like strawberry, my favorite."

"How very nice! Let's save them for supper tonight." Violet glanced around. "Obadiah, did you do all thi—?"

"He's taking the surrey around back, Mama. He left our stuff on the walkway."

"You all bring in the rest of our things; then you may head for your rooms and start unpacking. I'll find out what he's planning to do next. Get on with you now."

"Who cleaned the house and brought the flowers, Mama?" Eunice couldn't resist asking as she collected her satchel. "Do you think it was Mr. Watson?"

"Perhaps," Violet allowed. "But I'm pretty sure he didn't bake those pies."

Jughead was tethered to the hitching rail. With pricked ears and quivering nostrils, he watched Violet walk past. He looked friendly enough, though his blue eye had a glassy look. "Hello," she greeted. The horse shook himself, sending up a cloud of trail dust.

Violet hurried to the barn. The surrey was parked under an overhang. Obie had just finished hanging the harness on the barn wall. "Will that harness fit another horse?"

"If not, we'll trade for one that fits." He began to rub down Barabbas.

As he worked, Violet looked around. "This is a nice barn. Do you think we could keep a cow in here with the horses?"

"Yes."

Violet's eyes returned to Obie. His faded blue shirt had come untucked in places, though his suspenders strapped it against his trim body. The sleeves were rolled up above his elbows, revealing muscles that swelled and stretched as he worked over the horse. He must have removed his red combinations for the summer—his shirt's open neck revealed a strip of white undervest.

For the first time that day, Violet recalled Nick's accusations about Obie's past. Was he really a legendary gunman? Had he killed several men?

Obadiah Watson was certainly a strong, tough man, but she could not imagine him as a killer. Leaning against a post, she asked softly, "Obadiah, are you the one who filled in the potholes, cleaned up the house, and brought the flowers and pies?"

"Al, Myles, and I fixed the drive, but Caroline Schoengard and Mamie Bristol did the rest. Like you said, word travels fast in this town." Violet could not read his face, for he was hidden behind the horse. He emerged a moment later, brushing his hands down his jeans, then led the horse past her and tied him in an open-backed stall. "I'll return with your things in a few hours. The horse'll be fine until then. I watered him already."

"Obie?" Her voice was low.

He paused in the barn doorway but did not turn to face her.

"I want you to know that I'm eternally grateful. I don't know what I would have done without you today. I am certainly in need of Christian charity, and you have been more than kind. I'm sorry I shouted at you earlier." Violet twiddled her fingers nervously as she spoke. "I don't usually lose my temper so easily. I don't know what ails me lately."

She saw his chest expand in a deep breath. He said, "I'll be back," then continued outside.

Violet followed slowly, letting her eyes drift upward as she emerged from the shadowy barn into the sun-spattered freshness of the outdoors. Branches waved gently overhead, their leaves flashing from green to silver. In the woods beyond the house, Violet spotted the white trunks of birches among the stolid gray oaks, basswoods, maples, and elms.

Obie skidded Jughead to a stop before her and asked, "Thought of anything else you need while I'm in town?"

"As a matter of fact, I need two more blankets. Please have Mr. Russell put them on account for me. I will pay him as soon as possible. Thank you!"

Obie nodded and gave a short wave. Violet was startled when Jughead suddenly reared almost straight up, came down with a snort, and clattered away. She had heard that cowboys were amazing riders, but such a thing had to be seen to be believed.

As she ascended the front steps, the thought struck her that Obie had been showing off for her like a schoolboy for a girl he admired. She smiled, glancing back at the place she had seen him last, and felt her spirits rise. *Maybe he does like me more than a little.*

"Mama, I'm hungry." Samuel met her at the front door. "When are we going to eat?"

"In a few minutes. Mrs. Sidwell packed us a few things for dinner. When our supplies arrive, I'll cook us a hot meal. I ordered plenty of food."

"Do you know how to use this stove?" Beulah asked.

"It's much like the one in Grandma Fairfield's kitchen. Here's the water reservoir," she said, moving into the kitchen. "Here's the oven, and here's the firebox. Look, someone has put kindling in it, all ready to light. We might as well heat some water for coffee." She wanted to offer Obie a cup when he returned.

"I'll fill the kettle," Eunice offered, eager to try out the newfangled pump.

"Thank you, dear. Now, where are the cooking utensils stored?" Violet began to explore the kitchen cabinets. There was little to find. "I'll be thankful when our possessions arrive from the East."

"Did you send for them already, Mama?"

"I wired for them. They could arrive any day."

"I was so afraid you would decide to sell this house," Beulah admitted. "I saw Mr. Houghton after school one day, and he tried to make me ask you to sell. He told me all kinds of stories about how awful it is to live on a farm and about how much work we'd have to do."

Violet frowned. "Mr. Houghton doesn't know what is best for our family. Mr. Watson says that we need to accept and enjoy the gifts God sends and not worry. God will enable us to survive here, I'm certain."

"Uncle Obie says he'll teach me to be a farmer," Samuel announced, already chewing on a chicken leg he had sneaked from the basket Amelia had sent.

"Did he?" Violet smiled her pleasure.

"He says he'll teach me to fish, too."

"Samuel, you shouldn't call an adult by his first name," Beulah chided.

"All the kids call him that. He likes it," Samuel defended himself. "I'm not being disrespectful. It's all right, isn't it, Mama?"

"If Mr. Watson doesn't mind, it's all right with me."

Eunice spread a cloth on the rough table, and Violet unpacked their dinner. "Mama, why does Mr. Watson help us like this?"

"He is trying to obey God's command that believers are to provide for widows and orphans."

"Isn't the church supposed to do that?"

"Mr. Watson tells me that many church members have pitched in to help us. Mrs. Schoengard and Mrs. Bristol cleaned the house, baked those beautiful pies, and brought the flowers. Wasn't that kind of them? Let's ask our blessing, children, before we talk anymore."

They held hands around the table as Violet quietly asked God to bless their food and their home. "Amen."

"Maybe he wants to marry you, Mama, like Mr. Houghton does."

Violet's eyes flew to her son's face. "What makes you say that, Samuel?"

"I heard some ladies talking in Mrs. Sidwell's parlor the other day while you were away. They said they would lay bets, if they were men, that he'd have you hog-tied within a month. They said he needs your money."

"Mr. Watson?" Violet felt a tightness around her heart.

"No, Mr. Houghton. They said he's a fortune hunter. Are we rich, Mama?"

The tightness eased into a relieved sigh. "Hardly. We have a tidy nest egg in the bank, but we are far from rich." Violet gave her son a steady look. "Why were you eavesdropping, Samuel?"

"I didn't mean to. I was in the broom closet, and its back wall leans up against the parlor. Once all those ladies arrived, I was afraid to move in case I knocked something over. Mrs. Sidwell threatened to flay me alive if I disturbed her Aiders' meeting. What does 'flay' mean?"

"I believe it means to skin something. No wonder you were afraid to move." Violet smiled in spite of herself. "Please pass the carrots, Eunice."

⟞⟐⟝

The family was outside making plans and exploring when hoofbeats sounded in the drive. Everyone hurried to greet Obie, but a lone horseman appeared instead. Violet and the children slowed to a disappointed walk.

"Howdy!" Nick Houghton shouted a greeting. His broad-shouldered physique made a striking picture astride a rangy bay. The sweat-drenched horse huffed noisily, drooping its head as soon as it stopped. Thick spume dripped from its mouth.

Nick swung down, tossed the reins around the rail, and approached Violet. "I heard about your move and made haste to offer my aid. Need help unloading supplies?"

Violet took a step back. Nick moved closer. She had to tip her head back to look him in the eye. "Our supplies have not yet arrived, but thank you for the kind thought."

"You know I worry about your safety, Vi, but I will try to restrain myself from voicing my doubts." He captured her hand and squeezed it until Violet thought her bones might break.

"Nick, please, my hand!" she exclaimed.

"So sorry, my dear. I hardly know my own strength." There was a strange light in his eyes—as though hurting her had given him pleasure.

He slapped his hat against his leg and looked around. "Got plans to rent out the fields? Could bring in a decent income that way."

"I have no plans at the moment. One thing at a time is all I can handle, and today I plan to move into my new home."

"Ah," was Nick's only reply. Violet studied his face while he studied the house. Nick's features were fine at first glance, but there was something missing. She wasn't sure which quality he lacked, but whatever it was, it was important.

"Someone's coming," he observed, turning away.

"It must be Mr. Watson with our supplies," Violet brightened. At the sight of Obie on the seat of a loaded wagon, relief washed over her. She discovered that her hands had been balled into fists. Did Nick intimidate her so much? A moment ago he had casually demonstrated his vastly superior strength. If he wished to frighten her, he had succeeded.

Obie's pair of brown mules waggled their long ears when Samuel skipped, shouting, beside them. Obie hauled them in and leaped down, and Samuel gave the wiry cowboy an ecstatic hug.

"Uncle Obie, guess what we found? A whole nest of garter snakes! Mama says not to touch them, but I want to keep one. They were right alongside the toolshed."

"Better obey your mama, Sam. We'll get you a better pet than a snake. Come help me unload this stuff. We've got a mess of work to do here, and I need a man's help."

Obie nodded coolly to Nick and tipped his hat to Violet and the girls. "Please tell us where to put it all, ma'am." Then his eyes fell upon Nick's exhausted horse, and Violet saw a shadow of anger cross his face.

"Sam, before we start, how about you walk Mr. Houghton's horse till he cools, then give him a drink."

"Yes, sir." Eager to prove himself capable, Samuel pulled the gelding's reins loose and led him across the yard.

Violet couldn't help fluttering slightly, and Obie caught the anxious movement. "I know that horse, ma'am. He won't harm your boy. He's a fine animal. Too fine to be ridden hard and left standing in the hot sun."

Nick's face went white, and his lips almost disappeared. "What about your mules, Watson? Gonna leave *them* standing in the hot sun?"

"Sam will care for them next," Obie said. Lifting a covered bucket from the wagon bed, he turned to Violet. "Brought milk. I'll set it in the springhouse right off. We'll keep you supplied until you get a cow."

Nick swore outright. "What gives you the right to barge in here and distribute your second-rate largesse?"

Already on his way toward the creek, Obie turned to answer, but Violet spoke first. "God gives him the right. He is representing the church body by caring for a widow in need, and I appreciate his help. He has given to us freely, just as the Lord provides for His own. Now, if you truly desire to be helpful, Mr. Houghton, you may begin by unloading those sacks of flour and sugar. I want them in my pantry. Beulah will show you exactly where when you get them inside."

Violet and Eunice unpacked some lighter items while Nick hoisted a hundred-pound flour sack up on his shoulder. Big man though he was, he seemed nearly crushed by the sack's weight. He staggered inside and dropped it heavily on the kitchen floor, panting like his winded horse.

"Oh!" Beulah exclaimed. "Watch what you're doing! You might have broken it, and then what a mess we would have. Please slide it over here against the far wall."

Violet hid a smile behind her hand at Nick's sulky expression. Rubbing his shoulder and grimacing, he poured himself a cup of coffee and relaxed at the table, watching while Obie brought in the other sacks and the trunk.

Samuel doggedly worked beside his hero, carrying in smaller items and placing them at Beulah's command. One word of praise from Obie was enough to make the boy's thin face glow with satisfaction.

At last the wagon was empty and the pantry was full. "Where did Mr. Watson go?" Violet brushed flour from her hands and removed her apron.

Beulah sprawled across a kitchen chair, her face smudged with flour. "I don't know. After he brought in that last load, he went back outside with Samuel. I heard him say something about cleaning up. Maybe he went home."

Violet's brow wrinkled. "Without a word to me? That isn't like him. Are the beans cooking?"

"Yes, Mama. I put in the salt pork, onions, and carrots just like you said. Eunice has to make the corn bread, doesn't she? I'm tired."

"You've done your part, dear. I'll handle the rest. Thank you so much!" Violet kissed the girl on her damp forehead and accepted a hug in return.

The kitchen door stood ajar, and Nick lounged against the doorjamb. "Excuse me, please," Violet requested, but he only drew on his cigarette, observing her through narrowed eyes. Beyond him she could see afternoon sunlight touching the treetops and casting long shadows over the barn.

"Mr. Houghton, please let me pass. You're blocking the doorway." Certainly she could have used the front door, but she was tired and cross and did not feel like going out of her way for this inconsiderate oaf.

"What will you do for me if I move?" Nick smiled slowly, his eyes begging her to respond in kind.

He was like an overgrown, indolent boy. She caught a whiff of his sour breath. "Ask me what I won't do. I won't kick you in the shins," she replied.

"Oh, darlin', you're just asking for a lickin'," he blurted gleefully and grabbed for her.

Violet's bravado instantly evaporated. She dodged and ran behind the table. "No! Truly, I'm not."

Eyes alight, Nick moved into the room, spreading his arms as though to sweep her in. "Come to papa, sweet thing."

As he passed, Beulah stuck out her foot and tripped him. He didn't so much as glance her way, but eased around the table, crooning to Violet as though he were wooing a frightened horse. Violet broke and ran for the open door.

Nick gave her a fair head start and watched as she raced across the yard with billowing skirts. Grinning, he flicked his cigarette to the ground and pursued her in earnest. From the doorway behind him, Beulah hollered, "Mr. Houghton, leave my mother alone!"

Obie must still be around. But where was he? In the barn? Hearing pounding footsteps, Violet dodged and doubled back toward the barn door. Nick's outstretched hand just missed snagging her flying skirts. She heard his boots skidding in the gravel, and he chuckled appreciatively.

What have I gotten myself into? When will I learn to watch my tongue? He thinks I'm flirting with him!

"Obie?" she gasped. "Obadiah, where are you?"

Nick grasped her arm and hauled her to a stop. "Now, what would you be callin' him for, honey gal? Thought you said he went on home. You trying to fool me?" There was an edge to his voice. "You and I are just having a romp. That old cowpoke will mind his own business if he knows what's good for his health."

A chill trickled down her spine at sight of his expression. "Mr. Houghton, please, I'm sorry if I've given you the wrong impression. I truly don't wish to romp. It's been a long day, and I'm very tired—"

"Females that trick a man thataway have only one thing coming to 'em," Nick announced, blue eyes sparkling. He swept her up into his arms and marched toward the chopping block, an old stump.

"No! Oh, please, Nick, let me be! This isn't funny! What will the children think?" Violet struggled vainly as he placed her face down across his lap. "Go away! Please go home and leave us in peace." Her voice crackled with anger and frustration.

He lifted his hand, but suddenly hauled her upright to sit upon his knee. Violet's breast heaved from her exertions, drawing his prurient eye. "You've got the wrong spirit about this, honey. Don't sound so angry and scared; you make a man feel like a heel!" Twisting one of her arms behind her back, he wrapped his arm around her waist and squeezed until her heart pounded against his ribs. "Mmm, that's better. You're such a sweet little thing that you make me forget all about your dignity. I just want to cuddle you close and soak you in."

He tried to nuzzle her neck. Violet squirmed her other hand free and beat at his chest, then pushed at his face. Shaking with fear and rage, she tried to sound authoritative, but her voice was tear-choked. "Mr. Houghton, I have no wish to be cuddled by you, so kindly remove that notion from your head. I am not a toy to be dandled on your knee and handled at will. Release me at once, do you hear?"

"You heard the lady, Houghton."

Nick's hands went limp. Violet wrenched away, lost her balance, and sat down hard in the dirt. Still gasping for breath, she lifted her eyes to see Obie

TIME FOR A MIRACLE

standing just outside the open barn door. His eyes were glacial; his hands were alternately clenching and relaxing at his sides.

Nick seemed mesmerized by Obie's stare. Violet had never seen a man turn pale simply because another man glared at him. If she hadn't known better, she would have thought Obie was aiming a gun at Nick's heart. She jerked her gaze back to Obie; he held no gun. If he carried a weapon at all, it was not in evidence.

"Mr. Watson, we feared that you had gone. I. . .I want to invite you to stay for supper. It isn't much, but you're welcome to share it with us. You. . .I. . ." Her invitation sputtered to a sorry end. "Will you stay? Please?"

He glanced at her, and Violet thought she saw his eyes flicker with warmth. "I think it's time for Mr. Houghton and me to leave you. Perhaps another evening, Mrs. Fairfield." His eyes returned to Nick and frosted over again. "Houghton, give me a hand here, will you?"

Nick rose from the stump and slumped into the barn. A moment later he reappeared behind a battered wheelbarrow full of rotted boards and rusted, twisted metal. Obie supervised him closely. "Take it to my wagon and unload it into the bed."

Samuel followed the men through the barn doorway, carrying a sack that clanked whenever he dropped it, which happened about every third step. "Hi, Mama. Why're you sitting there? I got more horseshoes than you can shake a stick at!" he announced cheerfully. "Uncle Obie and me are cleanin' up a mess from behind the barn. I'm s'posed to put this junk into his wagon."

"Uncle Obie and I."

"Right. Why don't you come help Uncle Obie and I?"

"Uncle Obie and me, son."

"Mama, can't you make up your mind?"

She smiled weakly, tucking in her disheveled shirtwaist as she struggled to her feet. "It's not my rule, dear. I'll explain it to you someday soon, but for now let me take one side of that sack and we'll carry it to the wagon together."

For once, Obadiah Watson was not working. His eyes followed Nick's every move, and he seemed tense, like a set bear trap. Violet sensed that there was more to this situation than she understood. She did not fear Obie, but she knew better than to distract him for the time being.

After Nick muttered a farewell, mounted up, and rode away, Obie seemed to relax. He and Samuel finished clearing rubbish from behind the barn; then they fed and watered Barabbas. Violet wanted a chance to talk with Obie alone, but the opportunity did not arise.

"Are you sure you won't stay for supper?" she asked as he climbed to the wagon seat. "There is plenty, and we would enjoy having your company."

Obie turned, met her gaze, but seemed lost in thought. Sensing an inner struggle, she batted her eyes, hoping to tip the scales in her favor. His eyes crinkled in the almost-smile that so attracted her. "Thank you, but I don't want to outstay my welcome. I'll check on you again soon or send Al."

Violet nearly pouted. "I wish you would stay."

"Why?"

One of the mules grew restless; Obie controlled it with a few twitches of his fingers on the reins.

"I. . .well, I like you very much. I enjoy your company, and I feel safe when you are near."

Without a word, he looked deep into her eyes. No longer icy, his gray eyes spoke volumes. As she read them, Violet's heart thudded against her ribs and her breath came short.

He opened his mouth as though to put his thoughts into words but apparently changed his mind. Clucking to the mules, he quickly drove out of the yard, leaving Violet to stare after him, flushed in disappointment.

Chapter 8

Know ye not that. . .ye are not your own?
For ye are bought with a price: therefore glorify God in your body.
1 CORINTHIANS 6:19–20

"Obadiah, I hear I've got competition as your best girl." Hattie interrupted his reading of a psalm to comment. "Talk is, you've got a handsome widow hanging on your arm these days, a Violet Something-or-other. Tell me about her."

Obie tried to hide his surprise. Had people been linking his name with Violet's? How would she react to this? His emotions churned into a discomforting mixture of pride, fear, and inadequacy.

"What do you want to know?" he rumbled, keeping his eyes on the text.

"Are you plannin' to wed the woman? I hear she's a recent widow, but some marry while in mourning, you know, especially when there are children to consider. She has three, right?"

He nodded. "Two girls and a boy. Beulah is sixteen, Eunice is twelve, and Samuel is not quite nine. Good children, they are."

"So you have a mind to become a father, have you?"

His face twitched.

"Why so pensive? You'd make a fine husband for any woman. I've often told Cyrus it's a cryin' shame that no woman snapped you up long ago, but then I guess you haven't been lookin' for a wife until now. You think she's pretty?"

Staring down at the open Bible, Obie nodded.

"Someone told me that she ain't above average, but perhaps it was sour grapes talkin'. I sure would like to see her for myself. Think you could bring her out for a visit? You've got to have my blessing, you know."

"Miss Hattie, I don't know that Violet wants me for a husband. I think maybe she just needs help, and I'm. . .available and willing. I'm homely as a skinned possum and nothing to attract a woman like Violet, unless she's desperate."

"But you'd take her any way you can get her?" Hattie guessed wryly.

Shamefaced, he admitted, "I got it that bad."

"Just because she's pretty? She'll be old and ugly someday, like me. You'd better have more reason than lust of the flesh for marryin' at your age."

One side of his moustache lifted. "I'll bring her to meet you; then you'll know. She's wonderful, Hattie. Sweet, kind, a good mother, hard worker, and she loves the Lord with all her heart. She loved her husband enough to follow him out here. . . ." He fell silent lest he reveal more than necessary about the real Jeremiah.

"I want to meet this woman afore I hand out any more advice. If she don't see what a prize you are, she ain't worth your time, honey. Any woman that'd marry a man just to keep her kids fed—"

"She's worth everything, Hattie. You'll see."

Violet was doing laundry when Samuel's excited call reached her ears. "Someone's coming, Mama!"

Immediately Violet dropped Samuel's Sunday shirt back into the tub, dried her hands on her apron, ran to the door, ran back and removed her apron, ran back to the door, checking her hair and tucking in stray strands, and tried to compose herself by taking a long, quivery breath. Smoothing her hands down her skirt, she stepped outside to greet the guest.

It was Albert.

Violet extended her hand in greeting, concealing her disappointment that he wasn't Obie. "Hello again, Mr. Moore."

"Cousin Buck calls me Al, and I'd be pleased if you did, too." Albert gave her a charming smile as he took her hand. "Buck is helping out at the Updahls' and the Thwaites' today, so he may not have time to come here."

Violet's smile faded. Hattie Thwaite again?

"Hello, Al!" Coming from the barn, Samuel tried a handstand, but fell over backwards. Unabashed, he hopped up and hurried to greet the older boy.

Albert chuckled. "Hello, Samuel. You look happier than when I last saw you. Cousin Buck tells me you're a hard worker."

"Please come inside and have a drink, Al," Violet invited.

"Thank you, ma'am. Sam, thanks, but don't bother about my horse. She's in the shade, and she's not thirsty yet." Albert followed Violet into the house with Samuel at his heels. "Sure is good to see a family in this big house." He politely waited for Violet to join him at the table before sitting down. Sipping his water, he glanced around curiously.

"I haven't been off the farm much lately, but I've heard rumors that Nick Houghton wants to buy this place—or else marry you and get this place in the bargain. He's the type to seek a rich wife."

"But we're not rich! Mama says all we have is an egg in our nest," Samuel announced.

Albert shrugged and gave him a crooked smile. "You've got this place. You're rich enough even without an egg."

"I hope I can make enough profit from the farm to keep us all alive. I haven't any knowledge whatsoever about farming," Violet confessed. Albert was only about seventeen or eighteen, but, like his cousin, he inspired trust.

"You don't need to farm, really. Sharecropping might be your best option. Cousin Buck mentioned that to me." Al drank the rest of his water and set the cup on the table. "Lease your land to farmers, then share in the proceeds from their harvest. It's simple." Then he smiled, his dark eyes twinkling. "Or you could marry a farmer and let him handle the work."

Violet fiddled with her cup. "Are there farmers in the area who might be interested? In sharecropping, I mean," she added hastily.

He grinned. "We could take on a field or two, and your neighbors on the west and north may well snatch up the offer. You might also rent land for grazing. It won't bring as much, but it wouldn't have to be cleared and plowed. And I know one farmer who might be interested in that option. . . ."

Violet waved her hand in dismissal, trying not to smile. "Samuel dear, please go find your sisters. They may not know that Al is here. They're in the garden, I think."

"All right, Mama." Samuel gulped down the last of his water and ran outside, leaving the kitchen door wide open. "Beulah! Eunice!" his voice faded away.

Violet met Albert's candid brown eyes. "How long have you lived with. . . Buck?"

"Four years, ma'am. Ever since he quit the range and moved here. When he inherited his father's business, a mercantile in Los Angeles, he sold out, traveled east, and purchased the farm next to this one. I am my father's eldest son, but he has four other sons, so my parents didn't mind too much when I begged to leave California and join my cousin. I have always wanted to live in a land"—he waved one long arm—"like this, where four seasons come in cycle, snow falls in the autumn and stays till the spring, and trees grow tall and thick. I like to hunt whitetails, not jackrabbits."

Violet warmed to the lanky boy. "Do you enjoy working for your cousin?"

"Very much. He's made me his partner. Since he spends a lot of time doing God's work, Myles and I do a lot of the farmwork. We don't mind. Buck's work is important to him and vital to the community. He works like a slave when he needs to, like when we sow or harvest, and he always does his share of the milking. He's also the handyman—he can fix anything."

"He's a wonderful man, isn't he?" Violet mused.

"You really like the old guy, don't you?" Al looked eager. "I was afraid the interest was on his side only. A woman could look a long time and never find a better man."

"So I've been told. . .repeatedly. Do you. . ." She stared at her twiddling fingers. "Do you think he is interested in marriage?" She wanted to ask about Hattie Thwaite but couldn't think of a casual way to bring her into the conversation.

"He's never been interested before, but since you arrived, well. . .even Myles comments on how the boss dangles after you. Kind of like a moth to a candle, you know? The old man's smitten pretty hard, I tell you."

"He's not old," Violet protested.

Al's grin widened. "He's forty-two as of next week. Getting long in the tooth to think of marriage, though he can still whip me and Myles but good in a wrestling match. I'd be pleased if you two married; though it does seem strange. I mean, he's always been so shy of women."

From the corner of her eye, Violet spotted movement at the kitchen door. "Come in, girls, and greet our guest."

Albert rose and bowed. "I am honored to meet again the lovely Misses Fairfield." He lifted his eyes to their faces.

Violet almost laughed aloud. Her girls were evidently swept off their feet by such charm. Beulah, the practical and unromantic, actually fluttered her lashes as she curtseyed in return. Violet suddenly wondered how Beulah might look with her hair up. She was nearly seventeen, after all, and the long brown braids did look childish.

"Want to go down to the pond, Al?" Samuel invited.

"For a while, yes. I hear you want to learn how to fish."

"I sure do. Uncle Obie promised to teach me."

"Please be careful around the water, children." Al and the girls were really too old for such a reminder, but Violet couldn't help being a mother.

When the noisy chatter faded away, Violet stared out the window toward Obie's house. Her fingers tapped restlessly on the windowsill.

"Lord, am I wrong to feel this way?" she murmured aloud. "All I seem to think about anymore is. . .men. It seems so silly and childish—yet I can't help myself."

Ignoring the laundry that awaited her attention, she went to her room and picked up her Bible. Rubbing the worn, soft leather cover between her hands, she spoke aloud again. "I don't want to make a wrong choice. Lord, is it Your will for me to remarry, or am I being selfish and weak?"

Sitting on her blanket bed, she scooted back against the wall and opened the Bible. "As I recall, the apostle Paul gave instructions concerning widows in several places. Let me see." She ruffled through pages until she found First Corinthians seven. Reading avidly, she frowned. "Paul seems to think it best if a man never marries and a widow never remarries. Is my longing for a husband a sign of weak faith? I don't want to be divided in my loyalty to You, Lord, and I certainly don't want to come between You and. . .well, I'll be honest about this. . .between You and Obadiah. As a bachelor, he is free to serve others as You direct, but if he were married to me, he would be concerned about me and my children first."

She ruffled through more pages, arriving at First Timothy. "Now here Paul advises young widows—I hope I still fit into the 'young' category—to marry and have children lest they get themselves into trouble through idleness. I have known widows that ought to have remarried," she mused.

Looking up at the ceiling, Violet said, "Now here we have a quandary. An unmarried man is better off if he doesn't seek a wife. A young widow is better off if she marries. But how can she marry without causing an unmarried man to lose his bachelor status? Hmm? I wish I had Paul here; I'd give him a piece of my mind for being so ambiguous. I guess what I can gather from all this is that I need to pray for Your will, seek to glorify You, obey Your direct commands, then wait and see what happens. I promise not to be one of these widows that 'waxes wanton.'"

Violet prayed, opening her heart to the Lord about many matters. Afterward, feeling happy, content, and a bit guilty for neglecting her chores, she descended the stairs. Afternoon sunlight poured through the western windows, reminding her that curtain fabric needed to be a top priority on her next shopping list. Singing softly, she began to prepare supper, scrubbing a garment or two during free moments.

Lord, everyone assures me that Obie is interested in me; but then he spends so much time with this Hattie Thwaite. Does he intend to marry her? I could be misreading his intentions toward me. I also need to ask him about his prison record and hear the story straight. It's not right for me to drag information about him from everyone else.

While wringing out Beulah's chemise, she stopped and sighed toward the ceiling. "I'm doing it again, aren't I, Lord? Obie this, Obie that. Am I setting myself up for disappointment? Please give me wisdom in this matter."

Through the open door she saw Al and her children walk toward the front of the house, laughing and chatting like old friends. Al had stayed far longer than his original intent. His poor horse was undoubtedly tired of waiting for him.

Horse. Violet suddenly remembered Barabbas in the barn. Had anyone fed or watered that horse today? Drying her hands on her apron as she removed it, she hurried to the front door just in time to see Albert and his horse disappear into the trees.

Violet considered asking one of the children to care for Barabbas, but shook her head, recalling those pinned ears and wicked teeth. If anyone were to brave the horse's anger, it would be she. "Eunice," she called. "Please come watch the hash while I care for the horse. Samuel, I could use your help."

Barabbas squealed angrily as they entered the barn. "I'm so sorry," Violet crooned, slipping alongside him in the stall. She reached for his halter, intending to lead him outside. "I completely forgot about you. We're not used to having animals to care for."

The gelding flung his head up and crowded her against the wall. One of his big hooves ground into her foot. Violet let out a pained grunt.

"Mama, are you all right?" Samuel was frightened. "Why don't we just bring him a bucket of water?"

After pushing the beast off her foot, Violet ran from the stall. Barabbas was tied up, but his heels were free, and she had seen him try to kick Obie. "Good idea. Help me pump some, would you please?"

Some of the water spilled while she lugged the bucket inside, but there was plenty left. The horse allowed her into his stall and drank eagerly. Violet smiled, listening to him slurp and gulp. He paid no attention when she slipped away. "Samuel, dear, he must be hungry, too. Would you get him a forkful of hay?"

Samuel tried to fling the hay over into Barabbas's manger, but it kept hitting the top of the partition and falling back. "Let me try." Violet took the pitchfork from him, scooped up the hay, and gave a mighty heave. The hay landed on top of the wall.

"Watch out, Mama!" Samuel tugged on her arm, but he was too late. The hay fell back toward them, scattering over the floor.

"Whoever designed this barn was a dunderhead," Violet grumbled. Much of her hair had come unpinned and straggled into her face. Hay sprouted from her hair and clothing, making her itch unbearably.

Flushed and irritated, she had no choice but to go back into the stall with the horse. She raked up the hay and gathered it into her arms. Barabbas was eager to have the hay, snatching mouthfuls of it before she could stuff it into his manger. His cheek muscles bunched and relaxed right before Violet's nose. "Well, that wasn't so bad." She stroked his shining flank as she turned to go.

Then something struck her on the back, knocking her forward. With an involuntary shriek, she staggered out of the stall and landed on the wooden floor. On hands and knees she waited to catch her breath. There was a sharp pain in her back.

"Mama! What happened?" Samuel ran and skidded on his knees to her side. "Are you all right?"

"I think. . .I'm all right." Violet crawled forward, out of reach of Barabbas's heels, then braced one hand on the wall and looked back. The horse was still eating like. . .well, like a horse. He ignored her. Shock began to pass, and rage set in. Tears burned her eyes and overflowed.

Worried, Samuel touched her back. "Your dress is ripped, and there's blood."

Violet slowly stood up. "You stupid, horrid, vicious horse!" Her shaking voice rose in volume and pitch. "If I had a gun, I'd shoot you right between the eyes, you nasty, rotten, ungrateful—"

A shadow fell through the open doorway. "Mrs. Fairfield?"

Violet's tirade concluded long before her anger was expended. She sucked in a noisy sob.

"Uncle Obie, Mama got hurt!" Samuel shouted. "Come quick!"

Violet heard quick steps; then Obie gripped her arms. "What happened?" She didn't want him to see her in a rage, but her anger was still hot.

Calming herself, she began quietly, "We were feeding the horse, and. . .Obie, you'll be angry with me, but I forgot all about him until a few minutes ago! Still, that's no excuse for—"

He slowly released her arms. His worried eyes took in her tears and her disheveled appearance. "Samuel said you were hurt."

"I put hay into the manger, and when I turned around something hit me on the back and knocked me down. He bit me and tore my dress!" She reached for her back with one hand, but couldn't touch the spot that hurt. Temper flared again. "He's a monster! You should just shoot him and save someone else the trouble." She shook a fist at the horse's backside. Barabbas's tail swished in total unconcern.

Obie whirled her around. "Excuse me, ma'am, but your injury should be checked. You've got buttons missing, and you're bleeding."

"I understand. Go ahead." Violet reached up to pull her tangled hair out of the way. For the moment, she was too upset to care about modesty. Tears still trickled down her cheeks, and she was helpless to stop them.

"You want *me* to. . .to. . . ?" he stuttered, dumbfounded. He cast a helpless look at Samuel.

"What's wrong, Uncle Obie?" Samuel asked. "Mama's mad enough to shoot *Barabbas,* not you."

"I. . .uh. . .can you unbutton those top buttons, Sam? My. . .uh, fingers aren't so good at it."

"I'll try." Samuel unbuttoned the top few buttons of his mother's dress. "I'd call Beulah, but she'd probably faint. She can't even take a splinter out of my finger without getting sick." He pulled the fabric aside to expose the injury. "Ooh, yuck!"

"What?" Violet gasped.

Obie's voice was tight. "It's a nasty bite."

"Is it bleeding much or just bruised?" Violet tried to reach over her shoulder and touch the sore place, but she couldn't reach from that direction, either. She turned around just in time to see Obie disappear through the doorway.

"Where is he going?"

"He pulled out a handkerchief. I bet he went to get it wet. Mama, that bite looks nasty. There's a big purple ridge and teeth marks. It's disgusting!"

"He got me right between the shoulder blades. I never could reach that spot." She reached an arm back and tried to touch the spot from beneath, but felt only the edge of her chemise. How embarrassing! But it was a clean one, trimmed with lace, and at least that stupid horse hadn't ruined it. She wiped her sleeve across her face, but new tears replaced the ones she wiped away.

"Mama, if you don't need me anymore, I want to go outside for a while. May I check on my robin's nest?"

"I'd rather you stayed here for a few more minutes." She gulped on another sob. As her anger ebbed, a feeling of weakness took its place. She felt exposed and distressed.

"You're gonna have a big bruise, I bet." Samuel poked at his mother's back, and she flinched.

"Hey, be gentle, Sam." Obie appeared, holding a damp handkerchief that was folded into a pad.

"I didn't touch the bite," Samuel defended himself.

Obie gently gripped Violet's shoulder. "This will be cold," he warned, and pressed the pad upon the bite.

Violet gasped. Trying to hide her reaction to the pain, she asked, "Is it still bleeding?"

"A little. You should soak it in Epsom salts and paint it with iodine when you get the chance."

"I like putting iodine on cuts," Samuel said, watching closely.

"No, you don't. Not on your own cuts," Violet tried to chuckle, but the attempt was weak. Everything about her felt feeble.

Obie was gentle with the cloth. "Let's get you inside where you can sit down, Violet."

"All right." Appreciating his tender care, she laid her hot, damp cheek against his hand. "Thank you."

"Does it hurt very much?" His soft voice made her feel like crying again.

"Not terribly much. I just feel so. . .so weak. Don't know why I'm such a ninny. I'm not mortally wounded."

"You've had a shock. Here, take my arm, and we'll head for the house. The girls can get you cleaned up. Someone needs to take care of you, for certain."

Violet gratefully wrapped both hands around his arm and leaned her head against his shoulder. "You're doing a good job of it."

"May I go now, Mama?" Samuel fretted, bored with the proceedings.

"All right. Don't go far; supper should be nearly ready."

"Can you make it to the house, do you think?" Obie asked, concerned, as they reached the open barn door.

"I'm sure I can. I'm not *that* badly hurt." Violet tipped her head back. "You're such a dear!" Rising on tiptoe, she pressed her lips to his cheek and heard him inhale sharply.

"Mama!" Beulah stood just outside. "What are you doing?"

Chapter 9

By love serve one another.
GALATIANS 5:13

Facing her outraged daughter, Violet quietly said, "Mr. Watson has been very kind. I simply kissed him on the cheek."

Beulah frowned, her dark eyes taking in her mother's unkempt appearance and Obie's obvious discomfiture. "We have company. Didn't you hear the horse outside?"

"No, I didn't. Who is it?" Her unbuttoned dress suddenly slid down her shoulder; she pulled it firmly into place with her free hand.

Caroline Schoengard stepped into view. "Hello, Obie. Didn't mean to take you unawares, Violet. I brought over some vegetables from our garden."

"How kind of you! Mr. Watson was just helping me with the horse. He bit me right on the back—the horse did, I mean," Violet stammered. She felt hotter than ever, but she recovered her dignity enough to shake her visitor's hand.

The pastor's wife looked as though she might laugh. "I see. Are you all right?"

"I think so. It hurts some." Violet's tears brimmed again.

"It needs to be looked after right away," Obie stated bluntly. "I'm glad you're here, Caroline." He took hold of Violet's shoulder and turned her to show Caroline her back. Violet let her face rest against his chest for one blessed moment.

Caroline sobered immediately. "Oh, Violet, I'm so sorry! Obie's right; that needs immediate attention. I've got time to stay a spell. Ma Schoengard is keeping the boys for me again and fixin' supper."

Violet wanted to stay right where she was, but she lifted her head and moved away. "Thank you, Caroline. Please join us for supper."

Caroline took Violet's other arm, and Obie released her. She wasn't sure whether or not she should invite Obie to join them, but he made the decision for her.

"Good evening, ladies. I'll take Barabbas to my place until I can trade him off."

"Obie, thank you again—and tell Al thank you for the milk he brought. We enjoyed having him here today." Violet tried to smile normally.

Obie grumbled something.

"Pardon?" Violet asked.

"He was supposed to care for your horse while he was here." He headed toward the barn, looking like a thundercloud.

Beulah took her mother's other arm and whispered, "Mama, I'm sorry I shouted at you. I didn't know. . ."

"I understand, and you're forgiven." She squeezed the girl's arm. More tears poured down her cheeks. In her present mood, everything seemed to make her cry.

Obie led the wild-eyed horse from the barn. The ladies stopped for a moment to watch. Barabbas snorted, lunged, and did his best to escape, but Obie quieted him with a firm hand and a low command. "Should never have left you here. What was I thinking?"

Holding the lead rope, Obie mounted his paint. "Ma'am, Mrs. Schoengard, Miss Beulah." He tipped his hat to each lady in turn, then rode away with Barabbas trotting behind.

❦

Violet lay facedown on her bed of blankets, since her actual bed hadn't arrived yet, and winced as warm water trickled down her sides. Caroline had found Epsom salts among Violet's supplies and was serving as self-appointed nurse. "I'm sorry to get your bed wet, my dear. You have other blankets, I hope?"

"Yes, we do. Don't worry about it. It just tickles, that's all."

"You'll be sore for a few days, I'm sure. You're really more bruised than cut, which is good. Less chance for infection to get into your skin." She shifted her seat on the "bed," groaning, "How can you sleep on this? I wouldn't be able to move in the morning."

"It's not that bad once you get used to it. Besides, I just received word that our furniture and other baggage should be arriving early next week. I'm so excited!"

"I'm sure nearly everyone in the area will want to help you bring it home and set up house. We can give you a proper housewarming then. Your moving here took everyone by surprise—we hardly did a thing to help out."

"But," Violet protested, "the pies, the flowers, and all the work that was done around the house to prepare it for us—I would call that quite a lot. We felt very welcomed indeed!"

Caroline smiled. "Oh, honey, just you wait. We'll have a proper shindig for you. I'll spread the word around. Not a dance this time, although you do have the ideal front room for it. We'll just have a party while bringing in your fancy things."

"Not so fancy, really, but they mean a great deal to me. I have many pieces that belonged to my parents. They've been in storage for years, since we've been living at my in-laws' house."

Caroline lifted the cooled compress and replaced it with a warm one. "Why didn't you move out here with Jerry in the first place? He never mentioned his family. Folks were mighty surprised when you showed up here."

Violet wriggled, irritated by her soggy chemise. "They were surprised?"

"Lots of folks scratchin' their heads. Jerry was a good man in his way, I'm sure, but. . .well, you're a handsome and refined lady, and. . ."

Violet studied the wall, noting cracks in the plaster. "It's hard to explain, Caroline. In fact, I can't really explain it all right now; however, I think the truth will come out in good time."

Caroline laid a sympathetic hand on Violet's arm. "You don't have to tell me, you know, if it's painful for you. I'm just a nosy woman who asks too many questions. Now, Violet, I'm going to dab iodine on your cuts, so prepare yourself."

Violet clenched her teeth but couldn't wait to answer. "Caroline—ouch! You don't understand. I was very happily married, but that seems like a lifetime ago. Oooh! I wish I could tell you, but I can't yet. Please, Caroline, you don't need to feel sorry for me. It isn't necessary. Except for this iodine, I'm not in any pain."

"Well, maybe now you're ready to begin a new life," Caroline decided, replacing the bottle's stopper. "I hope and pray that you'll find it here, Violet." She grinned. "You now have a purple blotch that contrasts fetchingly with your lovely white skin. By the way, I couldn't help seeing that kiss today. Maybe my matchmaking prediction wasn't so far off after all."

Violet rolled her eyes. "I simply kissed his cheek. Samuel was with us until a moment before you arrived. It wasn't as improper as it must have looked. I don't understand why Beulah flew into a frenzy. I thought she knew me better than that!"

"She was playing the part of mother, I think. It did look suspicious, you two coming out of the barn with your untidy condition and unfastened dress. I think she reacted before she thought it through, that's all."

"And what do you think? Was I. . .out of line to kiss him like that?"

"We–ell, he is a bachelor, and. . .quite susceptible."

"You're right. At my age, I should know better." Violet felt tears threatening again.

"Are you in love with him, honey?"

"I. . .I think I may be. . .learning to love him."

Caroline's blue eyes looked troubled. "I could tell you a few things about him, but I don't want you to get the wrong idea. I mean, some of the things I know sound bad, but Obie is. . .well, he's simply a good man. David thinks the world of him. Our boys adore Obie, and he is wonderful with them."

"He loves children. I don't think you could tell me anything that would lower my opinion of him, to be honest. Obie is gentle and kind—he's no killer, I'm sure!"

"Violet, I think you ought to know that some people believe Obie was involved in your husband's death—because of his past record, you know. No serious accusations have been made, for there is no proof or real motive—but the talk is out there. If you were to marry Obie, it might increase."

"He had nothing at all to do with Jeremiah's death. I know that for a fact."

"I'm glad to hear it, Violet. He deserves your faith in him, I'm sure."

There was a knock at the door, and Eunice pushed it open with one foot. "Supper is served. We decided to bring it up to you, since Mama can't come down."

"I probably could have come," Violet protested, "but thank you for the thought. Just set it on the floor here, and I can reach it."

Eunice glanced at her mother's back and made a face. "Poor Mama! Beulah told me what happened. I'm glad Uncle Obie and Mrs. Schoengard were here to take care of you. I wouldn't have known what to do, and Beulah says she felt faint just from looking at your back." She arranged the steaming plates on the floor and handed two napkins to Caroline.

"Wish I could see it," Violet grumbled. She lifted her face to accept a kiss from the girl. "Supper smells wonderful, dear. You're becoming an accomplished cook."

When their plates were cleared, Caroline gathered them up and stood. "I hate to leave, but I don't want to drive home after dark. Oh, before I forget, I mentioned your idea about a 'Care Committee' to David, and he really likes the idea. I imagine he'll mention it to Obie."

Violet gingerly sat up, holding her chemise and blanket to her chest. "Thank you for all the help, Caroline. I don't know what we would have done without you."

"God sent me today, I'm sure. Now you stay put and rest for a while, do you hear?" Caroline eyed Violet narrowly. "How'd you keep such a fine figure after three children, anyhow? My figure went to pieces after the twins, and I can't seem to get it back together."

Violet's smile was slightly crooked. "I got pretty hefty a few years back, but I realized I only made myself depressed when I couldn't fit into my clothes. I stopped eating so many sweets, and I work hard around the house. That's all."

"It's just not fair. Guess I'll hafta love you anyhow."

"You'd better."

Chapter 10

*With all lowliness and meekness,
with longsuffering, forbearing one another in love.*
EPHESIANS 4:2

"Mama, guess what!" Samuel burst into the house, leaving a trail of dirty footprints. His jacket and trousers were filthy, but his face was beaming. A strong fishy odor filled the kitchen.

"What, dear?" Violet restrained a gasp of horror lest she dash his joy. She laid aside her mending and caught the boy before he could do further damage to her floor.

"I caught seven fish, and five of them are big enough to eat. Uncle Obie helped me scale and gut them. Would you cook them for supper tonight?" Samuel was ecstatic. Violet could not recall ever seeing the boy more thrilled.

"That's wonderful, Samuel! Yes, I will cook them, and I'm sure they'll be delicious. Now I want you to take a bath. I'll call Beulah to fill the tub, and afterward you will put on some clean clothes. Is Mr. Watson still here, or did he leave?"

"I think he's still around. Why can't my bath wait until after supper, Mama? I want to tell him good-bye."

"Bath first. Maybe he'll stay for supper; I'll go ask him. You start getting ready for your bath." She found Beulah in her room, piecing a crazy quilt with scraps from Eunice's cast-off dresses. "Honey, please draw Samuel a bath—I want to invite Obie to supper tonight, and I've got to catch him before he leaves."

Without waiting for a reply, she clattered downstairs and out the front door, her heart racing. Jughead stood waiting at the hitching rail, saddled and ready to go, but dozing with one hind leg cocked. Violet bravely patted his shoulder in passing. "I'm glad to see you're still here." After that painful bite, she was more wary of horses than ever, but Jughead was different. He belonged to Obie.

She found Obie bent over the outside pump, sluicing slime from his fishy hands. "Obie, I'm glad you're still here! Please—"

The noise of running water drowned her voice, and at the sight of her, he interrupted, "Mrs. Fairfield, I'm sorry Samuel is so dirty. There was little I could do to clean him up short of dunking him under the pump—"

She shouted, "Oh, don't worry about that; I've seen worse. Please stay for supper tonight and sample some of Samuel's fish. He would be very pleased." The water slowed to a quiet trickle, and her voice lowered to match it.

He looked tempted but glanced down at himself. "I'm not so presentable myself, ma'am." Fish scales sparkled among the dark hairs on his forearms. Every exposed inch of his tanned skin glistened with sweat, which had trickled through dirt on his temples, leaving muddy streaks. He smelled, if possible, worse than Samuel.

"Couldn't you clean up and come back? We've hardly seen you this week. I would love to cook a nice meal for you." Violet stepped closer and saw his eyes dilate.

"If you're sure," he wavered.

"I'm very sure. I've wanted to have a good talk with you—I mean, to get to know you better. You're always so busy, and. . .well. . ." Violet started to flounder. "It seems as if you visit Hattie Thwaite nearly every day. Is she. . .I mean. . .I need to know, do you. . .are you. . .sweet on her?"

Obie's startled expression softened into a wide smile, showing his slightly crooked white teeth. "I sure am, but she's already taken."

"Taken?"

"She and Cyrus celebrated their fifty-eighth anniversary in March. You know Cyrus from church, don't you?"

"I. . .I never heard his last name," Violet faltered, feeling her face grow hot.

"I just sit with her and help out around their farm sometimes. If you like, I'll take you to meet her. Hattie has been asking to meet you, and Cyrus loves children."

"I see. I would. . .I would like to visit them." She could not meet his gaze and turned to flee.

"Wait, Violet," he spoke softly. "Don't be embarrassed. I'm glad you asked me. I like it that you're direct. I like. . .most everything about you."

Violet paused and lifted tear-wet eyes. "But I'm so. . .I've been chasing you like a. . .a wanton widow!"

"It's a new experience for me, being chased by a beautiful woman. I don't have much of a mind to run, so be careful you don't catch something you'll want to throw back." His eyes looked dark and suddenly serious.

She nodded, unable to speak.

"I'll be back for supper."

She nodded again, stiffly.

"Are. . .are you sure you want me to come back tonight?"

This time she smiled weakly and nodded.

❦

Standing in front of the wavy old mirror, Obie straightened his string tie and stared critically at his reflection. He had never been one to care about his looks, but tonight his ordinary appearance annoyed him. "Wish You could have seen fit to gift me with a few more inches and pounds, Lord," he sighed. "I do look scrawny as a plucked banty rooster and about as handsome. Not a likely match for a blue-eyed beauty."

He didn't dare voice the thought aloud, but he wondered if Violet could possibly endure his touch, let alone enjoy it. His rough, scarred hands against her white skin? Even the thought of it started a fire burning within him, and he winced, knowing he should not allow himself to entertain impossible dreams. Grimly he forced the memory of her smooth white back out of his thoughts. Yet he possessed one memory that could be cherished always—the touch of Violet's lips upon his cheek, a gift she had freely given.

Obie looked into his reflection's eyes and shook his head. "Was she really jealous of Hattie?" A smile lifted the corners of his moustache. "Maybe I do have a chance, after all."

Before riding away, he checked on Treat's pups. The fuzzy babies no longer stayed inside their box but wandered around the tack room. They bounded to greet Obie and yipped their delight. "Where is your mother? Deserted you again, has she?"

Treat now took every opportunity to escape her motherly duties and catch a few moments of uninterrupted sleep. Obie had already sighted her, curled up on a fallen horse blanket just outside the calves' stall.

"Poor li'l tykes, left all alone in here to pillage and destroy." A well-chewed bridle strap caught his eye, and he sighed, shaking his head. He hoped Violet would forgive him for inflicting one of these destructive little creatures upon her household; he intended to present Samuel with a pup as soon as they were old enough to leave their mother. For several minutes he patted roly-poly little bodies, scratched a freckled tummy, and stroked soft ears, yet they still protested when he left them.

"Soon one of you will get all the attention you want," he promised. He could already picture Samuel with a fuzzy pup in his arms. That boy needed a good dog.

Back at Fairfield's Folly, Obie unsaddled Jughead and loosed him into the paddock. The delightful aromas emanating from the house made his mouth water. It had surprised him to learn that Violet could cook. She seemed like the type of fine lady who would have kept servants.

The door opened for him before he could knock. "Good evening, Mr. Watson," Beulah said formally and dropped a curtsey.

Obie pulled off his hat. "And to you, Miss Fairfield."

Then Eunice appeared in the doorway. "Hi, Uncle Obie! Come on in and make yourself at home. Mama outdid herself tonight. We've got fish and corn bread with honey and jam, fresh greens and cooked carrots and two pies for dessert! Do you like cream on your pie? Al brought us some this morning along with the milk and eggs. He and Beulah sat in the parlor and talked until it got too hot to stay indoors."

"Is that so?" Obie grinned at the girls, surprised to see Beulah's olive cheeks flush. He had not realized that a youthful romance might be brewing under his very nose. "Sounds like quite a feast. So your mama is a good cook, is she?"

"The best. Father's friends used to invite themselves over for dinner sometimes, but Mama never minded. She likes to cook for people who like to eat."

"Then she'll like cooking for me." Obie hung his hat on a wall peg. The house was warm, though every window stood open to catch the evening breezes. A fly buzzed in lazy circles around the entry hall. "Where's Samuel?"

"Still bathing. He wouldn't get himself clean, so Mama took over scrubbing his neck. He still stinks of fish, but you don't. You smell nice. Is that cologne?"

"Not too strong, is it?" He asked, rubbing at his freshly shaven neck. "Al said ladies like it."

"This lady does. I can't smell it unless you're close by."

Beulah had allowed her sister to do all the talking, but now she put in a question. "Al uses cologne?"

"No, he doesn't. I've had this stuff for a long time, but never used it before. I can't even remember where I got it. Maybe from Hattie or another lady at the church."

"Would you like some water? We have no ice since we just moved here, but our well water is cool."

"Yes, thank you. Sounds good."

Eunice went to fetch the drink. Beulah finally offered, "Want to come into the kitchen and sit down? We haven't any chairs besides the kitchen chairs and benches."

"Sure."

Violet entered the kitchen from the laundry room a few minutes later, wiping her hands on her black taffeta skirts and leaving long water streaks. She apologized for being late and instantly put the girls to work serving supper. Samuel sulked in, looking freshly scrubbed, his dark hair plastered against his head except for one stubborn tuft on top. He cheered quickly at the sight of Obie.

"Did you empty your bathwater?" Violet asked. Samuel hadn't, so Obie volunteered to help him. They dumped the tub beside the back door to water the hollyhocks.

The family talked as they prepared to eat, including Obie in their discussions. He watched Violet as she moved about the kitchen, realizing that she had dressed up for the occasion. She had styled her hair in a fancy way, with curls dangling here and there. Her rustling gown was almost skintight in the bodice, with what looked like an immense pile of cloth drawn up to perch at the back of her hips. Her trim waist and full bosom rose gracefully from this virtual mountain of cloth. Obie thought it an odd style, yet he felt that Violet would look fabulous in almost anything.

Flies and yellow jackets buzzed about the dining room, attracted by the aroma of fried fish. Everyone fought to keep them off the food. Violet asked Obie to offer thanks, which he did in his quiet way. After the "Amen," their eyes met across the table, and she smiled, increasing his heart rate.

All three children tried to dominate the conversation.

"Mama, Clementine's brother William told Sybil's brother Hank that he wanted to ask me to the basket social they have every fall to raise money for school functions. I think he's very handsome, but I don't like the way he flirts with every girl he talks to." No longer stiffly silent, Beulah talked whether or not anyone listened.

"I wouldn't like that either, dear. It's a little early to be thinking about fall functions, don't you think? Eunice, please don't hum at the table. Yes, I do like your singing, but it's not polite to sing at the table; you know that. Now, what did the fish do, Samuel?"

"This one stole Uncle Obie's bait twice before he hooked it and let me reel it in. We could see it under the water. I tell you, this fish was mighty powerful. It made my rod bend, and I thought I lost it once, but Uncle Obie helped me get its head up and keep it away from snags. He had to dig the hook out of its throat with pliers, 'cuz it swallowed the worm right down, and his hands got all bloody. It flipped and struggled in the creel for a long time before it died, too."

Eunice gagged on the bite she had just put into her mouth. Covering her lips with a napkin, she choked until Beulah thumped her on the back. "Oh, Samuel," she groaned. "Don't talk about how a fish died while we're eating it. That's horrid!"

"Mama, please make him stop," Beulah joined in. "It's so ungenteel."

"All right now, you children be quiet and eat politely for a while," Violet decreed. "Whatever happened to 'Children should be seen and not heard'?"

Obie hid a grin with his napkin. He met Violet's apologetic eyes and shook his head slightly to indicate that he didn't mind them. She smiled in relief and gave him a helpless little shrug.

Perspiration dotted Violet's upper lip and made her smooth forehead shiny, but Obie thought he had never seen anyone more lovely. The supper was as delicious as promised, and the pies! Obie had a slice of each, shoofly and custard, with plenty of cream.

The girls cleared the table, but Obie insisted on helping with cleanup duty, wiping dishes and putting them away at Eunice's direction. Once Violet backed into him, her voluminous skirt engulfing his legs. He nearly dropped a tin plate.

"Excuse me, Obie. This isn't the most practical of gowns for daily life, but I get so tired of my plain black skirts. I wore this to my parents' funeral—they were well-to-do, and I needed a stylish gown. I haven't had any use for it since, however."

"Mama, you look like a dream in it, as you well know. All that taffeta!" Beulah chided her parent.

"All that fabric must weigh a lot. I don't see how you can stand wearing that rig in this heat," Obie commented.

Violet looked hurt. "It isn't that heavy, and the taffeta breathes easily."

A strained silence followed. The girls hung up their dish towels and left the room, chatting casually.

"Violet," Obie gripped her arm gently. "I didn't intend to hurt your feelings. You do look. . .like a dream, as Beulah said. I'm not one to appreciate style, I guess, but you always look just fine to me."

She gave him a prolonged view of her thick lashes before lifting them to display her stunning eyes. He released her arm and swallowed hard.

"Thank you. I need to learn which styles you do admire. We know very little about each other, really."

"I'll do my best to answer any question you want to ask."

"Isn't there anything you want to learn about me?"

Obie felt the tide of red creep up his neck again. "Yes, many things."

"Come, let's sit down at the table, and I'll pour the coffee. Would you like more pie?"

"No, thank you. It was great, though. Best I've ever eaten, I think. Where did you learn to cook?"

"My mother taught me. She believed that every woman should know basic housekeeping skills. It was a good thing, for Jeremiah and I could never afford to pay a cook. I always cooked for our family." Violet poured amber coffee into the two cups.

"Not only beautiful, she can cook!" Obie smiled bashfully, turning his cup between his rough hands and studying the steam.

Violet sat beside him in Samuel's chair. "Do you think I'm beautiful? I realize that true beauty comes from within, but I have always wanted to be pleasant to look at."

"Surely your husband told you how lovely you are. A man would have to be blind not to see. . ." He lowered his eyes back to his cup, afraid of saying too much.

"Thank you," Violet breathed, her eyes alight. "I know you'll think I'm vain, but I try so hard to look my best. It is good to know that you. . .approve."

"How's your back?"

Wondering about his train of thought, she answered, "Healing nicely. Caroline nursed me well. I still feel stiffness if I bend over or reach my arms up, but it doesn't hurt anymore."

"Did you want to ask about my past?" Again, Obie abruptly changed the subject.

"Yes, if you don't mind. I've heard several versions of your story, but I want to hear it from you. I know that you were accused and convicted of robbing a gold shipment and that you were in prison at a place called Yuma. The sheriff told me that much."

"What else have you heard?"

"Nick Houghton told me some nasty things about you, but I considered the source and disregarded everything he said. I can't believe that you killed anyone, let alone shot a man from a running horse like he said you did."

Obie straightened abruptly. "Houghton said he had *seen* me shoot a man from a running horse?"

"Yes. . .well, he intimated that he had; then he dropped the subject when I questioned him," Violet said, puzzled by Obie's reaction. "So I assumed he was making it all up. He said that you shot a man from a running horse while lying on your back. Is that even possible?"

"Nick Houghton. Could it be?" Obie mused quietly.

"*Have* you shot a man on a running horse?"

"Only once."

"While lying flat on your back?"

"Yes."

"And killed him? You really have killed people?" Violet gulped.

"Yes, I really have. Not for many years, but I have killed at least five men and wounded many others. I'm not proud of that fact, but it's the truth."

"During the war?"

"No, I was in prison during the War Between the States. Before that I worked as a hired gun for a time, along with Boz. We fought in several battles against Indians or outlaws. I've never killed in cold blood or in anger, and I haven't shot anyone since Yuma, since I became a believer. The last man I killed was Edwin Bolton, the older brother of the man who impersonated your husband."

"Oh!" Violet's voice was small. Each time he said the word "killed," a knife pierced her soul.

"I was imprisoned for Edwin's murder and for the murder of the men who carried the gold shipment. Edwin and his two younger brothers had stolen the gold and killed the four guards. I was too late upon the scene to save those men, but I shot Edwin as he tried to escape. Problem was, he had already shot my horse and got me in the leg, so I couldn't chase the other two or leave the scene. I was found there the next day with the five bodies and no gold. The two remaining Bolton brothers claimed that they had surprised me committing the crime. Although the gold was never found, it was assumed that I had stashed it somewhere. It was my word against theirs, and their father was important in that community. I didn't stand a chance, no matter how improbable their version of the story sounded. Except for one godly man who pled my cause, I would have been hanged for a crime I didn't commit."

"Oh!" Violet's eyes were enormous.

"That man came faithfully to visit me in prison. I was bitter at first, naturally; but, after a year or two, God softened my heart. I prayed with Burt to receive Christ, and he discipled me for two more years until his death. Burt Squires had never been strong, and the desert heat finally killed him. I missed him something awful, but after he died, I started sharing my faith with other prisoners and the prison guards, and before long there was a group of us that met together to pray and study the scriptures. It was a great place to grow in grace and knowledge of my Lord and Savior." Obie smiled, though his eyes held a hint of sadness.

"How long were you there?"

"Ten years."

"Ten years!" Violet mouthed the words in sympathetic horror.

"After my release, I went back to being a cowhand, hiring out with a cattle outfit in the Rockies. I met up with Boz Martin, who had become a lawman. I told him my story and asked for his help; he told me about my father's death. So I traveled back to California, sold Dad's business, and brought Al with me out here. We settled here because one of Boz's friends, a federal marshal, had given him a tip that one of the Bolton brothers had been seen near this area. I'd been praying for years that God would somehow clear my name, and this seemed like part of His answer. Al and I bought a farm and settled down; Boz got the job as Longtree's sheriff. Problem was, I didn't recognize Charles after so many years. Lived and worked right near the man and never knew him."

"Did he have the gold?"

"We think so. He wrote a letter before he died, but we couldn't read it. Boz sent it off to be analyzed, and we hope it contains a full confession. The gold isn't important to me, but my reputation is. Boz has been working the case for me all these years, trying to put the pieces together. He's a true friend."

"What about the other brother?"

"We think Patrick is still in the area. Charles told us that Patrick shot him and that he didn't recognize his own brother."

"You shot Edwin from a running horse while lying flat on your back?"

"Yes, and only his two brothers saw it."

"Are you thinking what I'm thinking?" Violet's eyes were frightened.

"But we have no way to prove it unless Charles's letter points to the man." Obie touched Violet's hand. "Don't be afraid. He would have nothing to gain by harming you. He probably believes that the gold is hidden around your house or property. He might hope to gain it by marrying you."

"And he killed his own brother in cold blood?"

"Patrick was always the most vicious of the brothers. He was only a boy at the time of the robbery, yet he shot at least two of the guards."

"Nick seems to enjoy inflicting pain."

"Has he harmed you?" Obie's voice was sharp.

"You saw him. . .pawing me that day. He twisted my arm and left bruises. See?" She pulled up her sleeve to reveal large yellow-gray spots on her forearm. "I do bruise easily; but these marks have lasted a long time, and they really did hurt. He frightens me. I've asked him many times to leave me alone, but he will not be discouraged. I don't think he's quite normal."

Obie sat back and folded his arms across his chest, brooding. "I want you to stay out of town for the next few days, to avoid Nick Houghton. He probably wouldn't hurt you, but don't take chances."

"He could come here, though, Obie. He has come before, and when I saw him in town a few days ago, he said he would visit again soon. He doesn't wait for an invitation, and he doesn't listen when I ask him not to come."

"Do you want to move back to Amelia's? Would you feel safer there until he's behind bars?"

"No. I only feel truly safe when I'm with you. Nick is deathly afraid of you, Obadiah. He's big and blustery, but at heart he's a coward. That's what makes him dangerous, I think."

Obie suddenly rose and paced across the room. "I was wrong to leave Barabbas with you, and I don't want to be wrong again. If you ever need me, Violet, give three shots and I'll come running."

"I don't know how to shoot a gun."

Obie looked upset, but he only said, "You should learn."

"You could teach me. There is a rifle in the hall closet, though I haven't seen any bullets for it."

Obie followed her to the entryway closet, carrying a candle to light their way. She opened the door and pulled out a rifle. "This must have belonged to Mr. Bolton."

Obie exchanged the candleholder for the gleaming weapon. "Winchester '73—a fine rifle. Wonder why he didn't take it with him." Stretching up as far as he could reach, he felt around on the closet shelf and pulled out a box. "Here are the shells." Violet watched in fascination and some horror as he levered ammunition into the rifle. "Keep it loaded and handy at all times."

"But what about Samuel? I don't want him playing with a loaded gun!"

He gave her an impatient look. "Of course not. I'll teach all of you to shoot. A boy needs to learn respect for guns early on. We'll store it on an empty chamber." He lifted the rifle to his shoulder and peered down its length.

"If you say so." Her voice sounded small.

He looked down at her and recognized the fright in her eyes. "Don't be afraid of me, Violet."

"You look so. . .so natural with that gun, so tough and sure. It makes me afraid that I don't know the real you, the Obadiah Watson that was a legend in the West."

"Legend in the West? Whatever gave you that idea? I was just a two-bit gunman until the Lord taught me better. I'm a good shot, but I've seen better. I don't carry a gun now, except for hunting. It isn't necessary in Longtree, thank the Lord. You know the real me, Violet. The old Buck Watson is gone forever, washed away in the blood of the Lamb." He stood the rifle back in the closet and closed the door. "Any more questions?"

"Why do people call you Buck?"

"My second name is Buckley, my mother's maiden name. When I was a kid, I thought Buck sounded tough, like I wanted to be. After I met the Lord, I didn't want to sound tough anymore. Obadiah means 'servant of the Lord,' and that's what I want to be. Some people can't break an old habit, and they still call me Buck. I don't mind it, but Obadiah better defines who I am now."

"I like your name, Obadiah Buckley Watson."

He said nothing. What was that look in her eyes?

"Are you afraid of me, Obie?" She sounded confused. "You seem nervous. I thought you. . .well, had an interest in me. I mean, this afternoon you said you wouldn't run if I chased you, but right now you look poised for flight."

Those curls dangling around her face reflected the candle's glow. Black taffeta caught the light and emphasized her every curve. Her skin looked flawless. Her eyes were dilated, mysterious, and inviting, and he could hear her soft breathing.

"Why?" he suddenly cried. "Why would you chase me? One day you'll take a good look at me in broad daylight and send me packin' with a flea in my ear. I'm no fit match for you, Violet Fairfield."

"Nonsense!" Those lovely eyes flared into anger. "What do you think I am—a proud socialite who thinks everyone beneath her notice? I'm an ordinary woman with many flaws. I'm not looking for a perfectly handsome man; I need a friend and companion—someone to love who loves and needs me. You never saw Jeremiah, the real Jeremiah; but he was no Adonis, let me tell you. He was tall and skinny as a rail, with an Adam's apple that caught your eye first thing. But he had a sweet smile and a heart of gold, and I loved him. That's all that matters! Maybe I was mistaken about you. I guess an old bachelor wouldn't know what marriage is all about. Good night, Mr. Watson."

She swept past him, opened the front door, and waited for him to take the hint. Troubled, he sneaked a glance at her face in passing. Tears sparkled upon her white cheeks, but she coldly refused to meet his gaze.

"Please be patient, Violet. This is all new to me. Uh, thanks for supper."

Chapter 11

*And let us not be weary in well doing: for in due season
we shall reap, if we faint not.*
GALATIANS 6:9

True to her promise, Caroline Schoengard spread the word about the arrival of Violet's household goods at the train station. Only hours after her possessions were unloaded on the platform, farm wagons began to roll down the Fairfield driveway, each one loaded with furniture or crates. "Delivery Day," Caroline called the impromptu celebration; and people from miles around joined in the fun, leaving their daily house- and farmwork behind to help out a needy widow.

Violet met some neighbors and became better acquainted with others. She flitted about, giving instructions and asking advice. It felt strange to her, having so many people around her house, but Caroline made introductions, trying to put Violet at ease. The Schoengards spent most of the day unloading and unpacking in Violet's kitchen, while Obie and Al set up bedsteads and carried in the mahogany sideboard, several chests of drawers, a highboy, and the davenport. The ladies set up a cold luncheon on tables in the yard, and several men whitewashed the house's exterior.

The children had a wonderful time running in and out of doors without worrying about tracking in dirt; Violet was too distracted to notice them. Samuel played with the Schoengard and Blackthorn boys. While keeping watch over the tiny tots, Beulah and Eunice chatted with some girls they knew from school and church.

❧

Al took frequent breaks to talk with Beulah, and during a stroll to the pond after lunch, he brought up a subject that concerned him. "Is your mother angry with my cousin? He's been quiet ever since he dined with you all last Saturday. He won't tell me what happened, but something's wrong. He's been sending me with your milk and eggs—not that I mind, you know, but I can't help wondering."

"I noticed that he hasn't been coming around. Mama seems sad, too. I think she misses him, but she hasn't told me if they argued. Maybe they'll work out their differences today."

"Not if they continue like they've been, avoiding each other."

"Sort of childish, don't you think?"

Al chuckled. "I bet they'll marry within the month. What do you say?"

Beulah shyly dropped her eyes. "You're probably right. Mama adores him, I know. She's been fretting today because Nick Houghton is here. He frightens her. Did you hear how he grabbed her once and threatened to spank her? Can you imagine anyone trying to spank Mama? He's not a good man."

"My cousin won't let him touch her again."

Beulah looked skeptical. "Don't mistake me, I admire your cousin greatly, but could he stop a large man like Mr. Houghton from harming Mama?"

Al leaned against a tree, tipped back his hat, and folded his long arms. "I wouldn't worry on that score. Miss Beulah, has anyone ever told you how beautiful your eyes are?"

Evening shadows were long when the Schoengard wagon rattled away. Scott, Bernie, and Ernie waved to Samuel until trees hid them from his sight. "Now you hurry and get into bed," Violet ordered her exhausted boy. "Just think—a real bed again! It's all set up in your room. Hop to it."

Violet admired the gleaming white clapboards of her house's exterior. Only the trim still needed touching up, and she had a feeling it would be taken care of without a word from her. What a wonderful community this was! Her heart overflowed with thankfulness for the Lord's provision.

It was pleasant to enter the sitting room and see her old Turkish rug on the floor in front of her mother's cherished horsehair davenport. A painted screen covered the cold hearth. A few pieces of china glistened from the china dresser; much of it was not yet unpacked. Violet stood in the doorway and admired, sighing with satisfaction. It felt like home.

"It's beautiful, Mama," Beulah said over her mother's shoulder.

Violet reached up and hugged her daughter's head against her own. "Isn't it? God has been very good to us."

"I remember seeing some of this furniture when we visited Grandma and Grandpa Carrington that time when I was about six. Eunice and Samuel don't remember any of it. We lived with Father's parents for so long, and before that I only remember moving around a lot. I hope we stay here always. I really like it here."

"I'm glad."

"Do you plan to marry again, Mama?"

Startled, Violet turned to study Beulah's face. "Why do you ask?"

"You've been so droopy all week since Obie hasn't come around. It's obvious that you admire him, Mama. I wasn't born yesterday."

Violet couldn't help smiling. "How well I know! And what do you think about the notion of a stepfather?"

"If it were Obie, I wouldn't mind. I think Father would have liked him. He's kind of rough and rugged, but he's got a kind heart."

"It doesn't hurt that he has a handsome young cousin, does it?"

"Mama!" Beulah peeked up through her lashes, smiling guiltily.

Violet chuckled. "Get to bed, girl, and tell your sister to hit the hay. We've all had a big day." Violet gave Beulah a gentle smack on the backside as the girl turned to go.

"Mama?" Samuel called from upstairs. "Can Uncle Obie stay to hear my prayers?"

Violet had not realized that Obadiah was still in the house. She hadn't seen his wagon in the yard; it must be back near the barn. Trying to keep her voice calm, she replied, "Yes, dear. I'll be up to tuck you in later."

After considering her feelings and weighing her options for several lonely days, Violet had reached a few important conclusions. Although in general she disliked violence and violent men, she understood that Obie's upbringing and circumstances had formed him into the sort of man who felt comfortable around guns and uncomfortable around women. If she loved him, she would have to accept him the way he was. He could never change his past. And she did love him, oh yes, indeed.

He had asked her to be patient—a difficult proposition for Violet. She wanted to settle their relationship now, if not sooner. If his hesitation was due to concern that she could not truly care for him, she could easily put an end to that misconception. She was mortified by the idea of throwing herself at him, but if it was the only way. . .

On the other hand, what if she ended up frightening him away forever?

Still dithering, she entered the kitchen to brew coffee. Nick Houghton stood at the counter, pouring a cup, which he extended to her with a winning smile. "Already brewed. I thought you might be ready for a cup about now. Quite a day, eh?"

Violet struggled to keep dismay from her face. "Mr. Houghton, I didn't know you were still here. Thank you for your help today." She had never actually seen him helping, though he had supervised while the other men worked.

"Have a seat, doll. You need pampering after a day like this. You like your coffee with cream only, right?"

⟋⟍⟍⟋

Obie helped Samuel tuck freshly ironed cotton sheets around his bed and arrange the blankets. "I like this so much better than my room at Grandfather Fairfield's house. It never felt like my room, really. Uncle Obie, do you have sisters? Mine are all right, I guess, but they think I should obey them just like I obey Mama. It's no fun having three mothers and no father."

"I have no sisters or brothers, but lots of cousins."

"Where are they?" Samuel climbed up and lay on top of the blankets, for the night was warm.

"In California or in New Mexico Territory, except for Al. He's like a little brother, I suppose." Seated on the wooden floor with forearms across his upraised knees, Obie glanced around the small room.

"What happened to your parents?"

"My mother died when I was five. Then I lived with my pa for a while and we traveled around. I was their only child."

"Was your father sad when your mother died?"

"Very sad."

"I don't remember Father much. He left us when I was little. Would you leave your family if you didn't have to, Uncle Obie?"

Obie considered his answer carefully. "I would never want to leave my family, but perhaps your father felt compelled to leave you behind until he had a home for you. A man feels responsible for the safety of his family."

"Have you ever been married?"

Obie shook his head.

"My mother likes you."

Obie shifted position. "She's a fine woman."

"If you married her, you could live here with us, and we could go fishing every day."

"You'd like that, would you?"

"I'd like that a lot. Do you think she's pretty? I do."

"Very pretty." Obie began to rise.

"What's the matter, Uncle Obie?"

"Uh. . .nothing. I was just thinking about. . .something. You'd better say your prayers if you want me to hear 'em."

"Yessir." With a bounce, Samuel scrambled into a kneeling position, folded his hands, and closed his eyes. "Lord, thank You for sending Uncle Obie to us. Please make him marry Ma so we'll have a proper family. Amen. Oh, and please help me to catch lots of fish tomorrow, and I sure would like a dog. Amen."

Obie picked up the candle. "I'd best be getting on home."

"Don't leave before Mr. Houghton does!"

Obie stopped short. "Houghton is still here?"

"I saw him climbing the attic stairs while you were digging through boxes for my tin soldiers. He came down awhile ago. What's he looking for, Uncle Obie? He snoops around when he thinks no one's looking. I don't want him here without you. He scares Mama."

"Unless she tells me to leave, I'll stick around." He ran one hand back over his short hair.

"Obie, was my father murdered?"

"No, but don't you say a word about it to *anyone*."

"I won't. I'm glad he's in heaven. Beulah says he used to talk about heaven a lot, like he was wanting to go there."

"I'm glad to hear it. Now you'd better get to sleep, Sam, or you won't be much help to your mama in the morning. It's late."

"What time is it?"

Obie pulled out his railroad watch. "Nearly ten o'clock." He shook his head. "I must be crazy, stayin' so late."

He stepped through the open door and spotted a startled face in the dark doorway across the hall. Eunice, clad in a billowing dressing gown, stood obviously listening in on their conversation. Caught red-handed, she smiled sheepishly. "I like hearing you talk," she defended herself. Long braids dangled on either side of her round face. "I won't tell anyone what I heard; don't worry. I heard Mr. Houghton talking to Mama down in the kitchen, and I know she doesn't want him around. I'm glad you're still here."

Obie gently tugged at one brown braid. "Me, too. Now you get to bed, young lady."

He stepped lightly on the stairs, shielding the candle with one hand. The house seemed very still. He silently pushed open the kitchen door. Violet had fallen asleep at the handsome oak table with her head on her arms. Nick sat across from her with his back to Obie, head tipped, draining a silver bottle. Obie let the door shut with a snap.

Nick shoved the flask inside his vest and quickly picked up his cup of coffee. "Thought you'd never come down. Are the young'uns asleep?"

"Nearly. Looks like your excitin' company was too much for Mrs. Fairfield."

It was supposed to be a joke, but Nick's eyes narrowed. "Watch your tongue, Watson, and keep your nose out of my business."

Obie's brows lifted. He poured himself a cup of coffee, then pulled out a chair and straddled it. "Didn't know I had meddled in your business, Houghton." He kept his voice low to avoid disturbing Violet. From this angle he could see her parted lips and closed eyes.

"Your intervention here is unwelcome. Understand?" Nick growled thickly. His nose glowed cherry red, and his eyes were somewhat glazed. Obie watched him with a wary eye.

"Tell me what you mean by 'intervention.'"

Nick swore with feeling. "You've been buzzin' around Violet like a fly around a horse, workin' more at her place than at your own. What're you hopin' to gain by it?"

"The Lord told us to care for widows—"

"Yeah, yeah, I heard that already. Look, you dried-up, flea-bitten, bow-legged old cowpoke, if by any chance you're thinking marriage, I give you fair warning that I laid first claim on this treasure."

Nick let his gaze rest on Violet's disheveled hair, and his voice grew slightly husky. "There's a fire burnin' somewhere inside this prim and proper little lady, and I mean to find it. She stole my heart that first day at the train station with one glance from those baby blue eyes, and I mean to have her if it's the last thing I do. She's been waiting for a man like me to come along and sweep her off her feet."

Obie's glance strayed back to Violet's face. Her eyes were open, and as he watched, she wrinkled her nose and grimaced. He quickly looked across the room, at the floor, anywhere to keep from smiling.

Nick stretched his long arms; then he laced his fingers behind his head. Suddenly amiable, he suggested, "You go on home, Watson. I'll sit with Violet until she wakes up."

On cue, Violet stirred, sat up, and yawned, daintily patting at her open mouth. She started to stretch, glanced at Nick, and quickly put her hands in her lap. He wore a wolfish expression, eyes dilated, red lips apart. "What time is it?" she inquired.

Nick's voice was thickly solicitous. "After ten, my dear. I let you sleep for a while, but Watson came downstairs just now. Sorry he disturbed you. Want another cup of coffee?"

"No, thank you. Obie, did you get any pie?"

"Yes, ma'am. Thanks." Then he realized that she was silently begging him to stay and protect her. Their quarrel was gone and forgotten. "Come to think of it, I could just tuck in another piece about now. Caroline bakes a fine blueberry pie."

Violet chattered as she cut another slice and slipped it on Obie's plate. "I must remember to thank her this Sunday. She's been so good to me. We've become close friends, you know. The children and I visited at the parsonage a few days ago and had a wonderful time. Caroline makes the most beautiful crocheted doilies I've ever seen. She has promised to teach us how to make them."

As she handed Obie the pie and sat down, she hitched her chair closer to his. Nick's glittering eyes moved back and forth between their faces.

Violet chattered on. "Nick, is your horse in the paddock? Will you be able to see to saddle and bridle it? I'll get you a lantern, if you like."

"I'll manage."

Obie dawdled over a small bite of pie. Violet's skirt brushed his knee, and he caught a whiff of flowers. Under the table, she touched his leg with her hand, as if seeking reassurance. The bite of pie dropped from his fork, and he had trouble scooping it up again.

The silence stretched uncomfortably long. "Say, Violet," Obie blurted, "I've found a few horses that might please you."

"Oh? Tell me." She eagerly accepted the new topic.

"Kauffman's dark bay gelding would do. He's got Morgan blood, and he's gentle as a lamb. And the Eversons have a gray—"

"I've been thinking of buying the bay myself," Nick interrupted.

"I doubt Rob would sell him to you." Immediately, Obie winced. He had not considered his words before speaking.

Nick leaped to his feet, flushed with sudden anger. His bloodshot eyes flared. "Explain that remark, Watson!"

Obie calmly studied the man towering over him. "Don't do anything rash, Nick. Remember where you are—inside a lady's home. I'll fight you tomorrow if that'll make you happy, but sit down for now."

From the corner of one eye, Obie saw Violet's hand flutter up to her throat. She tried to speak normally, but sounded breathless. "Nicholas, I think you'd better start for home. You have a long ride ahead, and it's late."

He turned upon her. "You tryin' to get rid of me? You—" He spouted off a string of invectives so coarse that Violet clapped both hands over her ears and cried out.

Slowly Obie rose to his feet and circled the table. "Get out of this house, Houghton. Don't do anything you'll regret tomorrow when you're sober."

Nick reached inside his jacket and pulled out a small gun. Before he could level it, Obie batted his arm up and away. Violet didn't even have time to scream.

Boom. A left fist to Nick's belly—Nick appeared to fold in half. Thunk. A right to his jaw—the gun clattered to the floor. Ashen-faced, Nick slowly toppled backward and cracked his head against the seat of a chair. His large body went limp.

Obie stood looking down at the still figure, shaking his right hand and flexing its fingers. He glanced up at Violet. "I'm sorry."

Violet stared at Nick, then at Obie, and gulped. "I thought he would kill you!"

Bending over, he picked up the gun. "That's likely what he had in mind." He unloaded the derringer and tucked it under his belt in back.

"I'm so thankful you were here!" To Obie's amazement, she rushed to him and wrapped both arms around him. "Thank you, thank you," she murmured, nuzzling into the side of his neck. Slowly he lifted his hands and set them upon her shoulders, feeling her warmth through the cotton fabric of her dress. She was trembling—or was he trembling? He wasn't sure. He simply stood there, immobilized by the incredible pleasure of her embrace until she moved away. Covering her hot cheeks with both hands, she choked out, "I'm sorry—"

Dazed, he shook his head. "Don't be. It was. . .like heaven." Quickly he bent to examine Nick, touching a darkening bruise on the younger man's jaw and feeling the rising lump on the back of his head. "He should be fine except for a headache. I'll take him and his horse to my place for tonight."

"Won't he hate you tomorrow?"

"No more than he did today. His memories will be hazy, at best. He's sloshed."

Violet shook her head as if she didn't understand why he would say such a thing, so Obie reached into Nick's waistcoat and drew forth the silver flask.

"Whiskey. I'd better get the team hitched before he comes around."

"I'll hold a lantern for you. I just can't tell you how glad I am that you were here!" she repeated.

He was aware of her watching eyes while he hitched the sleepy, annoyed mules to his wagon. Her presence gave him pleasure, but his hands felt strangely clumsy. Might she offer another embrace before he drove away? Never could he have imagined how good she would feel in his arms. . . . He led Nick's hired horse to the wagon and tied it to the tailgate.

Without a word he returned to the house, slung Nick over his shoulder, and carried him to the wagon. Violet watched as he climbed up, hauled the limp man farther into the wagon bed, and carefully pillowed Nick's head on a saddle.

"I hope he didn't hit his head too hard when he fell," she remarked. "Nick has always seemed afraid of you; tonight he was too drunk to be cautious. You're amazingly strong and quick. You are good at everything you do, aren't you?"

Turning, Obie regarded Violet for a moment, but said nothing. He jumped down, and they stood face-to-face. The lantern he had hung from the tailgate swayed, casting fleeting beams upon her face.

She released her breath in a little gasp. "Thank you for. . .everything. Is your hand all right? I saw you shaking it and I meant to ask, but then I forgot."

"It's all right," he said gruffly. He walked around her and prepared to climb up to his seat.

"Are you still angry with me?"

He turned to find her right behind him. "I was never angry with you. It was the other way around."

"I'm not angry anymore." Once again she rose to her tiptoes and kissed his cheek. This time her lips lingered upon his skin, warm and delightful. He felt ignited down to his toes. "Good night, Obadiah Buckley Watson. You are a wonderful man." Her voice was husky.

He stared at her for an eternal moment, unable to move. Then his mouth seemed to open of its own accord. "Will you marry me?"

He thought the silence would never end. Almost he turned and ran, inwardly dying from the pain of certain rejection—but at least he had asked. He could never kick himself for being too shy to ask.

"Yes."

Shock rendered him speechless.

"I said 'yes,' Obie. Do you really want to marry me?" Her voice held a tremor as though she were afraid.

"More than anything. . .but I can't believe. . .you said 'yes'?" His voice kept cracking.

"I did. Here I was trying to be patient as you requested, and then you astonish me with a proposal! I never know what to expect from you, dear man."

"When. . .when do you want to get married?" His voice cracked again like an adolescent boy's.

"Soon. In a few weeks, perhaps." She was achingly beautiful by lamplight. He wanted to hold her, but the very thought of it made him weak in the knees. And yet. . .soon she would be his, entirely his!

"I'll speak with Dave tomorrow about. . .about a wedding." He wanted to say tonight, but that might be rushing things.

Violet nodded. "Good night, Obie."

"Yes, it is." It was time for him to leave before he embarrassed himself. "This is the best birthday I ever had."

"Birthday?" Violet gasped. "You didn't tell me. . ."

He turned and scrambled nimbly to his seat. His chest felt like bursting with the effort of containing his feelings. "I'm forty-two today."

"Well, happy birthday," she said quietly.

It was no good. He couldn't leave, for the mules were still tethered to the railing. Deliberately he climbed down and jerked the slipknots loose. Then, before he could talk himself out of it, he took Violet into his arms and kissed her. Once. Thoroughly.

Violet watched as he drove away; he could feel her eyes, could sense her presence.

Not until the wagon reached the open road did Obie release his pent-up exuberance. One wild whoop pierced the night.

Violet jumped in fright at the dreadful sound. She had never actually heard Apaches on the warpath, but that cry equaled her most vivid imaginings. She turned on the veranda's top step and stared toward the dark drive where Obie had disappeared.

"Obie?" she wondered aloud. She touched her still-tingling lips with her fingertips and chuckled. "I'm engaged!"

Chapter 12

For the LORD God is a sun and shield:
the LORD will give grace and glory: no good thing
will he withhold from them that walk uprightly."
PSALM 84:11

As she stepped into the upper hallway, Violet heard Beulah call softly. Entering the girl's bedroom, she asked, "What is it, darling?"

"Where have you been? I heard an awful racket downstairs, and then you went outside for so long, I thought you'd been kidnapped. What happened?"

Violet sat on the edge of her daughter's bed and set her candle on the table. "Mr. Houghton picked a fight with Mr. Watson."

Beulah pushed herself up on her elbows, her dark eyes wide with concern. "Is he all right?"

"He was unconscious when I last saw him." Violet couldn't prevent a smug smile from creeping across her face.

"Where. . . ? What. . . ? Mama, tell me what happened! How can you smile when Uncle Obie is hurt?"

"Obie is fine, my dear. Mr. Houghton is somewhat the worse for wear, however."

"Really? Obie knocked him out? But he's so much smaller than Mr. Houghton!"

"Obadiah Watson is worth a dozen Nick Houghtons."

"That's what Al said. So what did you do after the fight?"

"We hitched up the mules, loaded Mr. Houghton into the wagon bed, and got engaged."

Beulah sat upright. "You did what?"

"I promised to marry Obie Watson."

"Really?" Another voice chimed in from the doorway. "I knew it! Oh, this is marvelous!"

Violet chuckled. "Eunice, I might have known you wouldn't be asleep." She patted the bed, and Eunice hopped up beside her. Big, shining eyes peered from beneath the girl's ruffled nightcap.

Beulah asked, "Are you sure about this, Mama? He's nice, but he's kind of old."

"Old? Did your father seem old to you?" When the girls shook their heads,

106

Violet said, "Do you know how old he was?"

"About your age?" Eunice guessed.

"He was fourteen years older than I."

"Oh. How old is Obie?"

"Forty-two. Only five years older than I am. His gray hair makes him look older, but he is quite young and strong. I find him very attractive."

"Attractive? Mama, *really*!" Beulah exclaimed in shocked disbelief.

"Yes, really. You'll know what I mean when you fall in love. Now you get some sleep, girls. We have lots of work to do around here tomorrow. I want to finish planting the garden. Caroline brought more seeds today and gave me good instructions about what to do with them. We'll be late in the season, but it shouldn't matter all that much. I think gardening will be fun once we learn how it's properly done."

Beulah sighed. "Sometimes I wonder whether we're cut out for farm living. You were bitten by a horse, Eunice spilled carrot seeds all over the garden—"

"Oh no!"

"I didn't mean to, Mama. They just. . .flew out of my hand."

"And you can't even drive," Beulah continued. "Everyone has to bring us things or drive us here and there."

"I can too drive, and so can you. I just couldn't handle that dreadful Barabbas. Obie will find us a pair of nice, quiet horses. And once we're married, he'll do most of the driving and farming, so it won't matter if we're hapless city folks. We'll learn."

"Will we still live in this house, or will we move to his farm?"

"We'll work those details out another day. I'll live wherever he wants me to live."

"You really love him, don't you, Mama?" Eunice glowed, though her eyes looked sleepy.

Violet smiled. "I surely do. He's a wonderful man."

"What will we do if Mr. Houghton comes around again before you're married?"

"I don't know. We'll cross that bridge when we come to it. I didn't intend to scare you two out of a good night's sleep. Remember that God is our true guardian and protector. Nothing can harm us while He keeps watch."

"I'm not afraid, just sleepy." Eunice yawned openly. "G'night, Mama. G'night, Beulah. See you in the morning." She hugged and kissed Violet before padding out of the room.

"Mama, you talk about God with more confidence since we moved here. It does look as though it was always in His plan for us to come here, doesn't it? I thought it was all a terrible mistake and that you were going to get your heart broken. Did you know all the time that Father wasn't really alive?" Beulah asked quietly.

"I was almost certain that he wasn't alive; but I had to come here, just in case. You know that I loved your father, don't you?"

"I have never doubted that. You were a good wife to him, and I'm sure you'll be a good wife to Obie. He knows God well, doesn't he?"

"Yes, he does. I think I'm learning to love God more as I learn to love Obie. Have you been reading your Bible, Beulah?"

"I will in the morning, I promise. You're right, Mama; God is very good to us."

"Good night, my dear."

~∞~

Before climbing into her parents' huge four-poster cherry bed that night, Violet finished transferring her clothing from Charles Bolton's old chest of drawers into a gleaming cherry highboy. "There, that's done. I'll be glad to get this eyesore out of the house." She slammed the chest's middle drawer with a flourish. It made a strange sound, not a hollow bang, but a muffled rattle.

"What in the world. . . ?" She pulled the drawer open again and tipped it up. Something slid to the back. . .but the drawer was empty. Curious, she thumped the bottom of the drawer and inspected it closely. A false bottom!

Within minutes she was seated on her bed, counting a pile of gleaming gold coins. She had no idea how much they were worth, for they appeared to be of foreign origin. Mexican, perhaps, but real gold for certain.

She could hardly wait to tell Obie.

~∞~

Violet spent the first half hour of the morning on her knees beside her bed, praising, thanking, and requesting wisdom. Then, revived and encouraged, she hurried downstairs to start the bread and fix breakfast. "Rise and shine," she caroled from the base of the stairs. "I have happy news to share."

Minutes later, Samuel capered around the kitchen, shouting with delight over his mother's engagement. "God answered my prayer! He did! He really did! We'll go fishing every day, and riding, and Uncle Obie has a dog. I want a horse of my own like Jughead."

Violet smiled and cracked an egg into the skillet.

Before that egg had cooked through, there was a knock at the front door. Violet left Beulah to watch the food and hurried to the entryway. She threw open the door. "Good morning!"

"That it is." Obie's broad back faced her. He turned quickly and held out a wriggling bundle. "I brought a pup for Samuel. Hope you still want one." He looked bashful, but she caught an ardent gleam in his eyes.

"Oh yes! He will be thrilled. Samuel," she called, stepping back to let Obie inside. "Come and see what Papa Obie brought for you."

A moment later, the frightened puppy was surrounded by fawning children. "Oh, he's so sweet!"

"Look at the little white streak on his nose. May I hold him, Uncle Obie?"

"Ask Sam; it's his dog. She's a girl, by the way."

Samuel laid claim to his pup and only grudgingly allowed his sisters to pet her. The black and white baby snuggled against his shirtfront. Violet recognized love at first sight when she saw it. "Why don't you take her outside on the grass and let her have a sniff around?"

"I got to think of a name." Samuel obediently carried his puppy down the steps and headed for a grassy spot.

Beulah turned her attention to Obie. "By the way, congratulations, Uncle Obie. . .or, like Mama said, Papa Obie. Mama told us the good news last night. I'm very happy for you both."

"Me, too." Eunice gave him a quick hug. "I knew she loved you right off. She just had that look."

"She did?"

Violet flushed under his questioning gaze. "Girls, who is watching the eggs?"

Her daughters rushed back to the kitchen.

Obie fiddled with his hat, then shyly reached out to take Violet's hand. "You haven't changed your mind?"

Violet only smiled and towed him into the living room. Once the door was shut, she slipped her arms around his waist. "Never." Resting her cheek upon his chest, she felt content. "I do love you, Obie. Eunice was right."

"It's a good thing, since I already talked with the minister. I'm not about to let you off the hook," he tried to joke, but his voice trembled. "Violet. . ."

"Yes?" she lifted her head, but he gently pulled it back to his chest and hugged her tightly.

"I can hardly believe it—that you love me. Don't ever stop. I. . .I love you so much, it hurts. I've got this awful fear that something will happen, that I'll lose you somehow."

"Obie! Remember what you told me about God? How He's a loving Father and enjoys giving us beautiful gifts? Live what you preach, sir." Violet kissed his chin to take the sting from her words. "What did Reverend Schoengard say when you told him?"

"He wasn't surprised. I think Caroline dropped him a hint about us; or else I wear my heart on my sleeve. Could be both. Can you be ready for a wedding in a few weeks?"

"Yes. I don't want a big production since it is my second wedding. Just a simple service will do nicely. The sooner the better as far as I'm concerned. However, there is the matter of me being in mourning. Do you think it will matter? I wish. . .I wish everyone could know that you're not a murderer. I don't care what they say about me, but I don't want people to whisper about you behind their hands. It makes me angry, Obie."

"Violet, justice will come in God's time. If you don't want to marry me under a cloud, I'll understand. We can wait."

Violet pulled back to look into his worried eyes. "I don't want to wait. I was being silly again, Obie. It doesn't matter what people say, really. I know you're innocent, and that's all that matters."

Obie brushed her cheek with the back of one hand, then touched his lips to the spot. "You're so soft, and you smell so nice. . . ." His moustache tickled.

"Do you have plans for today?" Violet asked. The feelings his caresses produced in her had better be saved for after the wedding, she knew.

Reluctantly he released her but kept hold of her hand. "I hoped to take you to the Thwaites' with me. I drove my buggy with that idea in mind. Afterward we could take a look at the horses I'm considering. I want your opinion on them. Do you have time for an outing?"

"Yes, indeed! Let me tell the girls—oh, have you eaten yet? Would you like some biscuits and eggs?"

"No, thanks. You go ahead, and I'll spend some time with Sam and the puppy."

"I won't be long." She turned back once more. "What became of Nick Houghton?"

"Left him sleeping in the wagon, and he was gone this mornin' when we got up. He's not badly injured."

"That's not what I was concerned about."

"Don't worry, Violet. Go on now."

She gave him a quick kiss on the cheek, but he caught her wrist and pulled her back for a real kiss. To his great satisfaction, she showed no inclination to avoid his callused hands or to shrink from his embrace. Indeed, he was obliged to push her gently away. "Go on with you. . .and you'd best fix your hair again."

Obie took a deep breath as he stepped outside. A wedding soon, she'd said. Who'd have imagined such a thing? He could hardly wait to tell Boz.

"Thank You, God," he breathed, remembering Violet's admonition. "You are too good to me."

Chapter 13

For the love of money is the root of all evil.
1 TIMOTHY 6:10

Before we go, I have something important to show you." Violet beckoned Obie inside. "I almost forgot about it."

"What is it, Violet? We need to be going."

She laid a finger on her lips and beckoned more forcibly. "Just come, please."

He followed her upstairs and into the bedroom, looking increasingly uncomfortable when she closed the door behind him. "This isn't proper, Violet. I—"

"Look here." Violet pulled out a drawer, showed him the loose bottom, and pried it up to reveal the cache of coins. "I found them last night. There were several in each drawer to distribute the weight."

Obie was amazed. "So he did have the gold, and he didn't spend it all. It's not such a clever hiding place. I wonder why Nick didn't find it."

"The false bottoms were fastened in much more securely than they are now. Charles had packed the coins with lots of fabric to keep them from clinking. If I hadn't slammed the drawer last night, I would never have noticed. I thought this was just an extraordinarily heavy piece of furniture—silly me!"

"We'll take the gold to Boz this morning. I don't want you sleeping in the house with it another night."

"Will you let Nick know that we found it? Otherwise, he could come looking for it again. I'd rather have him know that his search is useless."

He nodded. "We'd better let Boz decide what to do next. Have you got a sack to carry it in?"

The flour sack of gold coins, though far from full, was very heavy; yet Obie hefted it easily. "All that suffering, pain, and death over this sack of metal. Strange, what the love of money will do to people."

"What will Boz do with it?"

"I don't know. That's for the law to decide."

He stashed the sack on the floor of his box buggy. Violet imagined that the buggy rode several inches lower, weighted down by gold. It made her feel uncomfortable. "Should we bring the rifle along?"

"I don't think it's necessary, Violet." Obie lifted her up to the seat. "I haven't carried a gun for years."

"But that man is loose somewhere nearby, mad as a hornet, no doubt; and we already know he's a killer. He might suspect that we found his gold. You know I don't care much for guns, but I think we ought to bring along that rifle, if only for the look of the thing. It might make an outlaw think twice."

"If I had wanted a gun today, I would have brought my own." Obie hopped up to the seat beside her. His face was cloudy, yet he did not start the horse.

"But you didn't know about the gold this morning. Please, dear, if only for my peace of mind? I hate to be a nag, but I just have this awful. . .premonition. I don't want something to happen to destroy our joy any more than you do." Violet was tempted to use her feminine charms to convince him, but she knew better.

Although Obie's jaw tightened, he hopped down and stalked into the house, returning a moment later with Charles Bolton's Winchester. He laid the gun at their feet. "Happy now?"

Violet felt guilty. "Yes, but I hate making you angry."

They traveled in silence for a while. It was an overcast morning, yet oppressively hot. "How far is it to the Thwaites' house from town?"

"About twenty-five minutes in a buggy. Jughead makes it in fifteen."

"This seems like a nice horse. She's a pretty color. What's her name?"

"Bess. She's tricky to harness—ticklish. You wouldn't want her." His voice held little expression.

"Oh." Violet felt like unwanted baggage. "Hattie won't think much of me if I've already made you angry. We're not even married yet."

He cast her a speculative look, and she saw some of the tension leave his face.

"What are you thinking? Will it be worth giving up your freedom to have a nagging woman in your house?"

"I think so. Al does his share of nagging, believe it or not. I. . .well. . .I know how you feel about my past, about violence and killing. . . A man should never carry a gun if he isn't willing and able to use it."

"From what I've heard, you're more than handy with a rifle."

"That's not the problem. If you had seen your face when I told you about. . . about my past. . ."

"You're worried that I'll be frightened of you if you have to use that gun? I'm sure I would be frightened in a gun battle. Who wouldn't be? But I've come to realize that guns themselves are not evil. In this wicked world, if only bad men used guns, they would rule over the rest of us. I trust you to do what is right and necessary for my protection."

Right there on the open road, he let go the reins with one hand, took her by the back of the neck, and kissed her lips. "Thank you."

She correctly interpreted his reaction as vast relief.

~∞~

"Got some things to turn in, Sheriff." Obie pulled Nick's derringer from his waistcoat and dropped it on the desk along with a handful of cartridges. "Took that offa Houghton last night."

"He pull it on you?" Boz picked up the gun and fingered the polished barrel.

"Tried to. Might wanta ask the doc what kind of bullet was in Charles's belly. I have a notion it might match this weapon."

"I've got the bullet from the postmortem. Looks like your notion is right." Boz reached into his pocket and displayed a small metal object on his palm. "Buck, you'd best watch your back. Houghton must know his goose is purt' near cooked."

"That's not all." Obie tilted the flour sack over Boz's desk and let a few coins drop out. "Convinced? Bolton didn't spend it all."

Boz rubbed a gold coin between his thumb and finger. "He said so on that envelope, but he didn't tell where he hid it."

"You got the report back on his letter? Why didn't you tell me?"

"Just got it yesterday. That envelope was loaded with information. Charles confessed to the gold shipment robbery, but said he didn't kill any of the guards. Patrick and Edwin shot all four of them. Patrick came up with the plan to blame the crime on you, Buck. The letter also said that Jeremiah Fairfield died in his sleep. Mrs. Fairfield, Charles took a letter from Jeremiah's pocket to get your address so he could forward your husband's personal effects. I don't know what happened to the letter."

"I wonder if his brother has it."

Both men looked at her. "Why?"

"Because he must have sent me that telegram, and how else would he have learned that I exist? He probably thought that my coming and exposing his lie would force Charles to move the gold. Charles kept that letter, and sometime recently his brother got hold of it. Nick Houghton didn't 'just happen' to come to the train station on the day of my arrival. Remember, he said that Jeremiah sent him there to pick up a package? He knew that I was coming that day either because he read my return telegram or because Charles told him so."

Boz looked impressed. "You're right, ma'am. I was just about to tell the most important information on that letter. Nick Houghton is Patrick Bolton."

Obie squeezed Violet's hand, and she moved closer to him, lifting her eyes to his face. "You're cleared, Obadiah. And it happened in God's perfect time, like you said."

Boz studied them for a moment. "It 'pears you been withholdin' information from me."

Obie announced proudly, "You're invited to the wedding, of course. We haven't set the date yet."

"Soon, very soon," Violet asserted.

After clearing his throat noisily, Obie gave Boz a slow grin and lifted two fingers. "Two miracles, Boz. Count 'em."

The sheriff frowned, drumming his fingers on the desktop. "I don't want you broadcastin' the news until we've got Houghton behind bars. Hear me?"

Hattie grabbed Violet's wrist, pulled her down beside the bed, and studied her face with watery eyes. "You were married how long to that Fairfield fellow?"

Violet felt uncomfortable. She didn't want to lie. "We were married nineteen years ago this July."

Hattie's eyes narrowed, and Violet's heart sank. Didn't Obie's friend approve of her?

"Why would a godly woman marry a no-account cad like Jerry Fairfield?"

"Jeremiah was a good and godly man, a faithful husband, and a loving father." Violet could not allow Jeremiah's name to be so unfairly maligned.

"Then why did he leave you all behind?"

"He wanted to settle here and build a house before sending for the rest of us. He didn't know what to expect from this area, whether there would be decent lodging or anything."

"Something in this story doesn't ring true. I'm sorry to call you a liar, Miz Fairfield, but there it is." Hattie leaned back on her pillow and regarded Violet narrowly. "Does Obadiah know the truth in all this?"

Violet nodded soberly. "He knows more than I do, Mrs. Thwaite. I can't tell you all I know. I promised not to talk."

She saw understanding dawn in Hattie's weathered face. "You promised Obie?"

Violet nodded again. "And the sheriff."

"Ah! Now I'm beginning to see the light. You're an elegant woman, like he said. Although, you're not so pretty as I imagined. You look durable enough. Can you cook?"

Hattie's comments pricked Violet's pride. "I'm a good cook, and I keep a neat house. I may not be pretty, but I'm well preserved for a woman my age."

"Maybe so. Got your own teeth, anyway. And a good corset hides a multitude of flaws. Are your children well behaved?"

"Most of the time," Violet spoke through clenched teeth, managing to simulate a smile. "They need a father, especially my son. He adores Obie."

Hattie nodded. "Well, come back and see me anytime. I imagine I won't see as much of Obie once he's under your thumb, but that's as it should be, I suppose."

Violet nearly choked.

"Obie, come get your woman. She's tired of me, and it's mutual."

Obie entered the room, giving Violet a quizzical glance. "You all right today, Hattie?"

"I'll survive another month or two, I imagine. This lady of yours makes me

114

look scrawny. I'd like her better if she weren't so shapely. Come 'ere and give me a kiss, boy."

Obie grinned and bent over for his mandatory kiss. "You're jealous, Hattie. Now you know how Cyrus must have felt all these years, watchin' you make eyes at a younger man. Turnabout is fair play."

As they left Hattie's stuffy little room, he whispered into Violet's ear. "Mind if we stay a bit longer? Cyrus needs help in the barn. If I don't take care of it, I'm afraid he'll attempt it himself."

Although she was more than ready to leave, Violet assured him, "You go right ahead. We can look at the horses another day, if necessary."

Cyrus gave Violet a sweet smile when she entered the kitchen. "Have a nice chat with Hattie? She's been looking forward to meeting you, Miz Fairfield. I guess you know we think the world of Obie. We're thankful he's found a woman to make him happy."

Violet smiled into the faded blue eyes. "I'm thankful he found me, too."

"I want to take a look at that pulley, Cyrus. Have a minute?" Obie inquired.

"If you're sure you don't mind, I'd be mighty grateful. Now you just make yourself to home while we're workin', Miz Fairfield. Hattie will sleep most of the morning. Sure you won't be lonely in here?"

"Not at all. Do you mind if I find something to cook up?"

"I'd consider it a favor if you did, ma'am. My cookin' ain't nothin' to brag on."

So, while Obie and Cyrus worked in the barn, Violet busied herself in the kitchen, mixing a batch of ginger cookies. That morning in town, Obie had stocked up on staples for the old couple—flour, sugar, cornmeal, and coffee.

"I sure hope Hattie improves upon acquaintance," Violet muttered, slicing ham for sandwiches, "for I expect I'll be spending considerable time here in the future. These people are almost like my new in-laws." She smiled grimly, recalling how easily Hattie had gotten under her skin. "She's a sharp one, that's for sure. But Obie loves her, so she must have a good side."

She pulled out a batch of cookies and slid in a new pan. The table was set with platters of sandwiches, tiny gherkins, carrot sticks, and warm cookies. Lettuce, cheese, and sliced tomatoes filled another plate, and a bowl of freshly mixed mustard made a sinus-clearing centerpiece. Obie enjoyed spicy food, she had recently discovered.

"Better call the men to dinner while those cookies bake," she told herself.

She found Cyrus and Obie in the barn loft, wrestling with an enormous hook. Both men had stripped off their shirts and were drenched with sweat, for the loft was like an oven. "I could bake a batch of cookies up here, I believe," Violet remarked from the top of the tall ladder. "Luncheon is ready whenever you are."

"Thank you, my dear." Cyrus immediately headed for the ladder.

"Do you happen to have any fresh milk?" Violet asked as he followed her down. "If not, we can drink water." She tried not to look winded when she reached the floor.

"We have fresh buttermilk. I'll fetch some from the springhouse." Cyrus looked exhausted, but his step was still springy. Violet watched him exit the barn, his undervest drooping from bony shoulders.

"I'm glad you called him down from there. I couldn't convince him to leave, and that heat could kill an old man in no time at all," Obie said from behind her. "It wasn't doing me any good, for that matter."

She turned to watch him wipe sweat from his face and neck with his wadded-up shirt. His once-white undervest clung damply to the hard muscles of his chest and arms. "I hope it rains soon and relieves this heat. You look pretty worn-out."

He smiled at her and moved closer; then he remembered his condition and stopped short. "Guess I'm too dirty to hug you."

"Come cool off up at the house. I've fixed a nice meal for everyone."

"You're amazing." He spoke sincerely, reiterating the words with his eyes.

"I love you, too." She reached up to kiss his lips. They tasted salty.

"Again?"

She gave him another, loving the way he closed his eyes to savor the kiss.

"Come on before the flies get our dinner." She took his hand and dragged him outside and toward the house.

"Bossy woman," he teased. Suddenly he stopped short, and she recoiled back into him as he had planned.

"Ooh, you're all wet!" She planted her hands against his chest and pushed away.

Laughing like a boy, he fell back. Violet heard something whiz past, and suddenly Obie dropped flat onto the ground. Immediately, there followed the sharp report of a rifle.

Chapter 14

Because he hath set his love upon me, therefore will I deliver him:
I will set him on high, because he hath known my name.

PSALM 91:14

With a cry, Violet fell to her knees beside Obie. To her infinite relief, he blinked, lifted a hand to his head, and brought it away damp with blood.

"Oh, thank God, you're alive!"

A shallow red crease passed just above his right ear. He grabbed Violet's arm and jerked her down beside him. There was no cover near. She cowered against him.

"Crawl toward the house," he commanded roughly. "I'll follow. He has to reload, unless he has two Spencers." It was a chance they would have to take.

"Where's our rifle?"

"Inside. Hope Cyrus made it safely to the house."

Violet obediently crawled, getting frequently tangled in her skirts and petticoats. Another bullet spattered gravel two feet in front of her. Obie jumped up, grabbed her around the body, and ran for the house, half-carrying Violet. They fell through the door, and Cyrus slammed it shut. They lay on the floor, panting and wide-eyed.

"Are you all right?" She sat up and reached for his head, but he brushed her off.

"Cyrus, where's my rifle?"

"Right here, boy. I've got me a Spencer, loaded and ready. I had just stepped into the house when I heard that first shot. Thought you were done for at first, I did. Hev you spotted the varmint?"

"No, but I can guess who it is. Violet, go to Hattie and keep away from the windows." Obie checked the rifle and levered a shell into position. All of the boyishness had left his face; to Violet he looked hard as nails and twice as sharp. Blood trickled down his neck, but he ignored it.

Violet crept away to sit beside Hattie's bed. To her surprise, the old lady reached for her hands. Frightened for their men, the two women clung together and whispered prayers.

"Cyrus, keep an eye peeled." Obie selected an old hat from a hook, placed it on a broomstick, and poked it up in front of the sitting room window—an old trick, but it worked. Glass showered around him as a shot shattered the window. The hat flew across the room.

Cyrus had been peeking from the next window. "I saw him, Obie. He's hidin' in the brush. See that old stump? The patch of saplings to the right of it."

"Bad choice. No solid cover." Lifting the rifle to the sill, Obie fired several rounds into the patch. A yelp of pain rewarded him. A figure suddenly leaped up and fled, limping, into the woods. Obie followed him through the sights of the rifle, but he did not fire. He could not shoot a man in the back, not even a bushwhacker.

Cyrus had no such compunction. His Spencer cracked once; the outlaw screamed and reeled into the brush, clutching his left leg.

"That'll slow him down," Cyrus cackled.

"Nice shot."

"Didn't think I had it in me, eh?"

Stepping carefully through crunching glass, Obie left the dining room. "Violet?"

"Obadiah, where's Cyrus?" Hattie sounded frantic.

"Right here, hale and hearty," Obie said, "He nailed that feller. All clear now, ladies."

"Is he dead?" Hattie shouted back.

"Nah, just wounded and runnin' for it," Cyrus answered.

"Are you sure he was alone?" Violet inquired from Hattie's doorway, her eyes dilated and teary.

"Yes. It was Houghton, just like we thought. Boz will round up a manhunt for him, I reckon. He's not going far on that leg," Obie answered, leaning the rifle in the hall corner.

Cyrus pushed past Violet and knelt down to comfort his wife. . .and to do some boasting. "Clear across the yard, he was, in that patch of birch saplings, and I pegged him in the laig. Don't tell me these old eyes hev lost their edge, woman!"

Obie's eyes begged Violet to understand. "The Lord watched over us and delivered us today. When we were outside, all I could think was that Nick might shoot you and that I was helpless to prevent it."

"God used you to protect me," Violet assured him. She wanted to hold him, to assure herself that her man was alive and well, but she felt strangely shy.

"I can shoot a rifle, but I couldn't make Houghton miss his shots. That was entirely up to the Lord."

"Do you think he'll come back?" Violet worried aloud. "What if he waits alongside the road and shoots at us while we drive home? What if he goes to my house and molests the children?"

"I'd be surprised if Nick tried anything else today."

She wrapped her arms around herself and shivered in spite of the heat. "Hold me?"

Obie immediately pulled her against him and gently rubbed her back. "I wasn't sure. . .I'm sweaty and bloody and dirty."

"I don't care. I need you." She slid her arms around his body, melted against him, and sighed. "You're good at comforting, you know. I hope you haven't made a practice of hugging frightened women."

"Never. You're no hardship to hold, Violet."

She smiled up at him, then immediately frowned. "You have little cuts on your face."

"From the window."

"Let me clean you up. I'll sweep the glass up later."

Seated on a kitchen chair, Obie munched on a sandwich while Violet dabbed iodine on his cuts and the bullet crease. She knew it must sting, but he never once flinched. Now that the crisis had passed, he seemed relaxed and cheerful. "Attempted murder is plenty to convict Houghton if we can put him before a jury. This time we've got a corroborating witness in Cyrus. Even if Charles's letter doesn't stand up in court, this attempt on our lives can't be ignored."

"If you say so," Violet said, distracted. She dabbed at a cut over his left eyebrow, thinking how horrible it would have been had that shard hit him in the eye. "I'm afraid this one will leave a scar."

"If you don't mind my ugly mug, another scar won't matter much. I've got my share of them."

She scanned his face. "Where? I don't see any."

"In places you can't see. Edwin Bolton shot my leg before I shot him. I also once got into a fight in prison—the guy had a Bowie knife. He might have killed me if the guard hadn't stopped him." His calm voice belittled the affair. He hauled his undervest off one shoulder to display a jagged white scar high on his hairy chest. "Nearly died of infection anyway, but God had other plans."

Violet slid her arms around his neck from behind. Laying her cheek against his, she whispered, "It frightens me to hear about it. Please be careful, for my sake."

"I will." He reached up to hold her forearms in place.

"Does your head ache?"

"Like thunder. I'm glad you nagged me about the rifle. You were right."

Violet lifted her head to stare in disbelief. "I've got me a man who'll admit when he was wrong? The Lord is truly good!"

"Come here." Obie pulled her onto his knee and rubbed his face against her hair even as he grumbled, "Sarcasm isn't appealing in a woman."

"I wasn't being sarcastic. I think you're wonderful."

"You'd better." Amazing himself with his own boldness, he kissed her temple, her cheek, and her neck below her ear. Violet shivered and closed her eyes.

He lifted his head. "Do you mind?"

"Your moustache tickles—but I love it. I'm glad you're not shy with me anymore. I was afraid I would have to throw myself at you. I'm not used to being so forward." Violet traced a heart on his chest with one finger.

He grabbed her hand and kissed her knuckles. "I'm still plenty shy, but I'm getting used to the idea that you like me. Sure you don't need spectacles?"

"I think you're beautiful, just like you think I am. God made us that way, so why fight it? It's perfect."

When footsteps crossed Hattie's bedroom floor, Violet leaped to her feet and straightened her gown. Sniffing the air, she suddenly rushed to the oven. "Oh no! That last batch of cookies burned to black crisps."

"Thought I smelled something strange," Cyrus remarked as he entered. "Hattie figured that was the way you usually cooked."

Violet's brows lowered; her lips tightened.

Obie laughed and shook his head. "That Hattie!"

Looking at him, Violet relaxed and began to smile. That Hattie, indeed. What a character!

Chapter 15

The LORD is known by the judgment which he executeth:
the wicked is snared in the work of his own hands.
PSALM 9:16

Days later, Violet and the girls were hard at work, sewing their dresses for the upcoming wedding. Violet's gown was simple in design, pale blue to match her eyes, with pearly buttons running down the fitted bodice. Beulah and Eunice had, eventually, agreed on pink taffeta for their dresses.

When the door knocker sounded, Violet hurried to answer and found Obie on the step. "This is a pleasant surprise! I didn't expect to see you today."

Without a word, he handed her the Saturday edition. Violet opened it and read the headline. CRIME SOLVED BY LOCAL SHERIFF AFTER TWENTY YEARS. She looked up at Obie.

"Read on."

Violet scanned the article with widening eyes. Although Nick Houghton had not yet been brought into custody, the news of his true identity had been leaked. A pair of curious reporters had unearthed a plethora of interesting information, including details that were new to Violet. Unable to continue reading while Obie stood there watching her, Violet asked, "Did they clear your name in this story? Does it tell about Charles's confession?"

He nodded, smiling calmly. "And you don't need to wear black anymore."

"Obie, I'm so glad! I mean, about your reputation, not about mourning clothes."

Hearing their mother's happy cries, Beulah and Eunice came running. "What happened?"

Violet reopened the newspaper. "Read this article; it will answer all your questions."

The girls took the paper and began scanning it with eager eyes. Violet indicated that Obie should follow her to the kitchen. Once through the door, she closed it behind him and snuggled into his arms.

He held her willingly, smiling at her evident need of his embrace. "Only a few more days, my dear."

"I wish we had set the date for today."

"What about these fabulous gowns I've been hearing about in painful detail? Could you have finished them by today?"

"We could have done very well without them. No one in town has seen our old clothing anyway, since we've been in mourning all this time."

"It's nice to have something new for a wedding, though, Violet. It is the beginning of our new life together. I'm glad you'll all have new gowns."

"You're so sweet. I don't deserve you," Violet sighed. "I made Samuel a new suit, too. He outgrew his old one."

"I bought myself a fancy set of duds. We'll all look so fine, we won't know each other."

"I'd know you anywhere," she protested, nuzzling into his neck again. He gently rubbed her back.

"Caroline needed this extra time to prepare for the reception she's planning. I know we didn't need a reception, but it gives her pleasure to do this for us. We can be patient for a few more days." Taking her by the shoulders, he resolutely stepped back. "Violet, I brought something else for you to see."

"Something besides the newspaper?"

He nodded. "Come outside."

Violet obediently followed him to the veranda. Two new horses stood patiently at the hitching rail with Jughead, a dark bay gelding and a plump gray mare.

"Look them over, Vi. They're for you."

She walked around them slowly, wondering what she was supposed to be looking for. "They both look fine, Obie. But once we're married, won't I be able to drive your horses? Why do I need these two?"

"You need your own pair. Try talking to them."

Violet spoke gently to the mare and reached for her face. The horse sighed, shifted her weight, and closed her eye. "She certainly seems calm enough. What's her name?"

"Dolly. She's been used as a brood mare for many years, but she's broken to drive. We should be able to work some of this weight off her in time. I don't think a dynamite blast could startle her."

"Isn't she rather old?"

"Only about twelve or thirteen. Lots of good years left in her. I got her cheap."

"You already bought her?"

"Both of them. Figured I could sell them again if I need to. Barabbas brought a tidy sum—enough for her and some left over. The gelding is broken to drive or to ride. He was a buy. I've had my eye on him for some time. He would make Samuel a good first horse."

"Do you think Samuel's old enough for a full-sized horse?" Violet felt a twinge of worry.

"Plenty old enough. This fellow is gentle as a lamb. He's around eight years old, has Morgan blood, and can cut cattle right alongside Jughead. . .not that we do much of that around here. He's smart as they come."

"Well, you know best. I like both of them better than Barabbas; that's for certain. Is there a place for them in our barn?"

"I put Myles to work in there this morning. We're doing some renovating. If we're to live here, I need space for my stock as well as for these two."

"Do you mind living in this house, Obie? I know you aren't wild about it."

"I've lived in worse places. I'm wild about you and the children; that's what matters." His contented smile reassured Violet.

"And Myles is. . . ?"

"Our hired man. You met him, Violet. Don't you remember?"

"So I did. Now that you mention it, I have been hearing some hammering and sawing noises. We were so busy, I didn't take enough notice to bother investigating." Violet felt somewhat dazed.

He gave her an odd look. "You need to get out of that house for a while. Have you been sleeping?"

"Not very well. Wedding jitters, I suppose. When I should be asleep, I keep thinking about all the things I need to do. Also, it bothers me to know that Nick is still wandering around out there somewhere."

He shook his head. "I can't believe they haven't found him yet. Where could a wounded man go? He left no trail that Boz could find. . .but then, Boz never was known as a tracker."

Taking the two lead ropes, he said, "C'mon. Let's hitch up and try these two out."

"But we only have one harness," Violet protested weakly.

"I put Dolly's harness in the barn. No more excuses. You can do this."

Obie insisted that Violet do the harnessing. The horses stood patiently, and she was soon convinced that they were ideal for her. Samuel came and joined them, thrilled with the prospect of two new horses along with a new puppy. He suggested the name "Rollie" for the gelding, "So they can be Dolly and Rollie."

"I like it," Violet agreed.

"May I ride with you?" the boy begged Obie. His puppy rollicked around his feet, tugging at his cuffs and bootlaces.

"If you're quiet and don't distract your mother."

"Go tell the girls where we're going," Violet requested.

Violet's knuckles were white as she clutched the reins and buggy whip, but she kept her voice calm. The two horses followed her directions willingly. Soon they were trotting up the drive.

Recent rains had cooled the air and freshened the trees and shrubs. The road was wet, but not too mucky for good driving.

"May we go to your farm and see the calves and piglets?" Samuel begged.

The puppy lifted her head into the breeze, standing beside Samuel on the rear seat. He kept a careful grip on her collar.

"Why not? They've grown since you were there last."

Treat gave them a hearty welcome, barking around the strange horses' feet. Rollie lowered his head slightly and snorted, but he didn't shy or try to bolt. Dolly ignored the ruckus entirely.

"Treat, I'm gonna shut you in the tack room if you don't knock off the noise," Obie growled. At that threat she closed her mouth but still whimpered and capered around the surrey until it stopped near the barn.

"Good driving." Obie hopped down and lifted his lady to the ground, taking the opportunity to hold her close for a moment.

"That was fun." Violet reached down to pet Treat's shaggy ruff. "Will Treat want to move to our house with you?" The dog's tail swept the air.

"I think she'll be fine here with Al. She's as much his dog as mine anyhow. We've got Samuel's dog now, if he ever gives her a name."

Violet was amazed at how quickly the calves had grown, especially the bull calf. "What did you name him?" she asked.

"Moo-Moo, of course." Al grinned, replacing his gloves after shaking Violet's hand.

"You can't be serious," she whispered, glancing toward Samuel, who was with Obie, admiring the piglets.

"Oh, but I am."

"What about when he grows into a huge bull? Moo-Moo?"

"Maybe then we'll call him Big Mo. Anyway, Samuel chose his name for us. We couldn't call him anything else." His voice rose. "You must like it better than Violet."

"I beg your pardon?"

Obie moved in on the conversation. "We'd better get home now. Al has work to do." He gave the boy a hard stare.

Al only grinned. "Buck tried to change her name after you came, but we still call her Violet."

"Who?"

"The heifer calf that was born the day before you arrived in town. Buck named her Violet because she was so pretty. Once you arrived, he thought you might not like sharing your name with a cow, so he tried to make Myles and me change her name to Tulip. Neither of us liked that name. She's too pretty for a Tulip."

Violet gave Obie an inquiring look and laughed to see him flush scarlet. "Why didn't you tell me?"

"Didn't want you to think I'd named a cow after you," he muttered. "I always liked the name Violet. It's my favorite flower."

"Maybe I would have felt honored," she teased. "After all, she is a pretty calf."

When they returned home, Violet unharnessed the horses, brushed them down, and turned them out to pasture, where they both proceeded to roll in the grass. "What was the use of brushing them? The silly things." She felt rather fond of the two animals, and she felt proud of her accomplishment. "I must say, I do need a bath now. I smell horse wherever I go, and I've a sneaking suspicion that I'm smelling myself."

"My favorite perfume," Obie remarked, and she smacked his shoulder.

Violet saw a striking difference in Obie's reception at church the next day. People who had once avoided him now sought him out to offer their apologies and shake his hand. Friends who had believed in him despite his reputation thumped him on the shoulder and declared their relief at his vindication. Everyone expressed hope that Nick Houghton would soon be safely apprehended.

The wedding announcement created yet another stir. People whom Violet had never previously met now greeted her by name and offered their best wishes for her happiness. Sorrow was expressed for her husband's death, but Violet suspected that some people got a thrill from the solved murder mystery, mistaken identities, and false conviction. Events that had caused tragedy for so many now provided welcome entertainment for the citizens of Longtree.

"It was shocking, the way they had to shuffle bodies in our sacred graveyard, that's all I can say. We all thought you were a shocking penny-pincher when you didn't buy a marble gravestone for your first husband, my dear, but of course we all understand now. That new marble stone should make your first man proud, if he can see it. I'm sure you must be glad to have him laid decently to rest."

"Yes, Mrs. Blackthorn, I am pleased that everyone knows the truth about Jeremiah. He was a wonderful man, and—"

"I'm right sorry about how people used to talk, Mrs. Fairfield. We thought all this time that you were married to that awful Jerry Fairfield, yet he wasn't Jerry Fairfield at all, but another man entirely. And Obadiah Watson isn't a murderer after all. It's so hard to believe! Well, to God be the glory, is all I can say," Leila Blackthorn babbled at length after the service. "I always said that any man my children liked so much couldn't be all bad, and now I'm proved right. Well, all I can say is, you just can't believe all you hear about people."

Violet tried to smile, but her face felt strained. She was relieved when the woman finally moved on to greet Obie.

"Don't worry yourself about it," Caroline advised, pulling gently on Violet's sleeve. "She'll get tired of talking someday."

"Well, all I can say is, I hope so," Violet whispered. She couldn't help giggling, and Caroline giggled back. They both tried to stop, but laughter kept erupting at odd moments.

"At last, they're finished," Beulah breathed in satisfaction, stepping back to view the completed wedding garments.

"Are you happy with yours?" Violet asked.

"Yes, Mama. You were right—I like this neckline better."

"You look lovely in your dress, honey."

"I love my dress, Mama. It's the nicest ever," Eunice volunteered without being asked.

Violet slipped an arm around each girl's waist and squeezed. "I love you both."

"Tomorrow you'll be Mrs. Watson," Eunice reminded her for the umpteenth time that day. "Aren't you excited?"

Samuel called from the kitchen. "Mama, come here, please!"

Violet went to the door. "What is it?"

"Come, please? My puppy keeps whining and barking at something outside."

Violet joined him at the open kitchen doorway and stared into the damp darkness. Rain fell in intermittent gusts, and wind rustled the cherry trees. At their feet, the puppy twitched her nose and whimpered softly.

"She won't go out, Mama. It's time for her to go out, but she won't budge."

"Try taking her out front."

Samuel did, and the puppy reluctantly followed him to the grass, did her duty, and hurried back into the house.

"I wonder what was bothering her," Samuel mused as he headed upstairs with the pup at his heels.

Violet watched them go, feeling uneasy. A dog's keen senses could detect danger where a human saw nothing unusual. She opened the hall closet and made sure the Winchester was handy. Three shots, Obie had said. She could do that much, though she had never yet managed to hit a target.

Before going to bed that night, Violet placed a bar over each door. She didn't usually lock her doors, but her uneasiness had increased as the evening passed. "One more day, and Obie will be here with me," she told herself, but that knowledge did little to ease her mind for the present.

As usual, Violet checked on each child before going to her bed. Beulah was already asleep; Eunice gave her mother a drowsy hug. Samuel was sprawled out, snoring softly. Violet was surprised to find the pup awake, standing on a chair with her paws on the windowsill. Black ears pricked, the little dog stared into the stormy night.

"Puppy, what do you see?"

The pup glanced at her, turned back to the window, and whimpered. She was too young to know what to do about danger. Her fur ruffled in the damp breeze.

Violet hesitantly approached the open window. Below lay the kitchen garden, her flower beds, and the back porch, but Violet could not see them through the darkness and rain.

Was that a movement near the porch? She listened intently, but heard nothing except rain beating upon earth, trees, and rooftops. The puppy growled.

Then Violet heard a man's voice. Her blood froze. The voice was impassioned, angry, but there was only one voice. Though she could not understand the words, Violet knew it was Nick Houghton.

She closed her eyes, prayed for courage, and lifted the window another inch. "Nick?" she called. "Nick, is that you?"

"Help me," came the desperate reply. "Please, help me!"

Violet padded downstairs in her bare feet, taking the puppy with her for moral support. Removing the rifle from the closet, she pointed it out an open window, aiming at the sky. Levering a shell into place, she squeezed the trigger. *Crack!* The gun recoiled hard. She fired twice more. The shots resounded through the trees, echoing countless times.

Violet set down the gun and began to cry.

Chapter 16

*The effectual fervent prayer
of a righteous man availeth much.*
JAMES 5:16

"Violet? Are you all right?" Obie's anxious call drifted through the night. Violet leaped up and rushed back to the window. "Obie, we're all right. Come to the house."

She unbarred the door and flung it open. A moment later she was crushed in a wet hug so hard that her feet left the floor. "Thank God," Obie wept in profound relief. He looked up at the three children, standing quietly behind their mother in their bare feet and nightclothes. "You're all well?"

Eunice shielded her candle from the wind. "We're fine, just scared half to death."

"Mama shot the gun, Pa," Samuel informed him.

"I know." Still clutching Violet tightly to him, Obie reached his other arm to embrace the boy.

"Are you cold, Pa? You're shaking really hard."

"Not so much cold as frightened out of my mind," he confessed, kissing the top of Samuel's head. He squeezed his eyes shut and buried his face in Violet's loose hair.

Al appeared quietly in the doorway, looking tall and dangerous with rifle in hand. "What happened, Miss Violet?"

Obie loosened his embrace enough for her to answer, "It's Nick Houghton. He's out by the back porch calling for help. I think he's delirious. Samuel's puppy warned me of danger. I looked out the window, and I heard a man crying out. He may be dying, Obie."

Obie was evidently reluctant to leave her, but he accepted Violet's offer of a lantern and followed Al back into the rainy night. The Fairfields went to the back door and peeked out. Al and Obie appeared around the corner, talking quietly.

Obie lifted the lantern, revealing a sodden figure sprawled at the base of the steps. Nick was quiet now, deathly quiet. His face was still and cold. Obie felt for a heartbeat. "Let's get him to the doctor."

"Take the surrey," Violet suggested. "Do you need help? Some hot coffee?"

"No, you all stay inside and keep dry. We'll be fine."

Al took time to glance around. Chunks of wood lay along the back of the house as though someone had planned to set it on fire. "Looks like he had evil intentions, but wasn't well enough to follow through."

"Vindictive to his dying breath. C'mon, Al, take his arms. I'll get his legs. To the surrey, quick. We'll hitch up afterwards."

The sick man groaned when they lifted him, but did not regain consciousness.

"Will you come back tonight?" Violet asked plaintively.

"Do you want me to?" Obie paused, water dripping from his hat brim.

"I guess it isn't necessary. . .just be careful, please."

"We will. Nick is dying, Violet. Pray for him."

"I will. Thank you both for coming."

Just before noon the next day, Sheriff Martin stopped by.

"Why, Sheriff Boz, what a pleasant surprise!" Violet invited him inside, but he shook his head. Rain trickled from every crease in his clothing.

"I won't mess up your house, ma'am. I came by to tell you that Nick Houghton died early this morning. He got blood poisoning from his injuries, the doc said. Obie tried to talk with him about God, but he was too sick or too stubborn to listen. Anyway, you all don't have to worry about him botherin' you no more."

"I'm. . .I'm truly sorry to hear that he didn't repent," Violet said softly. "Thank you for coming to tell me."

"We found this in his coat pocket." Boz extended a rumpled, discolored letter. "It's addressed to you back in Maryland. You were right about the letter; he did have it."

Violet's eyes widened when she recognized Jeremiah's precise script. The seal was broken.

"Mebbe this wasn't a good time to bring you a message from your first husband, on the day you're marryin' again, but I thought you ought to have it right away."

"Thank you, Boz. It was kind of you."

"See you at the wedding, ma'am. Obie made me buy myself a fancy suit. Never seen the like." Boz tipped his hat, descended the steps, spat into the flower bed, and mounted his waiting horse.

Violet spoke just above a whisper, "Dear Jeremiah, I still wish you had stayed home, but it's pointless to argue with you about it now. You did what you thought best, and that's all there is to it. I loved you, my dear. Good-bye." She stuffed Jeremiah's letter into a keepsake box and wiped her eyes.

There was a gentle knock at the bedroom door. "Mama, Reverend Schoengard will be here soon. Are you ready to go?"

"I'm ready, Eunice. Just taking a quiet moment."

"I'm sorry. I'll leave you alone," Eunice apologized. "I'm just so excited!"

Violet gazed around the room, trying to picture Obie beside her on the bed. She shook her head and smiled. It was impossible to imagine; yet soon it would come true. "I probably shouldn't have read that letter from Jeremiah on my wedding day. Now I'm feeling pensive. Lord, please help me to be cheerful and thankful for Obie's sake. I adore him, and I don't want even a hint of sorrow to mar our special day."

To everyone's relief, the weather cleared that afternoon. Reverend Schoengard showed up at four o'clock to take the Fairfield family to the parsonage, where they planned to dress. His wagon was soon loaded with people, fancy garments, and the children's overnight satchels. Samuel would stay with the Schoengards that night, and the girls planned to stay overnight with Amelia Sidwell to give their parents a short honeymoon.

At last the hour arrived, and the wedding party drove to the church. Violet gratefully took Reverend Schoengard's arm after he lifted her down from his surrey. Her legs felt too weak to support her. The church building was filled to capacity, and many people stood outside to listen to the ceremony through the windows.

God, are You here? This is kind of scary! Violet prayed inwardly.

"You look wonderful," Caroline, the matron of honor, whispered as she arranged Violet's hat and kissed her cold cheek. "Your eyes are like stars."

It was time. Violet clung to the pastor's strong arm and paced slowly up the aisle, following Beulah, Eunice, Samuel, who carried the rings on a pillow, and Caroline. She remembered to smile. Dimly, she saw Hattie's and Cyrus's faces among the throng and wondered at Hattie's presence. She must have been feeling much better. Voices drifted to her ears, commenting on her gown and her beauty.

Obie awaited her at the front of the church, looking remarkably dashing in his cutaway jacket, white collar, and ascot tie. The stark black and white set off his deep tan and silvery eyes and hair. Boz Martin, the best man, was similarly attired, and manifestly uncomfortable. His jowls had been scraped raw by the points of his collar; his moustache fairly glistened with wax.

The ceremony passed in a blur for Violet until the moment Obie placed the simple gold ring upon her finger, enveloped her hand within his, and repeated the timeless words, "With this ring, I thee wed. . . ." For the first time, she looked up into his shining eyes. He spoke the vow to her alone, pledging his life, love, and possessions. Their audience might not have existed as far as he was concerned. Her hand warmed to his touch, and the heat ran up her arm, spreading through her body and heart.

"Obie," she whispered. The love she shared with this dear man was another wonderful blessing from God. *Thank You, Lord.*

Guests thronged to the hotel dining room for the wedding reception, where they enjoyed Amelia Sidwell's sandwiches, fresh lemonade, and the cake Caroline had baked. Side by side in the hotel foyer, Violet and Obie shook hands with guests and smiled until their faces ached. Violet wanted to hold his hand or his arm. He was so near, yet so far away, for she was obliged to share him with all these people.

At last the crowd began to thin, and a few good friends stayed to help with the cleanup. Beulah, who had glowed with happiness when Al danced attendance on her throughout the reception, reluctantly changed into work clothes and helped Amelia clear tables.

"Papa?"

Obie turned to see Samuel's serious eyes looking up at him. He wrapped one arm around the boy's shoulders. "Yes, son?"

"Did you hear that I thought of a name for my dog? I want to name her Watchful, since she's such a good watchdog. Eunice says that's a man's name, like in *Pilgrim's Progress,* but I like it."

"I like it, too. I should think Watchful will be proud of her name."

"She warned Mama last night, you know." Samuel leaned into Obie's side, his expression adoring.

"Pretty amazing for such a little pup." He ruffled the boy's hair.

"Have fun with Scott, Ernie, and Bernie, my dear, and don't stay up talking too late," Violet advised, hugging her son.

"Good night, Pa. Good night, Mama."

Samuel joined the Schoengard children. Eunice was taking them back to the parsonage so Caroline and the pastor could work in peace.

Violet waved them out of sight, then collapsed into a handy chair. "Oh, my aching feet!"

Obie leaned toward her and whispered, "I'll give you a good rubdown when we get home."

"Like a horse?" she grinned.

"Same idea. No liniment."

Obie had loosened his tie and removed his coat, but he still looked the distinguished gentleman. Violet ran one finger down the crisply pleated front of his white shirt and watched his eyes widen. "I'll take that offer," she murmured.

"I'll get the buggy," he promised hastily, collecting his coat.

"Ahem."

Violet looked up to find Boz standing over her, his torturous collar hanging askew. "May I. . .kiss the bride?"

"Certainly." Violet lifted her cheek for his kiss. *So he actually does have a mouth under all that hair,* she mused.

He stepped back, flushing. "Never thought Buck could be so lucky, ma'am. You just lost me a bet, you know."

"I did?"

"Well now, maybe not a bet exactly."

Obie interrupted. "Boz, be truthful. It wasn't a bet at all. He made a promise that if God performed two particular miracles for me, he would believe. Are you going to honor your promise?"

Boz fingered his ruined collar. "I already have honored it, Buck. I couldn't sit by and watch such goin's-on without bein' convinced that you've got Someone high up workin' on your side. There was absolutely no chance that this crime would be solved after twenty years—yet everyone in town picked up a newspaper last weekend and saw the true story about the crime plastered all over the front page. Your name is cleared, and there's an apology to you from a government representative, believe it or not. They can't give you back those ten years, but they're sure eatin' crow aplenty."

"That's wonderful, Boz!" Violet gasped. "I mean about you becoming a believer. God has been so good to us—who could deny His grace and mercy?"

"That's not all, Miz Watson. The other miracle was that you agreed to marry this has-been cowpuncher. I don't know what you see in him, but I can't deny that he married you, fair and square. I haven't seen any signs of coercion, so I've gotta admit that God gave him the woman he asked for."

Violet grasped her husband's arm and gave him a look so full of love that Boz glanced away. "Guess I better start puttin' in an order for myself," he muttered.

At last the newlyweds were alone, driving along the road home beneath a sky littered with stars. Obie shifted the reins to one hand and slipped an eager arm around his wife's waist. "Happy?"

"Exceedingly happy, my dear," she sighed, resting her head on his solid shoulder. "It was a lovely wedding, wasn't it?"

"Thought the reception would never end."

"But it's just the beginning of our new life together. Um, is it safe for you to kiss me while you're driving?"

In answer, he proceeded to kiss her neck, ears, cheeks, and lips. Lost in pleasure, Violet responded fervently until a snort from Rollie brought her back to reality. "Aren't we almost to our driveway?" she protested in mild concern and amusement.

"Dolly knows where her manger is." But he reluctantly picked up the forgotten reins as the team entered the shadowy drive.

"I'll help unhitch and feed them," she offered. "But let's skip the grooming just this once, please? I don't want to smell like horse."

"Believe me, you don't," her husband was quick to assure.

Myles from Anywhere

Dedication

With love to Tom, Annie, Jimmy, and Peter Stengl.
I thank God for each of you every day. Every mother should be so blessed!
Thank you again to Paula Pruden Macha and Pamela Griffin—two living
proofs that long-distance friendship is possible. Love you both!

Prologue

1872

CHILD PRODIGY MISSING. STATEWIDE SEARCH UNDERWAY FOR MYLES VAN HUYSEN, MUSICAL STAR, read the headlines of the August 21 edition of the city paper. A passerby stepped on the newspaper where it lay crumpled beside the tent door, and a breeze lifted the top page, sending it drifting across the midway.

A boy glared at the paper from beneath the brim of his cap, hoping his prospective employer had not read it closely. Why did Gram have to make such a big deal about everything?

"You say you're willing to work hard, kid? How old are you, anyway?"

"Eighteen. Ain't got no family." He struggled to sound illiterate yet mature enough to merit the two extra years he claimed.

"Kinda puny, ain't ya?" The owner of the traveling circus chomped on his unlit cigar. "You're in luck, Red. One of our fellas went down sick a week back, and we've been struggling since. It ain't easy work, and the pay is peanuts, but you'll get room and board, such as it is. Go see Parker in the animal tent and tell him I sent you."

"Yes, Mr. Bonacelli. Thank you, Mr. Bonacelli."

"You may not be thankin' me when you find out what you'll be doin'. What's yer name, Red?"

"Myles Trent." It was his name minus its third element. If he so much as mentioned "Van Huysen" the game would end for certain.

"Hmph. I'll call ya Red."

Visions of becoming an acrobat or animal trainer soon vanished from Myles's head. During the next few months, he worked harder than he had ever worked in his life, cleaning animal pens. It was nasty and hazardous work at times, yet he enjoyed becoming friends with other circus employees. Whenever the circus picked up to move to the next town, everyone worked together, from the clowns to the trapeze artists to the bearded lady. It wasn't long before Myles began to move up in the circus world.

Bonacelli's Circus made its way south from New York, then west toward Ohio, playing in towns along the highways and railroads. During the coldest months, the caravans headed south along the Mississippi; spring found them headed north. Months passed into a year.

Lengthening his face to minimize creases, Myles wiped grease paint from his eyelids. Behind him, the tent flap was pulled aside. Someone came in. "Antonio?" he guessed.

"Hello, Myles."

His eyes popped open. A handsome face smiled at him from his mirror.

Myles froze. His shoulders drooped. He turned on the stool. "Monte."

The brothers stared at each other. Monte pulled up a chair and straddled it backward. "I caught today's show. Never thought I'd see my musician brother doing flips onto a horse's back. You've built muscle and calluses. Look healthier than I can remember." There was grudging admiration in his voice.

"The acrobats and clowns taught me tricks."

"I've been hanging around, asking questions. People like and respect you. Say you're honest and hardworking."

Myles's eyes narrowed. "I love the circus, Monte. I like making people happy."

"You're a performer. It's in your blood."

Myles turned to his mirror and rubbed blindly at the paint. "Why so pleasant all of a sudden?"

Monte ignored the question. "Gram wants you back. She's already spent too much on detectives. I'll write and tell her I found you before she fritters away our fortune."

"I'm not going back."

"I didn't ask you to. The old lady sent me to keep an eye on you. She never said I had to go back. . .at least not right away." One of Monte's brows lifted, and he gave Myles his most charming smile. "The Van Huysen Soap Company and fortune will wait for me. No reason to waste my youth in a stuffy office, learning business from a fat family friend. I think I'd rather be a circus star like my runny-nosed kid brother."

"You've seen me. Now get lost." Hope faded from Myles's eyes. "You'll spoil everything."

"Believe it or not, I do understand. That was no life for a kid. I've often wondered how you endured it as long as you did. Getting out of that Long Island goldfish bowl is a relief. Always someone watching, moralizing, planning your life—whew! You had the right idea. I could hardly believe my luck when Gram sent me after you."

"She trusted you," Myles observed dryly. "What are you planning to do?"

"Does this circus need more workers? I'm serious. This looks like the life for me."

Myles huffed. "Nobody needs a worker like you, Monte. Why don't you go find yourself a gaming hall and forget you ever had a brother?"

"Gram would never forgive me if I returned without you."

"You could tell her I'm dead."

Monte pondered the idea in mock gravity, dark eyes twinkling. "Tempting, but impossible. Family honor and all that. You'd show up someday, then I'd look the dolt at best, the knave at worst. Part of the family fortune is yours, you know. I wouldn't try to filch it from you. I'm not as rotten as you think, little brother. I do feel some responsibility for my nitwit prodigy sibling."

The next morning when Monte left his borrowed bunk, Myles was gone. No one had seen him leave. Running a big hand down his face, Monte swore. "Gotta find that crazy kid!"

⟨∽⟩

"Are you here with good news or bad, George Poole?" the old lady grumbled from her seat in a faded armchair. A few coals glowed upon the hearth near her feet. "I trust you have disturbed my afternoon rest for good reason."

"Yes, Mrs. Van Huysen. You may see for yourself." He thrust a newspaper into her hands and pointed at a paragraph near the bottom of the page. "An associate of mine in Milwaukee—that's a town in Wisconsin—heard of my quest, spotted this article, and mailed the paper to me."

"Kind of him," Mrs. Van Huysen said, fumbling to put on her glasses. Holding the folded-back paper near her face, she blinked. "For what am I looking?"

"This, madam. The article concerns a small-town farmer who, years ago, served a prison sentence for robbery and murder. Last summer, new evidence was discovered and the man's name was cleared of the crimes. Judging by the article's tone, this Obadiah Watson appears to be a fine Christian man. It is a pleasure when justice is served, is it not?"

"Yes, yes, but what has this to do with my grandsons?" Virginia Van Huysen struggled to keep her patience.

"Let me find the line. . .ah, right here. You see? The article mentions a certain Myles Trent, hired laborer on Watson's farm." Poole's eyes scanned his client's face.

"I fail to see the significance, Mr. Poole. You raised my hopes for this?"

"Don't you see, madam? Your grandson's name is Myles Trent Van Huysen. Oftentimes a man in hiding will use a pseudonym, and what could be easier to recall than one's own given name?"

"Have you any proof that this man is my Myles? And what of Monte? There is no word of him in this article. The last I heard from the boys, they were together in Texas. Isn't Wisconsin way up north somewhere? Why ever would Myles be there?" Pulling a lacy handkerchief from her cuff, Virginia dabbed at her eyes. "In Monte's last letter he told me that he had surrendered his life to the Lord. Why, then, did he stop writing to me? I don't understand it."

Poole tugged his muttonchop whiskers. "I cannot say, dear madam. The particular region of Texas described in your grandson's most recent letters is a veritable wasteland. Our efforts there were vain; my people discovered no information about your grandsons. It was as if they had dropped from the face of the earth."

137

"Except for the note your partner sent me about the game hunter in Wyoming." Virginia's tone was inquisitive.

"An unfortunate mistake on Mr. Wynter's part. He should have waited until he had obtained more solid information before consulting you. Be that as it may, Madam, unless this Myles Trent proves to be your relation, I fear I must persuade you to give up this quest. I dislike taking your money for naught."

"Naught?" Virginia lifted her pince-nez to give him a quelling look.

Poole nodded. "We at Poole, Poole, and Wynter are ever reluctant to admit defeat, yet I fear we may be brought to that unfortunate pass. It has been nine years since Myles disappeared and nearly six since Monte's last letter reached you. If your grandsons are yet living, they are twenty-five and twenty-eight now."

"I can do simple addition, Mr. Poole," Virginia said. "Have you given up entirely on that hunter?"

"The fellow disappeared. He was probably an outlaw who became nervous when Wynter started asking questions. You must keep in mind that your grandsons are no longer children to be brought home and disciplined. They are men and entitled to live the lives they choose. I fear Myles's concert career will never resume."

Virginia clenched her jaw and lifted a defiant chin. "I would spend my last cent to find my boys. Look into this, Mr. Poole, and may the Lord be with you."

Chapter 1

Shall not God search this out?
For he knoweth the secrets of the heart.
PSALM 44:21

Summer 1881

M ove over, Marigold."

The Jersey cow munched on her breakfast, eyes half closed. When Myles pushed on her side, she shifted in the stall, giving him room for his milking stool and bucket. Settling on the stool, he rested his forehead on Marigold's flank, grasped her teats, and gently kneaded her udder while squeezing. His hands were already warm since she was the sixth cow he had milked that morning. Marigold let down her milk, and the warm liquid streamed into the bucket. Myles had learned that it paid to be patient with the cows; they rewarded his kindness with their cooperation.

"Meow!" A furry body twined around his ankle, rumbling a purr that reminded Myles of a passing freight train. Other cats peered at Myles from all sides—from the hayloft, around the stall walls, from the top of Marigold's stanchion. Their eyes seldom blinked.

The plump gray and white cat had perfected her technique. She bumped her face against Myles's knee, reached a velvet paw to touch his elbow, and blinked sweetly.

"Nice try, you pushy cat, but you've got to wait your turn. I'll give a saucer to all of you when I'm finished."

"Why do you reward them for begging? It only makes them worse." A deep voice spoke from the next stall where Al Moore was milking another cow.

"Guess I like cats."

"I. . .um, Myles, I've got to tell you that I'll be heading over to Cousin Buck's farm after dinner. I've got to talk with Beulah today. . .you know, about my letter."

"I'll be there, too. I'm working in Buck's barn this afternoon—mending harnesses and such."

"Things have changed since Cousin Buck married Violet Fairfield last year and took over her farm, Fairfield's Folly," Al commented sadly. "I mean, in the old days he kept up with every detail about our farm, but he's too busy being a husband and papa these days."

"He doesn't miss much. Must be hard work, running the two farms." Myles defended his friend.

"I run this place myself," Al protested. After a moment's silence he added, "You're right; I shouldn't complain. I just miss the old days; that's all. Anyway, to give Cousin Buck credit, being Beulah's stepfather must be a job in itself, and now with Buck and Violet's new baby..." His voice trailed away. "Buck has made major improvements at the Folly farm this past year. Guess that's no surprise to you."

"I do have firsthand knowledge of those improvements," Myles acknowledged. "Working at both farms keeps me hopping, but I don't mind. I'm glad Buck is happily married. I've never worked for better people than you and your cousin."

"Since I'm taking the afternoon off, I'll handle the milking this evening. How's that?" Al asked. "Don't want you to think I'm shirking."

Myles smiled to himself. "Don't feel obligated, boss. You always do your share of the work. Be good for you to take a few hours to play."

"But you never do. Wish you'd relax some; then I wouldn't feel guilty."

"Maybe you and I could toss a baseball around with Samuel this afternoon." The prospect lifted Myles's spirits. He liked nothing better than to spend time with Obadiah "Buck" Watson's three stepchildren. The retired cowboy preferred to be called "Obie," but Myles had known him for years as "Buck" and found it impossible to address or even think of his boss by any other name.

"That would be great!" Al sounded like an overgrown schoolboy.

Myles stripped the last drops from Marigold's teats. Rising, he patted the cow's bony rump. "You're a good girl, Goldie." He nearly tripped over the pushy gray cat as he left the stall. With a trill of expectation, it trotted ahead of him toward the milk cans, where several other felines had already congregated.

Myles found the chipped saucer beneath a bench. Sliding it to the open floor with one foot, he tipped the bucket and poured a stream of milk—on top of a gray and white head. Myles smiled as the cat retreated under the bench, shaking her head and licking as much of her white ruff as she could reach. Another cat began to assist her, removing the milk from the back of her head. "Pushy cat, Pushy cat, where have you been?" Myles crooned.

He filled the saucer until it overflowed; yet it was polished clean within seconds. A few cats had to content themselves with licking drops from the floor or from their companions. Myles tried to count the swarming animals but lost track at twelve.

"Too many cats," Al remarked, emptying his bucket into a can.

"They keep down the rodent population," Myles said.

"I know, but the barn's getting overcrowded. There were a lot of kittens born in the spring, but most of them are gone. I don't know if they just died or if something killed them."

Myles squatted and Pushy cat hopped into his lap, kneading his thigh with her paws and blinking her yellow eyes. She seemed to enjoy rubbing her face against his beard. He stroked her smooth back and enjoyed that rumbling purr. Myles knew Al was right, but neither man had an answer for the problem.

"Say, Myles, what if. . .I mean, are you. . .do you have any plans to move on? Might you be willing to stay on here over the winter and. . .I'm not sure how to say this." Al ran long fingers through his hair, staring at the barn floor.

Myles rubbed the cat and waited for Al to find the words. He had a fair idea what was coming.

"I'm hoping to marry Beulah and take her to California with me—to meet my parents, you know. We would probably be gone for close to a year, and I can't leave Cousin Buck to run both this place and Fairfield's Folly alone. I would take it kindly if you would. . .well, run my farm as if it were yours, just while I'm away, you understand. I would make it worth your while. You don't need to answer me now; take your time to think it over."

Myles nodded. In spite of his determination to keep his own counsel, one question escaped. "Have you asked her yet?"

"Asked Beulah? Not yet." Al's boots shifted on the floorboards. "That's the other thing that worries me. She's. . .uh. . . I don't know that she'll take to the idea of a quick wedding. We've never discussed marriage. . .but she must know I plan to marry her. Everyone knows."

Myles glanced at his young boss's face. "Will you go if she refuses?"

Al looked uncertain. "I could marry her when I get back, but I hate to leave things hanging. Another man could come along and steal her away from me. Maybe I could ask her to wait." He collapsed on the bench, propped his elbows on his spread knees, and rested his chin on one fist. "She's really not a flirt, but I can't seem to pin her down. Every time I try to be serious, she changes the subject. What should I do, Myles?"

Myles rose to his feet and began to rub his flat stomach with one hand. "You're asking an old bachelor for courtship advice?" He hoped the irony in his voice escaped Al's notice. "I've got no experience with women."

"No experience at all?" Al's face colored. "I mean. . .uh. . . Sorry."

Myles shrugged. "No offense taken. I left home at sixteen and bummed around the country for years."

"What did you do to keep alive?"

"Any work I could find. No time or opportunity to meet a decent woman and had enough sense to avoid the other kind. When I drifted farther west it was the same. You don't see a lot of women wandering the wilderness."

"So where are you from?"

"Anywhere and everywhere." His lips twitched into a smile that didn't reach his eyes. "When your cousin hired me and brought me here to Longtree, that was the first time I'd been around women since I was a kid. Guess I don't know how to behave around females."

"I didn't know you were afraid of women. Is that why you almost never go to church or socials?"

Myles lifted a brow. "I didn't say I was afraid of them. More like they're afraid of me."

"If you'd smile and use sentences of more than one syllable, they might discover you're a decent fellow."

This prompted a genuine smile. "I'll try it. Any other advice?"

Al cocked his head and grinned. "That depends on which female has caught your eye. Want to confide in old Al?"

"I'd better cast about first and see if any female will have me," Myles evaded.

Al chuckled. "Too late. I know about you and Marva Obermeier."

"About me and. . .whom?"

"Don't look so surprised. Since the barn raising at Obermeiers' when you and she talked for an hour, everyone in town knows. She's a nice lady. If you want a little extra to hold and like a woman who'll do all the talking, Marva is for you."

"But that was—" Myles began to protest.

"Things aren't progressing the way you want, eh? You ought to spend evenings getting to know her family, getting comfortable in the home. Try teasing her and see what happens. Nice teasing, I mean. Women enjoy that kind of attention from a man."

"They do?"

A collie burst through the open barn door. Panicked cats scattered. Both men chuckled. "Good work, Treat."

Treat grinned and wagged half her body along with her tail, eager to herd the cows to pasture. "Cats are beneath your notice, eh, girl?" Al said, ruffling her ears.

Al carried the milk cans to the dairy. Myles untied the cows and directed Treat to gather them and start them ambling along the path.

Udders swaying, bells clanging, gray noses glistening, the cows did their best to ignore the furry pest at their heels. While Myles held the pasture gate open, Treat encouraged the little herd to pass through. Myles gave one bony bovine a swat before latching the gate behind her. "As usual, last in line. No wandering off today, my ornery old girl."

The sun was still low in the sky and already the temperature was rising. Myles swung his arms in circles to relieve the kinks. He glanced around. No one watching. He performed a few cartwheels, a round off, then a front flip to back flip in one quick motion. He straightened in triumph, flushed and pleased, arms lifted to greet the morning. The cows and Treat were unimpressed.

"Good thing you're used to my antics. Hey, Treat, maybe I'll see Beulah today." Myles slapped his thighs until the dog placed her front paws on them. He ruffled her fur with both hands. "What do you think, girl? Think Beulah will smile at me?"

Then his grin faded and his heavy boots scuffed in the dirt. Little chance of that while Al was around. Of all the stupid things Myles had ever done, falling in love with his boss's girl was undoubtedly the worst.

❧

Deep in thought, Beulah Fairfield dumped used dishwater behind her mother's gladiolus. Something jabbed into her ribs, and the last of the water flew skyward. "Oh!" She spun around, slapping away reaching hands. "Al, stop it!"

Al took the two back steps in a single bound and held the kitchen door for her. "Testy woman. Better make myself useful and return to her good graces."

She was tempted to suggest that he choose another time to visit, but her mother had chided her several times recently for rudeness. "Thanks." Beulah forced a smile as she entered the kitchen before him. His return smile seemed equally fake. "Is something wrong, Al?"

He let the door slam behind him. "Nothing much."

Beulah hung the dishpan on its hook and arranged the dish towels on the back of the stove to dry. "Would you like a cup of coffee?"

"Uh, sure. Yes, please."

"Please take a seat at the table, and I will join you presently."

In another minute, she set down his coffee and seated herself across the table from him. His forehead was pale where his hat usually hid it from the sun; his dark hair looked freshly combed. Beulah knew her apron was spotted, but she was too self-conscious to change to a fresh one in front of Al. Her hair must be a sight—straggling about her face. "I've been canning tomatoes all morning." She indicated the glowing red jars lining the sideboard.

Before Al could comment, Beulah's sister Eunice burst into the room. The hall door hit the wall and china rattled on the oak dresser. "It *was* your voice I heard in here! Why did you sneak around to the back door, Al? I was watching for you out front."

A black and white dog slipped in behind Eunice and thrust her nose into Al's hand, brushy tail beating against the table legs. "Watchful, shame on you! Get out of the kitchen." Beulah attempted to shoo the dog away.

"She's all right." Petting the dog, Al gave Eunice a halfhearted smile. "I didn't sneak. My horse is in the barn, big as life. I rode over with Myles. He's mending the whiffletree the horse kicked apart while we were pulling stumps."

"Myles is in our barn?" Beulah asked.

"Still want to go for a ride today, do you?" Al asked Eunice as if Beulah had not spoken.

The girl flopped down in the chair beside him. "Of course we want to ride with you. My brother has to finish cleaning the chicken pen, but he's almost done. I finished my chores. Won't you teach me to jump today? Please?" She laid her head on Al's shoulder and gave him her best pleading gaze, batting long lashes.

He chuckled and roughed up her brown curls. "Subtle, aren't you, youngster? We'll see. I'd better talk to your parents before we try jumping. To be honest, Blue Eyes, I want to talk with your sister in private for a minute, so could—"

The door popped open again, this time admitting Violet Fairfield Watson, the girls' mother, with a wide-eyed baby propped upon her shoulder. "Would one of you please take Daniel while I change his bedclothes?" She transferred the baby to Beulah's reaching arms. "Thank you, dear. Hello, Albert. Will you stay for supper tonight?"

"I. . .um, thank you, but no, not tonight, ma'am. I. . .I've got to do the milking. I promised the kids we'd go for a ride this afternoon, but then I've got to get home and. . .and get some work done."

Violet gave him a searching look. "Hmm. Is something wrong, Al?"

Blood colored his face right up to his hairline. "Actually, yes. I got a letter from my mother yesterday. She wants me to come home to California. I'm the oldest son, you know. It's been five years since I was last home, and my folks want to see me again."

"I see." Violet Watson sent Beulah a quick glance before asking Al: "Do you plan to leave soon?"

"I'm not sure, ma'am. That depends. . .on a lot of things. I'll have to work out a plan with Cousin Buck—Obie—for care of the farm. I can't expect Myles to handle everything alone for so long. I mean, he's just a hired hand."

"How long is 'so long'?" Eunice asked, her expression frozen.

"I don't know. Could be up to a year. The train fare between here and California is no laughing matter. I have to make the visit worth the price."

"Yes, you do need to speak with Obie about this, Al." Violet looked concerned. "That is a long time to leave your farm."

Al held out his hands, fingers spread. "I know, but what else can I do? They're my parents."

"But, Al, a whole year? What will we do without you?" Eunice wailed.

Wrapping one long arm around the girl, Al pressed her head to his shoulder. "Miss me, I hope. I'll be back, Blue Eyes. Never fear."

Rocking her baby brother in her arms, Beulah watched Al embrace her sister. *No more pokes in the ribs, no more mawkish stares. I wonder how soon he will leave?*

Baby Daniel began to fuss. Beulah took the excuse to leave the kitchen and wandered through the house, bouncing him on her hip. He waved his arms and kicked her in the thighs, chortling. She heard the others still talking, their voices muffled by intervening doors.

My friends all think I'm the luckiest girl in the world because Al likes me. He is handsome, nice, loves God, has his own farm—he'll make a great husband for someone. But that someone isn't me!

She strolled back into the hall, studying the closed kitchen door. No one would notice if she slipped outside. Snatching a basket from a hook on the hall tree, she headed for the barn. Her heart thumped far more rapidly than this mild exertion required. Shifting Daniel higher on her hip, she reached for her hair and winced. No bonnet, and hair like an osprey's nest. Oh, well; too late now. If she didn't hurry, Myles might finish his work and leave before she had a chance to see him.

A tingle skittered down her spine. Without turning her head, she knew that Myles stood in the barn doorway. The man's gaze was like a fist squeezing her lungs until she gasped for air. Daniel squawked and thumped his hand against Beulah's chest. He managed to grasp one of her buttons and tried to pull it to his mouth, diving toward it. Beulah had just enough presence of mind to catch him before he plunged out of her arms.

One ankle turned as she approached the barn, and she staggered. Daniel transferred his attention to the basket hanging from her arm beneath him. He reached for it and once more nearly escaped Beulah's grasp. "Daniel, stop that," she snapped in exasperation, feeling bedraggled and clumsy.

"Need a hand?"

Swallowing hard, Beulah lifted her gaze. A little smile curled Myles's lips. One hand rubbed the bib of his overalls. The shadow of his hat hid his eyes, yet she felt them burning into her.

"I came for eggs," she said, brushing hair from her face, then hoisting Daniel higher on her hip. "For custard."

"Your brother Sam headed for the house with a basket of eggs not two minutes back."

"He did?" Beulah felt heat rush into her face. "I didn't see him."

Daniel grabbed at a button again, then mouthed Beulah's cheek and chin. She felt his wet lips and heard the fond little "Ahh" he always made when he gave her kisses. Unable to ignore the baby's overtures, she kissed his soft cheek. "I love you, too, Daniel. Now hold still."

When she looked up, white teeth gleamed through Myles's sun-bleached beard. "Thought Al was with you."

"He's in the kitchen with my mother and Eunice. Daniel and I came out for the eggs. Are you—will you be here long?"

"Might play baseball with Samuel and Al. Glad you came out for a visit."

Myles appeared to choose his words with care, and his voice. . .that rich voice curled her toes. Did he know she had come outside in hope of seeing him? Why must her mind palpitate along with her body whenever Myles was near? She was incapable either of analyzing his comments or of giving a lucid reply.

"You haven't been to our house for a while, and I haven't seen you at church all summer."

His smile faded. He took a step closer, then stopped. Did Myles feel the pull, almost like a noose tightening around the two of them and drawing them ever closer together? She had never been this close to him before. Only five or six feet of dusty earth separated them.

Tired of being ignored, Daniel let out a screech and smacked Beulah's mouth with a slimy hand. Pain and anger flashed; she struggled to hide both. "Daniel, don't hit."

The baby's face crumpled, and he began to wail. Sucking in her lip, Beulah tasted blood. "I think it's time for his nap." She spoke above Daniel's howls. "I'll try to come back later."

Myles nodded, waved one hand, and vanished into the barn's shadows. Beulah trotted toward the house, patting Daniel's back. "Hush, sweetie. Beulah isn't angry with you. I know you're tired and hungry. We'll find Mama, and everything will be fine."

Al held the door open for her. "What are you doing out here? What's wrong with the little guy?"

"Where's my mother?"

"Upstairs. You going riding with us?" he called.

"No, you go on. I've got work to do." She barely paused on the bottom step.

"Play ball with us later?"

"Maybe." Beulah hid her grin in Daniel's soft hair.

Once Daniel was content in his mother's arms, Beulah returned to the kitchen to work and ponder. Sure enough, a basket of brown eggs waited on the floor beside the butter churn. Samuel must have entered the kitchen right after she left it.

Beulah found her mother's custard recipe on a stained card and began to collect the ingredients. *I'm just imagining that Myles admires me. Probably he watches everyone that way. I scarcely know the man. No one knows much about him. He could be from anywhere—a bank robber or desperado for all we know. It is ridiculous to moon about him when I can have a man like Al with a snap of my fingers. Myles is beneath me socially—probably never went to school. Could never support a family—we would live in a shack. . .*

Al's words repeated in her mind: *Just a hired hand. Just a hired hand. Just a hired hand. . .*

Chapter 2

And when ye stand praying, forgive,
if ye have ought against any:
that your Father also which is in heaven
may forgive you your trespasses.
MARK 11:25

Custard cooled on the windowsill. Untying her apron, Beulah peeked through the kitchen window. Outside, a baseball smacked into a leather glove. She heard her brother Samuel's shrill voice and good-natured joking between Al and Myles. *He's still here!* She hung her apron on a hook, smoothed her skirts, and straightened her shoulders. Once again, her heart began to pound.

Eunice slammed open the kitchen door. Damp curls plastered her forehead; scarlet cheeks intensified the blue of her eyes. "We had a great ride, Beulah! You should have come."

Beulah wrinkled her nose.

Eunice splashed her face at the pump. "It hurts Al's feelings that you never want to ride with us."

"I'm sure I don't know why."

Lifting her face from the towel, Eunice protested, "But you're supposed to want to spend time with him. People in love want to be together all the time, don't they?"

"How would I know?" Beulah said. "And I can't see how being in love would make me want to ride a horse. Hmph. You need a bath. I can smell horse from here."

"You're mean, Beulah." Eunice rushed from the room.

Beulah rolled her eyes. Pinching her cheeks, she checked her reflection in the tiny mirror over the washbasin. "Guess I didn't need to pinch my cheeks. They're already hot as fire."

Beyond Beulah's kitchen garden, the two men and Samuel formed a triangle around the yard. The ball smacked into Al's glove. He tossed it to Samuel, easing his throw for the boy's sake. Samuel hurled it at Myles, who fielded it at his ankles, then fired another bullet toward Al. Around and around they went, never tiring of the game.

"Hi, Beulah!" Al greeted her with a wave. "Want to play? We've got an extra mitt."

"No, thank you." *He must be crazy.* "Don't want to spoil your fun."

"We would throw easy to you," Samuel assured her.

"I'll watch." Beulah moved to the swing her stepfather, Obie, had hung from a tall elm. After tucking up her skirt lest it drag in the dust, she began to swing. The men seemed unaware of her scrutiny. They bantered with Samuel and harassed each other. Her gaze shifted from Myles to Al and back again.

Al's long, lean frame had not yet filled out with muscle. A thatch of black hair, smooth brown skin, beautiful dark eyes, and a flashing smile made him an object of female fascination. How many times had Beulah been told of her incredible good luck in snaring his affection? She had lost count.

Leaning back in the swing, she pumped harder, hearing her skirts flap in the wind. Overhead, blue sky framed oak, maple, and elm leaves. A woodpecker tapped out his message on a dead birch.

Sitting straight, she wrapped her arms around the ropes and fixed her gaze upon Myles. He was grinning. Beulah felt her heart skip a beat. Myles had the cutest, funniest laugh—a rare treat to hear. What would he look like without that bushy beard? He had a trim build—not as short and slim as her stepfather Obie, but nowhere near as tall as Al.

The ongoing conversation penetrated her thoughts. "So are you planning to go, Al? Will you take me with you? I've always wanted to see a circus. I bet my folks would let me go with you," Samuel cajoled.

Al glanced toward Beulah. "I was thinking I might go. It's playing in Bolger all weekend. The parade arrives tomorrow."

Samuel let out a whoop. "Let's all go together! Eunice wants to go, and you do, don't you, Beulah? Will you come, too, Myles? Maybe they'll ask you to be a clown. Myles can do lots of tricks, you know. Show 'em how you walk on your hands. Please?"

Beulah's eyes widened.

Myles wiped a hand down his face, appearing to consider the request. "Why?"

"I want you to teach me. C'mon, Myles! Beulah's never seen you do it."

She saw his gaze flick toward her, then toward Al. He fired the baseball at Al, who snagged it with a flick of his wrist. "You can walk on your hands? Where'd you learn that trick?"

"I worked for a circus once. The acrobats taught me a thing or two."

Beulah fought to keep her jaw from dropping.

"No kidding? I'd like to see some tricks. Wouldn't you, Beulah?" Al enlisted her support.

Beulah nodded, trying not to appear overly interested.

Myles studied the green sweep of grass. "All right." He removed his hat. "Can't do splits or I'll rip my overalls," he said with a sheepish grin.

"If I tried splits, I'd rip more than that," Al admitted.

Myles upended and walked across the yard on his hands, booted feet dangling above his head. He paused to balance on first one hand, then the other. With a quick jerk, he landed back on his feet, then whirled into a series of front handsprings, ending with a deep bow. His audience cheered and clapped.

"Amazing!" Al said. "I never knew you could do that."

"Your face is red like a tomato," Samuel said.

Beulah met Myles's gaze. Did she imagine it, or did his eyes reveal a desire to please? Heart pounding again, she managed an admiring smile. "Who needs to see a circus when we have Myles?"

He seemed to grow taller; his shoulders squared. "You would enjoy a real circus."

"So let's go!" Samuel persisted. "Beulah, you've gotta help me ask Mama. With Myles and Al taking us, I'm sure she'll say we can go."

"Do you want to take us?" Beulah asked, carefully looking at neither man.

"It might be fun," Al wavered.

"I do." Myles's direct answer took everyone by surprise. "I'm going for the parade and the show."

❧

Beulah and Eunice hurried into the kitchen. Beulah tied her bonnet beneath her chin, setting the bow at the perfect angle. "Does this bonnet match this dress, Mama?"

Violet cast her a quick glance. "It's sweet, dear."

"Now you stay close; no wandering off by yourself," she warned Samuel while combing back his persistent cowlick. "Being ten does not mean you're grown up." The boy squirmed and contorted his face.

Obie watched them from his seat at the kitchen table, his chest supporting a sleeping baby Daniel. Amusement twitched his thick mustache.

"I'll behave, Mama," Samuel said. "Do you think there will be elephants in the parade, Pa? Maybe bears and lions! Myles used to be in the circus. He says it was lots of work. I think I'd rather be a preacher when I grow up."

His stepfather lifted a brow. "Preachers don't have to work, you figure?"

"Reverend Schoengard doesn't work much. He just drives around visiting people and writes sermons."

Obie chuckled. "Our pastor more than earns his keep. You don't get muscles like his by sitting around all the time."

Eunice was still braiding one long pigtail. "I'm so glad it stopped raining! Now it's all sunny and pretty—the perfect day for a circus. Are they here yet?" She hurried to the window and peered toward the barn.

Obie tipped back his chair and balanced on his toes. "They're hitching the horses to the surrey. Should be ready soon."

"Can I go help, Pa?" Samuel begged.

"Ask your mother."

"You may. Try not to get too dirty." Violet released her restless son. "I'm trusting you to keep your brother in line, girls. Don't get so involved with your friends that you forget to watch Samuel."

"We won't, Mama," Beulah assured her mother. A crease appeared between her brows. "Our friends? I thought just the five of us were going."

Obie grinned. "I imagine half our town will head over to Bolger this afternoon. Circuses don't come around every day."

"Here come Al and Myles!" Eunice announced, bouncing on her toes.

Beulah bent to kiss Daniel's soft cheek. "Bye, Papa and Mama. Take care and enjoy your free day."

Al was less than pleased when Samuel squeezed between him and Beulah on the surrey's front seat. "Can't you sit in the back? It's crowded up here, and I need elbow room."

The boy's face fell. "Can't I drive a little? Papa lets me drive sometimes. The horses know me."

"I'll climb in back," Beulah offered quickly, rising. When she hopped down, one foot tangled in her skirt and she sat down hard in the dirt, legs splayed. Her skirt ballooned, displaying a fluffy white petticoat and pantaloon. Horrified, she clapped her arms down over the billowing fabric and glanced toward Myles. He was loading the picnic basket behind the surrey's rear seat. Had he seen?

"But, Beulah," Al protested. "I wanted to—Are you all right?"

Beulah scrambled to her feet and brushed off her dress, cheeks afire. "I'm fine."

"I'll drive, if you like," Myles said. "I don't mind sitting with Samuel."

Al looked abashed. "I don't either. It doesn't matter, really." He settled beside the boy and released the brake. "Climb in."

In the surrey's backseat, Eunice had one hand clamped over her mouth. Her shoulders were shaking. She looked up, met Beulah's eyes, and started giggling again. Beulah felt a smile tug at her mouth. Frowning to conceal it, she climbed up beside her sister and smoothed her skirts. "Stop it!" she hissed.

"You looked so funny!" Eunice nearly choked.

Myles hauled himself up to sit on the other side of Eunice. He must have visited the barber that morning. His beard and hair were neatly trimmed. He watched Eunice mop her eyes with a crumpled handkerchief, but made no comment.

Beulah leaned forward. "Are you excited to see a circus again, Myles?"

He looked at her with raised brows. "Guess I am. It's been a long time."

Conversation flagged. While Samuel chattered with Al, the three in the backseat studied passing scenery with unaccustomed interest. Beulah longed to talk with Myles, but about what? Her mind was blank.

After a while, Myles cleared his throat. "Lots of traffic today."

"Must be for the circus," Al said. "I think I see the Schoengards up ahead."

Samuel's ears pricked. "Scott is here?"

"You're sitting with us, Sam." Beulah leaned forward to remind him.

"I know. I know," he grouched, pushing her hand from his shoulder.

The streets of Bolger were already crowded. People lined the road into town, standing in and around buggies and wagons. Al parked the surrey beside a farm wagon, easing the team into place. "We can see better from up here," he explained, "and we've got shade." He indicated the surrey's canvas top. "Did you bring water, Beulah?"

Samuel stood and waved his arms, shouting. "Here it comes! I see it!"

A roar went up from the crowds, and Beulah clutched her seat. The horses objected to the commotion. Al had his hands full quieting the rearing animals.

"May want to drop back," Myles advised. "Especially if this circus has elephants."

"You all climb out," Al growled. "Don't want Sam to miss the parade."

Beulah climbed down, but Eunice chose to remain in the surrey. "Al needs company," she said. "You three can find us after the parade."

Grabbing Samuel's hand, Beulah tried to find a place with a clear view. "This way," Myles said, waving to her. He found a front row spot for Samuel, and Beulah clutched her brother's shoulders from behind.

Two elephants wearing spangled harnesses led the parade. Pretty women rode on the beasts' thick necks, waving to the audience. A marching band followed, blaring music that nearly drowned out the crowd's cheers. Beulah watched clowns, caged beasts, a strong man, fat lady, a midget, and several bouncing acrobats. Costumed men shouted invitations. "Come and see the circus! Come to the show!"

Beulah clapped and waved, smiling until her cheeks ached. The crowd pressed about her and waves of heat rose from the dusty road, but she was too enthralled to care. Samuel hopped up and down, waving both arms. "It's a real lion, Beulah! Do you see it? And that huge bear! Was it real?"

When the music died away and the last cage disappeared into the dust, Beulah stepped back—right on someone's foot. Hands cupped her elbows; her shoulder bumped into a solid chest. "Oh! I'm so sorry," she gasped.

"We'd better find Al and Eunice," Myles said. His eyes were a dusty olive hue that matched his plaid shirt.

Beulah shivered in the heat. "Yes. Yes, of course." He turned her around and started walking, guiding her with one hand at her elbow. Beulah walked stiffly; she was afraid to wiggle her arm lest he remove his hand.

Samuel capered beside them, turning cartwheels in the trampled grass. "Have you ever seen a bear that big, Myles? And they've got two elephants, not just one. This is the greatest circus! Did you see those men wearing long underwear do back flips? Why don't they wear clothes, Myles?"

Myles chuckled. "Not underwear, Sam. They wear those snug, stretchy clothes to make it easy to move. It's a costume, you could say. There's the surrey."

He waved an arm at Al.

Samuel took off running toward the surrey. "Did you see it? Weren't the elephants great, Eunice?" His sister agreed.

Al's smile looked forced. "We could see pretty well from here. Too well for the horses' peace of mind. They don't care for elephants and lions. I'm hungry. Ready to dig into that supper basket?"

∼∞∾

Myles followed the Fairfields and Al into the big tent and took a seat at one end of a bench. Ever since the parade, Al had hovered over Beulah like a dog over a bone. Now he made certain she sat at the far end of the bench. Beulah looked up at Al just before he sat beside her. Myles lifted a brow. That pout of hers was something to see.

Although Myles knew he was a far from impartial observer, he was certain something had changed between Al and Beulah. True, they had never been a particularly affectionate pair, but they appeared to enjoy an easy camaraderie.

No more. Beulah seemed almost eager to escape Al's company. Her attention wandered when he spoke, and her gaze never followed his tall form. Al's dark eyes brooded, and his laughter sounded strained.

Perhaps they had quarreled. It was too much to hope that their romance had died away completely. Everyone in town knew that Al and Beulah would marry someday. Everyone.

Myles studied the sawdust center ring, arms folded across his chest. There was a tightness in his belly. He tried to rub it away. Not even the familiar sounds and smells of the circus could alleviate his distress.

"Are you hungry again, Myles?" Eunice asked over Samuel's head. "We could buy some popcorn."

He tried to stuff the offending hand in his pocket, then crossed his arms again. "I'm not hungry, but I'll buy you a snack." Rising, he approached a vendor and returned with a sack of buttered popcorn. "Don't know how you can eat again so soon, but here you go." Eunice and Samuel piled into the treat, knocking much of it to the floor in their haste.

"Hey, look. Isn't that Marva Obermeier?" Al pointed across the tent. "If you hurry, you could find a seat with her, Myles. We'll join up with you later."

The well-meaning suggestion was more than Myles could endure. Without a glance at Al or Beulah, he turned and left the tent. Stalking around the perimeter of the big top, ducking under guy wires, he made his way toward the living quarters.

Evening shadows stretched long on the trampled grass between tents and wheeled cages. From the shadows of one caravan, a large animal gave a disgruntled rumble.

"You there! Mister, the public is not going back here," an accented voice called from behind him.

Myles froze. It couldn't be! He turned slowly, studying the approaching clown. No mistaking that green wig and the wide orange smile. "Antonio? Antonio Spinelli!"

The clown halted. Myles saw dark eyes searching his face. "Who are you?"

"Myles Trent. I'm the boy you taught how to tumble years ago. You used to call me Red, remember?"

Antonio stepped closer, his giant shoes flopping. "Red? The bambino who feared the heights and the bears?" He held out a hand at waist level then lifted it as high as he could reach and gave a hearty chuckle. "My, how you grow!"

Myles gripped the clown's hand and clapped his shoulder. "I never expected to see you again, Antonio. You're a sight for sore eyes! How's your wife?"

"Ah, my Gina, she had a baby or two or three, and now she stay in the wagon while the show it goes on. We do well, we five—two boys and a dolly." The proud father beamed. "I teach them all to clown as I did you, Red." He scanned Myles once more. "You looka different with that beard on you face. And your hair not so red anymore. You marry? Have a family?"

Myles shook his head. "No. I've got a girl in mind, but she doesn't know it yet."

Antonio laughed again. "You wait until my act, she is over; then you come and see Gina. Tell us all about your ladylove. Yes?"

Myles nodded. "For a quick visit. I'm here with friends."

"This girl in your mind?" Antonio guessed.

"Yes. Problem is, another fellow has her in mind, too."

Antonio pulled a sober face, ludicrous behind his huge painted grin. "That a problem, yes. Now you must put yourself into the lady's mind, that's what! I must run. You stay." He pointed at Myles's feet.

"I'll wait." Myles nodded.

The little clown hurried toward his entrance. Soon Myles heard laughter and applause from the big top, then screams of delighted horror. The aerialists must be performing. He imagined Beulah watching the spectacle, and his smile faded. *If only I could sit beside her, enjoying the show through her eyes.*

The Spinelli family lived in a tiny red coach parked behind the row of animal cages. Myles had to duck to keep from bashing his head on the ceiling, and his feet felt several sizes too large. The redolence of a recent spicy meal made his eyes water.

Antonio's wife Gina was thrilled to see him, kissing him on both cheeks. She shoved a pile of clothing from a chair and told him to sit, then plied him with biscotti, garlic rolls, and a cup of rather viscous coffee. Myles took one sip and knew he wouldn't sleep all night. It was a pleasure to hear the Spinellis' circus stories, yet he could not completely relax and enjoy their company.

A tiny girl with serious dark eyes claimed his lap and played with his string tie while he talked. "This is our Sophia," Gina explained. "The boys, they are helping with the horses. Such a crowd tonight! Never did I expect it in the middle of nohow."

"Nowhere," Myles mumbled.

"We had a problem with the bear today. Did you hear?"

"Gina." Antonio shook his head. "We are not to speak of this."

She touched her lips with red tinted nails. "Oh, and I was forgotting. You will not think of it." She shook her dark head and changed the subject. "So you work at a farm? You are happy at this farm, Red?" Gina had put on weight over the years, yet she was still an attractive woman.

Myles shifted little Sophia to his other knee. "I am. I hope to acquire land of my own before long and raise a family along with cattle and crops."

Gina nodded. Her mind was elsewhere. "And you were such the performer in those days! Our Mario is much like him, don't you think, Antonio? Such a fine boy you were, and how we missed you when you disappeared. It was that brother who chased you off, no? Never did I care for him, though he was your flesh and blood. What become of that one?"

A tide of bitterness rose in his soul. "Monte is dead." Antonio's intense scrutiny produced an explanation. "He was shot by bandits in Texas. Gambling debts and cattle rustling."

The little clown nodded. He had not yet removed his wig and greasepaint. "And you cannot forgive this brother."

Myles sniffed. "Why should I forgive him? He's dead."

"For your own peace of mind. You have the look of a man carrying a heavy load, Red. It will break you, make you bitter and old while you are young."

Myles made a dismissive movement with one hand and watched his own leg jiggle up and down. "I'm starting over here in Wisconsin. The past is gone, forgotten."

"You have not forgotten; oh, no. Grudges are heavy to carry. The past will haunt you until this burden you give to God. Remember how the good Lord tells us that we are forgiven as we forgive others? Why should God forgive you when you will not forgive your fellowman?"

Myles placed the dark-haired "dolly" on her feet and rose. "I'd better return to my companions. It was a pleasure to see you again, Gina." Gloom settled over his soul.

After Myles made his farewells, Antonio accompanied him back to the midway. Darkness had fallen, making support wires and ground stakes difficult to see. Myles felt the need to make casual conversation. It would not be right to leave his old friend in this dismal way.

"This seems like a successful circus," Myles said, ducking beneath a sagging cable. "Are you satisfied with it?"

Antonio shook his head. "Ever since Mr. Bonacelli, he sell out, things not go so well. Lots of us come from Bonacelli's Circus—some of the animals, even.

The new owner, he cut the pay and the feed to make a profit. The animals not so happy anymore."

"Is the bear the one that came at me while I was cleaning his cage?" Myles grimaced at the memory of falling through the cage doorway with hot breath and foam on his heels.

"The very same." Antonio frowned. "He's a bad one, sure. You were right to fear the beast. He only get meaner as he get old. He ripped up our animal trainer we had who liked his corn liquor too well."

"I can believe it. Was it the same bear that made trouble today?"

Antonio glanced around. "Not to speak of this!" he whispered.

"Those cages don't look sturdy. I wouldn't want my little ones playing near them if I were you."

Antonio nodded and pushed Myles toward the main entrance. "Gina keeps the bambinos to home. You not to worry, my friend. Ah, it looks like the show, she is over. You had best find your friends quick. Is this lady with the yellow hair the one who lives in your head?"

Myles glanced up to see Marva Obermeier approaching. "No. She's just a friend." But a moment later Marva was attached to his arm. Myles introduced her to Antonio, attempting to be polite. The clown's eyes twinkled.

"I didn't know you knew any clowns, Myles," Marva chattered in her amiable, mindless way. "Wasn't that a tremendous show? It was so exciting when..." Myles tuned her out, scanning the passing crowds.

He spotted Al's broad gray hat. "Al!" Waving his free arm, he gave a sharp whistle and saw his friend's head turn. "Over here!"

Marva was excusing herself. "My papa is beckoning—I must go. It was nice to meet you..."

Myles tuned her out again, focusing on Al until he spotted Beulah behind him. "Here she comes—the tall girl in the blue dress. Beulah Fairfield."

Antonio regarded Myles with evident amusement. "Your other lady friend is gone. Did you notice?"

Myles glanced around. Marva had disappeared. "Did I tell her good-bye?"

"You did." Still grinning, Antonio turned to study Beulah.

Myles made his introductions all around. Samuel was thrilled to meet a real clown and plied the man with questions. Antonio answered the boy patiently.

"How long ago did you two know each other?" Beulah asked.

"This fine fellow was but a lad with hair like fire," Antonio said, eyes twinkling.

"It has been about eight years," Myles said. "Antonio and his wife were newly married. Now they have three children."

"Myles tells me he has thoughts of family for himself." Antonio wagged one finger beside his ear. "Time, she is passing him by."

Myles felt his face grow hot.

Al gruffly reminded them that home was still a good drive away. Antonio bade the Fairfields and Al farewell. Beulah held the clown's hand for a moment. "It was so nice to meet an old friend of Myles. His past has been a mystery to us, but now we know you, Mr. Spinelli."

Beulah's smile had its usual effect: Antonio beamed, shaking her hand in both of his. "But mine is the pleasure, Miss Fairfield, to meet such a lovely lady. Red is a mystery to Gina and me always—so secretive and shy! But in him beats a man's heart, I am knowing. He is needing a great love to banish these burdens he carries and fill his life with laughter and music."

Myles knew a sudden urge to hurry the little clown away before his heart's secret was broadcast to the world. Al relieved his distress by hustling Beulah away. "Give them time alone, Beulah. They haven't seen each other in years. We'll meet you at the surrey, Myles."

As soon as they were out of earshot, Antonio shook his head mournfully. "And this Al, your fine friend, is the other whose heart beats for Beulah. For him it is a sad thing, Red. She must be yours."

Myles lowered one brow. "What makes you say that?"

Antonio waved at the starry sky. "I read it in the stars? But maybe the stars, they are in a young lady's eyes." He laughed and patted Myles's arm. "You will have joy, Red. Gina and I, we will remember you and your Beulah in our prayers each night. Remember what I say about forgiveness—I know this from living it, you see. Don't imagine you are alone. Everyone has choices in life. Think of Beulah—you cannot offer her an unforgiving heart. The poison in you would harm her."

The man was like a flea for persistence. Nodding, Myles pretended to ignore the stinging words. "You will write to me? I live in Longtree, the next town over."

"I not write so good, but Gina will do it. Maybe when the season ends, we come to see you and your little wife."

Myles smiled and hugged the smaller man's shoulders. "Thank you, Antonio. You have given me much-needed encouragement."

Buck met the tired travelers in front of the barn and helped unhitch the horses. "Why are you up so late, Papa? Is Mama still awake?" Eunice asked sleepily.

"Mama and Daniel are asleep. Get ready for bed quietly, children. Go on with you now." Buck shooed his flock toward the house. "We've got church in the morning."

"Thank you, Al. Thank you, Myles. It was a wonderful circus," Beulah paused to say. Her eyes reflected the surrey's side lamps.

"You're welcome," they each replied.

"See you at church," Al called after her. "May I come pick you up?"

Myles jumped. That would be a sign of serious courtship. Hidden in the shadows behind the surrey, he gritted his teeth and braced himself for her reply.

"Thank you for the offer, but no, I'll see you there," Beulah's voice floated back. "Good night."

Al smacked a harness strap over its peg and tugged his hat down over his eyes. Without a word, he led his horse from its stall and saddled up. Myles felt a pang of sympathy for his friend.

Buck finished caring for the team while Myles saddled his mare. "Got a job for you Monday," Buck said.

"What's that?" Myles asked.

"We got two pasture fence posts snapped off; musta been rotted below ground level. I found Mo among our cows. He may be only a yearling, but he's all bull. I propped up the fence well enough to hold him temporarily; but we've got to replace those posts soon."

"I'll run the materials out there," Al promised.

"And I'll fix the fence," Myles said.

Chapter 3

Let all bitterness, and wrath, and anger, and clamour,
and evil speaking, be put away from you, with all malice.
EPHESIANS 4:31

Clutching a novel under one arm, Beulah peeked into her mother's room. "I'll be at the pond if you need me, Mama."

Bent over the cradle, Violet finished tucking Daniel's blanket around his feet. Straightening, she turned to smile at her daughter. "Enjoy yourself, honey. Would you bring in green beans for supper tonight? Samuel caught a dozen bluegill this morning, and beans would be just the thing to go with fried fish."

"He's getting to be quite a fisherman," Beulah observed. "Whatever will we do when school starts up and we lose our provider? You're right, beans sound delicious—or they would if I were hungry. Is Papa around, or did he go into town today?"

Violet led the way downstairs. "He went to help Myles repair the fence the bull broke. Which reminds me...I know it's asking a lot of you, dear, but would you be willing to carry water to the men? They're way out at that northwest pasture beyond the stream."

Beulah followed her mother into the parlor. "Of course I will, Mama. I'm going out anyway."

"You're a dear! You might take along some of those cookies you baked."

Beulah felt slightly guilty about her mother's gratitude, since her motive was not entirely altruistic. "That's a good idea. If I hurry, I'll still have time to read a chapter or two."

Violet settled into a chair and picked up her mending. "Darling, I want you to know that I've noticed your efforts to be cheerful and kind, and so has Papa Obie. You're my precious girl—I want other people to see and appreciate your beautiful spirit along with your pretty face."

"Do you really think I'm pretty, Mama?" Beulah tried to see her reflection in the window. "Everyone says I look like my real father, and he was homely. At least, I remember him as kind of ungainly and bony with big teeth."

"You have your father's coloring and his gorgeous brown eyes. Your teeth may be a bit crooked, yet they are white and healthy. You have matured this past year, and I think you must have noticed that boys find you attractive. Al certainly does."

Beulah looked down at her figure. "I guess so. I wonder why men are attracted by a woman's shape. When you think about it, we're kind of funny looking."

Violet laughed. "Trust you to say something like that! As for me, I'm thankful that men find women attractive and vice versa. It makes life interesting."

"So it isn't wrong for a girl to enjoy looking at a man?"

"Wrong? Of course not," Violet answered absently. "I enjoy looking at my husband."

"When a girl is interested in a man, what is the best way for her to let him know it?" Beulah perched on the edge of the sofa. "A subtle way, I mean. Without actually saying so."

Violet looked at the ceiling, touching her needle to her lips. "Hmm. Subtle. How about meeting his gaze and smiling? A touch on his arm, perhaps. Touching can be hazardous, however. A lady doesn't want to touch a man too much or he will lose respect for her."

Beulah's lower lip protruded and her brows lowered as a certain memory of a clinging blond recurred. Her mother's advice seemed faulty. A shy man like Myles might be different. He might prefer a woman who took the initiative. "How does a lady know if a man returns her interest?"

Violet's lips twitched. "She will know. Most men are straightforward."

"But how will she know for certain? If a man stares at a girl, does that mean he is interested?"

"That depends on the stare." Violet frowned. "Who has been staring at you?"

"It's a respectful gaze. Don't worry." She hopped to her feet. "Thank you, Mama. I'd better hurry before the day is gone."

Although she took a shortcut through a stretch of forest, the trek to the back pasture was more arduous than Beulah had anticipated. She crossed Samuel's log bridge over the brook, then hiked up the steep bank, nearly dropping the water jug once.

"Why did I think this was such a good idea?" she grouched, hoisting the jug on her hip. "I'll be a sweaty mess again before he sees me." Mosquitoes and deerflies hummed around her head, dodging when she slapped at them. Her arms ached until they felt limp, and her feet burned inside her boots.

Through the trees she caught sight of Papa Obie's mustang Jughead and open pastureland beyond him. The horse's patches of white reflected sunshine as he grazed. Wherever Jughead was, Beulah was certain to find Obie nearby.

Sure enough, there were Obie and Myles, ramming a new post into a hole. Both men had removed their shirts; their damp undervests gaped open to reveal sweaty chests. Suspenders held up faded denim trousers, and battered hats shaded their eyes.

"Hello," she greeted, picking her way between stumps. "I brought water and cookies."

"Beulah!" Obie straightened. "You're an angel of mercy. We've needed a drink yet hated to stop before we finished this post." He exchanged a glance with Myles. "Let's take a break." Myles nodded, and the two men sat on nearby stumps.

Wiping his face with a red kerchief, Obie drained the dipper in one long draught. "Thanks."

Beulah's hands trembled as she handed Myles the dipper. Hazel eyes glinted in his dusty face. He, too, poured the water down his throat and wiped his mustache with the back of one hand. "Thank you."

"More?"

Each man accepted two more drinks, and the jug felt much lighter. Then they gobbled up her molasses cookies. "These are delicious, Beulah. . .but then your cookies always are," Obie said.

She peeked at Myles to see if he agreed. "My favorite." He lifted a half-eaten cookie.

Satisfied, she settled upon a low stump near Obie's feet and arranged her skirts. "How much longer must you work in this heat? Is this the last post?"

"Yes. Once we brace this post and attach the crossbeams, we'll be done. Nasty work." Obie shook his head, betraying a former cowboy's natural aversion to fences. "Myles did most of it before I got here. Planned that well, didn't I?" He grinned at the hired man, and Myles acknowledged the teasing with a smile.

"Ready?"

Myles nodded, and the two returned to their work.

Beulah stayed. Myles never spoke to her, but several times she caught his eye and smiled. He did not smile back. Her heart sank. *He is in love with Miss Obermeier! Whatever shall I do?*

"Beulah, would you bring me the hammer?"

She hurried to comply.

"If you would hand me that spike. . ." Obie requested next.

This time she hovered. "May I help?"

"Not now," Obie puffed. "Better stay back."

Myles lifted the rails into place, and Obie hammered in the spikes. The hair on the hired man's forearms and chest was sun-bleached. Sweaty hair curling from beneath his hat held auburn glints. His trousers bagged around slim hips.

From this close range Beulah could locate his ribs and shoulder blades. Sinews protruded in his neck and chest as his muscles strained. When Mama was pregnant with Daniel, Beulah once sneaked a peek at a human anatomy book in the doctor's office. Myles might have posed for the model of muscles and bones, so many of them were visible beneath his skin.

He glanced up; Beulah looked away, too late. Her body already dripped sweat; now she burned on the inside. *What must he think of me, staring at him like a hussy?* She strolled away, fanning her apron up and down. Grasshoppers fled buzzing before her.

When the last rail was in place, Beulah helped the men gather their tools. Obie loaded his saddlebags. "Thanks again, Myles." He swung into Jughead's saddle. A wisp of grass dangled from the gelding's mouth. "Will you see Beulah home, then check on Cyrus Thwaite for me? He hasn't been eating well since his wife died, and I want to make sure he's all right."

"Yes, sir, I will."

Obie's silvery eyes smiled, and one brow arched. "You two take your time. Behave yourselves."

Now what did he mean by that? Beulah wondered.

Jughead sprang into motion, hurdling brush and stumps in his way. Within moments he had disappeared from view.

Beulah looked at Myles. "Why didn't you bring a horse? I thought cowboys preferred to ride. Or are you really a clown?" she tried to tease.

Wiping one sleeve across his forehead, he clapped on his hat. Every inch of exposed skin glistened red-brown, and his undervest was sopping. Though he was pleasing to behold, Beulah tried to remain upwind.

"First a clown, then a cowboy, now a farmer." One grimy hand began to rub his belly. "No point in making a horse stand around while I work. The boss was in town this morning; he needed a horse."

"Don't forget your shirt." She scooped it up and held it out.

"Thanks." He slung it over his shoulder and picked up her water jug.

He wouldn't even meet her eyes. Beulah's temper rose. "You don't need to escort me home. You must be tired." She picked up her book.

"Let's cut through Mo's pasture."

Not twenty yards down the sloping pasture, placidly chewing his cud, lay Mo. Shading her eyes, Beulah cast a wary glance at the dormant bull. "Is it safe?"

"He knows me." Myles bent to step through the fence rails. "Come on."

She slipped through the fence easily enough, but her skirt caught on a splinter and Myles had to release it. Beulah kept glancing toward Mo. The bull watched them walk across his field. Slowly he began to rise, back end first.

"Myles, he's getting up!" Beulah caught hold of Myles's arm.

He looked down at her hand on his arm, then back at the yearling Jersey.

Clutching his arm, she let Myles direct her steps and kept both eyes on the bull. Mo began to follow them, trotting over the rough ground.

"Any cookies left?" Myles asked.

"Some broken ones. Why?"

"Mo likes sweets. Don't be frightened, child. He's too small to harm you."

Child!

When the bull approached to within a few yards, it bawled, and Beulah let out a yelp. "Here, give him the cookies!" She shoved the sack into Myles's hands, then cowered behind him. The man's cotton undervest was damp beneath her hands, but the solid feel of him was reassuring. Beulah could hear her own heartbeat.

Myles extended a piece of cookie. "Come and get it, Li'l Mo. You've had your fun, scaring Beulah. Now show her what a good fellow you are."

Shaking his head, the young bull pawed the ground and gave a feinting charge. Myles held his ground. Mo stretched toward the cookie, nostrils twitching. When the bull accepted the treat, Myles took hold of the brass ring in its nose. "Good lad." He stroked Mo's neck and scratched around the animal's ears. "This is one fine little bull."

Beulah began to relax, peeking around Myles's shoulder. "I can't believe he was once a tiny calf. Samuel named him 'Moo-Moo.' Remember that day when my mother drove us to your farm—Al's farm—by mistake? Or were you there that day?"

"I was there. I helped deliver this fellow that very morning." With a farewell pat for Mo, Myles turned to Beulah. "I remember how cross you looked that day. You've got a pretty smile, but your pout is like nothing I've ever seen." His grin showed white through his beard.

Beulah gaped, hands dangling. She took a step back and tucked her hands under her elbows. "I—I was not cross; I was worried."

"With your lip sticking out and your eyes stormy, just like now." His hat shaded his face, yet Beulah caught the glint in his eyes.

She covered her mouth with one hand, conscious of her overbite. Eyes burning, she turned and picked up the water jug. If Myles knew how she felt about him, he would laugh, and the whole town would know about Beulah's infatuation within days. Marva would regard her with pity and mild amusement.

"Are you all right, Beulah?" Myles took two steps in her direction. "I didn't mean to hurt your feelings."

"I'm not angry; I'm hot." Water sloshed in the jug. Beulah eyed the sweaty man. "You look hotter." Without pausing for reflection, she dashed the water into his face.

Water dripped from his nose and beard and trickled down his chest. "Did I deserve that?"

He didn't seem angry. A nervous giggle escaped before Beulah could stop it. "You needed a bath."

His eyes flared, and Beulah knew she had better get moving. Picking up her skirts, she dashed for the fence, intending to vanish into the forest. But an arm caught her around the waist. "Not so fast." Without further ceremony he tossed her over his shoulder and picked up the empty jar. Her book flew into the tall grass.

"What are you doing?" she gasped. "Put me down!" He surmounted the fence without apparent difficulty and headed into the woods.

Beulah found it hard to breathe while hanging head down over his shoulder, and her stomach muscles were too weak to lift her upper body for long. In order to draw a good breath she had to put both hands on his back and push herself up. "Myles, a gentleman doesn't treat a lady this way! Please put me down. This is…improper," she protested. The grasp of his arm around her legs was disturbing, the solid strength of his shoulder beneath her stomach even more so. There was a roaring in her ears.

"Very well." He hefted her and flung her from him. Beulah fell with splayed arms and horrified expression only to land with a great splash. She had enough presence of mind to shut her mouth before water closed over her head.

Flailing her arms, she managed to right herself, but her face barely cleared the surface when she stood on the rocky bottom. The source of the roaring sound was now clear: The stream poured into this little pool over a lip of rock suspended twelve feet above the surface. The churning water tugged at Beulah's billowing skirts, and bubbles tickled her arms.

"How dare you!" she gasped, sudden fury choking her. "I could have drowned!"

An exaggeration, but the sharpest accusation she could think of at the moment. She had to shout for him to hear her.

Myles stood above her, his boots planted wide, arms folded on his chest. Dapples of sunlight played across his hat and shoulders. "It's not deep," he protested. "I swim here often." His smile was infuriating.

"I can't swim with my boots and clothes on," she blurted, then choked on a mouthful of water. "You…you monster! You are no gentleman!"

"I had not observed you behaving like a lady."

"Ooooh!"

Desperate for revenge, she thrashed over to the steep bank and reached for his boots. One frenzied hop and she caught hold around his ankles. No matter how hard she tugged, he remained unmoved. She paused, gasping for air. "Where are we? I've never seen this place."

"Just over half a mile above the beaver pond. The waterfall made this hole, perfect for swimming. It's one of my favorite places on earth."

Beulah tried to look over her shoulder at the lacy waterfall, but her bedraggled sunbonnet blocked her view. Hoping to catch Myles unaware, she gave his feet another sharp jerk, lost her grip, and slid back into the pool. Sputtering with fury, she surfaced again, arms thrashing. Her teeth chattered, although the water was not terribly cold. "Help me out of here!"

He frowned, considering, then removed his hat and boots. After stacking his garments well out of Beulah's reach, he dove into the pool and disappeared.

Beulah let out another little screech, then scanned the pool for him with narrowed eyes. He should pay for this outrage.

He did not come up. Beulah began to feel concerned. Had he hit his head on a rock? "Myles?" she inquired.

"Myles, where are you?" She stepped forward, took a mouthful of water, and coughed. "Myles!" Her hands groped, searching for his body. This pool was too shallow for safe diving. Panic filled her voice. "Myles!"

" 'Ruby lips above the water blowing bubbles soft and fine, but, alas! I was no swimmer, so I lost my Clementine.' " The voice in her ear was a rich baritone.

"Oh!" Beulah's anger revived. "You are dreadful! I thought you had drowned— that's what you wanted me to think!" Even more infuriating was her helpless condition. It was difficult to appear righteously angry when her face barely cleared the surface. Exertion and excitement made her huff for every breath. "How can you be so mean? First you say I'm ugly, then you drop me in the water fully clothed, and then you pretend to drown? And I thought you were a nice person! You're horrible! Cruel!"

"Who said you're ugly?" He caught her by the waist and lifted until her head and shoulders rose out of the water. His hair lay slicked back from his high forehead. She could count the freckles on his peeling nose.

"Let go of me!" The grip of his hands sent her heart into spasms. Her corset's ribs bit into her flesh. She pulled at his fingers, kicking wildly.

He shook her. "If you don't hold still, I'll drop you back in the pool and you can find your own way out."

Her struggles ceased. She gripped his forearms, feeling iron beneath the flesh. *I can't cry! I must keep control.*

"Now who said you were ugly?"

"You did. That was unkind! I can't help having crooked teeth any more than you can help having red hair and freckles!"

He blinked. She saw his eyes focus upon her mouth. She clamped her lips together.

"I never noticed that your teeth are crooked."

"But you said. . ."

"I said I'd never seen a pout like yours. It's like a tornado brewing. Wise people stay out of your way." He grinned. "I would never call you ugly. Your temper, however, deserves that designation, from all I hear."

Beulah gaped into his face.

"Go ahead and flay me alive. I can take it." He smiled.

Her mouth snapped shut. The backs of her eyes burned.

"I've got to put you down for a minute. My arms are giving out." He turned her to face away from him. She placed her hands on top of his at her waist, thankful for her trim figure and sturdy corset.

Hefting her back up, he slowly walked toward the far side of the little pool. As they passed the waterfall, Beulah looked up and felt spray on her face. "Wait!"

Myles stopped, lowering her slightly. Beulah reached out and touched the sheet of falling water, surprised by its power. "Ohhh, this is wonderful!" Rainbows glimmered in the misty water. She lifted her other hand, straining her upper body toward the falls.

"I can't hold you like this anymore," Myles protested, then let his arms drop.

Startled, Beulah caught hold of his wrists and began to protest; but Myles pulled her back, wrapped his arms around her, and supported her against his body so that her waist was at his chest level. "Go ahead and enjoy the waterfall," he ordered from between her shoulder blades.

Beulah's pounding heart warned her that she had exceeded the bounds of ladylike deportment. "Have you ever walked beneath it?"

"I have." She was sliding down within his grasp.

"Can you walk through it while holding me?" She looked over her shoulder at him and recognized the intimacy of the situation. His arms pressed around her waist and rib cage. He lifted his knee to boost her higher in his grasp.

"Are you—are you sure—are you sure you want me to?"

Chapter 4

Seek ye the LORD while he may be found,
call ye upon him while he is near.
ISAIAH 55:6

P lease do!" she begged.

His arms shook both with strain and with excitement. Knowing he should flee temptation, Myles found himself unable to deny Beulah's request. Hopefully she would attribute his strangled voice to physical effort.

Again hefting her higher in his grasp, he walked toward the waterfall, feeling stones turn beneath his feet. Keeping one arm wrapped over his, Beulah lifted her other arm over her head to greet the cascade as it tumbled over their heads. Water filled their ears, noses, and eyes, dragged on their clothing, and toiled to pull them under. When they emerged on the far side, Beulah coughed. Water dribbled from her every feature. She had slipped down within his grasp, her bonnet was gone, and her arm now clung around his neck. Long eyelashes clumped together when she blinked those glorious brown eyes. Her smile lighted up the grotto. "I will never forget this, Myles."

She was a slender girl, yet she felt substantial in his arms, better than anything he had ever imagined. Oh, but she was lovely with her questioning eyes and her lips that seemed to invite his kisses! Her free hand crept up to rest upon his chest; she must feel the tumult within. His breath came in labored gusts.

Shaking, he gripped her forearms and shoved her away. He shook his head to clear it, reflecting that another dunk under the waterfall might benefit him.

"Myles—" she began, then fell silent. Although she was obliged to cling to his arms to keep from sinking, he felt her withdrawal. Her chin quivered with cold.

God, help me! I love her so, the wild little kitten.

Without another word Myles hoisted her into his arms, this time in the more conventional carrying position, and slogged across to the far shore. When Beulah turned to crawl up the bank, he caught a glimpse of her face. "Beulah?"

Her booted foot slipped and thumped him in the chest. With a soft grunt, he caught hold of her ankles and gave her an extra boost until she could sit on the mossy bank.

Water streamed from every fold of her clothing. Her hair dripped. Her face was crumpled and red. Her woeful eyes turned Myles to mush.

"Are. . .are you all right?" Assorted endearments struggled on his lips; he dared not speak them aloud. He touched her soggy boot, but she jerked it away, staggered to her feet, and rushed off along the bank of the creek.

When Myles emerged from the forest near Fairfield's Folly, Watchful rose from her cool nest beneath the back porch and came to greet him, tail waving. Thankfully she was not a noisy dog. Myles left the jug on the porch and turned to leave, but the kitchen door opened.

"Hello, Myles."

Myles removed his hat as he turned. "Hello, Mrs. Watson."

Violet Watson cradled Daniel against one shoulder, jiggling him up and down. "My, but it's hot today! I happened to see you out the kitchen window." Her blue eyes scanned him. "I see you've been for a swim."

"Yes, ma'am."

"I must admit, a dip does sound tempting. So Beulah reached you men with the water and cookies?"

"Yes, ma'am. Please extend my thanks for all of her thoughtfulness."

Violet smiled. "I'll do that. She must still be reading at the pond. That girl does love to read, and she seldom finds time for it these days. I'm afraid I depend greatly on her help around the house. Maybe I need to give her more afternoons off like this."

Myles nodded, feeling dishonest. He knew Beulah had returned home already, for he had followed her wet trail through the forest. She must have sneaked inside. "I enjoy reading, too."

"Really? Do you also enjoy music? Beulah and I are both fond of music, but we have so little opportunity to hear good music around here."

His ears grew warm. "I enjoy music." Realizing that he was rubbing his stomach, he whipped the offending hand behind his back. Violet didn't seem to notice.

She leaned against the doorframe. "I play the piano a little. Obie bought me a lovely instrument for Christmas, you know, but I do not do it justice. Beulah plays better than I do. Do you sing or play an instrument?"

"Yes, ma'am."

"I'm thinking of planning a music party after harvest, just for our family and a few friends. Might you be willing to join us?"

"I'd be honored, ma'am." Myles shifted his weight. "I must be going. Have an errand to run."

"Are you going to see Cyrus Thwaite? That poor man has been so lonely since his wife died. I'm certain he doesn't eat well. Let me pack you a sack of cookies for him."

Myles handed over the empty cookie sack. Little Daniel reached for it, trying to bring the strings to his open mouth.

When Violet returned the full sack, she gave Myles a sweet smile. "Good-bye, and thank you."

Myles's mare whinnied as she trotted up the Thwaite drive. "Hello the house!" Myles called. Swinging down in one easy motion, he left his mare's reins hanging. A knock at the door brought no response. Myles entered, feeling mildly concerned. Cyrus seldom left his farm since his wife Hattie died last spring.

Myles scanned the kitchen, taking a quick peek into the pantry. The sacks of flour and sugar he had delivered the week before had not been touched. Only the coffee supply had been depleted. Dirty cups were stacked in the dry sink, but few plates had been used. He set Violet's sack of cookies on the table.

"Cyrus?" he called, quickly inspecting the rest of the untidy house. Stepping outside, Myles felt the relief of fresh air. A breeze had risen, swaying the birches beyond the drive. "Cyrus?" he bellowed, heading for the barn.

There—he heard a reply. From the barn? Myles broke into a jog. Chickens scattered as he approached the barn door. The cow lowed, turning her head to gaze at him. "Why aren't you out at pasture?" Myles left by the barn's back door. "Cyrus, where are you?"

"Here, boy." Cyrus waved from across the pasture. He appeared to be leaning on the handle of a spade. At his feet lay a gray mound. Two vultures circled overhead, and crows lined the nearby pasture fence. The swaybacked old mule must have keeled over at last. But by the time Myles crossed the field, he realized that the animal had met a violent death. Its body was mauled.

"What happened?"

Cyrus lifted a long face. "You know how he could unlatch doors; he musta let hisself out last night, poor ol' cuss. Myles, I may be crazy, but this looks like a bear's work to me." He lifted a silencing hand. "I know there ain't been a bear in these parts since Hector here was a long-eared foal, but what else could break a full-growed mule's neck like this?"

Myles studied the claw marks on the animal's carcass. "Why would a bear want to kill an old mule? Surely it might have found better eating nearby." A suspicion popped into his mind.

"Mebbe it's sick or wounded or plain cussed mean. Would ya help me bury what's left Hector?" Cyrus looked halfway ashamed to ask. "Cain't jest see m'self leavin' him for the vultures and coyotes. Thought I'd bury him on this here knoll."

Myles nodded and returned to the barn for another spade.

To give Cyrus credit, he worked harder at eighty than many men worked at thirty; but his body lacked the strength to lift heavy loads of dirt. All too soon he was obliged to sit down. "Was a time I could work like you, Boy, but that time is long past." He wiped his forehead with a grimy handkerchief. "I been putting lots of thought into what's to become of this here farm. Hattie wanted to leave it to Obie, but I don't see much point in that. He's already got more land than he can work."

Myles paused for a breather, leaning on his spade. One callused hand absently rubbed his belly. "You might sell it and live in town. Bet you'd enjoy living at Miss Amelia's boardinghouse, eating her good cooking morning and night. Lots of company for you there."

Cyrus looked pensive. "You paint a tempting picture, Myles boy. I reckon I'd like that mighty well, but I can't see myself selling this farm. Hattie and me built it up when we was young, expecting we'd have a passel of young'uns. Never did, though. I figure this land is worth more to me than it would be to a stranger. It's played out. We planted it so many years, took all the good right out'n it."

Myles began to dig again. "I hear there're ways a man can put soil right again by planting other things like beans and peas in it. Some scientists claim it'll work."

Cyrus shook his white head. "I'll never see the backside of a plow again. But if you had a mind to buy, I might reconsider selling. I'd rest easy knowing it was in your hands, Myles." His eyes drifted across the weedy pasture to stump-ridden fields beyond.

"If I—" Myles stopped working to stare at his spade. "You'd sell to me?"

"That sounds about like what I said, don't it? This place needs someone who'll put work and love into it. You've done a sight of work hereabouts already, but I know you've been itching to do more, to make the place what it oughta be. You're a good man, Myles Trent, and I think you're a man God will use—no matter if folks claim you don't believe in Him. I know better."

Myles met the old man's gaze. "How do you know?"

"You're plumb full of questions that demand answers, and you ain't the kind who'll quit before he finds them answers. God promises that a man who seeks Him will find Him, if he searches with all his heart."

Myles shifted his grip on the handle. "I can't buy your place, Cyrus. No money. I've laid a little by each year, but not enough."

Cyrus pondered, deepening the lines on his brow. "Don't know why, but I got this feeling about you and my farm, Myles. I think God has something in mind, though I cain't begin to tell you what it is."

A deep sigh expanded Myles's chest. When he exhaled, his shoulders drooped. "Unless He plans to drop a fortune into my lap, I'll be a hired hand till the day I die."

"You might could marry rich," Cyrus suggested with a wicked grin. "Naw, I don't mean it. You find yourself a good wife and make this place into a proper home again."

Myles quickly began to dig. Cyrus chuckled. "Why is finding a wife such a chore for you young fellers? I just up and asked Hattie to wed me and got us hitched. No fuss and feathers about it, yet we stayed happy together sixty years.

Bet there's more'n one lady in town who'd be eager to accept a fine feller like you. Why not chance it? Might want to wash up first; try hair oil and scented soap. Females like such things."

"A man doesn't want to marry just any woman," Myles objected. His thoughts whirled.

Scented soap. Van Huysen's Soap.

Money. His money.

Farm. His farm?

"Why not? One woman is same as another." Cyrus's grin displayed almost toothless gums. "Comely or homely, fleshy or scrawny, they kin all keep a man warm on long winter nights. Hattie was never what you might call comely, but then I weren't no prize winner myself!" He cackled. "One woman—that's all you need."

When the hole was deep enough, Myles dragged the carcass over and shoved it in. "That should be deep enough to keep varmints from digging ol' Hector up," he said. Cyrus helped him fill in the hole and tamp it.

"Hope that bear took off for foreign parts," Cyrus remarked. "We don't need a killer loose in these woods."

"I'll warn our neighbors about the possibility of a renegade bear. Want to come to supper at Miss Amelia's boardinghouse with me tonight?"

Cyrus's faded eyes brightened. "That'd be fine. You got a buggy?"

"We can hitch my mare to your buggy," Myles said. "I'll talk with Buck about getting you another mule or horse. You can't stay out here alone with no transportation."

⁓⊗⁓

On the way to town, Myles's mare tossed her head and tucked her tail whenever he clucked to her. "Cholla takes being hitched to a buggy as an insult," Myles explained when Cyrus commented on the mare's bad mood.

"Is she yours or Obie's?"

"Mine. Caught and tamed her myself out in Wyoming. Not so pretty to look at, prickly like the cactus she's named for, but she's got legs like iron and a big heart." Myles fondly surveyed his mare's spotted gray hide, wispy tail, and unruly mane.

"And a kind eye. You can tell a lot about a horse by its eyes," Cyrus added.

Miss Amelia Sidwell greeted them at her boardinghouse's dining room door. "Pull out a chair and tuck in. Evenin', Myles. You been taking too much sun."

"You're looking pert today, Amelia," Cyrus commented. "Fine feathers make a fine bird."

Miss Amelia appeared to appreciate the compliment, favoring the old man with a smile. Her blue-checked apron did bring out the blue in her eyes. "What brings you to town, Cyrus? Ain't seen you in a spell." Her voice was as deep as a man's.

"Your cooking draws men like hummingbirds to honeysuckle," Myles assured her, straddling his chair. He returned greetings from other diners, most of whom he knew.

A stranger stared at him from across the table. Myles nodded, and the gentleman nodded back, then looked away.

Amelia scoffed. "Hummingbirds, indeed. More like flies to molasses, I'd say." She ladled soup into Cyrus's bowl. "Got more of you blowflies than I kin handle these days. I'm thinkin' of hiring help."

"You, Amelia?" Boswell Martin, the town sheriff, inquired in his wheezy voice. "I can't imagine you finding help that would suit. What female creature ever found favor in your eyes?"

Never pausing in her labors, Amelia snapped back, "Miss Sidwell to you, Boz Martin—and I'll thank you to keep your remarks to yourself. If that's a chaw in your cheek, you'd best get yourself outside and rid of it. I never heard tell of a man eating with tobacco tucked in his cheek, looking like a hulking chipmunk. If you don't beat all!"

The sheriff meekly shoved back his chair and stepped outside while the other diners struggled to hide their mirth. Myles again met the gaze of the dapper gentleman with bushy side-whiskers. The two men shared an amused smile.

"I ain't never seen you before, Mister." Cyrus directed his comment toward the stranger. "You new in town or jest travelin' through?"

"I arrived in town Tuesday," the gentleman replied. "I am George Poole, lately from New York. I have business in this area."

"Welcome to Longtree, Mr. Poole." Cyrus and Myles reached across the table to shake the newcomer's hand. Poole's handshake was firm, his gaze steady.

The sheriff returned to the table and began to shovel food into his mouth.

"Boz?" Cyrus said. "I lost my mule today—looked like a bear's work."

Sheriff Martin gave the old man a skeptical look, still chewing.

Cyrus forestalled the inevitable protest. "I know there ain't been a bear in these parts for twenty years, but I know what I seen. The varmint broke ol' Hector's neck and left huge claw marks. I'm thinking you ought to organize a hunt before the critter tears up more stock."

Martin nodded and spoke around a mouthful of stew. "I'll get right on it."

"Don't talk with your mouth full," Amelia ordered, reaching over the sheriff's shoulder to place a freshly sliced loaf of bread on the table. Within moments the platter was empty. "You lot behave like hogs at a trough," the gratified cook growled.

"Talk of bears puts me in mind. . .that circus left Bolger this morning," one diner said. "I heard rumors they lost an animal in this area. Did you hear anything about it, Sheriff? Last thing we need in these parts is a roaming lion."

This time Boz swallowed before he spoke. "Nope. Ain't heard a thing."

Again Myles recalled his circus friend Gina Spinelli's slip of the tongue about a rogue bear, but he said nothing. Surely a missing circus bear would have been reported to the authorities. Or would it?

Mr. Poole turned his steel blue eyes upon Miss Amelia. "That was a wonderful meal, madam. The best meal I've eaten in many a year."

Amelia fluttered. "Why, thank you, Mr. Poole. I'm right glad you liked it. I've got apple dumplings and cream in the kitchen."

"May I take my dessert later this evening? I'm afraid I cannot swallow another bite at the moment." He laid his folded napkin beside his empty plate and pushed back his chair. When he stood, the top of his head was on a level with Amelia's eyes.

Work-worn hands smoothed her starched apron. Myles noticed that her gray hair looked softer than usual; she had styled it a new way instead of slicking it back into a knot. "Certainly, Mr. Poole. You let me know when you're ready for your dessert."

Poole excused himself from the table and left the room, apparently oblivious to the stunned silence that followed Amelia's reply. "But, Amelia—" the sheriff protested.

"Not another word from you." She withered him with a glance. "Not a one of you what cain't fit in your dessert when it's offered. A fine gentleman like Mr. Poole isn't used to stuffing his face, so's a body must make allowances." With a sweep of her skirts, Miss Amelia returned to her kitchen.

Sheriff Martin scowled. "That woman's gone plain loco. A few bows and compliments, and even the best of women plumb lose their heads."

"Jealous, Boz? Maybe you'll get further with the lady if you try bowing and complimenting." Old Cyrus chuckled. "Wouldn't hurt to bathe if you're right serious about courting."

Boz's already florid face turned scarlet. "Reckon she'd take notice?"

"A woman likes it when a man takes pains on her account. Amelia likes things clean and neat."

"Clean" and "neat" were two terms Myles would never have applied to the sheriff. He was startled by the concept that Sheriff Martin wished to court Miss Amelia. Not that the man was too old for marriage—Boz hadn't yet turned fifty. But hard-boiled Martin had never struck him as the marrying kind.

Then again, what made any person wish to marry? A craving for love and companionship, he supposed. The longing to be needed, admired, and desired. The urge to produce children to carry on one's name. Myles could appreciate the sheriff's inclination.

"I'm thinkin' on asking her to the church social Friday," Boz growled, shoving food around on his plate. "How you think I oughta go about it, Cy?"

Enjoying his new role, Cyrus sized Boz up, rubbing his grizzled chin. "You need to head for the barber for a shave and trim, then buy yourself new duds. And no tobacco. Amelia hates the stuff. Might better drop it now than later."

Boz rubbed his plump jowls with one dirty hand, making a raspy noise. He nodded. "I'll do it." Amid raucous ribbing from the other men at the table, the sheriff rose, hitched up his sagging belt, and headed for the door.

"No dessert, Boz?" Amelia stood in the kitchen doorway, a loaded plate in each hand.

"Not tonight. Got business to attend. Thank you for a wondrous fine meal, *Miss Sidwell*." Boz bowed awkwardly and made his exit.

Shocked by his unaccustomed formality, Amelia stared after him, shrugged, and plopped dumplings in front of two diners. When she served Myles and Cyrus, she fixed Myles with a shrewd eye. "You takin' Marva Obermeier to the church social, Myles? She's counting on it."

The fork stopped halfway to his mouth, then slowly returned to the plate. "Miss Obermeier?" His stomach sank. "Why would she expect that?"

"You'd be knowing better than I," Amelia snapped and headed back to her kitchen.

Myles gave Cyrus a blank look. The old man lifted a brow. "It's all over town, Myles. Didn't you know?"

The dessert lost its appeal. "I think I've only talked to her twice."

"You mean to say you ain't sweet on her?"

"No. I mean—yes, that's what I mean to say; no, I'm not sweet on her. I hardly know the woman."

"I reckon you'll be getting to know her real soon." Cyrus chuckled.

Chapter 5

Wrath is cruel, and anger is outrageous;
but who is able to stand before envy?
PROVERBS 27:4

C yrus was no prophet, but he came uncomfortably close. And "uncomfortably close" was an apt description of Marva herself. The blond lady was not unattractive; in fact, in her rosy, plump, blond fashion, she was pretty.

"I'm so happy to see you here tonight, Myles. You've been neglecting church lately." She wagged a finger in his face and moved a step closer. "My papa says I should claim you for my partner at charades."

Myles took a step back. "Why is that?"

"He says you're a natural performer. Have you ever been on the stage?" Marva spoke above the noisy crowd, leaning closer.

"In a way," Myles hedged, shifting backward. "Have you?"

Marva chuckled in her throaty way. "I? Not unless you count school recitations. I play piano in church, but that's different. No one looks at me. Are you warm, Myles? Would you like to step outside for a while?" She stepped closer to make herself heard.

"No, no, I'm fine." Myles moved back and bumped into the wall. He cast a desperate glance around, only to spy Beulah across the room. She sipped lemonade from a cup, then laughed at a comment from her companion. Myles felt a pinch in his chest at the sight of Al's broad shoulders and smooth dark hair. So Beulah had come to the social with Al. The romance must have revived.

"Myles?" He heard someone repeating his name and struggled to focus on Marva's blue eyes.

"Myles, are you all right? You look pale all of a sudden."

"Maybe I do need fresh air." He walked to the door, wishing he could bolt. Across the porch and down the steps, between small clusters of talking, laughing people—fresh air at last. He drew a deep breath and lifted his gaze to the evening sky. A few pink stripes still outlined the horizon; stars multiplied above them.

"It's a lovely night, Myles. I'm glad you brought me to see the sunset." Marva spoke at his elbow, linking her arm through his. "Do you want to take a walk?"

Considering his options, he accepted. "Why not?" He started across the yard surrounding the building that served Longtree as both church and schoolhouse.

Marva trotted to keep up. "Slow down, Myles! We're not racing. Wouldn't you like to stroll away from other people where we can talk?"

"The games will start soon. Wouldn't want to miss them." Myles shortened his stride, but maintained a rapid gait.

Marva began to puff. "I had no idea you enjoyed games so much, Myles. Aren't we rather old for such things?"

"You never outgrow having fun. They're having a spelling competition to-night along with charades." Fun was the farthest thing from his mind at the moment. Surviving the evening without a broken heart would be challenge enough.

When they returned to the steps, Myles escorted Marva through the door. A large woman greeted her. "Marva, darling, you look lovely tonight. I'm sure Myles thinks so!" Without waiting for a response, she rambled on. "I was just saying to Ruby that your recipe for corn fritters is the best I've ever tasted. You add bits of ham to the mix, right?"

While the women discussed cooking, Myles melted into the crowd. "Pardon me. Pardon," he repeated, trying not to be pushy. Arriving at the refreshment table, he reached for a glass of lemonade.

"Hello, Myles." His outstretched hand froze in place as he recognized the pink taffeta dress across the serving table. Slowly his gaze moved up a slender form to meet eyes like chips of black ice. Beulah held a ladle in one hand, a cup in the other. "Are you having a pleasant evening? Miss Obermeier looks particularly lovely tonight, flushed from the cool night air."

Myles wanted to return a snappy remark about Beulah's equally blooming complexion, but his mouth would not cooperate. Was it her beauty that immo-bilized him, or was it her chilly stare?

"Would you like two cups of lemonade?"

"One will do. Uh, do you need help? I mean, with serving?" He worked his way around the table until he stood at her side. Was this a good time to apologize for throwing her into the pond?

She studied his face with puzzled eyes. "No, but you could offer to fetch more lemonade. Mrs. Schoengard and my mother are mixing more at the par-sonage. We spent half the day squeezing lemons. I never want to do that again. Caroline Schoengard, you know, the pastor's wife?" she added in answer to his blank look.

"Oh. Yes. Are you having a nice time?"

"It's all right. Far more people showed up than were expected. Poor Mrs. Schoengard was distraught until Mama offered to help. Will you get the lemon-ade for me? This bowl is nearly empty."

"Right away." He thought he heard Marva call his name as he stepped out the back door, but he pretended not to hear. What a joy this evening would be if he could spend it at Beulah's side! How he longed to partner her at games, to share casual conversation and develop a friendship, to have talk circulate town that Myles Trent was sparking Beulah Fairfield.

Violet met him at the parsonage door. "Why, Myles, how nice to see you!"

He doffed his hat. "Beulah sent me to help. Is the lemonade ready? Her bowl is empty."

"Wonderful! Caroline," Violet called back over her shoulder, "people are drinking the lemonade even without ice."

"I haven't heard any complaints," Myles said. "Lemonade is a treat. Just right to wash down the sandwiches and fried chicken."

"Hello, Myles." The pastor's wife appeared in the kitchen doorway, wiping her hands on a towel. "A Chicago friend of my husband shipped the lemons to us. Wasn't that kind? Far more than our family could use." A lock of blond hair clung to Caroline's forehead.

"You must get off your feet for a while, Caroline," Violet fussed over her pregnant friend.

"I'm fine." Caroline ignored her and led Myles to the kitchen. "Thank you for the help, Myles. We were about to send for someone to carry this kettle."

Myles wrapped his arms beneath the kettle's handles and lifted. Lemonade sloshed against his chest. Violet gasped. "I knew we should have put it into smaller containers. I'm sorry, Myles. That thing is so heavy—"

"It's all right. If you'll open the door. . ." Myles walked through the house, across the dark churchyard, and up the church steps. Violet and Caroline called further thanks after him, but he was concentrating too hard to reply.

Beulah backed away from the serving table while Myles emptied his kettle into the cut glass punch bowl. Only a few drops trickled down the kettle's side to dampen the tablecloth. Several gray seeds swirled at the bottom of the bowl. "There." Myles set the kettle on the floor and brushed at his shirt. Already he felt sticky.

"You've spilled lemonade all down the front of you; but then, you've probably noticed," Beulah remarked.

"I couldn't help it. Did pretty well coming all that way with a full kettle."

Beulah picked up a napkin and rubbed at his spotted sleeve. "Yes, you did. Thank you, Myles." Her gaze moved past him. "Marva is looking for you."

He cast a hunted glance over one shoulder. "Guess I'd better run. If she asks, tell her I got covered in lemonade and decided to go home."

"You mean, for good?" Beulah's eyes were no longer icy. Her hand touched his forearm. What was it about her mouth that made him think of kissing every time she spoke to him? "Won't you come back?"

Myles placed his other hand over hers and squeezed. "By the time I came back, the party would be about over. It's all right. I'm no socialite anyway. Never have been."

Someone asked for a cup of lemonade. Beulah poured it with shaking hands while Myles admired the downy curve of her neck. The pastor stood up to announce the start of the spelling match, and the milling crowd began to shuffle.

"If you leave, how will Marva get home?" Beulah asked beneath the buzz of conversation. He bent to listen, and her breath tickled his ear. His hand cupped her elbow. Did he imagine it, or did she lean toward him?

"The same way she came, I guess. Why?"

Beulah bit her lip, studying his face. Myles swallowed hard. Suddenly she bent over the table to wipe up a spill. Her voice quivered. "People never will learn to clean up after themselves. Thank you for your help tonight."

"My pleasure. And Beulah. . ." His courage expired.

"Yes?" She looked up for an instant, then dropped her gaze and licked her lips.

"Miss Beulah, may I have some lemonade?" Across the table, a little girl smiled up at Beulah, revealing a wide gap between her teeth.

"Certainly! Looks like you've lost another tooth, Fern. Are you competing in the spelling bee tonight?"

"Of course, Miss Beulah. You sure do look pretty. Wish I could put my hair up."

"It won't be too many years until you can. And thank you."

Beulah filled another cup. "You were saying, Myles?" She took hold of his wrist and pulled his hand away from his stomach. He hadn't even realized he was rubbing it again.

Heat rushed into his face. "Nothing important. I'll see you around." He didn't want to sound like an echo of little Fern. Beulah wasn't just pretty, she was beautiful tonight with her gleaming knot of dark hair, satin skin, full red lips, and those eyes that took his breath away. . .but he had no idea how to tell her so without sounding foolish.

She faced him. "Oh. Well, good night." Her lips puckered, suspiciously resembling a pout. A fire kindled in Myles's belly, and his hands closed into fists. The intent to drag her outside and bare his soul, come what may, began to form in his mind.

"Ready for the spelling bee, Beulah?" Al asked, sliding behind the table to join them. "Hey, good to see you here, Myles! I saw Marva a minute ago. Better start making your move; you know, like we talked about." He gave Myles a wink and an elbow to the ribs.

"Oh. Yeah," Myles said.

"Myles is just leaving," Beulah said in a voice like ice cracking. She linked arms with Al. "I've been looking forward to this all day," she cooed, gazing up with limpid eyes.

Al blinked in surprise, then grinned. "Me, too!"

Myles stared, his fists tightening.

"Don't stand there like a stone statue, Myles; go find Marva," Al advised.

"You and I have the prettiest gals in town."

Myles skulked out the back door, his heart dragging in the dust. He vaulted to his mare's back and wheeled her toward the street.

"Leaving already, Myles?"

"Sheriff Boz? What are you doing out here?" He reined Cholla to a halt. She champed her bit and pawed at the gravel road.

"Patrolling the town. It's my job."

"Miss Amelia turned you down," he guessed. "I saw her with that New York man tonight."

Boz hooked his thumbs in his sagging gun belt. "Marva turn you down?"

"I've never asked her anything," he grumbled. "Better luck next time, Boz."

"Nothing to do with luck. I been praying for a good wife, and Amelia's the one God showed me." He rubbed his chin. "It'll just take time to convince her."

∽✸∾

"But, Beulah, you promised to be my partner!"

"I told you, I've got a headache. Ask Eunice; she's good at charades." Beulah slumped into a chair behind the serving table and rubbed her temples. "You already won the spelling competition. Isn't that enough?"

Al propped big fists on his hips. "How can a headache come on that fast?"

She shot him a sour look. "You expect me to explain a headache? It's all this noise, and I can hardly breathe."

He folded his arms across his chest and stared down at her. "I'd be happy to take you outside. Beulah, the games won't be any fun if you don't play. I'll sit with you until you feel better."

"No! Please leave me alone. I think I'll go over to the parsonage and ask Mrs. Schoengard if I can lie down."

Al helped her to her feet. "I'll walk you there."

He was so considerate that Beulah could not be as uncivil as she felt. As they passed the line of tethered horses and buggies, she looked for Myles's spotted mare. Cholla was gone. "Does Myles really plan to court Marva?" The question could not be restrained.

"I guess so. I. . ." Al gave her a sideward glance. "Why?"

"I wondered why he left so abruptly right after you advised him to 'make his move.'"

One side of Al's mouth twitched. "No matter what the man says, I think he's afraid of women. He's all right with girls like you and Eunice, but a real woman scares him speechless. Maybe I'll give him more advice and see if I can help."

Beulah reared back. "Albert Moore, I'm eighteen now, and I'll have you know that I'm just as much a woman as Marva Obermeier is!"

"Don't you think I know you're a woman? Beulah, that's what I've been trying to talk with you about these past few weeks, but you'll never give me a chance." On the parsonage steps, Al pulled her to a halt and gripped her shoulders.

Beulah flung his hands off. "That was a cruel thing to say, Al," she raged. "Myles doesn't see me as a little girl, even if you do! Leave me alone. I don't want to talk to you tonight."

The door swung open. Violet appeared, pulling on her gloves. "Is the party over? I was just heading that way—Beulah?" She stepped back as Beulah rushed into the house, gripping her head between her hands.

Chapter 6

Casting all your care upon him; for he careth for you.
1 PETER 5:7

Beulah was in her kitchen garden picking yet another batch of green beans for supper when Al caught up with her late the following afternoon. "I did it." He slapped a pair of leather gloves against his thigh.

"Did what?" Beulah asked coldly, adding two more beans to her basket.

"I finally told Cousin Buck about my mother's letter and my plan to go to California. He's disappointed in me for 'running out on my responsibilities,' as he phrases it. But, Beulah, when *will* be a good time to go back? My parents will die of old age before it's ever a convenient time."

"It is a difficult situation for you," Beulah agreed, trying to forget her grudge and be courteous. "I imagine Papa will calm down and begin to see your side of the situation. Presently he is thinking only of the work involved for him in keeping two farms running. Do you think you might sell off stock?"

"Our Jerseys? Never! We've worked years to build up our herd. Now that we have a silo for storing feed, we can keep our cows producing milk over the winter. This is not the time to cut back."

"But if there is no one to milk the herd, I can't see—"

"Myles will be here to milk them. Now that the creamery has opened, our farms should start pulling a profit instead of barely keeping us out of debt."

"Then this is poor timing for you to leave your farm, Al. It sounds to me as if you need to make serious choices about which is more important to you, your farm or seeing your parents."

"Nonsense," Al said. "After we bring in the crops, one man can keep the farm going over the winter. There's no reason Myles can't keep things rolling until my return. He should be pleased to have a steady job. During the past few winters he's had to cut ice blocks on the lakes or work up north in the logging towns to support himself."

Beulah turned back to her beans. "Papa Obie says Myles has worked hard for three summers and has little to show for it. Papa thinks you and he ought to grant Myles some land to start up his own farm, or at least give him a partnership. I heard him talking about it with Mama." There was a buoyant feeling in her chest when she spoke Myles's name.

A line appeared between Al's thick brows. "I don't like that partnership idea. Myles is a good fellow, hardworking and honest, but the Bible says we should not be unequally yoked together with unbelievers."

"Myles is not a believer?" Her voice was dull, giving no evidence that an ice pick stabbed at her heart.

Al lifted a significant brow. "Buck hopes that in time God will reach Myles's heart, but I haven't seen any change." He reached over to pick himself a ripe tomato. "If Myles wants land of his own, he should homestead somewhere. There is plenty of land for the taking in this country if a man has the ambition to find it for himself. Why should I give him any of mine?"

"I thought you wanted him to stay here and milk your cows. He can hardly homestead for himself while he's doing your work." *Myles cannot leave, not ever!*

"True," Al admitted. "But he has plenty of time; he's not old." He tossed and caught the tomato with one hand.

"You're younger than Myles," Beulah observed.

"Why are you so interested in Myles Trent?" The tomato slipped from his hand and smashed into the dirt. "First last night, and now today."

"What are you talking about?" Her cheeks flamed, but perhaps Al would not see. "I simply think your attitude is selfish. Kindly stop destroying my produce."

For a moment she heard only puffing noises as Al struggled to restrain hasty words. When he spoke again, his voice was humble. "I'm sorry I said that about Myles; he's a good fellow. Beulah, please. . .I didn't come here to argue. I need to talk with you. It's important."

"Al, I've got to go make supper; I've taken far too long picking these beans. Mama must be wondering if I ever plan to come back inside." She moved along the row of vegetables toward the house.

His mouth dropped open. "But, Beulah—" He started trotting along the outside edge of the garden to intercept her. "Honey, I tried to talk with you last night and you put me off. We can't go on like this! I've got something important to ask. Don't you want to hear?"

"Some other time, Al. I'll see you later." With an insincere smile, she darted up the steps.

Staring after her openmouthed, Al suddenly flung his hat to the ground and let out a roar. "That cuts it! I'm not even sure I want to marry you anymore, you. . . you. . .*woman!*"

∞

"So when are you getting married?" Eunice asked, plopping down on Beulah's bed.

"What?" Beulah stopped brushing her hair and stared at her sister.

"Didn't Al ask you to marry him?"

"Whatever gave you that idea? Do you want me to marry Al?"

"If you marry him, he can't go away." Eunice wrapped her arms around her knees and flung her head forward. Her brown hair, several shades lighter than Beulah's, draped over her knees and arms, hiding her face.

Beulah began to braid her hair. "I don't want to marry Al, Eunice." Red-rimmed eyes gazed from the mirror. Lack of sleep was catching up with her.

The girl's head popped up. She stared at Beulah between wavy locks. "That's silly. Everyone knows you're in love with Al. He's been courting you almost since we arrived in Wisconsin."

"I'm not in love with Al, and I don't want him to court me."

Eunice tossed her hair back. Anger sparked in her ice-blue eyes. "You're afraid to go to California, aren't you? I wouldn't be afraid. I'd go anywhere with Al."

"Then you marry him." Beulah smacked her brush down on the dressing table and rose. Her nightdress fluttered around her legs as she paced across the room. "I don't want to marry Al whether he goes or stays, Eunice. He is not the man I love." She rubbed her hands up and down her bare arms. What had happened to her gentle little sister? What had happened to the entire world? Everything seemed strange and mixed-up.

"Then who is? I can't imagine anyone nicer or handsomer than Al. You haven't got a heart, Beulah. I don't think you'll ever get married."

Beulah swallowed the lump in her throat. "I would rather be an old maid than marry a man I don't love. What has gotten into you, Eunice? This isn't like you."

Biting her lips, Eunice sprang from the bed and rushed out of the room. Beulah heard the girl's feet thumping along the hallway.

Beulah lay in bed, staring toward the ceiling. *It's not as if I've never bickered with Eunice before, but this fight was different. What is wrong with me? Why do I hurt so much inside?*

There was a quiet knock at the door. "Come in."

Light streamed from the candlestick in Violet's hand as she peeked into the room. "I've just come from Eunice's room, and she told me of your quarrel. Beulah, do you need to talk?"

Beulah nodded, and a shuddering sob escaped. Rolling over, she buried her face in her pillow and cried out her misery. Warm hands rubbed her shoulders and stroked her hair.

At last Beulah turned back, mopping her face with a handkerchief. "Oh, Mama, I'm so unhappy."

"I know. Papa and I have been concerned about you."

"I don't know what to do."

"Tell me."

Beulah blew her nose and propped up on one elbow. She thought for a moment. "I don't know where to begin."

"Why not begin with what hurts?"

Beulah bit her lip. "I'm in love, Mama. . .and oh, it hurts so much! He sees me as just a girl—at least, Al says he does. And I think he doesn't respect me anymore because I touched him too much. And Al says he isn't a believer—but I can't believe he could be so nice and good if he isn't."

Violet frowned. "That cannot be true. Al has always proclaimed his faith in Christ, and we have no reason to doubt him."

"Yes, but he says Myles isn't. Mama, do you think he really wants to marry Miss Obermeier?"

Her mother blinked. "Beulah, do you mean to say you're in love with...Myles Trent?"

Beulah nodded.

"Oh, my!" Violet's shoulders drooped. "I had no idea. Papa told me..."

"Told you what? Don't you like Myles, Mama?"

"Of course I like him. He's a good man. Obie thinks highly of him. It's just that..." She couldn't seem to put her thoughts into words.

"He's only about twenty-five, and I'm eighteen now. Oh, Mama, just looking at him sets my soul on fire! I know he isn't handsome like Al, but he's so...so..."

Violet sighed. "I understand. He has the same masculine appeal as your papa. It's something about these cowboys, I guess. What did you mean by 'touched him too much,' Beulah?" Her voice sharpened.

Beulah studied her wadded handkerchief and confessed the waterfall story. "He didn't kiss me or anything, Mama, but I wanted him to." Her eyes closed. "Mama, he's so strong and gentle! It was the most wondrous moment of my life... and the worst. I can't help thinking about him all the time and wishing he would hold me again."

Violet brushed a hand across her eyes. "Oh, dear. I had no idea... What kind of mother am I to let this go on under my nose?" Her hand dropped to her lap, and her shoulders squared. "Darling, you know that Myles has told your papa little about his past. It's not that we don't like him, but I fear he may be hiding from the law—you know, under a false name."

Beulah bolted upright. "Mama, how can you say such a thing? Myles has always been honest. Papa and Al trust him. And he is so polite. I know he has an air about him—sort of mysterious and dangerous, I guess—but that doesn't mean he is a criminal!"

The line between Violet's brows deepened. "I don't mean to accuse him, dearest, but we cannot be too careful with our daughters. You are a beautiful young woman, and it sounds to me as if you tempted Myles almost beyond his strength to resist. If he does intend to marry Marva—which would perhaps be best for all concerned—you need to leave him alone."

"Mama, how can you say it would be best for him to marry Marva? I told you that I love him!" Beulah caught her breath on a sob.

Violet stood up and began to pace across the room. "But, Beulah, what about Al? Eunice tells me that you don't want to marry him, but, darling, he is steady and dependable—he's your friend, and he loves you. I can't help thinking...Well, to be perfectly candid, my dear, you have a tendency to be contrary. Are you certain you're not deciding against Al simply because everyone expects you to marry him?"

Beulah wrapped her arms around her knees and glowered. "Mama, Al is my friend, but he is more like an irritating brother than a lover. When we first met he treated me like fine china; then he got used to me and started acting like himself, and, honestly, Mama, he is so immature and annoying! I can think of few prospects worse than facing Al across the breakfast table every morning for the rest of my life."

Violet stared, shaking her head. "Oh, dear," she repeated. "I must talk with Obie. We may have to let Myles go...and that would be difficult, what with Al leaving for California soon. How could we find a replacement?"

Beulah scrambled to her knees, clasped her hands, and begged. "Mama, please don't send him away! He has done nothing wrong—it was entirely my fault!" She thumped a fist into her quilt. "And why shouldn't I marry him if I love him? Even if he sinned in the past, he is an honest man now, and he would be a good husband to me."

Violet seemed to wilt. "Beulah, how can you even consider marrying a man who does not love and serve God? I knew you had strayed from the Lord these past few years, but I thought you understood how vital shared faith is to a marriage."

Beulah sat back on her heels and hung her head. "You won't even give Myles a chance, will you, Mama? How can you be so sure he isn't a believer? He doesn't drink or swear or gamble, and there is goodness in his eyes." Resting her head upon her knees, she began to cry again.

Violet sat down and stroked the girl's long braid. "Beulah, I do want to give Myles a chance—he is a fine young man, and I can see why you admire him. I will ask your papa to talk with him about his faith and about his intentions toward you. But in the meantime, I think it would be best if you spent more time with your girlfriends and stayed away from Myles Trent. Not that we will ban him from the house, but..."

"Do you mean I have to hide if I see him coming?"

"I simply don't want you to seek him out, dearest. If he approaches you, be gracious, of course, as I have taught you. Darling, I will be praying for wisdom and guidance—for your papa and me as well as for you."

She bent to kiss Beulah's damp cheek.

Chapter 7

Let nothing be done through strife or vainglory;
but in lowliness of mind let each esteem other
better than themselves.
PHILIPPIANS 2:3

Thank you for coming, Mrs. Watson. And thank you for bringing Beulah. Maybe soon we'll be working on her wedding quilt." Sybil Oakley waved good-bye from her front porch as Violet clucked her gray mare into a quick trot.

Beulah waved to her friend until trees hid the girl from sight. "It's hard to believe Sybil is getting married." Beulah sighed.

"She has grown up quickly this past year. You know, many women would have flown into a temper if you'd pointed out flaws in their quilts. Sybil accepted your criticism graciously."

Beulah fanned herself. "I wasn't trying to be unkind."

"Neither were you trying to be kind. Darling, you must learn to think before you speak, or you'll chase away all your friends. You're gifted in many ways: beauty, talent, and intelligence. You don't need to point out other people's faults to make yourself look better."

Beulah was silent. The mare's hoofs clopped along the road, sloshing in occasional puddles. Maple and birch trees were beginning to show patches of yellow and red.

"I'm sorry, Mama. I'll apologize to Sybil next time I see her." Her voice was quiet.

"I've noticed that Al doesn't talk to you when he comes over. Did you quarrel with him, too?"

Beulah braced herself for a pothole in the road. "Not exactly. I think he's mad because I won't let him talk mushy to me. He tries to get romantic, and it makes me uncomfortable. He is my friend, and that's it."

"Have you told him how you feel?"

She wrinkled her nose. "No, but if he doesn't catch on by now, he's dumber than I think."

"Don't be unkind," Violet said. "You haven't told him about your infatuation with Myles, have you?"

"Mama, of course not! It's none of his business—and besides, I don't want to make him mad at Myles. I haven't seen Myles since the church social." Beulah felt glum.

"I did hear that he had dinner with the Obermeiers the other night. I hope he settles down with Marva. She needs a good man to love and spoil."

Beulah closed her eyes against a stab of jealousy.

∽∾∾∾

Singing to herself, Beulah wiped off the table. There was a quiet knock at the open kitchen door behind her. "Samuel is outside. He can play until dark," she called.

"Beulah?"

She spun around, putting a sudsy hand to her heart. "Myles?" It came out in a squeak. "I—I thought you were one of Sam's friends come to play. Papa Obie and Mama are at Cyrus Thwaite's house this evening, and Eunice is at a friend's house. It's just the boys and me at home," she babbled. "And the baby is asleep. I haven't seen you in weeks! Did you need to see my papa?"

Behind him, the sky was pink and filmy gray. A bat darted above the fruit trees, and a fox yapped in the forest. "No. I came to see you. I brought this." He held out a book. "Found it in Mo's pasture this morning. You dropped it that day, didn't you?"

That day—only the most important day of Beulah's life. Feeling conscious of her bare feet and loose braid, Beulah wiped her hands on her apron and reached for the book. "Thank you." It smelled warm, like sunshine and wildflowers. The cover was warped, and the pages looked wavy.

"It got wet."

"I can still read it." She looked up.

What would Mama do? Shoulders back. Head high. Cool, even tones. Gracious and hospitable. "Will you come in for coffee and cookies?"

His boots shifted on the floorboards. "First I need to. . .to apologize for throwing you in the creek. That's been weighing on my mind. You were right to be angry—my behavior was inexcusable."

Beulah watched his right hand rub circles on his flat stomach. Why did he always do that? It made her want to touch him. *I can't love a man who doesn't serve God. I can't! Gracious and hospitable, that's all.*

"I forgive you. It was my fault, too. I threw water at you first."

"No hard feelings?"

She glanced up. The entreating look in his eyes reminded her of Samuel. "Would I ask a man to carry lemonade for me if I held a grudge against him?"

Myles smiled. "Guess not. Or maybe you knew I'd spill it all over myself and wanted to get back some of your own."

Beulah opened her mouth to protest, but Myles laughed. "I'm teasing. You're easy to provoke."

Warmth filled Beulah's heart and her cheeks. "So they say. I'm trying to improve. I wish you would smile and laugh more often. Your laugh makes me want

186

to laugh. Now will you come in for coffee and cookies?"

His eyes twinkled. "Thank you. I will."

She lowered her chin and one brow. "What's so funny?"

"You. I'm glad you're back to normal. Those elegant manners make me nervous."

Beulah laughed outright. Forgetting her resolve to be aloof, she grabbed him by a shirt button and dragged him into the kitchen. Planting a hand on his chest, she shoved him into a chair. "Sit. Stay."

He seized her wrist in a lightning motion. "Bossy woman. If you request, I am your humble servant. If you order. . ." He shook his head. "Another dunk in the creek might be imminent."

"You use awfully big words for a hired hand." Beulah tugged at her arm. "Is that a threat?"

"A warning."

"I guess your apology wasn't genuine." She pouted, thinking how nice it would be to slip into his lap. He smelled of soap and hair oil. "Don't you want to be friends?"

Pressure on her arm brought her closer. "Is that what you want from me?" The low question set her heart hammering. His face was mere inches from hers. Beulah licked her lips.

Scrabbling claws skidded across the floorboards; then Watchful shoved her face and upper body between Beulah and Myles. Panting and wagging, the dog pawed at Myles's chest.

He released Beulah to protect his skin from Watchful's claws. "Down, girl. I'm glad to see you, too." He forced the dog to the floor, then thumped her sides affectionately. Glancing toward the door, he said, "Hello, Sam."

Samuel stamped his boots on the porch, tossed his hat on a hook, and flopped into a chair. "Howdy, Myles. You come for cookies?"

"Just trying to sweet-talk your sister into giving me some. See if you can influence her."

Beulah propped her fists on her hips. "Not necessary. Samuel, you wash your hands first and bring in the milk, please." She moved to the stove and poured two cups of coffee.

The boy made a face at her back but obeyed.

"Bossy, isn't she?" Myles observed.

"You said it!" Samuel pumped water over his soapy hands, then ran outside to the springhouse.

Beulah's spine stiffened. She set a steaming cup in front of Myles. "Sugar? Milk?"

"Black is fine."

She felt his gaze while she took cookies from the crock and arranged them on a plate. "I'm not bossy," she hissed.

"Do you prefer 'imperious'?" His eyes crinkled at the corners. "You're rewarding to tease, and you somehow manage to be pretty when you're cross. Unfair to the male of the species, since you seem to be cross much of the time. I have observed, however, that your smile is to your frown what a clear sunrise is to a misty morning. Each wields its charm, yet one is far more appealing than the other."

Confounded by this speech, Beulah settled across from him. She was pondering an answer when Samuel clattered up the steps, carrying the milk. "Save some for me," he protested, seeing Myles pop an entire cookie into his mouth.

Still chewing, Myles wrapped his forearms around the plate of cookies and gave Samuel a provoking smile. "Mine."

Samuel pitched into him. Myles caught the boy's arms and held him off easily, but Samuel was a determined opponent. Beulah watched helplessly as they wrestled at the table. She rescued Myles's coffee just in time. "Boys, behave yourselves!"

The chair tipped over, and Myles landed on the floor, laughing. "Truce," he gasped. "I'll share."

Samuel was equally breathless and merry. "I beat you," he claimed. He thumped Myles in the stomach, and the man's knees came up with a jerk.

"Samuel! Don't be mean!" Beulah jumped to her feet. "Are you all right, Myles?"

Samuel gave her a scornful glare. "Don't be silly. I couldn't hurt him."

Myles sat up, resting an arm on his upended chair. "Aw, let her protect me if she wants to. I like it." Rubbing his belly, he smiled up at Beulah, and she felt her face grow warm.

Myles and Samuel talked baseball and fishing while they finished off the cookies. Sipping her coffee, Beulah listened, watching their animated faces and smiling at their quips and gibes.

"So where's Al?" Samuel looked at Beulah, then at Myles.

Beulah collected the empty dishes and carried them to the sink. Leaning back in the chair with an ankle resting on his knee, Myles stroked his beard. "Reckon he's at home."

"Why didn't he come with you?"

"He didn't know I was coming."

"He was here last night," Samuel said. "Eunice and I played marbles with him. Do you want to come play catch with me tomorrow?"

"Just might do that. Better enjoy free time while we have it. Harvest starts in a few days, and from then on, we work like slaves." Myles rose and stretched his arms. "Guess I'd better get on back."

"Bye, Myles." Samuel left the room without ceremony.

Taking his hat from the table, Myles twisted it between his hands. "Thank you for the cookies and the good company, Beulah. Can't remember when I've had a nicer evening."

"I can't either." Beulah clasped her hands behind her. "I'm glad you came over." She backed away, giving him room to pass.

His eyes searched her face. "So am I." He clapped on his hat and disappeared into the night.

Chapter 8

He healeth the broken in heart,
and bindeth up their wounds.
PSALM 147:3

Rapid footfalls approached the main barn from outside. "Myles? Al? Is anyone here?" Beulah called.

"I'm here," Myles answered. He set aside the broken stall door and rose, brushing wood shavings from his hands. "Al is out. Do you need him?"

Beulah stopped in the barn doorway, eyes wide, chest heaving. "I...well..." She hopped from one foot to the other, her gaze shifting about the barn. "Oh, what can it hurt? I need your help! Please come quickly, Myles."

"Are you ill? Hurt? Come, sit down here." He indicated the bench.

"No, no, I need help," she panted. "I found a cat caught by a fishhook down near the beaver dam. Do you have something I can use to cut it loose?"

A cat? Myles put his hammer into his neat toolbox and selected a pair of pliers. After plucking his hat from a hook on the barn wall, he pulled it low over his forehead. "Lead on."

"I hope I can find the cat again." Beulah was beginning to catch her breath. Her bound braid hung cockeyed on the side of her head; her sunbonnet lay upon her shoulders.

"We'll find it." He followed her outside into blinding sunlight.

She pulled her sunbonnet back into place and retied the strings. "Do you like cats? I've never been fond of them, but this one purred when I touched it. Even if it hissed at me, I still couldn't leave it to die. Could you?"

"Of course not." Myles frowned, seized by a premonition.

When they entered the forest Beulah took the lead. Myles followed her slim form through the trees, keeping close behind her. He heard the cat wailing before they crossed the dam.

"Lucky you heard her instead of some hungry animal." Myles pulled aside branches. Sure enough, there was a familiar round face with the white blotch on the nose. Sorrow and horror formed a lump in his throat. "Hello, girl. How long have you been here?" He snipped away a tangle of line until only a short piece dangled from the cat's mouth. Slipping one hand beneath her, he lifted Pushy free of the brush and cradled her in his arms. That rumbling purr sounded again, and the cat closed her golden eyes. Myles rubbed behind her ear with one finger, and she pushed her head into his chest. Dried blood caked the white bib beneath the cat's swollen chin. She made a little chirruping noise, her usual greeting.

He felt movement within her body, and the lump in his throat grew, making it difficult to speak. "I think she's expecting kittens."

"Really?" Beulah breathed out the word. "Can you help her, Myles?" She stroked the cat's side, then let her hand rest on Myles's arm.

"I'll try. Let's take her home."

Back in the barn's tack room, he dug with one hand through a box of medical supplies until he found a bottle of ointment. "Please find a blanket to wrap her in."

Beulah returned empty-handed. "The only blankets I can find are stiff with horse sweat and covered in hair. Will my apron do?" she asked, untying it.

He wrapped the cat in Beulah's calico apron, securing its legs against its body so that it could neither scratch nor squirm. Pushy let out a protesting howl, but relaxed and began to purr when he rubbed her head.

Beulah looked amazed. "This is the friendliest cat I have ever seen!"

Myles gave her a quick smile. "She's a special one. She won't stay wrapped up long, so we've got to work quickly. You hold her head up and her body down while I cut off the end of the hook."

Beulah did as she was told and watched him work. The cat struggled when Myles had to dig for the hook's barb, which protruded beneath her chin. Then *snip* and the barb fell upon Beulah's apron.

"Now we must hold her mouth open so I can slip out the rest of the hook." Myles demonstrated how he wanted Beulah to hold the cat under her arm. Once she had the cat in the right position, he pried its mouth open and struggled to grip the hook with the pliers. Pushy squirmed, gagged, and growled. Myles heard claws shredding Beulah's apron. His hat landed upside down on the floor.

"Got it." Myles held aloft the bit of wire and string. "Better get cotton over that wound before. . ."

Too late. Blood and pus oozed from the wound and dripped upon Beulah's lap. Myles snatched a cotton pad from the worktable and pressed it against the cat's chin. "Sorry about that."

Beulah said nothing. Her eyes were closed.

"Beulah? You. . .uh, might want to clean your dress there." He dropped cotton wool on the spot.

"I–I'm not very good around blood," she whispered.

Myles snatched the cat from her lap and pushed Beulah's head down toward her knees. "Lower your head until the faintness passes."

The apron dropped to the floor. Pushy struggled, trying to right herself. Her claws raked across his chest. "Yeow!" Myles tucked her under his arm, and she relaxed. "Stupid cat."

"Do you think she will live?" Beulah's voice was muffled.

"I hope so. Although I'm sorry about your dress, it's a good thing all that mess came out of her jaw. I'll put ointment on her face and hope her body can heal what we can't help."

"I've been praying for her." Beulah lifted her head. Her face had regained color. She took the jar of ointment and removed the lid.

"Have you? Good."

"Do you believe in God, Myles?" Beulah held out the jar.

"I believe there is a God."

She smiled. "I thought you must. Al said you weren't a believer."

He found it hard to meet her gaze. "Al can't be blamed for that. I guess I've been fighting God. Painful things happened in my past, and I blamed Him." Myles dipped a finger into the ointment. "I've had a lot of talks with Buck—Obie—about God."

"I know who you mean. All of Papa's old friends call him Buck—it's his middle name. So you don't blame God now?"

Myles evaded the question. "It isn't logical to blame God for the evil in the world."

"Feelings are seldom logical," Beulah said.

His hands paused. "True. Which is why it's dangerous to live by one's feelings." Myles held Pushy's head still as he smoothed ointment over her chin. She resumed her cheery purr.

"Pushy here must wonder why I am hurting her, yet she trusts me. This simple cat has greater faith than I do." There was a catch in his voice.

"She is your cat, Myles?"

"She lives in our barn. I named her Pushy because she finds ways to get me to pet her and feed her. I realize now that I hadn't seen her around for days, yet I didn't think to search for her." He fixed his eyes upon Pushy, trying to hide his face from Beulah. She would think he was foolish to become emotional over a cat. Pushy closed her eyes and savored his gentle rubbing.

So lightly that he scarcely felt it, Beulah skimmed his hair with her fingers. "You can't be everywhere and think of everything the way God does, Myles. I'm sure Pushy forgives you. You didn't intend to let her down. It was a human mistake."

"We humans make a lot of mistakes." Bitterness laced his voice.

"My mother says that's why we need to be patient with each other." She sighed. "People can be so annoying, and my first reaction is to say something nasty. My mother says it's because I'm proud and think myself better than other people."

Myles lifted his head until he could feel Beulah's touch. "Do you?"

"Think myself better? Sometimes I do," she said so softly he could hardly hear. Her fingers threaded through his hair. "Deep inside I know I'm not better, though. I don't like being mean."

Her touch made it difficult to concentrate. Myles closed his eyes. "You're being nice to me right now. My grandmother used to rub my head like this."

"You look as if you might start purring." Beulah laughed.

Hearing laughter in her voice, he smiled. "P-d-d-r-r-r. I can't do it like Pushy does."

Pushy climbed from his arms into Beulah's lap, tucked in her paws, and settled down to purr. The two humans paid her no attention. Myles shifted his weight and sat close to Beulah's feet. She put both hands to work, rubbing his temples and the nape of his neck. "I've got chills down my spine, this feels so good," he said, letting his head loll against her hands.

"Your hair ranges in shade from auburn to sandy blond."

"Yeah, but it's still red hair."

"Did you used to get teased about it?"

"My nickname was 'Red.'"

"The clown called you that, I remember."

"Antonio and everyone else at the circus. Wish I had dark hair and skin that didn't freckle."

"Like mine?"

"Yours or Al's."

"I used to get teased about my big teeth and about being skinny." She spoke quietly. "I've never told that to anyone but my mother before."

"It hurts, being teased." He reached back and patted her hand.

After massaging his shoulders for a few minutes, she touched the left side of his chest. "Is this your blood or Pushy's?"

Myles looked down, surprised to see a spot of red on his tan shirt. "Mine, I think. She scratched me."

"You had better put ointment on it," Beulah advised. She held out the jar.

Myles unbuttoned three shirt buttons, then his undervest and glanced inside. "It's nothing." He covered it up.

"Let me see."

"Yes, Mother." Feeling sheepish, he exposed the triple scratch, which was reddened and puffy. "I thought you couldn't bear the sight of blood."

"Turn this way." Beulah leaned over the sleeping cat and wiped a fingerful of ointment into the wound until his chest hair lay smeared and flattened across the scratches. "I've never done this before." She pursed her lips in concentration. Myles tried to swallow, but his mouth was too dry.

She looked up and smiled. "There, that should feel better soon." The smile faded. "Did I hurt you? I tried to be gentle. Those scratches are deep."

"Uh. . .Pushy needs a drink." His voice sounded like gravel in a bucket. "I'll fetch milk from the springhouse." Myles scrambled to his feet and rushed from the barn, shaking his head to clear it. The temptation to haul Beulah into his lap and kiss her had nearly overcome his self-control.

He lifted the bottle of milk from its cold storage in the little man-made pool. Conflicting thoughts raced through his mind.

She doesn't know. She thinks I'm a Christian man like Buck and Al. If she knew me, really knew me, would she trust me, touch me with her dear hands? Myles shook his head, teeth bared in a grimace. *Antonio said I'm poison—full of bitterness and hatred. I would destroy her, the one I love. God, help me! I don't know what to do!*

He rubbed his face with a trembling hand. *Yes, I do know what I should do. If I were an honorable man, I would tell her to leave me alone, tell her to marry Al and be happy.*

When he returned to the barn, Beulah still sat on the bench with Pushy in her lap. The girl's eyes were enormous in her dirty face, and she was chewing on her lower lip. She opened her mouth, but Myles spoke first. "Sorry I took so long. Let's see if Pushy can drink this."

"She's asleep."

"I imagine she'll wake when she smells the milk. Set her on the floor here." He filled the chipped saucer.

Myles was right. Pushy was desperate for the drink, yet she could not lap with her swollen tongue. She sucked up the milk, making pained little cries all the while.

"I thought you were angry with me when you rushed outside," Beulah said.

"Why would I be angry?" Myles kept his eyes upon the cat.

"I shouldn't have touched you like that; you won't respect me anymore."

He let out an incredulous little huff, smiling without real humor. "Won't respect you? That's unlikely." He stared at a pitchfork, unwilling to grant her access to his chaotic thoughts. *Do you know what your touch does to me? Do you dream about me the way I dream about you? Could you be content, married to a wretched, redheaded hired man? What would you think if you knew my past?*

"Does your stomach hurt?"

Myles snatched his hand from his belly.

"Eunice says you must be hungry a lot because you rub your belly so much."

He felt warm. "Nervous habit."

After several saucers of milk, Pushy made an effort to groom. As soon as she lifted her paw to her mouth she remembered the impossibility of using her tongue, but she wiped the paw over her ear anyway.

"Do you think her kittens will live?"

"I felt one moving while I held her. Unless she eats, she will not have milk enough for them." Squatting, Myles rubbed the back of the cat's neck with one finger, and the purr began to rumble. "I'll chop some meat for her tonight. It will have to be soft and wet. I'll keep her in my room until she is well. Poor Pushy. I think she has wanted to be my pet all this time, but I was too busy to notice how special she is."

"You *are* too busy. I hardly ever see you. I wish you would come by for coffee again some evening. My parents wouldn't mind." Beulah rose and shook out her rumpled apron. "I think even I would enjoy having a cat like this one. She's special."

Rising, Myles watched her fold the stained garment. She looked smaller without that voluminous apron. Her simple calico gown complemented her pretty figure. The sunbonnet hung down her back.

The ache in his soul was more than he could endure. *I'm not an honorable man. Al can't have her! I want Beulah for my wife. Whatever it takes, God. Whatever it takes.*

"Would you like to own Pushy?"

"I'm sure she will be happiest here with you." Beulah smiled. "I don't think my mother would want a cat. We already have one animal in the house, and that is enough. I had better be going home now. No one knows where I am. Take care of Pushy, Myles. . .and thank you for coming to her rescue. You may think I'm bossy, but I think you're wonderful!" Rising on tiptoe, she kissed his face above his beard.

He slipped his arms around that slim waist and pulled her close. Her face rested within the open vee of his shirt; her breath heated his skin.

"Why did you do that?" Myles asked gruffly, his cheek pressed against her head.

"I saw my mother kiss Papa Obie that way not long after we met him." She sounded defensive. "She told me she did it to demonstrate gratitude for his kindness."

"No wonder Buck is besotted with your mother." Eyes closed tight, he spoke into her hair.

"I was trying to show affection." Beulah's arms wriggled free and slid around his waist. "Now I understand why Mama likes it when Papa holds her. It's nice."

When her hands pressed against his back, he released her and stepped away. "Come. I will walk with you as far as the dam."

Beulah looked shaken. Myles could think of nothing to say, so they walked in silence.

"Did I shock you?" she asked meekly.

"No."

Beulah had been walking ahead of him on the narrow path, but now she stopped to face him. "I wish I knew what you were thinking. Sometimes I feel as if you are laughing at me on the inside. I must seem young and naive to you."

"Believe me, I'm not laughing," he said. "Do I seem old and dried up to you?"

"Of course not, but you never seem happy. Even when you smile and laugh, there is sadness in your eyes." She tipped her head to one side and searched his face. "Do you ever wish you could talk with someone about. . .about things?

I don't think I really know you, Myles. You're like a carrot—most of you is underground."

His lips twitched at her choice of analogy. Fear of overwhelming her prevented him from revealing even a fraction of his desire to be known and loved. "I'll let you know when the carrot is ready for harvest."

"Now I know you're laughing at me!" Dark eyes accusing yet twinkling, she gave him a little shove and hurried away along the trail. "Good-bye, Myles."

"Beulah?"

She glanced back.

"You can demonstrate gratitude to me anytime you like."

Aghast, she turned and ran into the woods. He chuckled.

Chapter 9

Thou openest thine hand,
and satisfiest the desire of every living thing.
PSALM 145:16

Myles found the Bible in the bottom of an old saddlebag, smelling of mildewed leather. A spider had nested on the binding—years ago from the looks of it. The title page bore his name in his brother's hieroglyphic script: "Myles Van Huysen, from his brother Monte, 1875."

His squared fingertip caressed the page. "Monte." Memories assailed him: A childhood filled with Monte's derogatory name-calling and cruel tricks whenever Gram's back was turned. Years of adolescent jealousy and competition. Then Monte showing up at the circus—mocking, yet for once honest about his feelings and plans.

Myles stared vacantly at the saddlebag. In Monte's final days something had happened to change him, to turn him from his reckless ways. Was it the shock of finding himself a hunted man? Was it the realization that someone wanted to kill him? Myles shook his head. Danger had never fazed Montague Van Huysen.

He recalled faces around the campfire, cowboys of assorted sizes and colors squatting to drink scalding coffee before heading out to keep watch over the herd. Monte had smiled, a genuine smile containing no scorn, when he handed over the brown paper parcel. *"Happy Birthday. The boys gave you a lariat, so I got you something you didn't want. It took me years to stop running from God; hope you're quicker to find Him."*

Now, clutching the Book to his bare chest, Myles closed his eyes. "You were right, Monte. I didn't want it. Nearly tossed it away when I saw what it was. Wish I had. Stupid to carry an old book around with me all these years."

He opened it at random. "Isaiah. Never could make heads or tails of those long-winded prophets." Frowning, he looked at the heavy log beams overhead. "All right, God," he growled, "*if* You exist, explain Yourself to me. Beulah says I'm unhappy. Antonio says I'm carrying a burden of unforgiveness. I don't see how I can be held responsible for the wickedness of other people!"

Rising, Myles began to pace back and forth across the small room, his Bible tucked under one arm, a finger holding his place. "I'm not the one who sinned. First my mother gave up on living and left me to Gram. Then Gram favored Monte and made me work like a slave. Monte never gave me a moment's peace;

then he followed me around the country all those years as if he really cared what became of me. It's his fault he got killed—" A surge of emotion choked Myles's voice. Grimacing, he struggled to hold back tears. Vehemently he swore.

Sorrow and loss were incompatible with his anger at Monte. Myles clenched his fists and screwed up his face. "I hated him, God! Do You hear me? I hated him! I'm not sorry he died." A sob wrenched his body. "I hate him for being such a fool as to get himself killed. I hate him for being an outlaw. I hate him for being so kind to me right before he died, just so I would mourn him!" Tears streamed down his face and moistened his beard.

He climbed onto his bed, taking the Bible with him. Flat on his back with the Book lying open on his chest, he continued, "You tell me to forgive people if I want to be forgiven. Ha! What they did was wrong, God! I can't pretend it wasn't and absolve them from guilt." Self-righteousness colored his voice, yet speaking the words gave him no relief. "They didn't ask to be forgiven. They weren't even sorry. I hope they all burn in hell. What do You think of that?"

He pressed upon his aching stomach and groaned aloud. Antonio's words rang in his head: *"You cannot offer Beulah an unforgiving heart."* Poison. Hatred. The bitterness was eating him alive from within.

"Can You offer me anything better?" he demanded.

If I want God to explain Himself, I'd better read what He has to say. He's not going to talk to me out loud. As if this Book could answer any real questions.

His finger was still holding a place in Isaiah. Myles opened the Book, rolled over, and focused on a page. " 'Ho, every one that thirsteth, come ye to the waters, and he that hath no money; come ye, buy, and eat; yea, come, buy wine and milk without money and without price,'" he read aloud.

How can he that has no money buy something to eat? His soul was thirsty, but this couldn't be speaking about that kind of thirst. Myles read on: " 'Wherefore do ye spend money for that which is not bread? and your labour for that which satisfieth not? hearken diligently unto me, and eat ye that which is good, and let your soul delight itself in fatness.'"

So maybe it really is talking about feeding the soul. I suppose spending "money for that which is not bread" means trying to fill the emptiness inside with meaningless things. Maybe only God can fill that aching void, the hunger and thirst in my soul.

His gaze drifted down the page. " 'Seek ye the LORD while he may be found, call ye upon him while he is near: Let the wicked forsake his way, and the unrighteous man his thoughts: and let him return unto the LORD, and he will have mercy upon him; and to our God, for he will abundantly pardon.'"

Myles stared into space and brooded. Much though he hated to admit it, his hatred and anger were wicked. He was that unrighteous man who harbored evil thoughts. He was in need of pardon.

He read on: " 'For my thoughts are not your thoughts, neither are your ways my ways, saith the LORD. For as the heavens are higher than the earth, so are My ways higher than your ways, and my thoughts than your thoughts.'"

Myles snapped the book shut, eyes wide. A chill ran down his spine. There was his answer: God does not need to explain Himself. Period.

Myles suddenly felt presumptuous. Insignificant. Like dust. He tucked the Book under his bed, blew out the lamp, and lay awake until the early hours of morning.

If Buck Watson was surprised when Myles started asking him questions about scripture, he didn't say so. The two men spoke at irregular intervals, sometimes drawing a simple conversation out over hours.

"There are parts of the Bible I can't understand," Myles said as he raked hay on a newly cut field. He felt small beneath the dome of cloudless blue sky. Trees surrounding the pastures flaunted fall colors, reminding him of the passage of time.

"Such as?" Buck prompted.

The two worked as a team, tossing hay into a wagon. The mule team placidly nibbled on hay stubble. Myles looked at other crews around them, their burned and tanned backs exposed to the autumn sun. "I was always told to obey God's commands and He would take care of me. But the Bible tells many stories about good people who were killed or tortured. I've had bad things happen in my life. Wicked people seem to reign supreme; tornadoes, floods, and droughts come; and God sits back and does nothing. The Bible says God is the Author of good, not of evil. I know He knows everything and doesn't have to explain Himself to us lowly people, but my head still wants to argue the point."

"Man has free will to choose good or evil, and those choices can affect the innocent. The whole earth suffers under the curse of sin, and we all feel its effects. Sometimes God intervenes; sometimes He doesn't."

"But why? If He's all powerful, loving, and holy, why doesn't He prevent evil or crush wicked people?" Myles stabbed too hard, driving his pitchfork into the earth.

Buck considered his answer, brows knitted. "There are things we won't know until we reach eternity. You see, Myles, our faith is based not upon what God does but upon Who He is. God tells us that He is just, loving, merciful. We must take Him at His word and know that He will do what is best. He doesn't explain Himself. He doesn't guarantee prosperity and good health. But He does promise to be with us always, guiding and directing our lives for His purpose. Once you place your faith in Him, you will discover, as I have, that He never fails, never disappoints. He will give you perfect peace if you will accept it." Buck forked hay atop the mound in the wagon bed.

"Peace." Myles studied Buck's face and beheld that perfect peace in action. God's reality in Buck Watson's life could not be denied. There was no other explanation for the man.

Myles lifted his shirttail to wipe his sweating face. Over the course of the day, he had peeled down to an unbuttoned shirt. Buck worked shirtless; his shoulders were tanned like leather beneath his suspender straps. "I do want the kind of peace you have," Myles admitted. "I know I'm a sinner, but I'm not as bad as some people."

"When you stand before God, do you think He will accept the excuse that you weren't as bad as some other guy? What is God's requirement for entrance into heaven?"

"I don't know," Myles grumbled.

"Then I'll tell you: Perfection. No sin. None."

Myles jerked around to face his boss. "But that's impossible. Everybody sins. If that is so, then nobody could go to heaven."

A slow smile curled Buck's mustache. "Exactly. The wages of sin is death, and we are all guilty. Doomed."

Myles shook his head in confusion. "How can you smile about this? You must be wrong."

"No, it's the truth. Look it up for yourself in Romans." Buck's gaze held compassion. "But here is the reason I can smile: God loves us, Myles. He is not willing that any should perish. You see the quandary: God is holy—man is sinful. Sin deserves death—we all deserve death. No one is righteous except God Himself. Do you know John 3:16?"

Myles thought for a moment. "Is that the one about 'God so loved the world'?"

Buck nodded. " 'For God so loved the world, that he gave his only begotten Son, that whosoever believeth in him should not perish, but have everlasting life. For God sent not his Son into the world to condemn the world; but that the world through him might be saved.' "

Myles stared into space. "I think I'm beginning to see. . ."

"I would suggest that you start reading the book of Matthew. Read about Jesus, His life and purpose. He is God in the flesh, come to save us. Ask God to make it clear to you."

Myles climbed atop the pile in the wagon, arranging and packing the hay. His brow wrinkled in thought.

"Jesus died in your place, Myles, so you could go to heaven," Buck shouted up to him. "He loves you."

To Myles's irritation, tears burned his eyes. He turned his back on Buck and worked in silence. His work complete, Myles jumped down and leaned against the wagon wheel. A muscle twitched in his cheek, and his body remained taut. "I still have questions."

Gray eyes regarded him with deep understanding. "Nothing wrong with that. God wants you to come to Him with your questions."

Myles glanced at his friend and drew a deep breath. "Buck, I haven't forgotten your past. I don't know how you continued to trust God all those years, especially while you were in prison through no fault of your own."

"I had my ups and downs," Buck said. "Times of despair, times of joy. But I clung to God's promise to bring good out of my life. Sometimes that promise was the only thing I had left."

"But didn't you hate the men who did it to you? I mean, they're all dead now. You've had your revenge. Although I never understood why you went and tried to lead that rat Houghton to God before he died. I should think you would *want* him to rot in hell!"

Buck stopped working and studied Myles. "Hmm. I see." He rested both hands atop the rake's handle. "I tried hating, Myles. For months, I hated and brooded in that prison, vowing revenge on the lying scum who put me there. Then a friend read me a parable Jesus told about forgiveness; you can find it in the book of Matthew, chapter eighteen. That story changed my life."

Myles grunted. Forgiveness again. He didn't want to hear it.

Buck took a deep breath. "Myles, it comes down to one question: Are you willing to make Jesus your Lord or not?"

Myles stared at a distant haystack and brushed away a persistent fly. There was one thing he could do to make his past right. "I must return to New York."

Buck lifted one brow. "Oh?"

"I'll never have peace until I let my grandmother know where I am and apologize for running away. I can't bring my brother back for her, but I can give her myself. This is something I know God wants me to do." Myles slipped a hand inside his open shirt and scratched his shoulder. "Maybe I should write a letter. If I go back, I might lose everything that's important to me here."

Buck looked into his soul. "Beulah?"

"You know?"

"I'm not blind. Her mother asked me to question your intentions."

Myles swallowed hard. "What about Al?"

"Wrong question. What about Myles? Listen to me, my friend. You can't make your heart right with God. Only Jesus can do that for you."

Myles's head drooped. "I know I'm not good enough for Beulah. A friend told me once that I would poison her with the bitterness in my heart. I've got to work this thing out with God."

Buck crossed his arms, shaking his head sadly. "Until you do, better leave Beulah alone."

Myles lifted his hat and ran one hand back over his sweaty hair. Then he nodded. Climbing into the wagon seat, he loosed the brake, called to the team, and headed for the barn. Buck moved to a new spot and began to rake.

Al and his crew waited near the barn to unload hay into the loft. After turning his load over to them, Myles watered his team at the huge trough. One mule ducked half its face beneath the water; the other sucked daintily. Myles pushed a layer of surface scum away with one hand, then splashed his face and upper body with the cold water. Much better. He slicked water off his chest with both hands, then plastered back his unruly hair.

Just as he finished hitching the team to an empty wagon, Beulah's voice caught his attention. There she was at the barn, serving cold drinks to the hands. Slim and lovely, dipping water for each man and bestowing her precious smiles. Myles suddenly noticed his raging thirst. Eyes fixed upon Beulah's face, he started across the yard.

Better leave Beulah alone.

Myles halted. Shaking his head, he closed his eyes and rubbed them with his fingers. The woman was like a magnet to him. Buck was right to warn him away from her. *Guess I'll have to do without the drink.* He jogged back to the wagon, leaped to its seat, and slapped the reins on the mules' rumps. "Yah! Get on with you."

"Myles!"

Shading his eyes with one hand, he looked back. Beulah ran behind the jolting wagon, her bonnet upon her shoulders. Water sloshed from the bucket in her hands. "You didn't get your drink. You can't work in this heat without it."

Myles hauled in the mules and wrapped the reins around the brake handle. She hoisted the bucket up to him. Myles took it, holding her gaze. "Thank you." Lifting the dipper several times, he drank his fill.

"Why didn't you come talk to me?" she asked. "I've hardly seen you for days and days. How is Pushy? Any kittens yet?"

"Not yet. She's healing well. She. . .she sleeps between my feet." Myles lost himself in the beauty of Beulah's eyes.

"Myles, are you feeling all right? Maybe you've had too much sun." Accusation transformed into concern. "Why don't you come inside for a while? Your face is all red."

Temptation swamped him. What would it hurt to relax for a short time? When Beulah's gaze lowered, he realized that he was rubbing his belly again. She smiled when he began to button his shirt. "Don't bother on my account. You must be roasting." She touched his arm. "Your skin is like fire. Maybe you need another dunk under the waterfall."

Startled, Myles met her teasing gaze. "I washed in the trough. I'll be all right. Buck is waiting for me." His skin did feel scorched where her hand rested on his arm, but it wasn't from sunburn.

The smile faded as her eyes searched his face. "If you're sure. . .Myles, what's wrong?"

"I can't talk with you, Beulah. Not until—You don't even know me, who I really am."

"I know all I need to know. Did my mother tell you not to talk to me?" She sounded angry.

He studied her delicate hand, wondering at its power to thrill or wound him. "No."

"You're still coming to our music party Friday, aren't you?"

"I'll be there." He handed her the bucket. "Better get back to work." Holding her gaze, he tried to smile. "You, too. Lots of thirsty men around here."

She nodded and watched him drive away.

Streams of milk rang inside a metal pail. Al spoke from the next stall. "I've got to leave soon in case we get an early snow. Thanks for all your help preparing this place for winter."

Myles grunted.

"I've given up on marrying Beulah. I don't know why I ever thought she'd make me a good wife. She's pretty, but looks aren't everything. A man wants a woman to be his friend and companion. Beulah flirts one minute and treats me like anathema the next. She about snapped my head off this afternoon. Something was tweaking her tail, that's certain."

Myles chewed his lip. "She hasn't been herself lately. She's got lots of good qualities."

Al snorted. "At the moment I'd be hard-pressed to name one."

"She's your friend. Don't say anything you'll be sorry about later, Al. Just because she isn't meant to be your wife doesn't mean she's not a good woman."

Al grumbled. "I know you're right. But still, I'm thanking the Lord that He prevented me from proposing marriage. What a fix I would be in if she had accepted!"

Myles leaned his head against a tawny flank, fixed his gaze upon the foamy milk in his bucket, and drew a long breath. "I'm thanking Him for the same thing."

"What did you say?"

"I said I'm thanking God that you didn't propose to Beulah."

"Thanks. Say, when did this come about, you talking to God?" Al's grinning face appeared above the stall divider.

"Recently. Been talking to Buck a lot. I've got a past that isn't pretty, but I know I need to make things right. I wrote a letter to my grandmother. Plan to mail it tomorrow when I go to town."

"Will you be able to keep my farm going this winter?"

"Not sure I should make promises at this point, Al."

He sighed. "I guess I understand. Wish I had peace about going to California. I don't feel right about it, and God isn't answering my questions."

As soon as he was alone, Myles allowed a grin to spread across his face. He punched the air in delight, kicked his feet up and stood on his hands, then dropped to his knees. "Thanks, God! I can hardly believe it, but thanks! Soon as I gave in to You and wrote that letter—whizbang! Al is out of the running! Now if I can sell my part of the soap business and buy Cyrus's farm, then. . ."

"Myles, good to see you."

Pausing on the boardwalk in front of the general store, Myles stared at the speaker. The voice was familiar, but the face? "Sheriff Boz?"

Gone was the tobacco-stained walrus mustache. Looking pounds thinner, Boz Martin sported a crisp white shirt and string tie. The star pinned to his vest sparkled. His gun belt no longer completely disappeared beneath an overhanging paunch. He grinned, showing yellow teeth. Myles had never before seen the man's mouth.

"Don't know me, eh?"

"I haven't seen you at Miss Amelia's in a while."

"Been staying away. I'm hopin' she'll be surprised, too."

"I'm sure she will be. You look. . .fine."

Boz stood taller, puffing out his chest. "Town's jam-packed with drifters, harvest workers. Lot of riffraff, if you ask me. We had to break up a fight at the Shady Lady last night. You hear about it?"

Myles shook his head.

Boz deflated slightly. "I'll be just as glad when that lot moves on. That New York character, Mr. Poole, left town last week, so I've got hopes Amelia will notice me again. Poole was mighty interested in you, Myles. Can't know why."

"How do you mean, 'interested'?"

"Asked a lot of questions around town. You going to Buck and Violet's party tonight? I can't make it, and neither can Amelia."

"That's too bad. Seems like half the town was invited. The Watsons have a lot of friends."

Peering intently across the street, Boz rose on tiptoe, fingering his gun belt. "That Swedish family south of your place lost a pig a few nights back. Looks like Cyrus's bear ain't left the county after all."

Myles turned to see what was distracting Boz, but saw nothing unusual. "Be glad to help on a hunt. We've been keeping our stock close to the barns, just in case."

"Ain't Al headin' west soon? Hear he's taking Beulah with him."

Myles fingered the letter in his pocket. "Al's catching the train south tomorrow. He's traveling alone."

Boz shifted to one side, frowning past Myles. "That so? Those two make a purty pair."

Blinking in surprise, Myles studied his friend's vacant expression. Another curious glance over his shoulder cleared up the mystery. On the walkway near the livery stable stood Miss Amelia, conversing amiably with the town barber. Myles shook his head and grinned. "Actually, Boz, I'm planning to elope with Beulah tonight after the party. We're moving to Outer Mongolia to open a millinery shop for disgruntled Hottentots."

"Yup. I saw that match coming almost as soon as she stepped off the train."

Myles chuckled. "Never mind. I'll see you later."

Still distracted, Boz waved two fingers. "Later, Myles."

When Myles left the general store, Boz had joined the conversation across the street. Smiling, Myles shifted his bundle under one arm. *Good old Boz. Hope he gets his Amelia.*

The letter was in the mail. Soon Gram would know both where Myles was and what had happened to Monte. *Is that enough, God?*

Cholla dozed at the hitching rail with her eyes half shut. "Howdy, girl. Bought myself new duds for tonight. Hope you'll recognize me all duded up." The horse rubbed her ears against his hand and lipped his suspender strap. Myles's voice trembled with anticipation. "Think I'll stop at the barber next and get me a shave. Don't know if Beulah likes my beard or not, but I'm through hiding my identity. Maybe tonight I'll tell her about my past. Maybe she'll like the sound of 'Beulah Van Huysen.'"

"Myles!"

He turned on his boot heels. A buxom figure in a calico dress hurried along the boardwalk. Myles stiffened. He wanted to run, but his boots had grown roots.

"Goodness, but it's warm today," Marva panted, waving a hand before her flushed face. Her eyes were vividly blue. "They say it's going to storm tomorrow, maybe even snow, but I can't believe it! The trees still have most of their leaves. Mr. Watson got his corn in, didn't he? I saw the reaping machine pass our farm yesterday on its way out of town. Papa got our crops in days ago, but then he doesn't farm that much acreage."

She pressed white finger marks into his forearm and shook her head. "You're so brown, Myles, like an Indian! It's not good for fair-skinned people like us to take so much sun. I hope you wear your hat and shirt all the time."

Behind Marva, the Watson buggy stopped at the railing. Samuel and Eunice remained in the buggy while their mother stepped down and tethered her horse.

"Hello, Marva, dear. So good to see you. Hello, Myles," Violet said in her gracious way.

"I'm looking forward to the party tonight, Mrs. Watson," Marva said as Myles tipped his hat. He tried to smile, but his face felt like dried clay. Marva chattered on, "This will be the social event of the season, I'm certain. I'm inviting Myles to join our family for supper before the party."

Violet gave Myles a look. "How nice! I look forward to seeing your parents, Marva. Is your mother better?"

"Much better, thank you. She and I have practiced a duet, and my papa brought out his fiddle for the occasion. I also look forward to hearing Myles sing. He has a marvelous voice." Marva took Myles by the elbow and pressed close.

Myles attempted to disengage his arm, but she clung tenaciously. Heat rose in his face.

He saw one delicate eyebrow lift as Violet met his gaze. "I, too, anticipate hearing you sing, Myles. Good day to you both."

Without moving away, Marva rattled on as if she had never been interrupted. "I'm sure you must be longing for good home cooking. It's been weeks since you visited us, and my papa keeps asking where you've taken yourself. I told him you've been harvesting for nearly everyone in the county, but he won't be happy 'til you join us for a meal. We can have supper first, then drive to Fairfield's Folly together." The dimple in her right cheek deepened. "What's your favorite pie?"

"Blackbottom. My grandmother used to bake it." Pushing at her hands, he detached himself from her grip. "Miss Obermeier, I really don't—"

"I'll do my best to equal your grandmother's pie. Where are you from, Myles? You seldom speak about yourself." Her gloved hand rested on his chest.

"There's little to speak of." Myles tried to slide the conversation closer to his horse. "Miss Obermeier, I don't think you—"

Marva followed. "Good friends don't use titles, Myles. Please call me Marva. I like to hear you speak my name."

"I must go now. Work doesn't wait for a man." Perhaps it was rude to mount Cholla then and there, but Myles was desperate to escape. Tonight was the night to let Marva know that his heart had already been bestowed elsewhere. His problem was how to communicate any message at all to a woman who never stopped talking.

"Be there at five." Marva rested her hand on his knee in a proprietary way. "Don't forget."

"I'll come after the cows are milked." He spun Cholla around.

Eunice and Samuel waved as Myles passed their buggy. "When's the wedding, Myles?" Eunice teased, and Samuel clasped his hands beside his face and batted his eyes in a fair imitation of Miss Obermeier. Had Myles not been so irritated, he might have been amused.

Glancing over his shoulder, he saw Marva laughing and waving at him. What had gotten into the woman?

Cholla sensed his anger and wrung her tail in distress. As soon as she passed the outskirts of town, Myles let out a "Yah!" Cholla leaped into a full gallop.

Chapter 10

*Beloved, let us love one another: for love is of God;
and everyone that loveth is born of God, and knoweth God.*
1 JOHN 4:7

Miss Obermeier finished playing a hymn. A patter of applause trickled through the room as she returned to her seat between Myles and her mother. She leaned over to whisper to Myles. He inclined his head to listen. Marva's pale hair gleamed, and her fair skin contrasted with Myles's ruddy tan.

"Wonder why Myles didn't wear his new duds," Al muttered as Cyrus Thwaite began a mouth organ solo of "Camptown Races."

Beulah met Al's gaze. "He bought new clothes?"

He nodded. "Today. A fancy suit, like for a wedding. Told me he had an announcement to make. I'm guessing there will be a wedding soon."

Beulah jerked as if she had been slapped.

"Maybe it didn't fit," Al mused. "Too bad. Marva looks like a queen, and Myles looks like. . .like a farmhand. I've got to help the man loosen up."

Eunice leaned around Al, frowning and holding a warning finger to her lips. "Don't be rude!" she whispered.

Beulah took shallow breaths. *I won't look. I cannot bear to see Myles sitting with that woman.* Her heart had started aching the moment she saw Myles hand Miss Obermeier down from a buggy, and the pain grew steadily worse. Marva's parents already seemed to regard Myles as a son-in-law.

He never made me any promises, yet I thought there was something special between us. Maybe he does think of me as a child to be amused.

Biting her lower lip, Beulah smoothed the skirt of her sprigged dimity frock. She had been so proud of this dress with its opulent skirts and tiny waist. Violet had fashioned a ruffled neckline that framed the girl's face, revealing the delicate hollow at the base of her throat and a mere hint of collarbone. Now the white ruffles seemed childish.

Marva's royal blue satin gown showed off her white shoulders. Beulah wondered that Marva could keep her countenance in front of Reverend and Mrs. Schoengard. "I think her dress is improper for an unmarried lady."

Al gave her a wry look. "Trust you to say so."

"Shh!" Eunice leaned forward again.

Beulah flounced back in her seat. *I was excited to have Myles come tonight. Now I wish he had stayed home. I wish I had never met the horrible man.*

David and Caroline Schoengard rose to stand beside the piano. Violet settled on the stool and opened her music. "We will sing 'Abide with Me,'" Caroline announced in a trembling voice.

Beulah watched the pastor shape his mouth in funny ways as he sang the low notes. Mrs. Schoengard was now heavily pregnant. Their voices were pleasant, but once in a while Caroline strained for a high note and fell short.

Al shifted in his seat and tugged at his stiff collar while the Schoengards returned to their seats. "Is it almost over?" he whispered.

The only people present who had not yet performed were Al, Myles, and Obie. Beulah knew her stepfather could not carry a tune. He attended Violet's party to be an appreciative audience, he said. And Al would "rather be dead than warble in front of folks."

"Myles, will you play for us?" Violet requested. "Don't be shy; none of us are music critics."

Myles rose, approached the piano, and turned to face his small audience. Candlelight flickered in his eyes and hair. "I'll play, but I have something to tell all of you afterward." His gaze came to rest upon Beulah. "Something important."

She sucked in a quick breath, lifting one hand to her throat.

Myles placed the piano stool and seated himself. He drew a deep breath and flexed his fingers, seeking Beulah's gaze. The message she read in his eyes at that moment banished her jealousy and insecurity.

He began to play a lively composition. His hands flew across the keyboard with complete mastery. Broad shoulders squared, heavy boot working the pedal, he looked incongruous, yet perfectly at home. His very posture denoted the virtuoso.

Myles completed the piece with a flourish. "Schubert," he said into the ensuing silence. A murmur stirred the room's stuffy air as people audibly exhaled.

"Wow," Al said.

"That was unbelievable, Myles," Violet said. "Never before in my life have I heard—"

"I had no idea you knew how to play piano," Marva protested. "You always let me play and never said a word!"

"You never asked me," Myles said. "This is what I planned to tell you all tonight. My true name is Myles Trent Van Huysen, and during my childhood I was a concert pianist and singer. At age sixteen I ran away, and many years I have wandered the country seeking purpose for my life. Thanks to Buck Watson, I found that purpose here in Longtree. I apologize for keeping my identity a secret all this time. I was wrong to deceive you. With God's help, I am doing my best to make reparation to those I have wronged."

Obie and Al approached Myles with outstretched hands. Beulah watched the men clap Myles on the shoulders and embrace him, expressing forgiveness and acceptance. Soon everyone had gathered around the piano, eager to greet this new Myles.

Beulah joined the crowd, trying to appear happy. What did this mean? Was Myles planning to leave town and return to his concert career? He suddenly seemed far away and beyond her.

"Sing for us, Myles," Violet pleaded.

"Yes, please do," other voices chimed in.

"A love song," Marva requested.

"A love song." Myles appeared at ease in his new role of entertainer. . .but then, the role was not new to him. Acrobat, pianist, singer—what other surprises did the man hold in store? Was there anything he could not do?

Beulah recognized the tune he began to play, but never before had she heard such elegance in the old, familiar words. Myles affected a Scot's accent that would fool any but a native. His voice was smooth, richer than butter.

"O, my love's like a red, red rose,
That's newly sprung in June."

Beulah felt herself blush rose red when Myles caught and held her gaze.

"As fair art thou, my bonnie lass,
So deep in love am I,
And I will love thee still, my dear,
Till a' the seas gang dry."

He was singing the love song to her! Beulah gripped the piano case with both hands, feeling the music reverberate in her soul.

"And fare thee weel, my only love,
And fare thee weel a while!
And I will come again, my love,
Tho' it were ten thousand mile!"

The song ended. Myles lowered his gaze to the keys, releasing Beulah from his spell. "Hope you like Robbie Burns," he spoke into a profound silence. "It was the only love song I could think of at the moment. I know some opera, but didn't think you'd care to hear me sing in Italian."

Beulah drew a deep breath; it caught in her throat.

"Never cared much for fancy singing, but that beats all," Al admitted. "I think I'd be pleased to listen for as long as you cared to sing—and in any language you choose."

"How long has it been since you played the piano?" Violet asked.

Myles figured for a moment. "More than nine years. It's a gift, I guess—being able to play any song I hear. I didn't play those pieces flawlessly, of course, but usually I can play and sing almost anything after hearing it once or twice."

"Amazing! I heard no mistakes. Myles, you have thrilled our souls. Thank you for sharing your gift," Violet said. "I hope you know that you are part of our family, whatever your name."

The entire group murmured agreement.

"If anyone is thirsty or hungry," Violet continued, "we have cider and cookies in the kitchen. You are all welcome to stay as long as you like."

Everyone seemed to relax, and conversations began to buzz. Cyrus and Pastor Schoengard asked Myles to play requests, which he obliged. Strains of "My Old Kentucky Home" and "It Is Well with My Soul" accompanied the chatter. Samuel chased another boy into the parlor, laughing and shouting. Their mothers shooed the boys outside.

Beulah drifted toward the kitchen and claimed a cup of homemade cider. The drink felt cold and unyielding in her stomach, so she left her cup on the counter. She wanted to wander outside amid the fruit trees, but the night was cool and her dress was thin. She could retire to her room for the night, but that would negate any chance of talking with Myles. Wrapping a shawl around her shoulders, she took refuge on the porch swing.

The front door opened and closed. "May I speak with you?"

Startled, Beulah looked up. Moonlight shimmered on a full skirt and fisted hands. Marva's face was hidden in shadow.

"Yes."

The other woman joined her on the swing, making it creak. A moonbeam touched Marva's beautiful hair and traced silver tear streaks on her face. Muscles tensed in her round forearms as she repeatedly clasped her hands.

"Myles loves you." Marva gulped.

Beulah had no idea what to say. *Dear God, please help me to be kind and good.* She pulled her shawl closer and saw Marva do the same. They would both freeze out here on the swing.

"Are you going to marry Al?" Marva asked.

"No."

"Why not?"

"I don't love him that way."

Marva sighed. "You're so young. Do you have any idea what you want in a husband?"

"I know that I don't want to marry a man who is like a brother to me."

"So you would steal a man from another woman?"

Beulah stiffened. "Of course not! What a—" She nearly choked on her own hasty words. Maybe Marva's insinuation was unkind, but it was the desperate charge of a broken heart. What might Beulah be tempted to say under similar circumstances? She felt sudden sympathy for Marva.

"You already had Al. Why did you try to steal Myles from me?" Tears roughened Marva's voice.

"I didn't know you loved him, Miss Obermeier. I wasn't trying to be cruel to you, honestly!"

Marva covered her face with her hands. "It's not fair! It's just not fair."

Beulah patted Marva's shoulder. "My mother tells me that God is always fair. If He doesn't allow you to marry Myles, then He must have someone better in store. You've got to trust Him, Marva. He doesn't make mistakes."

Marva lowered her hands and sucked in a quivering breath. "You're nothing like I thought you were, Beulah Fairfield. Everyone talks about your sharp tongue and quick temper. They must be jealous. You're really a sweet girl." Her tone was doleful. "No wonder Myles loves you. You're both pretty and nice."

"So are you," Beulah said. "Just now I asked God to help me be kind; it doesn't come naturally to me."

Marva gave a moist chuckle. "Me, neither. I came out here wanting to scratch your eyes out! It's easy for you to talk about God bringing someone better along; but when you get to be twenty-six with not so much as a whisker of a husband in sight, you'll know how I feel. Of course, you're likely to be married and a mother several times over by the time you're my age."

She stood up, leaving Beulah in the swing. "When my parents come outside, will you tell them I'm in the buggy?"

"I'll tell them. Are you sure you're all right, Marva?" She followed the older girl down the steps.

Marva shivered. "I'll recover. Humiliation isn't fatal."

"I don't know. I've come close to dying of it more than once."

Marva reached out and hugged Beulah. "Maybe my heart isn't as broken as I thought it was. I feel better already. Myles is a wonderful man, but he never did seem to care for my cooking, and sometimes when I talked to him I saw his eyes kind of glaze over. Guess I'd better be patient and wait for God's choice instead of hunting down a man for myself."

Beulah found it hard to restrain a giggle, but Marva waved off her efforts. "Go ahead and laugh. I know I'm silly." She grinned. "You know, I once even considered Sheriff Martin as a marriage prospect. I didn't consider him long, but the thought crossed my mind."

"Marva, he's old enough to be your father!"

Marva chuckled. "I know. Oops, here come my parents. You'd better get inside before you freeze. I'll see you at church, Beulah."

⌾

"I would take it as a favor if you would sing in church," Reverend David Schoengard said in a hushed voice. "God could mightily use a talent like yours."

"I hope He will," Myles replied. "When the time is right, I will let you know."

"Don't wait too long," David advised.

"I am still learning what it means to honor Jesus as Lord. You know that story about the lost sheep? That's me."

"The church door is open to lost sheep."

A small boy tugged at the pastor's leg. "Dad, Ernie hit me."

"Excuse me a moment, please." David squatted to listen to his son.

Myles scanned the room.

"Looking for Beulah?" Al asked. Leaning one elbow on the piano, he sipped a cup of cider. "She's talking with Marva, I think. I spotted the two of them on the porch swing not long ago. If you need help splitting up a cat fight, call on me."

"How did you—"

"Please, don't ask! Anyone with half an eye could have read the look on your face while you sang to Beulah tonight, old friend. I'm thinking you'd better soon have a serious talk with Buck, or he'll be after you with the shotgun." Al's grin was pure mischief. "I'm also thinking I'll have to miss that train tomorrow. Don't you want me to stand up at your wedding?"

"You're not angry?"

"Naw. When two people are right for each other, it's obvious. And vice versa. Beulah and I blended like horseradish and ice cream. You'll be good for her; she needs someone to keep her in line. You should have seen her writhing in jealousy when you showed up with Marva tonight." Al chuckled. "She must have been dying when I talked about what a handsome couple you and Marva made."

Myles felt his face grow warm. "I intended to tell Marva tonight—"

"I don't think you need to say a word. She knows. Her parents just left. They looked pretty sad."

His shoulders slumped. "They're good people, Al. And Marva's a nice lady. I feel bad about hurting her."

Al shrugged. "Some of us are slow to catch on. I wasn't the quickest hog to the trough, myself. Don't know why I couldn't see the attraction between you and Beulah before now. It sticks out like quills on a porcupine. But there will be another girl for me—one who appreciates my humor and thinks I'm great." He grinned.

Myles had to smile. "You're chockfull of brilliant analogies tonight. Porcupine quills?"

"So are you going to talk with Beulah or not?"

<hr/>

He found Beulah on the porch swing. Watchful lay at her feet. The dog flopped a fluffy tail. "Isn't it too cold for swinging?" Myles asked.

Huddled beneath her shawl, Beulah stared up at him. "I guess it is. I needed a place to think, but I've discovered that the front porch isn't private."

Myles leaned a hip against the railing, gazing out past the barn. His left leg jiggled up and down. "Al told me Marva talked to you."

"She was crying at first, but when she left she was laughing. I like her, Myles.

She is funny and nice. I think she could be a friend."

He shifted against the rail. "I was planning to explain to her tonight. About you and me, I mean."

Her voice was too bright. "I enjoyed your singing. I don't understand why you hid your talents for so long."

The comment interrupted his train of thought. "It's a long story."

From somewhere beyond the barn came a commotion. Watchful lifted her head, ears pricked. Myles followed the dog's gaze, but saw nothing. Hackles raised, growling softly, the dog trotted down the steps and headed for the barn. The white tip on her tail was visible after the rest of her disappeared.

"Myles?" Beulah stopped swinging and leaned forward. "What is it?"

Watchful began to bark. Myles had never heard such a noise—the dog sounded frantic, terrified. His ears caught the bawling of cattle, trampling hooves.

"I don't know, but I'm gonna find out."

Running feet approached, and two small figures appeared in the moonlight. Myles heard the boys panting before he could identify Samuel and his buddy, Scott Schoengard. "Myles!" Samuel said, stumbling up the steps. "There is something big in the yearling pen—something that roars!"

Chapter 11

We roar all like bears.
ISAIAH 59:11

I called Watchful, but she won't come. Go save her, Myles! That monster will kill her!" Samuel was sobbing.

Myles threw open the front door. "Buck! Al! Trouble at the barn."

Buck snatched up a lantern and a rifle, tossing another gun to Myles. Al caught up with them halfway across the yard. The yearling pen was ominously quiet except for Watchful's shrill yelps. Leaning against the split rail fence, Buck lifted the lantern. On the far side of the pen, many wide eyes reflected the lamplight. A young cow bawled.

"Watchful, come." The stern command brought the collie to heel, ears flattened, tail between her legs. Every hair on the dog's body stood on end. She still yammered at intervals. "Hush, Watchful." Instant silence. She pressed against Buck's leg and shivered.

Buck unlatched the gate, and the three men stepped into the pen. Myles felt the hair on his nape tingle. A cursory examination of the corral revealed that the invader was gone.

Buck studied the muddy ground with a practiced eye. He pointed out bunches of woolly hair on a fence post along with glutinous streaks of blood. "It was a bear."

Myles counted the cattle. "One yearling missing. The Hereford-cross with the white patch on his left hip."

Al measured a print in the mud with his hand. "That was one big bear. It lifted that steer over the fence."

"We'll track it come morning. I don't follow giant bears into dark forests," Buck said with grim humor.

Al crossed his arms. "That monster could have come after one of the children."

"Sam and Scott were playing near the barn," Myles said. He swallowed a wave of nausea at the sudden mental picture of what might have been. "God must have been protecting them. I'll be ready for the hunt first thing tomorrow, Buck."

"Me, too."

Buck lifted a brow at his cousin. "Don't you have to get ready for your trip, Al? Your train leaves at four o'clock tomorrow afternoon."

Al glowered at the ground. "Might know I'd have to miss the fun. All right. I'll feed and milk in the morning, one last time, so you two can hunt."

Something cracked in the darkness near the gate. Watchful's ears pricked. The men spun around, guns lifted. A ghostly figure drifted closer. "It's me—Beulah."

"What are you doing?" Al snapped. "Don't you know there's a bear out here somewhere?"

Beulah clutched her shawl. "I didn't know until now." Her voice sounded small.

"Back inside, Beulah," Buck ordered. "Your mother will worry."

"I'll escort her." Myles stepped out of the corral.

"No lingering."

"Yes, sir." Myles had never before heard that protective note in Buck's voice. He followed Beulah toward the kitchen door. She drifted beneath the apple trees, crunching leaves beneath her feet.

"I love all our trees and the beautiful fall color, but now comes the hard part—raking," she said in a quivering falsetto. "Did you like the cider? My mother and I made it from our apples."

Myles touched her arm. "Beulah."

She turned. Her eyes were dark pools in her pale face. "Oh, Myles, you aren't really going to hunt that bear, are you? I'm frightened!"

She cared! "I've hunted bears before. Buck and I will hunt this one down in no time. A few shots and it'll be over."

Her hand fluttered up to rest upon his chest. Myles wrapped his fingers around her upper arm. "Buck told me not to linger, but I must tell you tonight. I love you, Beulah. I want to marry you. I want it more than anything." His voice cracked.

He heard her suck in a quick breath. "Do you know God yet, Myles? Mama and Papa both told me to wait until you gave your life to Him. You said something tonight about making your peace with God's help. Did you mean it?"

"I did. I do. I wrote to my grandmother and apologized for running away. I imagine she will contact me soon, and I expect to make a quick trip to New York to wrap up business affairs." His voice trembled with eagerness. "I'm planning to buy the Thwaite farm, Beulah. For us. You and me. How does that sound?"

He wanted to hold her in his arms, but the rifle in his right hand made that impractical.

Beulah touched his beard with two fingers. "It sounds wonderful. . .but are you sure you want to be a farmer? You can do so many things. I've never known anyone like you."

"I'm sure." He leaned the rifle against the back steps and took Beulah into his arms. "Are you sure you want to marry a farmer?"

She captured his face between her hands and gently kissed his lips. "Please don't go away, Myles. Not ever."

"What?" he mumbled, conscious only of his need for another kiss. Her lips warmed beneath his, and her hands gripped his shoulders. Myles kissed her again and again until the cold, dark world faded away. Nothing existed except Beulah, sweet and pliant in his arms.

The kitchen door opened, catching them in a beam of light. "Beulah, it's time for you to come inside," Violet said.

The couple sprang apart, wide-eyed and breathing hard. Beulah grabbed for her falling shawl and rushed past her mother into the house.

"Myles, I believe you need to talk with Obadiah before you meet with Beulah again."

Myles heard the iron behind Violet's mild tone. Gathering his scattered self-control, he nodded and picked up the rifle. "This is Buck's."

Violet took it from him. "Al is waiting for you out front." She started to close the door then paused. "I know you love my daughter, Myles, and I'm not opposed to the match. But as her mother, I must be careful of her purity."

Guilt swamped him. "I understand. I am sorry, ma'am. It won't happen again."

"See that it doesn't. Good night, Myles Van Huysen."

❧

Myles stepped into predawn darkness, feeling the chill through his wool coat and gloves. A recent dusting of snow on the ground might make tracking more difficult. Cholla was displeased to see him so early, but she accepted her bit after Myles warmed it in his palm. "We're on a hunt, girl. Like old times."

Cats waited around Cholla's stall, making noisy petition for milk. "Sorry, friends. No milk this morning." Myles thought of Pushy, still sleeping on his bed, and grinned. These cats would rebel for certain if they knew she got her own saucer of cream each morning and evening.

He tied a scabbard to his saddle and shoved his loaded rifle into it, then packed extra cartridges into his saddlebags. "Hope we're back in time to escort Al to the station." He would miss his young boss and friend.

Cholla broke into a canter, tossing her head and blowing steam. Myles hauled her back to a jog. "Too dark for that pace, my lady. We'll get there soon enough."

Buck waited in the yearling paddock. By the first light of dawn, he studied the bear's spoor. Buck nodded greeting as Myles joined him. "Big bear, like Al said. Amazing claw definition for a blackie. I'd say it was a grizzly if I didn't know better."

"Powerful, whatever it is, to carry off a yearling steer. It obviously has little fear of man."

"Makes my heart sit in my throat to think how the children have walked and ridden about the property at all hours these past weeks. And all the while this monster was afoot."

Myles had been having similar thoughts. "Have you heard the rumors that a bear escaped from the circus? If this is the bear I think it might be, our lives have been in constant danger. That grizzly hated people."

Buck swung into his saddle. His jaw clenched in a grim line. "Whether it is or whether it isn't, our job is to end the creature's life."

The bear's trail was easy to follow; it had dragged the carcass through grass and brush. Less than a mile up the creek, they found the remains of the young Hereford crossbreed. "There lies our next year's winter beef supply," Buck grumbled, still on horseback. "This bear has an eye for a tender steak."

Jughead and Cholla snorted and shied at the strong scent of bear. "Steady, boy. That bear should be miles from here by now." Buck patted his gelding's neck, but the horse would not be quieted. "I don't like this." Buck exchanged glances with Myles, then studied the surrounding brush and trees. Plenty of hiding places for a bear.

Cholla reared slightly, eyes rolling. "What if it stayed around to eat from the kill again?" Myles asked and hauled his gun from its sheath.

Buck swung his mount around, rifle at the ready. "It could happen. This bear doesn't seem to follow standard bruin behavior. Let's see if he's still around." He gave a whoop.

"That should frighten every critter in the county," Myles chuckled. The laughter froze in his throat. Not twenty yards away, a huge cinnamon-brown form rose out of a patch of mist. The bear's roar was more than Cholla could endure. With a rasping squeal, she reared high, pawing the air. Myles forced her back down, but it was impossible to fire while fighting his horse. The bear made a short charge, then paused to rise up and roar again. Foam dripped from its open jaws.

A rifle cracked, and the bear flinched. Infuriated, it charged at Jughead. The mustang bolted with Buck sawing at his reins and shouting.

Myles brought his rifle around, but Cholla chose that moment to shy sideways into the trees. The shot went wild, and Myles lost a stirrup. Furious and frustrated, he decided to let the screaming horse loose and try his chances on foot. He leaped to the ground, and while the bear made a short dash toward Cholla, Myles fired. In his haste, he hit the hump on its back.

Instantly the bear spun around, spotted Myles, and charged with incredible speed. Myles caught a glimpse of flaming eyes, yellow tusks, and a red tongue. Without a thought he cartwheeled to one side, made a front roll, and propelled himself upward to catch hold of a tree branch. He swung his legs up as the bear charged beneath him, still roaring.

All well and good, but now his rifle lay on the ground. "Buck, I'm up a tree!" Could he be heard above the animal's fury?

The bear quickly figured out where Myles was and returned to the tree. Its roars were deafening, and it pushed against the tall pine, making it wave wildly.

Then, to Myles's horror, the bear began to shinny its great bulk up the trunk. Even as Myles scrambled to move higher, one great paw slapped into his leg and pulled. He let out a shout, clinging to the trunk with all his strength. "God, help me!"

Shots rang out in rapid succession. Buck stood ten feet away in plain view, pumping bullets into the beast's back. The bear gave another roar, then a grunt, and dropped to the ground in a heap.

Myles hugged the tree trunk, laughing in hysteria. Relief made his arms go limp. Had he eaten breakfast, he would surely have lost it. Pain knifed through his leg. "Thank You, God. I'm alive."

"Amen." Buck's voice sounded equally shaky. "You all right, Myles? I'm so sorry—I never dreamed my yell would bring the bear down on you like that. I thought he had you for a moment there."

"I think he got my leg. That beast went up a tree like a squirrel—I've never seen the like."

"It is a grizzly. I guessed it from the tracks, but I didn't believe my own eyes."

Myles tried to climb down the tree, feeling weaker than a kitten. His leg was wet. His head felt swimmy. "Check its neck, Buck. I have an idea he's wearing a collar, or used to be."

Buck bent over the carcass. "Biggest bear I've seen in years." He reached a hand into the coarse fur. "You guessed it, Myles. A leather collar with a short length of chain. Those rumors about the circus bear were true. I can't believe no one reported this!"

"No doubt the owner feared negative publicity. They probably expected to find the bear before they left, but he was too smart for them."

"Maybe he was smart, but a circus animal wouldn't know how to survive in the wild. Stealing stock was his only option. Look how skinny—no fat surplus for hibernation. He would never have lasted the winter. I can't help feeling a little sorry for the old bruin." Buck shoved the inert body with his boot.

"Not me. This isn't the first time that old buzzard came after me." Myles released his hold on a branch and dropped to the ground. His leg buckled. He fell to his knees and grabbed it. The hand came away red. "Buck, I need help."

Rushing to his side, Buck pulled out a knife and cut away the trousers. The smile lines around his eyes disappeared. "Looks nasty. Got to stop that bleeding."

Chapter 12

Peace I leave with you, my peace I give unto you:
not as the world giveth, give I unto you.
Let not your heart be troubled, neither let it be afraid.

JOHN 14:27

While Beulah mixed pancake batter, gazing dreamily through a frosty windowpane, she saw Jughead trot into the barnyard, riderless and wide-eyed. "Mama!" Dropping her work, she raced upstairs. "Mama, Jughead came home without Papa. Something bad has happened, I just know it!"

Violet nursed Daniel in the rocking chair. Her body became rigid; her blue eyes widened. "Let's not panic. Papa might have released Jughead for some reason." She bit her lip while Beulah wrung her hands. "Send Eunice over to tell Al. He'll know what to do."

Dead leaves whisked across the barnyard, dancing in a bitter wind. Frost lined the wilted flower border, and ice rimed the water troughs. His reins trailing, Jughead hunted for windfalls beneath the naked apple trees. Beulah's gentle greeting made the horse flinch and tremble. He allowed her to take his reins, however, and seemed grateful for her attentions. She patted his white shoulder, feeling cold sweat beneath his winter coat.

In the barn, Eunice was saddling Dolly. Excited and frightened, the younger girl chattered. "Can you believe how cold it is today? And yesterday I didn't even carry my coat to school. Good thing there's no school on Saturday or I wouldn't be home right now. Good thing Al hasn't left yet. Maybe he'll decide not to go to California after all. Maybe..."

Beulah tuned out her sister's prattle. If anything had happened to Papa or Myles...Beulah hauled Jughead's saddle from his back and hung it on the rack. Would Papa want her to blanket the horse now, or was Jughead warm enough with only his winter fur? Taking the gelding to his stall, she slipped off his bridle. The slimy snaffle bit rattled against his teeth, but Jughead was too good-natured to hold that against Beulah. He bumped her with his Roman nose and heaved a sigh, seeking reassurance.

Beulah patted his neck and rubbed his fuzzy brown ears, resting her cheek against his forelock. "Papa will be all right, Jughead. Don't worry."

"I'm leaving now, Beulah." Dolly's hooves clattered on the barn floor as Eunice mounted.

219

"Be careful. And hurry, Eunice."

After Dolly galloped up the driveway with Eunice clinging to her back, Beulah closed the barn door and returned to the house. Her face felt windburned when she removed her wraps.

Wandering from room to room, she looked for chores that needed doing. No one was hungry for pancakes, so she covered the batter. At last she decided to bake bread and cookies. The men might come home hungry. Her thoughts kept returning to Myles and Papa.

Dear God, please keep them safe! I love them both so much.

While the bread rose and the first batch of cookies baked, she sat at the table and tried to soak up the stove's radiated heat. Wind howled around the eaves and rattled the windows. Beulah shivered.

Violet entered the kitchen and sniffed. "It smells good in here, Beulah. You've been working hard." She spread a quilt on the floor and set Daniel on it, handing him a spoon and two bowls for playthings. Sitting at an awkward angle, he crowed and waved both hands in the air. He grinned at his mother, and Violet smiled back.

Beulah stared. "How can you be so calm, Mama? Papa could be in terrible danger out there, and it looks like snow again!" She waved a hand at the window.

"God is with him, Beulah. I've been praying since you told me about Jughead, and God assures me that He is in control. Remember Philippians 4:6–7: 'Be careful for nothing; but in every thing by prayer and supplication with thanksgiving let your requests be made known unto God. And the peace of God, which passeth all understanding, shall keep your hearts and minds through Christ Jesus.' If I chose to worry about Obie every time he went into a dangerous situation, I would be in a home for the insane by this time." Violet smiled.

Daniel leaned too far forward and fell on his face. Unfazed, he grabbed the spoon and batted it against a bowl.

Beulah studied her mother's expression. "But how, Mama? How can you trust God this way? You can't see Him, and you know that bad things happen sometimes."

Violet poured herself a cup of coffee. "When you truly know the Lord, you know that evil and pain are the farthest things from Him. He is all the joy and meaning in life, dearest. Without Him, life is nothing. It's the Holy Spirit Who gives us peace, Beulah, along with love, kindness, and every other spiritual fruit. He doesn't force Himself into our lives—we have to allow Him to fill and use us for God's glory."

Beulah removed the cookies from the oven and put in another batch. "Last night I asked God to help me be kind to Marva, and He did. I have given my life to Jesus, and I know He is working in me, but I don't have the peace I see in your life and Papa's. Most of the time I don't even want to be kind and good. Hateful things come out of my mouth before I think them through!"

Violet rose and wrapped an arm around her daughter's drooping shoulders. "Darling, don't you understand that all people are that way? None of us in our own strength can be always kind or loving or unselfish. Those traits belong to God alone. And yet God can use anyone who is willing to be used by Him. You say He helped you last night? Then you know He can change your heart when you allow Him."

"I'm willing right now, but I might not be tomorrow," Beulah admitted. "You know how ornery I am."

Violet squeezed the girl's shoulders. "Yes, the tough part is surrendering your will to His will. I understand entirely. Where do you think you got your ornery nature? It wasn't from your father."

"Then how do you do it, Mama? How can you be so full of faith and patience and everything?"

"Remember when Jesus talked about taking up our cross daily? He meant that every day we must die to ourselves and let Him live through us. That is the only way to have lasting peace and joy in your life—and it's the only way to have faith through any crisis. When you know God well, you will understand how completely He can be trusted with your life."

Beulah nodded, thinking over her mother's words. She sampled a cookie, chewing slowly. "Mama, I need to talk with you about Myles. Last night, right before you told me to—"

Watchful began to bark from her post at the back window.

"Someone is coming," Violet said. Both women rushed to look outside. Behind them, Daniel began to cry. Violet hurried back to pick him up.

"They're back!" Beulah exclaimed. "Al and Eunice are with them."

"Thank the Lord!" Violet rejoined her at the window.

"I'm going out there to greet them," Beulah declared. She hurried to the entry hall for a coat and hat, then rushed down the steps and across the yard. "Papa! Myles, are you all right?" Both men looked pale and drawn.

Obie caught her before she could spook the horses. "We killed the bear, but not until after he took a swipe at Myles. Got to get the doctor out here right away. Help us take Myles into the house, and I'll ride to town."

"I'll go with you," Al offered. "I'm not leaving today. I'll catch a train next week. I can't run off to California when Myles is hurt."

Nobody argued. Beulah rushed back to the house to inform her mother, and together they decided Myles should have Samuel's bed. The men carried Myles up the stairs just as Beulah tucked in the top bed sheet. The sight of his bloody boot and trouser leg stopped her breath for a long moment. "Oh, Myles!" she exclaimed. Her head began to feel light and foggy.

"It's not so bad. You should see the other guy." He gave her a crooked smile. "I'm pretty thirsty."

"I'll get you a drink. Do you want water or coffee or milk?"

"Water."

As she left the room, she heard her mother order quietly, "Al, help me cut the boot from his foot. Beulah, we need a basin of hot water."

"Yes, Mama." All the way downstairs and while she worked, Beulah prayed: *Lord, please fill me with your Spirit today and help me to show love, peace, joy, and every other fruit. Please help my dear Myles! Help the doctor to heal his leg like new. And please keep me from fainting when I see all that blood.*

She held the basin with towels to prevent sloshing water from burning her hands while she mounted the stairs. A bucket of cold water for Myles weighted her right arm.

"Put it there on the bureau," Violet said. "Thank you, Beulah. Al and Papa have gone for the doctor."

Beulah offered a dipper of well water to Myles. He propped himself on one elbow and drank. "Much better." When he returned the dipper, their hands touched. Beulah felt her lips tremble. She could not meet his gaze.

Beulah dropped the dipper into the bucket. On the floor at her feet lay the shredded shirt Obie had used to stanch Myles's blood. It was leaving a stain on the floorboards. Beulah closed her eyes and breathed deeply. *Don't think about it*, she told herself. She gingerly picked up the shirt and wrapped a clean sheet around it. Blood soaked through.

"You may toss out that old shirt." Violet was tearing a sheet into strips. "Then again, I suppose we can boil it and use it for rags."

Beulah trotted downstairs and put the bloody cloth in a pot to boil, then ran outside and was sick behind the withered perennial bed. Her head still felt light afterward, but at least her stomach had settled. The cold, fresh air helped.

"The bleeding has slowed," Violet was saying when Beulah returned to the room, "but you'll have to be stitched."

"I thought as much." Myles looked pale.

"Beulah, will you please check on Daniel?" Violet asked. "I think I hear him stirring."

Beulah gave Myles a longing look, then hurried to obey her mother.

Daniel had pushed up with both hands to peer over the side of his cradle. His little face was crumpled into the pout that always appeared just before he started crying. He grinned when he saw Beulah and flopped back down on his face, crowing and kicking at his blankets. Beulah melted. "Oh, sweetie, I do love you! I wish you would sleep right now, though."

"I'll take him for you, Beulah." Eunice stood in the doorway. Curls had escaped her braid to frame her round face, and the hem of her dress was soaked. Her blue eyes looked lost and lonely. "Is Myles going to die? You should have seen that bear. It was huge. Papa says it charged at Myles and he swung into a tree like a monkey." She wiped a fist across her eyes and sniffed. "Please let me take Daniel. I don't know what else to do." Tears clogged her voice.

A wave of love for her sister warmed Beulah's heart. "Myles lost a lot of blood, but I don't think he'll die. Of course you may take Daniel. You'd better change into dry clothes first. If you don't, you'll be coming down sick next thing, and we don't need that." Her voice softened. "Thank you for riding for help this morning. You're pretty wonderful."

Eunice's dimples appeared before her smile. She nodded and hurried to her room. Beulah settled into the rocking chair and cuddled Daniel close. He was too busy and awake to snuggle, so she let him sit up and amuse himself by playing with her buttons while she sang "Auld Lang Syne."

Eunice spread Daniel's blanket on the floor and set up his blocks before she took the baby from Beulah. "We'll be fine. I think the doctor is here; someone arrived just now."

"Thank God! And Eunice, Al decided he's not leaving today." Beulah smiled at the overjoyed expression on her little sister's face. "He'll catch the train next week."

Eunice caught hold of Beulah's skirt as she whisked past. "Beulah, I'm sorry I said you were heartless. You love Myles, don't you?"

Biting her lip, Beulah nodded. "But don't you tell anyone!"

The dimples appeared again. "I won't. He's not Al, but I like him a lot."

Peace filled Beulah's heart as she returned to Samuel's bedroom. Next thing she knew, she was being shooed from the room. How she wished Myles would request her presence! Not that Mama would have allowed such a thing. Not that Beulah could have endured the sights or sounds of a sickroom without passing out on the floor.

Beulah hurried to the kitchen to prepare more coffee and cookies for everyone. Someone—Eunice?—had removed the batch of cookies from the oven and punched down the bread dough. It was ready to bake.

Dear God, it's hard to be helpful when all I want is to be with Myles. I guess this is the best way for me to serve today. Please help me to have a cheerful attitude and to give thanks.

Obie and Al were grateful for the hot food. Beulah joined their sober conversation midway through and gathered that someone besides Myles was hurt. "*Who* got shot last night, Papa? What happened?"

Obie wiped his nose with a handkerchief. "The sheriff. One of those drifters who's been causing trouble in town all month had a drop too much at the tavern last night and took offense when Boz offered him a night's rest in jail. Before anyone could react, the man pulled a gun and shot Boz from point-blank range."

Blood drained from Beulah's face. . .again. "Will he live, Papa?" she croaked.

Obie shook his head. "They carried him home, and Doc dug out the bullet, but he's afraid it nicked a lung. Boz has powder burns on his chest, and he has trouble breathing."

Beulah bit her lips and screwed up her face. The tears overflowed anyway.

Obie patted her hand. "Miss Amelia is taking care of him while Doc is here with Myles. Boz couldn't ask for better care. We just need to pray. He has peace about eternity, thank the Lord." Obie drew a shaky breath and blinked hard. "He's my oldest friend. The deputy is keeping order in town for the present. The man who shot Boz is behind bars. I'm hoping to visit him after church tomorrow."

"I'll go with you," Al offered.

"You could take him some of my cookies." Beulah wiped her face with her apron and tried to smile.

Light snow fell Sunday, but Monday dawned clear and warmer. Eunice and Samuel threw snowballs back and forth as they left for school, but the snow blanket had dwindled to a few patches by noon.

While Mama nursed Daniel, Beulah peeked in to check on Myles. His foot lay propped on pillows. In repose, his pale face had a boyish look. His eyes opened, but Beulah slipped away before he spotted her. Violet had made it clear that Beulah was never to be alone with Myles in his sickroom.

Outside, Watchful began to bark. Beulah went to her own room and peered down at the driveway. "Mama, someone is coming. I don't recognize the horses."

Violet sounded harassed. "Would you greet our guest and make excuses for me, dear? I'll be down when Daniel is finished."

Beulah untied her apron and hung it on a hook, patted her hair, and opened the door. An elderly woman stood on the top step. Behind her, the buggy turned around and disappeared up the driveway. "Hello, dear. Is this Obadiah Watson's home?"

"Yes, it is."

Watchful suddenly rushed past the woman into the house, whisked Beulah's skirts, and bounded up the stairs. "I'm so sorry," Beulah gasped. "That was my brother's dog."

The lady straightened her bonnet. "Does a man named Myles Trent work here?"

"Yes, but he does not live here."

The lady's face fell. "But they told me...Oh, dear, and I let that hired rig go...I was so sure Myles would be here."

Beulah hurried to explain, "No, don't worry—you see, he is here right now. Upstairs in bed. He was injured the other day. Are you—Could you be his grandmother?"

The woman lifted a trembling hand to her lips. "Yes, I am Virginia Van Huysen. Is my grandson expected to live?"

Her tragic eyes startled Beulah. "Oh, yes!" she quickly assured. "He is recovering nicely. It was a bear that attacked him."

"I see." The woman looked bewildered. "My Myles was attacked by a bear?"

Beulah recalled her manners. "Please come inside. My mother will be down in a few minutes; she is caring for my baby brother. I'm sure Myles will wish to see you."

Mrs. Van Huysen gave her a weak smile and stepped inside. "I hope so. I'm sorry, child—it has been a long and tedious journey. My train arrived in town only this morning. Mr. Poole was supposed to meet me in Chicago, but he did not appear."

"I see." Beulah said nothing. She could neither ask questions nor remain silent. The lady seated herself on the horsehair davenport at Beulah's invitation. They sat and stared at one another.

"Would you like me to tell Myles that you have arrived?"

"He did not know I was coming." There was sadness in the woman's reply. "How old are you, child?"

"Eighteen. I am Beulah Fairfield. Obadiah Watson is my stepfather. Myles has worked for him these past three years, mostly during the summers."

"I am pleased to make your acquaintance, Miss Fairfield. You are a pretty child. Do you play the piano?" She indicated Violet's instrument.

"A little. Nothing to compare with Myles. He played for us the other night for the first time. It was amazing."

Mrs. Van Huysen lifted her brows. "So, he still can play. Hmm. Did he sing for you?"

Beulah could not help but smile. "Yes! It was wonderful. He told us that he was a concert pianist in New York, and he told us his real name for the first time. Did you receive his letter?"

"Letter? Myles has not written to me in years."

"But he did! Just last week. He wanted to apologize to you for running away to join the circus when he was a boy. Did Myles live with you always?"

"The boys lived with me after their parents died."

"I didn't know his parents were dead. My father died years ago, but my mother is happy with Mr. Watson. He is a good father to us." Beulah paused. "Did you say 'the boys'? Does Myles have a brother?"

Mrs. Van Huysen suddenly rose. "Please take me to Myles now. I can wait no longer."

Beulah led her to the staircase. "This way, please."

Mrs. Van Huysen worked her way up the stairs. Beulah wanted to offer her arm for support but feared rejection. "This way," she repeated, pushing open the door to Samuel's bedroom.

Myles appeared to be asleep. Blankets covered him to the chin, and his eyes were closed. "Myles?" Beulah whispered, moving to the far side of the bed. He did not stir. The room still smelled of blood, ether, and pain.

Mrs. Van Huysen stood at his other side. "Myles, my dear boy!" Her lips moved, but no other sound emerged. Tears trickled over her withered cheeks.

Beulah touched Myles's shoulder. "Myles, wake up. There is someone here to see you." Her own eyes burned. "Myles!" She gripped his shoulder and shook gently. Her fingers touched warm bare skin. Startled, she jerked her hand away.

His eyes popped open and focused on her face. "Beulah. I was dreaming about you." His hazy smile curled her toes. His hand lifted toward her face.

"Look who is here to see you, Myles," she whispered, unable to speak loudly. She glanced at his grandmother, and a tear slipped down her cheek.

Myles turned his head. Beulah saw his eyes go wide, and his mouth fell open. A moment later he was sitting up, clutching Mrs. Van Huysen and nearly pulling the lady from her feet. "Gram!" His voice was a ragged sob.

Beulah crept from the room.

Chapter 13

Thou wilt keep him in perfect peace,
whose mind is stayed on thee:
because he trusteth in thee.
ISAIAH 26:3

"You're so tiny, Gram. Did you shrink, or have I grown?" Myles asked.

Virginia patted his hand and smoothed his forehead, just as she had during his childhood illnesses. She smiled, but her expression was far away. "You must tell me about Monte sometime, Myles. Right now is convenient for me."

He pulled his hand out of her grasp and ran it over his rumpled hair. "I know. I've been hiding things too long, from myself. . .from everyone." He drew a deep breath and released it in a sigh, praying silently for strength. "This won't be easy."

Virginia watched him with sad yet peaceful eyes.

"Monte was wild, Gram. I know you thought he was a good boy, but it was all a sham. He loved to gamble, drink, and smoke. . .although I can say with confidence that he was never a womanizer. You raised us to respect women, and Monte kept that shred of decency as far as I know. With his charm, he might have been worse than he was."

Tears pooled in his grandmother's eyes, but she nodded. "I knew, Myles. It nearly broke my heart to see the way you two boys fought and despised each other. I prayed for wisdom and did everything I could to encourage love and respect between you. It never happened. For some reason, Monte considered you a rival from the day you were born."

Myles sat stunned. "You knew? I thought you doted on him."

"Certainly. I doted on the both of you. What grandmother doesn't dote on her grandsons, flawed though they may be?"

"Then why did you keep me isolated from everyone except private tutors and force me to practice for hours every day? It was a terrible life for a boy! I thought you hated me and loved Monte."

Virginia looked stunned. "I wanted the best for you, Myles. God gave you a wondrous gift, and I felt it my duty to give you every opportunity to develop and enjoy that gift of music. I thought your complaints stemmed from laziness, and I refused to listen. Oh, my dear, how wrong I was! My poor boys!" Wiping her eyes, she insisted, "Tell me about Monte. I must know."

"When you sent him after me, he took advantage of the opportunity to sample every pleasure the world had to offer. He was delighted to escape his responsibilities. He did plan to return someday, but then circumstances prevented it."

Virginia shook her head. "I knew I had lost him. Releasing him to find you was a last effort to show him that I trusted and respected him as a man. He proved himself unworthy, as I feared. He did write to me occasionally over the years, however, as you did. I never understood why that precious correspondence ended."

Myles absently unbuttoned his undervest. "The last place we were together was Texas; you knew that much. We had a steady job brush-popping longhorns for a big rancher. Monte started running with a group of gamblers. They were the ruin of him. It wasn't long before he started rustling a beef here and there to support his habit, and the boss became suspicious."

Tears trickled down Virginia's cheeks again, but she nodded for him to continue.

Myles twined a loose string around his finger and tugged. "Then all of a sudden Monte changed. I don't know exactly what happened—well, maybe I do—but anyway, one day he was wild, angry, and miserable; the next day he was peaceful, calm, and had this radiant joy about him. He told me that he had made his life right with God. I thought he had lost his mind. Both of us hated church and anything to do with religion, yet here was Monte saying he had found Jesus Christ. He tried to talk with me about God—even gave me a Bible for my birthday."

"Thank You, Jesus!" Virginia moaned into her handkerchief.

"One day we were riding herd, almost ready to start a drive north. Monte was across from me, hunting strays in the arroyos. A group of riders approached him. I took my horse up on a small bluff and watched. I had a bad feeling—something about the situation made me nervous. The best I can figure, the riders were men to whom Monte owed money, probably demanding payment. I saw Monte's horse rear up; Monte fell off backward and vanished. The sound of a shot reached me an instant later. Panic spread through the herd. Within seconds I was riding for my life, hemmed in on every side by fear-crazed longhorns."

The string broke free, and his button dropped beneath the blankets.

"And Monte?"

"I never found him, Gram. By the time we got that herd straightened out—a good bit smaller than it was when the stampede started—we were miles from the location of the fight, and it was pouring rain. I hunted for days, but found no trace of Monte or his mustang. The horse never returned to the remuda; it must have died in the stampede, too."

Virginia sobbed quietly.

"I don't know if the men who killed Monte were aware that I witnessed his murder, but I didn't take chances. I was nineteen, scared, stricken with regret and sorrow. I hightailed it out of Texas and never went back. Once or twice I thought about writing to you, but shame prevented it. Not until God straightened me out this summer did I have the courage to confess my role in Monte's death."

"You weren't to blame, Myles." The idea roused Virginia from her grief.

He sniffed ruefully. "Had I not run away from home, Monte would never have been in Texas."

"Then he most likely would have died in a back alley in Manhattan. It is not given us to know what might have been, my boy. We can only surrender what actually is to the Lord and trust Him to work His perfect will in our lives." Virginia's voice gained strength as she spoke. "Monte is safe with the Lord, for which fact I am eternally grateful. Myles, dear, can you ever forgive me for my failings as a grandmother?"

Myles nodded. A muscle in his cheek twitched. "I forgive you, Gram. You meant well." He blinked, feeling as if a small chunk had broken from the burden he carried. To his surprise, forgiving his grandmother was an agreeable experience. Love welled up in his heart, and he opened his arms to her.

Weeping and smiling, Virginia fell into his embrace without apparent regard for her dignity.

⁂

Beulah carried a tray upstairs and knocked at the closed door. The voices inside stopped, and Mrs. Van Huysen opened the door. "That looks lovely, dear. Thank you." She stepped aside, and Beulah carried the tray to the bureau.

"Are you two having a good visit? Were you comfortable last night, Mrs. Van Huysen?"

"Yes, dear. Thank you for the use of your bedroom. I'm sorry to put everyone to such inconvenience."

"It is no trouble. We are all pleased to meet Myles's grandmother."

More than a day had passed since Virginia's arrival. Beulah's family had begun to wonder if the two Van Huysens would ever rejoin the world.

Myles eyed the steaming bowls and the stack of fresh bread slices. "What kind of stew?"

Beulah felt her face grow warm. She gave his grandmother an uncertain glance. "Bear."

Virginia's face showed mild alarm.

Myles laughed aloud. "Poetic justice. I hope he was a tender bear. Don't worry, Gram; Beulah is the best cook in the state, with the possible exception of her mother."

"I don't doubt it."

"I hope it's good stew," Beulah said weakly. "Papa says the bear was skinny and tough. He showed me how to prepare it so it would taste better, but I don't know if you'll like it."

Myles shoved himself upright. "Beulah, will you ask Al to feed Pushy? She must be wondering what happened to me."

Beulah avoided looking at him. "Al says Pushy is lonely but well. She reminded him to feed her. No kittens yet."

"You need to take a look at the stitches in my leg, Beulah. There are fifty-seven. Doc did a great job of patchwork. Maybe you could learn a few new designs for your next quilt. Beulah sews beautiful quilts, Gram. She can make almost anything."

"Indeed?"

"Did you see the bear when they brought it in, Beulah? Wasn't he immense? You should have seen that monster climb a tree. He would have had me for sure if Buck hadn't packed him with lead. Say, that water looks good. Would you pour me a drink?"

Beulah felt his gaze as she poured two glasses of water from the pitcher. She glanced at his grandmother and caught an amused smile on the lady's face.

Virginia suddenly rose from her chair and smacked Myles's hand. "Stop that belly rubbing. Never could break you of that." She addressed Beulah obliquely. "Myles suffered chronic stomachaches as a child. He used to wake me every night, crying for his mother. At least he no longer totes around a blanket."

Myles slumped back against the pillows. "No secret is sacred."

Beulah smiled. He would be embarrassed for certain if she gave her opinion of his habit—she found it endearing.

"Myles was a sickly, scrawny child—all eyes and nose. It's amazing what time can do for a man. I never would have known you in a crowd, Myles—although one look into your eyes would have told me. Doesn't he have beautiful eyes, Beulah? They are like his mother's eyes, changing hue to suit his emotions. I would call them hazel."

"Sometimes they look gold like a cat's," Beulah observed.

"Has he told you that he was being groomed for opera? His beautiful voice, his ability to play almost any piece the audience might request, and his subtle humor packed in the crowds. He was truly a marvel—so young, yet confident and composed. Even as a little child, he was mature beyond his years. I thought I was doing the best thing for him, helping him reach the peak of his ability. How wrong a grandmother can be!" She shook her head sadly.

"We've already discussed this, Gram. It's in the past and forgiven, remember?" Myles sounded embarrassed.

"Myles told me about the letter he wrote last week." Virginia shook her head. "I never received it. My private detective, Mr. Poole, recently discovered Myles's whereabouts after long years of searching. I find it odd that Myles wrote to me even as I was coming to see him. But the Lord does work in mysterious ways."

"God told me to write to you, Gram," Myles said gruffly, "even though He knew you were coming."

"At any rate, I plan to telegraph Myles's old agent tomorrow and set up a return performance. The musical world will be agog; his disappearance made the papers for months. His reappearance will take the world by storm, I am certain."

"Gram," Myles began, sounding somewhat irritated.

Beulah backed toward the door. "That's wonderful. You had better eat before the stew gets cold. I'll be back for the dishes."

She heard Myles call her name as she ran down the steps, but she could not return and let them see her distress. *Myles is leaving!*

❧

"Beulah is a pretty thing and well-spoken," Virginia commented. "Exquisite figure, although I'm sure you have noticed that fact."

"I have."

"Your fancy for the child is evident, and even I can see why she attracts you." Her gaze shifted to Myles, and she pursed her lips. "The bluest blood in New York runs in Van Huysen veins."

"Blended with the good red blood of soap merchants, sea captains, and a black sheep or two. From all I hear, some of Beulah's ancestors might have looked down their aristocratic noses at one or two of my wild and woolly ancestors." His mustache curled into a smirk.

Virginia merely poked at her stew.

"So you like Beulah, Gram?" Myles dipped a chunk of bread into his stew and took a large bite.

"I suspect there is more to that inquiry than idle curiosity. Do you intend to wed the child?"

"I do." One cheek bulged as he spoke.

His grandmother considered this information. "Would she blend into our society, Myles? Her manners are charming, but they are country manners, nonetheless."

"If she won't blend in, then I wouldn't either. It's been a long time since I lived in your world." Myles ate with relish.

Virginia frowned. "Yours is a veneer of wilderness, I'm certain. Cultured habits will return, given the proper surroundings. I do hope you plan to shave soon. Facial hair does not become you."

"It was a disguise. Not a good one, but it fooled me." Myles smiled wryly. "All of this is immaterial, since, as you know, I do not intend to remain in New York. One farewell concert, sell the business, and back here I come to purchase a farm." His voice quivered with excitement.

Virginia lifted a trembling hand to her lips. "Um, Myles. . ."

"Buck Watson told me again and again that God blesses when we surrender our lives, and I'm living proof of that fact. It struck me one day that my resistance to facing my past was preventing me from having the future I

231

longed for. You can stay in Long Island if you like, Gram, or we could sell that old house and move you out here. There's room in the Thwaite farmhouse, and I plan to build on anyway. The farm needs money and work, that's certain, but neither should be a problem."

Virginia finally succeeded in breaking into his soliloquy. "About the business. . .there is something you need to know, Myles."

∞

Beulah scooped the mess of raw egg and shattered shells from the hardwood floor and dumped it into a pail. Goo had settled in the cracks between boards.

"I didn't mean to, Beulah. The floor was slippery, and I fell flat." Samuel hovered around her, shaking his hands in distress. "Mama needed those eggs. I feel awful."

Beulah sat back on her heels and sighed. "The chickens will lay more eggs tomorrow, I'm sure. We still have two from yesterday. Don't worry about it. I'm thankful you're not hurt."

Samuel crouched beside her. "Are you feeling all right, Beulah? Is Myles dying? Is Sheriff Boz dying? Why are you being so nice?"

Beulah frowned, then chuckled. "As far as I know, no one is dying. Papa says the sheriff is holding his own. I simply don't see any point in being angry about smashed eggs. You didn't intend to break them, and someone has to clean it up. I'm not busy right now like Mama is, so I'm right for the job."

Her brother laid a hand on her shoulder. "Thanks, Beulah. You're a peach." With a fond pat, he hurried from the room.

When the floor was no longer sticky, Beulah sat back with a satisfied sigh. "That wasn't so bad."

"Beulah," Samuel called from another room. "Mama wants you to collect the dishes from Myles's room. And can you set beans to soak?"

"I will." When the beans were covered and soaking, Beulah washed her hands and checked her reflection in the blurry mirror. Her hair was reasonably neat, and the chapping around her mouth had cleared. She touched her lower lip, recalling Myles's ardent kisses. "Will he ever kiss me again?" she whispered.

Glancing at the ceiling, she sighed again. *Lord, please give me peace about the future. I know You are in control, but I always want to know about things right now! Please help me to control my emotions around Myles and to seek Your will.*

Minutes later, Beulah knocked at the bedroom door. "Myles?"
Silence.

She pushed open the door. He lay with arms folded across his chest, staring out the window. "Myles, do you mind if I collect your dishes?"

He did not so much as bat an eye. Biting her lower lip, Beulah began to load the dinner dishes onto her tray. Mrs. Van Huysen had picked at her food. Myles must have enjoyed his stew.

"Please stay," Myles begged as Beulah prepared to lift the tray. He reached out a hand. She was startled to see that his eyelids were red and swollen.

"Myles, what's wrong? Where is your grandmother?" She wrapped his cold hand within both of hers. "Are you hurting?"

His other hand fiddled with a buttonhole on his undervest; the corresponding button was missing. "Yes." He pressed her hand to his cheek and heaved a shaky sigh.

"I'm so sorry!" Beulah settled into the chair beside his bed. "Would you like me to read to you?"

"No. Don't go so far away."

Beulah blinked. "Far? I'm right next to you. Where is Mrs. Van Huysen?"

"Lying down, I think. I don't care. Nothing matters anymore."

She reached out to feel his forehead. "You're cool and damp. Would you like another blanket?"

When she would have returned to the chair, he grabbed her around the waist and pulled until her feet left the floor. Sprawled across him, Beulah felt his face press into her neck. "Myles, let me go! What if my mother walked in right now? She would murder me!"

"I need you, Beulah. Just hold me, please! I won't do anything indecent, I promise."

Hearing tears in his voice, she stilled. "Myles, what is wrong?" Her hand came to rest on his upper arm. It was hard as stone. His entire body was as tense as a bowstring.

"Do you love me, Beulah?"

Her teeth began to chatter from pure nerves. Something was not right. She felt a terrible heaviness in her spirit. "Yes, I love you. I do. Myles, whatever is wrong? I'm frightened." Pushing up with one arm, she regarded his face. "You were bright and cheerful when I brought lunch. Is the pain that bad? I'll get Mama."

"No!" He gripped her wrist. His eyes were glassy and intense. "Will you marry me right away? We can start over somewhere else, maybe homestead a place."

She shook her head in confusion. "I thought you planned to buy the Thwaite farm and settle here. Why should we marry right away? You're acting so strange, Myles."

He emitted a bark of laughter. "Plans? I have no more plans. Not ever. Plans involve depending on someone else. I will never again trust anyone but myself. And you, of course. You'll be my wife. We can live by ourselves out West."

The dread in Beulah's chest increased. "Please tell me what has happened." She twisted her arm, trying to escape his viselike grip.

He suddenly released her and flung both forearms over his face. "Same old story. I trust someone, they let me down. Everyone I have ever depended on has failed me. Everyone. Most of all God. As soon as I start trusting Him even the slightest bit, the world caves in. If you desert me, too, Beulah, I think I'll crawl away and die."

She reached a hand toward his arched chest, then drew it back. "But God will never fail you. Why do you think He let you down?"

Myles sat up in a rush of flying blankets. Eyes that reminded Beulah of a cornered cougar's blazed into her soul, and an oath blasted from Myles's lips. His white teeth were bared. "Enough of this insanity! The entire concept of a loving, all-powerful God is absurd. A fairy tale we've been force-feeding children for generations. A superstition from the Dark Ages. I don't ever want to hear you talk about God to me again, do you hear?"

Beulah's mouth dropped open.

His fury faded. "Don't look at me like I'm some kind of monster! I need you, Beulah!" Flinging the blankets aside, Myles swung his legs over the far side of the bed and tried to stand on his good leg.

Seeing him sway, she sprang around the foot of the bed. "What are you doing? Myles, get back in bed or I'll call Papa." She stopped cold, realizing that he wore nothing but winter underwear. Hot blood flooded her face, and she rushed back to stand by the door.

He whipped a blanket from the bed and wrapped it around his waist. Jaw set, he hopped to the window and looked down on bare trees and blowing snow. "That's how I feel inside: cold, gray, and lifeless."

"That's because you've turned your back on God." Beulah was surprised to hear herself speak. "What happened to you, Myles? Why are you acting this way?"

He huffed. "I'll tell you what happened. For years Buck has been telling me about God, about salvation. Finally I decided to try this thing out, trusting God. I wrote to Gram. I started giving God credit for the good things happening in my life. I even started believing that He was with me. When I read the Bible it was as if He talked to me."

Beulah studied his broad shoulders and felt her dreams crumbling.

"I began to believe that He had wonderful plans for my life—marriage with you, the farm I've always wanted, and friends who like me for myself, not because I'm a Van Huysen. I've never wanted the money; I've been proud to support myself and lean on no one. . .except maybe Buck. But since God told me to reconcile with Gram, I figured He must intend me to make use of my inheritance. I didn't want much; just enough to buy a farm and set us up with a good living. Then I found out that you loved me—life was looking incredibly good. Gram came, asked me to forgive her, and I did. Great stuff. Everything coming together."

He fell silent.

Beulah settled into a chair, hands clenched in her lap.

"Then the cannonball drops: There is no money. The family friend who ran the Van Huysen Soap Company mismanaged it into bankruptcy, sold out to another manufacturer, and is now president of that company. He swindled it all away and left Gram holding massive debts. She sold off most of our stock and commercial properties to pay the debts, then mortgaged the family house to pay for the detectives who found me. There is no money. None."

Beulah tried to sound sympathetic. "Don't the police know how that man cheated your grandmother? Isn't there something you could do to help her?"

"There is no money to pay for lawyers, and apparently Mr. Roarke covered his legal tracks. It looks as shady as the bottom of a well, but no one can prove anything."

"Poor Mrs. Van Huysen. I can understand why you are upset. Had you been there to keep an eye on the business, this might not have happened to her."

Myles turned to fix her with a glare. "Don't you understand, Beulah? Gram is fine; she still has the old house and a small stipend to live on. The money lost was *my* money! This is the end of *my* dream. I have no money to buy a farm, and I can't support a family on my pay as a hired hand. We cannot stay here. Either I must return to New York and try to break back into the music world—which would not be an easy task no matter what Gram says—or I must head out West and find land to homestead."

Beulah's chest heaved, and her heart thudded against her ribs. That heavy, ugly feeling weighed on her spirit. "So when it looks like God is answering your prayers the way you want, you believe in Him. As soon as things don't go your way, you decide He doesn't exist? That isn't faith, Myles. That is opportunism. And I thought *I* was a selfish person! I don't care what you decide to do. Whatever it is, you'll do it without me."

Picking up the tray, she stalked from the room.

Chapter 14

And Jesus answered and said unto him,
What wilt thou that I should do unto thee?
MARK 10:51

Al entered the sickroom without knocking. "Myles, you won't believe what happened!" Spotting Mrs. Van Huysen, he pulled off his hat. "Hello, ma'am."

"Good morning, Albert," Virginia responded cordially.

"I sure enjoyed visiting with you last night. Myles, do you know this grandmother of yours whupped me at checkers? It was an outright slaughter."

"Myles never cared for the game," Virginia said when Myles remained silent. "He is good at chess, however." A moment later, she rose and gathered her embroidery. "I'll let you boys chat awhile." The door clicked shut behind her.

Al settled into the empty chair, long legs splayed. "It stinks in here. Like medicine."

Myles tried to scratch his leg beneath the bandage. The skin showing around the white cloth was mottled green and purple. "What's the news from town? Doc tells me it looks like Boz will pull through."

"If good nursing has anything to do with it, Boz will be back on his feet within the week. From all I hear, Miss Amelia treats him like a king." Al's eyes twinkled. "She had him moved to her boardinghouse, and her front parlor is now a hospital room. Nothing more interesting to a woman than a wounded man, but I guess you know all about that."

Myles grunted. "So what's your big news?"

Al slipped a letter from his chest pocket. "Today I got this letter from my folks asking me not to come west until spring. Can you believe it? Today! Think about it: If you hadn't let that bear rip your leg off, I would have been on my way by now and missed their letter. No wonder I didn't have peace about leaving! They don't even want me yet. I have no idea what I'll do with my farm next year, but it doesn't matter—God will provide, and I've got all winter to think and prepare. So if you need to go to New York, don't hesitate on my account."

Myles tried to smile. "That's good news, Al. I felt guilty about delaying your trip."

"Now that you're rich and all, you won't be needing a farm job, I reckon," Al said, looking regretful. "I feel funny about things I must have said to you in the last year or two, me thinking you had less education and fewer advantages than I had!" His grin was crooked. "That will teach me to judge people by appearance."

"You always treated me well, Al. You have nothing for which to apologize."

"Why are you so gloomy? Is your leg hurting?"

The innocent question sparked Myles's wrath. He bit back a sharp reply and folded his arms on his chest, staring out the window.

"Hmm. Beulah is moody, too. My powers of deduction tell me that all is not well in paradise."

"Shove off, Al. I'm not in the mood for your jokes." Myles scowled.

Al pursed his lips in thought. "Want to talk with Buck?"

"I want to get out of this house, pack up, and head for Montana."

"What happened, Myles? I thought your life was going great. Beulah loves you, you've cleared things up with your grandmother, you've got a music career and money to burn."

"I'm not rich, Al. The money's gone."

"Oh. All the money?"

"Every cent."

Al looked confused. "But Beulah wouldn't care whether you're rich or not. She loved you as a hired hand."

"Whatever I do, wherever I go, she says she's not going with me. Guess she only loved me if I stayed here in town." Bitterness left a foul taste in his mouth.

"That doesn't sound like Beulah. She could make a home anywhere if she set her mind to it, and she's crazy about you, Myles."

Myles gave a mirthless sniff.

"Sure you don't want to talk to Buck?"

"I know what he'll say. He will tell me I need to forgive those who have wronged me and give control of my life over to God. I've heard it all before."

Al lifted a brow. "Sooo, tell me what's wrong with that answer? Sounds to me as if the truth pricks your pride, pal."

Myles rolled his eyes.

"C'mon, Myles. Think this through. Are you content and filled with joy right now?"

Myles slashed a glare at Al, but his friend never blinked. "Fine. Don't answer that. Think about this: How could your life be worse if God were in control of it?"

Myles opened his mouth, then closed it. His head fell back against the headboard. "I've never had control anyway."

"Exactly. You're at the mercy of circumstances with no one to turn to. The only things you can truly control in your life are your behavior and your reactions."

"Sometimes I can't even control myself."

"Without God, we're all losers. Look at Buck. The stuff that happened to him was like your worst nightmare. He could be the most bitter, angry person you ever met, but he chose to trust God with his life, and look at him now!"

Myles nodded. "And you, too. You didn't get angry about Beulah."

Al shrugged. "It wouldn't have done any good to get mad. Anyone can see she isn't in love with me, and to be honest, my heart isn't broken. The point is, once you decide to trust God with things, He turns your messed-up life into something great. I'm not saying you'd have it easy from then on, or that all your dreams would come true; but no matter what happens, your life would be a success. The Bible says in First Peter, 'Humble yourselves therefore under the mighty hand of God, that he may exalt you in due time.' You can never lift yourself up no matter how hard you try."

After a moment's thought, Myles lowered his chin and shook his head. "I don't see it, Al. I understand that God is far above me, holy and just, almighty and righteous, but loving? I don't know God that way. Sure, He saved me from the bear, but look what has happened to me since."

"When was the last time you read about Jesus?"

"The last time I read the Bible? I was reading in Genesis the other night."

"I think you need to read the Gospels now. The Old Testament is important, too, but you need to understand about Jesus first. Where is your Bible?"

"At our house next to my bed. Don't bring it here, Al. I want to go home. Can you talk Buck into taking me home? It's driving me crazy, being here in the same house with Beulah. She hasn't spoken to me since we fought yesterday. Gram is good to me, but I'm getting cabin fever."

Al looked into his eyes and gave a short nod. "I'll talk to Buck."

⟨⟩

Beulah watched the wagon disappear up the drive. Her eyes were dry. Her heart felt as leaden as the sky. Returning to her seat, she picked up her piecework and took a disinterested stitch.

Violet observed her from across the parlor. "The house already seems quiet, doesn't it? I will miss having Virginia around to chat with. She is the most interesting lady. She refused my offer to stay here. I hope she will be comfortable at the men's house. They don't have an indoor pump, you know, and the furnishings are rather crude."

"Is Daniel sleeping?" Beulah asked in her most casual tone.

"Yes. Samuel is at Scott's house, and Eunice is reading. Did you hear Al's news?" Violet snipped a thread with her teeth.

"Several times over. I told Eunice first; then she told *me* about three times so far. I'm glad he's not leaving for a while. We would all miss him. I think Eunice has romantic feelings for Al."

Violet chuckled. "I've noticed. She has good taste. Maybe I'll have Albert for a son-in-law someday after all. I hope so. He's a dear boy."

Beulah concentrated on tying a knot. "She's only thirteen, Mama. Maybe I should have married him."

Violet's hands dropped to her lap. "Pardon?"

Beulah winced, wishing she had kept the stray thought to herself. "Al wouldn't marry me now if I proposed to him myself, and I'm not in love with him anyway, but I can't help wondering if I couldn't have been happily married to him. After all, lots of people make marriages of convenience and end up happy together. Al is annoying, but he's steady and safe."

Violet lowered her chin and stared at her daughter. "What about Myles?"

Beulah pressed her lips together and jerked at a tangle in her thread. "Myles is not the man I thought he was. He is selfish and bitter." She swallowed hard.

Setting aside her mending, Violet joined her daughter on the couch. "Tell me."

Beulah leaned against Violet. Her shoulders began to shake. Wiping her eyes, she grumbled, "I hate crying, Mama, but it seems as if every time I try to talk about something important, I start bawling."

"It's a woman's lot in life, darling." Violet pushed a lock of loose hair behind her daughter's ear and smiled. "I understand, believe me."

Between sobs and sniffles, Beulah poured out her heartache and disappointment. ". . .so I told him he could go without me. I thought he was kind and wise, Mama, but yesterday he acted like a brute. And all because of some money he doesn't have. I'm so thankful I found out what he is really like before I married him!"

Violet stared at the fireplace, pondering her reply. "So now Myles is a brute. All the good things you loved about him mean nothing."

Beulah wiped her eyes and nose with a handkerchief. "I could never be happily married to a man with such a terrible temper, Mama. He swore in my presence and never apologized!"

"If Myles has truly turned his back on the Lord, then I agree that you should not marry him. But if, as your papa believes, he is on the verge of surrender, it would be a shame for you to give up on him. He adores you, Beulah, and I think he would make you an excellent husband."

Beulah's head popped up. "Mama! How can you say that after what I just told you? He told me never to mention God's name in his presence again!"

"He was distraught. I'm sure he didn't mean it. I understand he had a long talk with Al about God this afternoon, and he plans to start reading the New Testament when he gets home today. Darling, every man has faults. I hope you realize that. Even Al would lose his temper, given the right provocation."

"Papa never shouts at you."

A dimple appeared near Violet's mouth. "No, but that's because he talks softly when he gets angry. The angrier he is, the softer his voice."

"You don't mean it, Mama," Beulah said, eyes wide.

Violet rubbed a little circle on the girl's back. "I mean every word. Darling, you had better learn quickly that only God can offer you complete security and contentment. No man can fulfill your every need, and most of them wouldn't want to try. The average man enters marriage thinking that a wife's purpose is to fulfill *his* needs. Unless you recognize the fact that all people are basically selfish, you will be in for a rude awakening when you marry. Myles has plenty of faults, but so have you, my dear."

"If people are so terribly selfish, how can a marriage ever be happy?"

"That's where the Lord makes a difference. In His strength, you and I can learn to love our men with all their human flaws and failings. That is one of the greatest joys of marriage: to give and give of yourself to please your beloved. Usually a good man will respond in kind, but you must understand that there is never a guarantee of this. Your part is to love at all times, without reservation."

Beulah wilted. "How can I do that, Mama? You know how selfish I am!"

"In the Lord's strength, dear. If you truly love Myles, you will accept him just as he is and be grateful for the opportunity to shower him with the love and attention he craves from you. There are few things in life more fulfilling than pleasing your husband, Beulah." Violet spoke with the authority of experience.

Beulah sat straighter. "I want to be exactly like you, Mama. You make Papa so happy that he glows when you're near. I want to make Myles that happy."

Violet squeezed her shoulders. "That's my girl! Now you keep on praying for Myles, and when he is ready to receive your love, I think you will know it."

Beulah hugged her mother. "You're wonderful. I feel so much better! Now, I have this idea for my wedding dress that I've been wanting to discuss with you. Do you have a moment?"

Eyes twinkling, Violet nodded.

⌇

Pushy kneaded a dent for herself in the middle of Myles's back. He groaned when she settled down. "You must weigh a ton, cat. When are you going to fire off those kittens?"

Pushy purred, vibrating against him. "You really missed me, didn't you?" Her affectionate greeting had warmed his heart.

He returned to his reading. The book was fascinating. For the first time in his life, Myles could visualize Jesus among the people, teaching, healing, loving.

The parable of the unforgiving servant in Matthew, chapter eighteen, struck a nerve. He recognized himself in the cruel, vindictive man who punished a debtor after he himself had been forgiven a much larger debt. The simple story was an eloquent reprimand and admonition.

"I understand, Jesus," Myles said, bowing his head. "This story is about me. Please forgive me for my anger at Monte. I want to forgive him as You forgave me. If he's there with You now, please tell him for me. Tell him I love him. I forgive Mama for dying and leaving me behind. She must have been terribly lonely after Father was killed in the war. And I forgive Mr. Roarke for swindling us, too. I don't imagine he's deriving much true pleasure from his ill-gotten gains. I feel almost sorry for him. You know that the real reason I refused to forgive people all those years was pride. I thought I was better than others. I was wrong."

Humility was an easy burden in comparison to the bitter load he had carried for so many years. Myles felt free and relaxed, yet still rather empty.

"Where is the joy, God? Are You really here with me? What's wrong with me? Maybe I'm spiritually blind."

Pushy purred on.

Sighing, Myles returned to the Book. The story enthralled him, and when he reached the end of Matthew, he continued on into Mark, absorbed in the story of Jesus from a slightly different perspective. His eyes were growing heavy when he reached chapter ten, the story of blind Bartimaeus begging at the roadside.

Then, for some reason, he was wide-awake. His mind pictured the pitiful man in rags who cried out, "Jesus, Son of David, have mercy on me!"

Jesus stopped and asked the fellow what he wanted. Jesus didn't overlook the poor and helpless among His people. He cared about the blind man.

Myles read the next part aloud. " 'The blind man said unto him, Lord, that I might receive my sight.

" 'And Jesus said unto him, Go thy way; thy faith hath made thee whole. And immediately he received his sight, and followed Jesus in the way.' "

Myles stopped and read it again. Slowly his eyes closed and his hands formed into fists. The cry echoed from his own heart. "Lord, I want to see! Please, help me to see You as You truly are."

He contemplated Jesus. "The kindest man who has ever lived. He came to reveal You to mankind. He was Emmanuel—'God with us.' God in the flesh. So You *are* a God of mercy, patience, and infinite understanding. Lord, I believe!"

Myles wept for joy.

Chapter 15

For I determined not to know any thing among you,
save Jesus Christ, and him crucified.
1 CORINTHIANS 2:2

His bandaged foot wouldn't fit into a stirrup, so Myles decided to ride Cholla bareback. A wool blanket protected his clothes from her sweat and hair, and he laid his walking stick, a gift from Cyrus Thwaite, across her withers. "Take it easy, girl," he warned, gripping a hank of her mane in one hand as he sprang to her back and swung his leg over. "I'm running on one foot, so to speak." The swelling had receded and the vivid bruising had faded to pale green and purple, but Myles could put little weight on the foot as yet.

"Myles, you be careful," Virginia called from the front porch as he passed. "Visit your friend and the barber and come straight home. Do you hear?"

"I hear." Reining in the fidgeting mare, Myles grinned at his grandmother. He could endure her motherly domination for the sake of her good cooking and excellent housekeeping skills—abilities he had never before known she possessed. "You're quite a woman, Gram."

"Away with your flattery," she retorted, not before he glimpsed her pleasure.

Cholla trotted almost sideways up the drive, head tucked and tail standing straight up. Its wispy hair streamed behind her like a shredded banner. "You're a loaded weapon today, aren't you?" Myles patted the mare's taut neck. "Sorry; no running. The roads are too icy."

A few miles of trotting took the edge off Cholla's energy. She still occasionally challenged her master's authority, but her heart was no longer in it. Myles felt her muscles unwind beneath him.

Although it was good to be out in the open again instead of cloistered in his stuffy room, fighting the horse drained much of Myles's strength. When he dismounted in front of Miss Amelia's boardinghouse, he lost hold of his walking stick. It clattered to the frozen mud. Cholla shied to one side, and Myles landed hard. His bad foot hit the ground. Clutching Cholla by the chest and withers, he gritted his teeth and grimaced until the worst pain had passed.

"Steady, girl," he gasped. Balancing on one foot, he scooped up his stick. It wasn't easy to tether Cholla with one hand, but he managed. Hopping on one foot, using the stick for balance, he made his way to Amelia's porch.

"What on earth are you doing, Myles?" Amelia said, flinging open her front door and ushering him inside.

"I came to see Boz," Myles gasped. "Isn't he here?"

"You come on into the parlor and sit yourself down." Amelia supported his arm with a steely grip. "That's where Boz keeps himself." She lifted her voice. "You got a visitor, Sheriff. Another ailing cowboy on my hands. Just what I needed. You two sit here and have a talk. I've got work to do." Leaving Myles in an armchair, she brushed her hands on her apron, gave each man an affectionate look, and departed.

Boz drew a playing card from his deck, laid it on a stack, and gave Myles a crooked smile. "How's the foot?" His right shoulder was heavily wrapped, binding that arm to his side.

"Mending. You don't sound so good." Myles shifted in his chair.

Boz did not immediately reply. "I ain't so good, Myles," he finally wheezed. "Bullet nicked a lung and severed a nerve in my shoulder. It kinda bounced around in there. Doc did his best, but he doesn't expect I'll regain the use of my arm."

Myles blinked and stared at the floor.

"I know what you're thinkin'," Boz said. "Not much good in a one-armed sheriff. I reckon God has other plans for my future."

Myles met the other man's steady gaze. Slowly he nodded, amazed by Boz's cheerful acceptance of his fate.

"Amelia says I can work for her. She's been needing to hire household help, and she cain't think of anyone she'd rather have about the place."

"You?" Myles stared blankly until he caught the twinkle in his friend's eyes. "Boz, are you joshing me?"

The former sheriff's face creased into a broad grin. "She reckons it wouldn't be proper for me to stay here permanent-like, so she proposed marriage."

Myles began to chuckle. Boz put a finger to his lips. "Hush! Let the woman think it was all her idea, at least until after we're hitched."

Myles sputtered with suppressed merriment, and Boz joined in. Soon the two men were wiping tears from their faces. Boz groaned, holding his shoulder and wheezing. "Stop before you do me in."

The door opened, and Amelia backed into the room carrying a tray. "I brung you coffee and cakes." Her sharp eyes inspected their faces. "Doc says the sheriff needs quiet. Hope I didn't make a mistake by letting you in, Myles."

"He's all right, Amelia. Laughter is good for what ails a man. What you got there? Raisin cookies?" Boz perked up.

"Yes, and snickerdoodles. Mind you don't eat more'n is good for ya, Boswell Martin."

Nearly an hour later, Myles grinned as he heaved himself up on Cholla's back. "Next stop, the store, then on to the barbershop." The horse flicked her ears to listen.

Thank You for leaving Boz with us here on earth, Lord, Myles prayed as he rode. *And thank You for giving him his heart's desire. He's waited a long time for love, but from the look in Amelia's eyes while she fussed over him today, he's found it.*

Myles picked up his mail at the general store. There was a letter addressed in strange handwriting. Curious, he paused just inside the doorway, balanced on his good foot, and ripped open the letter.

Dear Myles,

    Antonio tells me what to write, and I do my best.

    Antonio pray for you every day. He say have you dropped your burden yet? I hope you do, Myles. We want your best for you.

    You can write us here in Florida. We stay until summer season open. We want to visit you, but have not the money.

    Antonio want to know if the bear was found. He feel bad about keeping it secret. Our circus, it was bought by another man when the owner was put in jail. He cheat one man too many, Antonio say. Things better for us now, but we want a home that does not move.

    Antonio speak much of settling down to open a bakery. Is there need for a bakery in your town?

                        God bless you.
                      Antonio and Gina Spinelli

Myles determined to write back at his first opportunity. Antonio would be pleased to hear news of his mended relationship with God, and if any town ever needed a bakery, Myles was certain Longtree, Wisconsin, did.

As Myles rode past the parsonage, someone hailed him. He reined in Cholla and waited for the pastor to approach. "Hello, Reverend."

David Schoengard's ruddy face beamed as he stood at Cholla's shoulder and reached up to shake Myles's hand. "Good to see you about town. We've been praying for you. From all I hear, yours was a serious injury."

"Thanks for the prayers. God has been healing me. . .inside and out."

David's eyes gleamed. "Ah, so the lamb has found its way home?"

"More like the Shepherd roped and hog-tied an ornery ram, flung it over His shoulder, and hauled it home. I'm afraid I was a tough case, but He never stopped trying to show me the truth."

The pastor chuckled. "I understand. Are you ready to profess your faith before the church?"

Myles tucked his chin. "Is that necessary?"

"Not for your salvation, of course, but it would be a wonderful encouragement to other believers to hear how God worked in your life. I'm also hoping you'll honor us with a song someday soon."

Staring between Cholla's ears, Myles pondered. "I do need to ask forgiveness of people in this town. Guess this is my chance. I'll do it, if you think I should, Reverend."

"I appreciate that—and please call me Dave, or at least Pastor Dave. I'm no more 'reverend' than you are." He patted Cholla's furry neck.

Myles nodded. "All right, Pastor Dave. Do I need your approval on a song?"

"I'll trust you to choose an appropriate selection. And thank you. Caroline will be excited when I tell her you agreed to sing."

"How is she doing?"

"She has a tough time of it during the last weeks before a baby arrives, but she handles it well. My mother is at the house to help out. She and Caroline are great friends."

David cleared his throat. "If you don't mind me asking, how are things between you and Marva? Or is it you and Beulah? Caroline and I were never sure."

Myles scratched his beard and took a deep breath. "Marva and I are friends. There never was more between us. And Beulah isn't speaking to me at present. I. . .uh. . .let's just say she got a glimpse of Myles Van Huysen at his worst, and she didn't care much for what she saw."

"I see. Have you apologized?"

"Not yet. I haven't spoken with her since God. . .since He changed me. I don't know how to approach her. I mean, she pretty much told me to leave her out of my future plans."

"The change in you could make a difference, Myles. Faint heart never won fair maiden."

"Yes, I need to figure out a plan. Right now I'd better be on my way. I've got orders not to dawdle."

"Your grandmother?" David stepped away from the horse. "I enjoyed meeting her last Sunday. Quite a lady."

Myles nodded. "Beulah is a lot like her. Feisty." He smiled. "If you think of it, I could use a few prayers in that area, too. You know, for wisdom and tact when I talk to Beulah."

"Every man needs prayer in the area of communication with women," David said with a straight face. "See you Sunday." With a wink, he turned away.

Myles squirmed in the front pew, elbows resting on his knees, and rubbed one finger across his mustache. His chin felt naked, bereft of its concealing beard. His heart pounded erratically. Lines of a prepared speech raced through his head.

Marva Obermeier played the piano while the congregation sang. She never once looked in his direction. Myles could not sing. He knew he would be ill if he tried. Why had he volunteered to sing so soon? He wasn't ready. It was one thing to entertain a crowd for profit and another thing altogether to sing in worship to God while other believers listened.

"Relax, Myles. The Lord will help you." Virginia leaned over to pat his arm. He nodded without looking up.

Was Beulah here, somewhere in the room behind him? Would she change her mind when she saw how God was transforming his life, or had he forever frightened her away? With an effort, Myles turned his thoughts and heart back to God and prayed for courage and peace. *This is all new to me, Lord. I feel like a baby, helpless and dependent. Can You really use me?*

His foot throbbed. He needed to prop it up again. Pastor David was making an announcement. Myles tried to focus his mind.

"A new brother in Christ has something to share with us this morning. Please join me in welcoming Myles Trent Van Huysen into our fellowship of believers."

Myles rose and turned to face the crowd, leaning on his crutch. Expectant, friendly faces met his gaze. He swallowed hard. "Many of you know that I have been living a lie among you these past few years. Today I wish to apologize for my deceit and ask your forgiveness."

There was Beulah, seated between her mother and Eunice. Her dark eyes held encouragement and concern. She pressed three fingers against her trembling lips.

"My grandmother, Virginia Van Huysen, has prayed for me these many long years. She never gave up hope that God would chase me down. I stand before you to confess that I am now a child of God, saved by the shed blood of Jesus Christ. My life, such as it is, belongs to Him forevermore. I do not yet know how or where He will lead, but I know that I will humbly follow." His voice cracked.

Marva sat beside her father in the fourth row. Although her eyes glittered with unshed tears, she gave Myles an encouraging smile.

"I'm having difficulty even talking—don't know how I'll manage to sing. But I want to share my testimony with a song."

He limped to the piano. After leaning his crutch against the wall, he settled on the bench. This piano needed tuning, and several of its keys were missing their ivories. One key sagged below the rest, dead. Myles played a prolonged introduction while begging God to carry him through this ordeal.

Lifting his face, he closed his eyes and began to sing Elizabeth Clephane's beautiful hymn:

"Beneath the cross of Jesus I fain would take my stand. . ."

Myles knew that the Lord's hand was upon him. His voice rang true and clear. The third verse was his testimony:

"I take, O cross, thy shadow for my abiding place—
I ask no other sunshine than the sunshine of His face;

Content to let the world go by, to know no gain nor loss,
My sinful self my only shame, my glory all the cross."

The last notes faded away. Myles opened his eyes. His grandmother was beaming, wiping her face with a handkerchief. He collected his crutch and stood. Someone near the back of the room clapped, another person joined in, and soon applause filled the church. "Amen!" Myles recognized Al's voice.

Pastor Schoengard wrapped an arm around Myles's shoulder and asked, "Would anyone like to hear more from our brother?"

The clapping and shouts increased in volume. " 'Amazing Grace.' " It was Cyrus Thwaite's creaky voice.

" 'Holy, Holy, Holy,' " someone else requested.

Pastor David lifted his hand, chuckling. "This is still a worship service, friends. Please maintain order and do not overwhelm our new brother." He turned to Myles. "Will you sing again, or do you need rest?" he asked in an undertone. "Don't feel obliged, Myles. There will be other days."

Myles stared at the floor, dazed by this openhearted reception. He smiled at the pastor. "It is an honor." He returned to the bench and began to play, making the ancient spinet sound like a concert grand.

Chapter 16

But as it is written, Eye hath not seen, nor ear heard,
neither have entered into the heart of man,
the things which God hath prepared for them that love him.
1 CORINTHIANS 2:9

W hoa, girl." Myles hauled the horse to a stop and set the buggy's brake. On the other side of a pasture fence, Al and Buck kept watch over a smoldering fire, feeding it with branches and dead leaves. Smoke shifted across the sodden field, hampered by drifting snowflakes.

Myles hoisted a large basket up to the seat beside him, unlatched the lid, and peeked inside. Indignant yellow eyes met his gaze. "Meow," Pushy complained.

"I'll be right back, I promise. I need to talk to Buck for a minute. You should be warm enough in there." Leaving the basket on the floor, he climbed down and vaulted the fence, hopping on his good foot before regaining his balance.

Cold seeped through his layers of clothing. "Not a great day to be outside," he commented to the other men as he approached. "That fire feels good." He held out gloved hands to the blaze.

"Need to get rid of this brush before winter sets in for good," Buck answered, forking another bundle of dead leaves into the fire. Flames crackled, and ashes drifted upward. "This is the best weather for it. Little danger of fire spreading."

"Um, I need to talk with you, Buck. Do you have a minute?"

Al looked from Myles to Buck and back. "Need privacy? I can head for the house and visit the family."

Myles shifted his weight, winced at the pain in his leg, and tried to smile. "Thanks. Would you take the buggy, Al? I've got Pushy and the kittens with me—planned to let Beulah see them. I'm afraid they'll get cold."

Al smirked and shook his head. "You and those cats! All right, I'll deliver the litter to Beulah, but that's all. Should I tell her you're coming?"

Myles nodded. "Soon."

He stood beside Buck and watched Al drive away. The rooftop of Fairfield's Folly was visible through the leafless trees surrounding it. Smoke drifted from its chimneys. Myles could easily imagine Beulah working at the stove or washing dishes.

"How's the leg?"

"Better every day."

248

"Good. Violet is in town visiting Caroline and the Schoengard baby," Buck said. "Had you heard? Little girl, arrived last night, big and healthy. They named her Jemima after Pastor David's mother."

"That's wonderful! A healthy girl, eh?" Myles fidgeted. "Great news."

"Beulah is watching Daniel. Samuel stayed home from school; said he was sick. I have my doubts." A smile curled Buck's thick mustache and crinkled the corners of his eyes.

"Beulah is home?"

"That's what I said. Washing laundry, last I saw."

"I, uh, need to talk with you. About the future. I mean, about Beulah and me. I need advice."

Buck threw a branch on the fire. "I'm listening."

Myles shifted his gaze from the fire to the house to the trees and back to Buck. He crossed and uncrossed his arms. "I'm not sure where to begin."

Buck smiled. Sparks flew when he tossed a large pine knot into the blaze.

"I want to ask your permission to marry Beulah, but I don't know how soon I'll be able to support a wife. I must return to New York and give a concert tour. Along with a few remaining stocks and bonds and whatever is left from the sale of the family house after I pay off debts, the money I earn should be enough to purchase the Thwaite farm. Cyrus agreed to hold it for me. . .at least for a few months." Myles spoke rapidly. Realizing that he was rubbing the front of his coat, he stuffed the errant hand into his pocket.

"Do you plan to propose before you leave or after you return?"

"I don't know." Myles rubbed the back of his neck, pushing his hat over his forehead. "Do you think she will accept my proposal at all? I mean, I haven't spoken with her—not a real conversation—since the time she blew up at me. I can't leave without knowing, but at the same time it would be tough to leave her behind once we're engaged. What do you think I ought to do, Buck?"

"Have you prayed about this?"

"God must be sick of my voice by now. I've been begging for wisdom and guidance. I feel so puny and stupid. After years of regarding God with—I'm embarrassed to admit this, but it's the truth—with a superior attitude, I'm feeling like small potatoes these days."

"God likes small potatoes. They are useful to Him."

Myles shoved his hat back into place. His smile felt unsteady, as did his knees. "If Beulah won't have me, I'll set up housekeeping with my grandmother. Gram has decided she likes Longtree better than New York, believe it or not. Most of her old friends have died, and she prefers to live out her earthly days with me here. She's a great lady."

"That she is. And what are her plans if you marry?"

"She would be willing either to settle in town at Miss Amelia's boarding-house or to stay with us at the farm, whichever Beulah would prefer. Gram has money of her own, enough to keep her in modest comfort for life." Myles tossed a handful of twigs into the fire, one at a time. "Do you...do you think Beulah will see me today? I mean, is she still angry? I was terrible to her that day—I swore at her, threatened her, and manhandled her."

Buck shook his head. A little chuckle escaped.

"What are you thinking?" Myles asked in frustration.

"Beulah and her mother have been sewing a wedding gown these past few weeks while you've been stewing in remorse and uncertainty. She forgave you even before you professed your faith at church. Beulah's temper is quick, but she seldom holds a grudge. I hope you know what a moody little firebrand you're getting. That girl will require plenty of loving attention."

Myles gaped as a glow spread throughout his soul. "She's been making a wedding dress? For me?"

"Actually, I believe she intends to wear it herself," Buck said dryly.

Myles was too intent to be amused. "And I have your permission to propose?"

"You do. Violet and I are well acquainted with your industry and fidelity, my friend. You will be an excellent husband to our girl."

Myles stared at the ground, blinking hard. "And I had the gall to believe God had deserted me," he mumbled. Biting his lip, he turned away. "I don't deserve this."

Buck wrapped a strong arm around the younger man's shoulders. "I felt the same way when Violet accepted me."

"You did?"

Buck laughed aloud. "Go talk to the girl and decide together on a wedding date. It might be wiser to wait until your return from New York to marry; but then again it might be pleasant for the two of you to make that concert tour together—a kind of paid honeymoon. Beulah could be your inspiration."

Myles stared into space until Buck gave him a shove. "Get on with you. She's waiting."

⌒⌒⌒

Beulah jabbed a clothespin into place, securing Samuel's overalls on the cord Papa had suspended across the kitchen. The laundry nearest the stove steamed. Beulah tested one of Daniel's diapers. It was still damp.

"You could at least try to talk to me," she accused the absent Myles. "How am I supposed to demonstrate unselfish love to a man I never see?" Her lips trembled. Clenching her jaw, she stabbed another clothespin at an undervest but missed. "No one tells me anything. For all I know, he's going back to New York without me."

Recalling Myles's singing in church, she brushed a tear away with the back of one hand. "He was so handsome. I hardly knew him without his beard. He looked like a stranger. And oh, his song made my soul ache." Pressing a hand to her breast, she allowed a quiet sob. "You have changed his heart, haven't You,

God? Mama was so right. After all my accusations that Mama wouldn't give Myles a chance, *I'm* the one who quit on him at the crucial moment. Please let me try again, Lord."

Samuel's wool sock joined its mate on the line.

A whimper of sound escaped as Beulah's lips moved. "If you have changed your mind about me, the least you could do is come and tell me so. Oh, Myles, I love you so much!"

A lid rattled. "Who are you talking to, Beulah?" Samuel slipped an oatmeal cookie from the crock and took an enormous bite. Watchful sat at his feet, tail waving, hopeful eyes fixed upon the cookie.

Startled to discover that she was not alone, Beulah glared. "Myself."

"Finally found someone who wants to listen, hmm?" Samuel ducked when she threw a wet towel at his head. Laughing, he left the kitchen with Watchful at his heels.

"I thought you were too sick to go to school," Beulah yelled after him. "You'd better get in bed before Mama comes home."

She retrieved the towel, brushing off dust. Sighing, she decided it needed washing again. "My penalty for a temper tantrum."

Scraping damp hair from her face with water-shriveled fingers, she drifted to the window and stared outside. Movement drew her attention to her garden. A doe and two large fawns, dressed in their gray winter coats, nibbled at bolted cabbages. Resting her arms on the windowsill, Beulah felt her heart lighten. "Better not let anyone else see you," she warned the deer. "One of your former companions is hanging on the meat hook by the barn. We have plenty of venison for the winter, but you never know."

The animals' ears twitched. All three stared toward Beulah's window. After a tense moment, the doe flicked her tail and returned to her browsing. Then the three deer lifted their heads to stare toward the barn before springing away into the forest.

Watchful barked from the entryway, and Beulah heard a man's deep voice. Her hands flew to her messy hair, and her eyes widened.

"Al is here!" Samuel shouted. "He brought something in a basket."

"I'll be right there," she said, relaxing. It was only Al. "Why aren't you in bed, Sam?"

Samuel pounded upstairs, skipping steps on the way.

✍

Myles lifted his hand to knock just as the door opened. Al waved an arm to usher him inside. "Enter, please. I'm on my way out. I'll take my mare back and leave the buggy for you. Want me to stable Bess before I go?"

Myles nodded as he limped inside. "Thanks, Al." He swallowed hard. "Where is Beulah?"

Al's grin widened. "In the parlor. Sitting on your bear."

"My bear?" Myles stopped, puzzled.

"It makes a nice rug."

"Oh, the bear."

Shaking his head, Al laughed. "Go on. Talking to you is useless." He clapped his hat on his head and slammed the door as he left.

Myles licked his lips and took a fortifying breath. *Lord, please help me.*

He stepped into the parlor. A shaggy brown rug lay before the stone hearth. Beulah sat Indian-style in the middle of the bear's back, and in the hammock of her skirt lay Pushy and four tiny kittens. Firelight glowed in Beulah's eyes and hair. The cat purred with her eyes closed while her babies nursed.

"Myles!" Beulah's voice held all the encouragement Myles required. "You came."

Daniel lay on his back near the rug, waving a wooden rattle with one hand. At the sight of Myles, the baby rolled to his stomach and called a cheerful greeting. Myles bent to pick up the baby, enjoying the feel of his solid little body. Daniel crowed again and whacked Myles in the face with a slimy hand. Bouncing for joy, he dropped his rattle.

"I came. You like my kittens?" Favoring his left leg, he settled near her on the rug. Daniel wriggled out of his grasp and scooted toward the fallen toy. "I wanted you to see them before their eyes opened."

"They are adorable." Beulah lifted a black and white kitten. Its pink feet splayed, and its mouth opened in a silent meow. Pushy opened her eyes partway until Beulah returned her baby. "I love them, Myles."

Hearing a catch in her voice, he inspected her face. "What's wrong?"

"Does this mean you're leaving? You brought the kittens to me for safekeeping."

Myles noted the dots of perspiration on her pert nose, the quivering of her full lips. Tenderness seemed to swell his heart until he could scarcely draw breath. "No, my dearest. I simply wanted you to see them. I have just spoken to your stepfather, as your mother wisely advised."

Beulah's dark eyes held puzzlement. "You spoke to Papa?"

"Have you changed your mind, Beulah? Do you still wish to marry me? Can you forgive me for swearing at you and threatening you?"

She clasped her hands at her breast. "Yes, Myles! More than anything I want to marry you!" She started to rise then remembered the burden in her lap.

Chuckling, Myles scrambled to his hands and knees, leaned over, and kissed her gently. Below his chest, Pushy's purring increased in volume.

When he pulled away, Beulah's eyelashes fluttered. Her lips were still parted. He returned to place a kiss on her nose. "We need to talk, honey."

"Your mustache tickles."

Just then, Daniel let out a squawk. Startled, Myles and Beulah turned. Only the baby's feet projected from beneath the davenport.

"Oh, Daniel!" Beulah cried. "He rolled under there again. Would you get him, Myles?" She deposited kitten after kitten in the blanket-lined basket. Pushy hopped in and curled up with her brood.

After crawling across the room, Myles took hold of Daniel's feet and pulled him out from under the davenport. As soon as he saw Myles, Daniel grinned. "You're a pretty decent chaperone, fella," Myles said. "Better than Pushy is, at any rate."

Beulah hurried to scoop up her dusty brother. "He moves so quickly. I got used to him staying in one place, but now he's into everything."

"Can I come in yet? Are you done kissing?" Poised in the parlor doorway, Samuel wore a pained expression.

"Don't count on it," Myles said.

Beulah shrugged. "You might as well join us. You're no more sick than I am, you scamp. But at least this way you get to be first to hear our news: Myles and I are getting married."

Samuel stretched out on the bearskin, combing its fur with his fingers. "I know. I heard you."

"You were listening? Samuel, how could you?"

"Easy enough. I was sitting on the stairs." He lifted a gray kitten from the basket and cradled it against his face.

While Beulah gasped with indignation, Myles began to chuckle. He sat on the davenport and patted the seat beside him. "Come on, honey. It doesn't matter. We've got important things to discuss." After depositing Daniel on the rug for Samuel to entertain, Beulah snuggled beneath Myles's arm and soon regained her good humor.

While Samuel played with kittens and Daniel rolled about on the floor, the lovers planned their future.

Epilogue

January 1882, New York City

C urled into the depths of a well-cushioned sofa, Beulah shut her book, smiling. Snow drifted upon the balcony outside her window, mounding on the railings like fine white sugar. Closing her eyes, she sighed in contentment. *Thank You, Lord. Married life is better than I ever imagined.*

The Van Huysens had opted to stay in one of the older hotels in the city. Its old-fashioned splendor was sufficient to please Beulah without overwhelming her. At times, especially around the holidays, she had suffered pangs of homesickness. But Myles's adoration, combined with the knowledge that this tour was temporary, soothed her occasional feelings of inadequacy and loneliness.

She slipped a letter from inside the book cover. There on the envelope her new name, "Mrs. Myles Van Huysen," was written in Mama's neat script. Beulah ran her finger over the words. She was eager to share family news with Myles that night after the concert. He was currently at the theater, practicing.

"Beulah?" A familiar voice called from outside the hotel door. Virginia did not believe in knocking. Beulah hurried to let in her new grandmother.

Virginia bustled into the room, her arms filled with packages. "I've been shopping. Wish you had come with me, but I still managed to spend a good deal. I want you to try this on." After dropping several boxes upon a table, she shoved the largest in Beulah's direction.

"What have you done, Gram?" Beulah chuckled. "What will Myles say?"

"I don't care what that boy might say. It's my money, and I'll spend it as I like." Spying the letter in Beulah's hand, she said, "So you've heard from your mother again? How is everyone back home?"

The crisp inquiry warmed Beulah's heart. She kissed Virginia's cheek. "I love you, Gram. Mama says to tell you 'hello.' They are all well. Daniel is pulling up to stand beside furniture now. Sheriff Boz and Miss Amelia have set February fourteenth as their wedding day, so we should be home in time for the wedding. Um, let's see. . .Eunice found homes for all four of Pushy's kittens. Mama and Papa are letting her keep the black one, Miss Amelia chose the black and white girl, and Mr. Thwaite picked the gray boy. Believe it or not, Al decided to take the black one with white feet! After all his teasing Myles about liking cats, he now has a pet cat of his own."

"That's so nice, dear." Virginia smiled fondly at the girl. "Only a few days now until we'll all be on the train headed for Wisconsin."

"Will you be sorry to leave New York? You must miss your old house. Didn't it hurt to see strangers take it over?"

Virginia pursed her lips and gazed through the window at blowing snow. "For many years now New York has not seemed like home. Ever since the boys left me, I've been a lonely soul. My friends are all gone, and sometimes when I walked around that old house, I missed my dear husband Edwin so much. . . . I could picture John and Gwendolyn chasing up and down the stairs—they were our only children, you know. John was killed in the war, and Gwen died of cholera at age fifteen."

Shaking her head, she said firmly, "Dwelling in the past is detrimental to one's mental and spiritual health. Now I have Myles, you, and many friends in Longtree." Her expression brightened. "My life is in the future now. First in Wisconsin, then in heaven!"

Seeing Beulah dab at a tear, she started back into action. "Now take these boxes and try on the gown. It's only a short time 'til we must leave for the theater. Don't want to be late! I had a note from Mr. Poole this morning—he will be at the concert tonight. The man seems to take personal pleasure in Myles's success, which is not too strange considering his role in the boy's return to the stage. I hear it's another sold-out house. Myles's agent has been begging him to reconsider and stay on permanently."

Arms loaded with boxes, Beulah turned back to grin. "Poor man! He hasn't a chance against Cyrus Thwaite's farm."

Beulah perched on the edge of her seat, absently fanning herself. Her emerald taffeta evening gown rustled with every movement, but it was impossible to keep entirely still.

"Hard to believe it's snowing outside, isn't it?" Virginia leaned over to ask. She smoothed a bit of lace on Beulah's shoulder and smiled approval.

Beulah nodded in reply. The old lady's whispers were sometimes louder than she intended. Myles was singing a heart-wrenching aria from *Aida*, and Beulah wanted to listen.

"Hard to believe this is the last week of Myles's tour," Virginia commented a few minutes later while Myles performed Schumann's A Minor Piano Concerto. Again, Beulah nodded briefly.

After weeks of attending her husband's concerts, she still had not tired of hearing him sing and play. Each night Myles varied his repertoire. Always he sang opera, usually Verdi or Mozart; often he performed a few ballads and popular songs; most nights he took requests from the audience. Beulah's favorite part of each performance was discovering which hymn he would choose for his finale.

Tonight he sang "Holy, Holy, Holy." Beulah closed her eyes to listen without distraction. No matter how cross, irritating, or obstinate Myles might have been during the day, each night she fell in love with him all over again. He was so handsome, charming, and irresistible up on that stage!

"I think I'll head home now, dear," Virginia said while Myles took his bow.

Beulah stopped clapping long enough to return the old lady's kiss. "Thank you so much for this marvelous dress and the gloves and the reticule and everything! Your taste is exquisite. You are too good to me." Beulah smoothed the ruffles on her bouffant skirt.

"Child, it was my pleasure. I trust Myles will approve. I hope you know how thankful I am to have you for a granddaughter. Myles has excellent taste, too. Good night." She patted Beulah's cheek and bustled away. Although Myles often requested her to let him escort her home, Virginia maintained independence, insisting that she was perfectly capable of hailing a cab and returning alone to the hotel.

As soon as the red velvet curtain fell, Beulah gathered her things and hurried backstage. Myles waited for her in his dressing room, smiling in welcome.

"Do you like it?" Beulah twirled in place. "Gram bought it for me. Isn't she wonderful? Not that I'll find much use for an evening gown back in Longtree. Gram fixed my hair, too."

Myles's eyes glowed. "You are beautiful, my Beulah. More than any man deserves." His voice was slightly hoarse.

When he closed the door behind her, Beulah wrapped her arms around her husband's neck and kissed him. "Thank you, thank you for bringing me with you to New York. I wouldn't have missed this experience for the world," she murmured against his lips.

"You say that every night," he chuckled, pressing her slender form close.

"And every night I mean it," she insisted. Framing his face with her hands, she studied each feature. "Sometimes I miss your beard, but I do love how your face feels right after you shave."

"You're standing on my feet." He rubbed his smooth cheek against hers.

"That way I'm taller." She stood on tiptoe to kiss him.

He took her by the waist and lifted her off his feet. "How about if I bend over instead? These shoes were expensive, and my toes are irreplaceable." Smiling, he kissed her pouting lips.

Consoled, Beulah snuggled against him. "Darling, sometimes I don't want this honeymoon to end; other times I want so much to be back in Longtree, setting up our new home. But it will be hard to return to ordinary life after all this glitter and glamour."

"This has been a marvelous honeymoon tour, but I think we would soon tire of such a hectic lifestyle. Think of snowball fights, ice-skating on the beaver pond, and toasting chestnuts. We need to hike up the stream and visit our waterfall while it's frozen."

"And I am looking forward to experiencing everyday things as your wife,"

Beulah added. "Cooking breakfast for you in our own kitchen, washing your laundry, collecting eggs from our own chickens."

Myles hugged her close and rocked her back and forth. Secure in his arms, Beulah felt entirely loved.

"Yes, each day offers its own pleasures," he mused aloud. "Be content with the joys of today, darling. This tour has been successful beyond my wildest dreams. I know God paved the way, and I'm sure we can trust Him to plan the rest of our future as well. We're making memories right now that we'll treasure for the rest of our lives. God is very good."

Lonely in Longtree

Prologue

March 1891, Minocqua, Wisconsin

Need anything else, Mr. Van Huysen?"

"Just my mail, ma'am."

"You got a newspaper and some big envelopes," Mrs. Daniels observed as she handed his mail over the counter. "You should come into town more often. This community hops with activity even during winter. Dances, concerts, masquerades—you ought to get more involved."

He smiled at the widow. "I keep busy. I'm too old for masquerades and such anyhow."

"Nonsense. You need to find yourself a wife. No sense in a man staying lonely in his old age."

"Hope I haven't yet reached that stage." Was she fishing for a second husband herself? Monte paid cash for his groceries, picked up two heavy sacks, and made the first trip out to his waiting sledge. He covered the sacks with oiled tarps to keep them dry. Two more trips, and he brushed off his gloves.

Sunlight tried to break through the heavy overcast. Icicles like jagged teeth glittered on the eaves of the shop and of every building along Front Street. The snow near the train station and tracks was grimy with soot, and traffic had fouled the roads. So much for a pristine wilderness.

"Wake up, Buzzard Bait." He rubbed one horse's furry ears, then gripped the other by its soft chin. Giving a little shake, he lifted until its fluttering nostrils blew steamy-warm breath into his face. "No more nap, Petuniagal." He kissed the whiskery pink nose and straightened Petunia's tangled forelock. Both horses tried to rub their faces on his sleeves or his backside while he removed their blankets and checked their harness and hooves. "Watch it there, Buzz," he warned when the horse nearly knocked him sprawling.

The door of the general store squeaked open, and Mrs. Daniels stepped outside. "You dropped your newspaper, Mr. Van Huysen."

"Always dropping something." Monte tucked the paper under his arm. "Thank you kindly, ma'am."

"The roads are bad. You take care." The store mistress retreated into her small but warm building.

"Will do. I go mostly across the lakes anyway." But Mrs. Daniels had already closed the door. Monte climbed to the seat of his wagon set on runners, clucked to the team, and started off west along Front Street, passing a line of hotels and shops and circling the island's shoreline until he reached the landing. Other sleds and sledges had packed a smooth track down to the lake. The snow on top of the ice was light; his horses made easy work of it. Speeding across the level white plain, Monte found it hard to recapture a vision of blue summer lakes and lush green shoreline. Frigid wind burned the exposed skin around his eyes and found every niche in his outerwear armor. Weaving around islands, cutting across necks of land, he made his way back to his remote section.

Pride swelled his chest when he first glimpsed the tree-lined shore. No finer piece of land existed in the Northwoods, he firmly believed. Magnificent white pines towered above naked oaks, elms, maples, and aspens. Birch boles traced silvery streaks against the deep green of fir and spruce. At his approach, a group of deer startled into the trees, white tails bobbing and flashing.

Come spring, he would begin breaking ground for a lodge. A hunting and fishing lodge to attract the wealthy socialites of Chicago and Milwaukee. Unlike local logging towns, Minocqua staked its future on its natural beauty. Monte's dream lodge should help bring that bright future and prosperity to the Lakeland area.

He drove the team up a shore landing and along the lane he had labored to carve from his wilderness home. The horses stopped in front of his cabin and waited for him to unload. A mule brayed a noisy greeting from the paddock; Buzz whinnied in answer. Petunia only snorted. Inside the cabin, a dog bayed and scratched at the door.

"At least I don't come home to a quiet, empty house," Monte mused.

He made himself wait until evening before he opened the newspaper and put up his feet. Ralph the hound stretched on the hearth before a blazing fire. Monte lowered one foot from his stool to rub along the dog's side.

He snapped open the paper, tilted it to catch the oil lamp's beam, and started reading at the top of the front page. No article escaped his interest. Each week he found pleasure in reading accounts of mostly unknown people in a far-off town. Mr. and Mrs. Boswell Martin celebrated their ninth anniversary by traveling to Chicago to see an opera. Ole Sutton was robbed on the road just east of town; a drifter was arrested in connection with the incident. Mr. Gustaf Obermeier celebrated his sixtieth birthday with his wife, Elsa, and daughter, Marva.

A familiar name caught his eye, and he straightened in his chair. *Last week, Longtree's own Mr. Myles Van Huysen performed a benefit concert for Longtree Community Church, donating all proceeds toward a new and larger facility. The concert was a great financial success. . . .* Monte skipped over details about the proposed construction. *Mr. Van Huysen lives near town with his wife, Beulah, his children, and his paternal grandmother, Mrs. Virginia Van Huysen of Long Island, New York.*

Monte read the article three times, then stared across the room. Myles, still singing, but not for his own profit. He might have been rich and famous by now.

How did his grandmother feel about her prodigy grandson's choosing a farm over a brilliant career on stage? How would Gran feel about her miscreant older grandson's new life as proprietor and owner of a recreation lodge?

A wave of loneliness for family swept over him. He closed his eyes and rubbed their lids. How old would Gran be now? She had seemed ancient twenty years ago. Had it really been twenty years? Pretty near.

What if. . . ? He pursed his lips and stared into the fire. What if he were to advertise his new lodge in the *Longtree Enquirer*? What if Myles could be tempted to bring his family north for a vacation on the lakes? Myles had always enjoyed outdoor sports. Perhaps if Monte played up the family fun aspect of the lodge. . . Maybe he could run a family special. . . . He must get a piano. . . .

The idea had merit, yet the probability of luring Myles and his family to Minocqua was laughably remote. Only God could pull off such a miracle. And Monte didn't dare ask Him, since God would ask in return, reasonably enough, why he didn't simply take a train down to Longtree to mend fences with his estranged family. Why should the Lord perform a miracle to accomplish reconciliation when he could easily initiate it himself?

Moping, he skimmed through the personal ads: *16h. molly mule for sale. . . housemaid needed. . .farm auction.* Then one ad caught his full attention:

> *Single woman of good reputation, in possession of small but prosperous farm, requires godly man of solid character as husband. Must tolerate presence of elderly parents. I can manage a farm alone but would prefer companionship. I am healthy, average in appearance and education, and easygoing by nature. I neither expect nor desire romantic overtures. Interested parties may contact the* Longtree Enquirer *for further information. Lonely in Longtree*

❧

April, Longtree, Wisconsin

Marva dumped tepid dishwater over the edge of the porch, then hurried back inside, already shivering with cold. "I think the temperature's dropping again," she commented. "The days may be getting longer, but they aren't much warmer. I'll put a hot water bottle in your bed tonight."

"No need, dear. Your father has warm feet." From her rocking chair pulled up close to the stove, Marva's mother smiled and nodded. Her knitting needles never missed a click.

Papa snorted and shook his newspaper until it crackled. "What stuff and nonsense they print in this paper!" He scooted his slippers closer to the stove, dropped the outspread paper into his lap, and tapped it with his magnifying lens. His white beard trembled in indignation. "Some fool man wrote an answer to some fool woman's advertisement for a husband. Can you imagine anything more idiotic? The man could be anything—a drunkard, a murderer, anything!"

"Or the woman could be out to trap him for his money," Mother said.

Marva set the dishpan upside down on the drain board and wiped down the countertops, watching her damp pink hands with deep concentration.

"Our Marva would never need to advertise," Mother said dreamily. "Some man will come along and snatch her up one of these days."

Marva paused and stared through the kitchen window at the landscape of early spring. A bleak view: gray, cold, and muddy. Much like her own future.

At one time she had believed her mother's romantic predictions. At one time she had considered herself a prize. But then man after man had come into her life, and man after man had passed on to some other woman or some other town. Marva might have married a filthy deputy with a bullet head and barrel chest, but he had turned out to be crooked as well as repulsive. She might have given the nod to a certain buck-toothed, goggle-eyed farmhand by the name of Camarillo Nugget had she so chosen.

She hadn't been that desperate.

Not back then.

Back then she had trusted that God would fulfill the desires of her heart. Back then she had depended on Him to provide her with a husband.

The one worthy man she'd thought might ask to share her future had chosen a pretty young girl of nineteen instead. Not that she begrudged Myles and Beulah Van Huysen their happiness together, but no one could deny that Beulah's gain had been Marva's loss.

All these years she'd spent alone, watching other women bear children and raise them. God must have forgotten about Marva Obermeier. That was the best she could figure.

"Time for us to turn in, Mrs. Obermeier." Papa folded up the paper, rose and stretched with a crackle of joints, and thumped his broad chest with one fist. "I'm fishing in the morning. Ice is off the ponds now."

"Yes, dear." Mother immediately wound up her yarn and stashed her work into the little wooden bin at her elbow. "Fishing, fishing. Always fishing." But her voice held no rancor. Rising to her diminutive full height, she trotted over to kiss Marva good night and passed on through to the bedroom. Papa gave Marva a whiskery kiss on the cheek and a tender smile and then followed Mother.

Marva waited for the door to clank shut and listened to their voices rise and fall in nightly conversation. Lifting her hand to her cheek where their kisses lingered, she smiled faintly.

Before their light turned out, she picked up the discarded newspaper and spread it on the kitchen table. Bringing the lamp close, she turned it up so that its golden light pooled on the pages. At the bottom of page 4, she found the response:

LONELY IN LONGTREE

Lonely in Longtree: In answer to your advertisement posted in a March edition of the Longtree Enquirer, *I proffer myself as a candidate for the position. Age 38 this month, never married, of sound health and character, I am a God-fearing man. I lay claim to considerable wooded property in the north of the state and plan to build come spring. Your parents are welcome. Sell the farm and stock and travel north to God's country. Or come first and see if the climate and conditions suit. If you dislike pine trees and sparkling lakes, you'll hate it here. Lucky in Lakeland.*

✑

June, Minocqua

Monte walked out of the Bank of Minocqua with a spring in his step. He would have sung or shouted had anyone questioned his broad grin. But passersby paid him no attention, and the horses tethered at the hitching rail dozed in complete indifference. He considered a visit to the barbershop or blacksmith but settled on Daniels' General Store instead.

Passing the Minocqua House Inn, he tipped his hat to a passing woman who gave him a rather unfriendly stare. Perhaps he had better moderate his expression to pleasant rather than beaming. As he entered the store, Mrs. Daniels greeted him in her cheery way and immediately announced that he had a stack of mail waiting. "Two of them newspapers. Now that we've got *The Times* here in town, maybe you could cancel that other subscription."

"I could." He accepted his mail, rolled it into a neat bundle, and tucked it under his arm.

"I hear you placed a large order from Glendenning. Pine and cedar and oak, they say, and huge beams of it. You planning to build soon?"

"As soon as possible, ma'am. A crew will begin digging the basement tomorrow. I plan to have my resort up and running by next summer." He met her curious gaze with a pleasant smile.

"You know they've got the ferry running to the Hazelhurst road now, and a drugstore is going in across the way. This town is booming! I wish you luck with your resort, Mr. Van Huysen. What are you planning to call it?"

"I haven't yet decided."

"Did you have a nice visit to Wausau? Word is that you visited the land office and bought up your claim. Wherever did you get the money for that? Rumors are flying all over town!"

"I had a pleasant visit to Wausau, Mrs. Daniels, although the train north ran twenty minutes late. Ma'am, I'm thinking I don't need to subscribe to *The Times*. I've got you to keep me informed of all the local news."

She stared for a moment, then chuckled. "Mr. Van Huysen, you're such a card! Now you take care."

He paused in the doorway to tip his hat. "And you, ma'am."

Petunia waited for him at Doyle's Livery. As soon as he entered and spoke to the proprietor, he heard his mare's welcoming whinny. "It do beat all the way that animal fancies you," Michael Doyle said after sending his stable boy to bring the horse out and saddle her up.

Monte paid for his horse's overnight keep, then sat on an outside bench to wait. Summer traffic rattled past on Chippewa Street. He found it difficult to recall how the island had appeared just a few short years ago—a peaceful cathedral of towering pines, their lofty tops whispering secrets on every breeze. If only more of those trees had been spared to shade and beautify the new town...

Homesteaders and developers seemed intent on stripping their land of trees. He could not understand this compulsion. Why should progress always destroy beauty? Tourists flocked to Minocqua for its natural attractions. His lodge, he determined anew, would complement its surroundings and satisfy a tourist's hunger for nature unspoiled.

Recalling his two newspapers, he unrolled one and scanned its pages for a note from Lonely in Longtree. If another month passed without a response, he would give up. Responding to that ad had been a foolish whim anyway.

No reply in the older paper. Trying to ignore a sense of disappointment, he opened the second one. *To Lucky in Lakeland*—his breath caught.

Clop, clop, clop. "Here she is, Mr. Van Huysen."

Petunia butted her head into the open newspaper and nearly tossed it to the ground. Monte's flash of anger expired as soon as he glimpsed the mare's affectionate expression. "Rotten beast that you are," he said, hugging her head as she lipped his shirt buttons.

"I like your horse, Mr. Van Huysen."

"So do I, son." He slipped the lad two coins and a wink.

"Thanks!"

With his mail safely stowed in the saddlebags, he headed north on the Minocqua and Woodruff Road, letting Petunia choose her pace. "Thanks to your interruption, I didn't have a chance to read her response. I sure hope this isn't a good-bye letter or a 'no, thank you.' I reckon you think I'm crazy, girl, but this little correspondence is the most fun I've had in years. Well...woman type of fun, anyway. I'll admit I've had some fun reeling in a walleye upon occasion." He grinned and patted the mare's sleek neck.

Much of the enjoyment lay in anticipation. Playing games with himself, he put off reading the ad. Only after his stock had been fed and after a leisurely stroll with his hound along the lakeshore, listening to the warning warble of loons and the incongruously twittering call of a soaring bald eagle, did he allow himself the pleasure of satisfied curiosity. Settling into a chair on the shore, he snapped open the newspaper and read:

LONELY IN LONGTREE

To Lucky in Lakeland: Your offer intrigues, yet I find your suggestions improper at this point in our acquaintance. I would know more about a man than his age and property before I would travel anywhere to meet him. Please describe your situation in greater detail if indeed your offer is serious. Why should I leave my home and move north when I already possess a comfortable situation here? The name "Lucky" carries unattractive connotations. Do you gamble? Smoke? Drink? I require a man of virtue whose life reflects genuine fear of God, not lip service. Lonely in Longtree.

Monte gazed blindly across the lake...and smiled.

Chapter 1

Delight thyself also in the LORD;
and he shall give thee the desires of thine heart.
PSALM 37:4

Summer 1893

A blessed hush dropped over the train coach. Doubtful that the peace could last, Marva glanced from side to side, gently bobbing eight-month-old Ginny on her shoulder. To her right, Jerry, age eight, slumped against her arm. To her left, Joey, age four, dozed in his seat, still clutching a toy horse in each hand.

Marva heaved a restrained sigh. Ginny stirred, and Marva resumed patting the baby's backside. Motherhood was exhausting. . .and these weren't even her children. How did Beulah manage at home? Probably the children weren't as restive in familiar surroundings. The constant motion and clamor of the train, the cinder-thick air, the heat, and the press of humanity must be nearly unbearable to a child. It was bad enough for an adult who understood why such discomfort must be endured.

Not that Marva was certain of the reasons herself. This "vacation" had been anything but restful thus far. She felt like an unpaid nanny. . .although, to be fair, she had offered her help repeatedly. How could any decent person watch friends struggle to control and comfort their six restless and bored children and *not* offer to help?

She should have stayed home to care for the farm. Traveling in company with all married adults and children served only to emphasize her singleness. She should have seen her parents off at the train station with a wave and a blessing. Ridiculous to imagine that—

The front coach door opened, and Myles Van Huysen entered. He met Marva's gaze and smiled, making his way along the narrow aisle. After a quick glance at his sleeping offspring, he shook his head with a rueful smile. "How'd you do it? You're amazing, Marva," he said in hushed tones. "Want me to take over? Beulah finally got Trixie to sleep. Tim and Cy are with the Schoengard family."

The children might wake when she moved, but their father would simply have to handle that eventuality. Marva's every joint ached from hours of immobility. She handed Ginny to Myles, who cradled his baby girl expertly. Extricating

268

herself from between the two boys was more difficult, but Marva managed it with only a few minor mishaps—such as pulling the hair of the man seated in front of her when she grasped the top of his seat for leverage and crushing her hat when she reached up into the luggage rack overhead. Once in the aisle, she straightened her back and legs, expecting to hear the crackle and pop of petrified joints. But the train whistled at that propitious moment, so any evidence of fossilization was concealed.

Myles took her place between his boys. Jerry wrapped his hands around his father's arm and snuggled down to sleep again. Joey slumped across Myles's lap.

Feeling a sudden need for air, even the smoky air on the platform, Marva staggered to the back of the lurching coach and outside, where she clutched the railing and breathed deeply. As long as she didn't look down, the speed wasn't too dizzying. To her delight, trees obscured her view. When had the scenery switched from farmland to forest? Absorbed in entertaining the children and calming the baby, she hadn't so much as glanced out the train's windows in several hours.

The clacking of the rails changed in tone as the train crossed a bridge over a blue river, and then the train flashed back into the cool stillness of forest on the far side.

A gust of smoke swept over her. Coughing, she blinked cinders from her eyes and made a futile attempt to wave away the choking fumes. Her white shirtwaist was now gray with black speckles. Enough of enjoying the scenery. She hurried back inside.

Near the back of the coach, her parents sat peacefully reading and dozing. Mother smiled at Marva's approach. "No children?"

Marva pulled her small valise from the overhead rack. "Myles took them. I think I'll try to catch a few winks."

"Your father says we should arrive within the hour. Isn't the view splendid? I'm so thankful you came with us, dearest. I know you've always wanted to travel and see the world."

She'd been thinking more along the lines of New York, Boston, or even Paris, but the Northwoods would have to suffice for the present. Marva returned her mother's smile. "The trees are magnificent. What are you reading, Papa?"

He closed the book over his finger and gave her a sheepish grin. "It's a Western novel I borrowed from Timmy Van Huysen."

"Once a boy, always a boy." Mother patted his arm.

The book jacket portrayed a cowboy astride a rearing horse on a narrow ledge above a cliff. His rifle spouted lurid orange flame at an attacking mountain lion. Instead of remarking on the hero's obviously imminent demise or the lion's improbably scarlet mouth, Marva said only, "My, but he wears furry trousers."

"Those are chaps," Papa grumbled and returned to reading. "Women!"

"I'm thankful this is a fishing trip and not a lion-hunting expedition. I'm picturing you in furry chaps straddling a wild mustang." Marva smiled at the thought.

"Those days are long past for me." He glanced up at her again. "You used to enjoy fishing."

"Oh, perhaps I'll try it again if you wish, but this trip promises to be more of a babysitting ordeal for me than anything adventurous."

Although she had tried to keep her tone light, her mother's eyes narrowed. "Marva, you are under no obligation to watch anyone's children."

She tried to forestall a lecture. "I can hardly enjoy myself if I know Beulah is exhausted and miserable. I was merely funning. I'm sure I'll find time to catch a bluegill or two." She glanced around in search of empty seats. "If I'm asleep when we arrive, please don't leave me on the train."

"Wouldn't matter much if we did," her father said, "since Minocqua is the end of the line."

Three rows up, she plopped into a window seat and set her bag beside her. Across the aisle sat a pair of strangers, sleeping soundly from all appearances.

Marva opened her valise and dug around until she located an envelope. Holding it to her chest, she glanced around once more. No one was looking. She pulled out a few newspaper clippings.

Lucky in Lakeland. For two years they had maintained an awkward association by newspaper ads. Sometimes months had passed between notes, yet each time she had thought the correspondence might be finished, another note would appear in the paper. For two years she had waited for him to make some kind of move, some indication that he wanted their relationship to advance.

He often spoke of her and her parents coming north, but no definite invitation had been extended, no names had been exchanged. The entire situation was distressingly indefinite.

She squeezed her eyes shut.

Most likely, Lucky, as she now thought of him, had simply entertained himself for two years by encouraging a desperate spinster. Still, he sounded sincere. . . .

Lonely in Longtree: I am not a gambling man, and neither do I smoke or drink—although I indulged in all these vices in my distant past. God changed my life. I actually consider myself blessed but chose "lucky" for the alliteration. You are right to demand more information. In December of last year, I filed claim on a section within easy distance of several local towns, located on the shore of a sizable fishing lake, rich in wildlife and quality lumber, and, in short, representing my idea of heaven on earth. Having made substantial improvements to date, I recently purchased the acreage and intend to begin construction of a resort lodge. Might you take interest in such a venture? Lucky and Blessed in Lakeland.

She ran her finger over the yellowed slip of paper. The man might have deceived her these past two years. He might prove a fraud. But she still felt vindicated in writing to him on the basis of those four powerful words: "God changed my life."

Dear Lonely in Longtree, I intend to hire a cook, a housekeeping staff, etc. Your role here would be entirely your choice. I hoped you might enjoy the venture as much as I do. Construction has started, and the log walls are going up. I wish you could come and see. Plenty of room for your parents to either live in the lodge or have a comfortable cabin of their own. Do you enjoy reading? Lucky in Lakeland.

Back then he had sounded eager to meet her, to show her his lodge. But somehow their discussions had rambled away from relationship into surface matters. Discussions of reading preferences and leisure pastimes had their merits, yet the friendship had never deepened. Did Lucky possess depths of character? Or perhaps he was the type of man who would always keep a woman shut out of his inner life.

But what did she expect? Any woman silly enough to bypass convention and advertise for a husband in the newspaper shouldn't expect a perfect match. Any woman sinful enough to bypass God's leading and strike out on her own couldn't expect rich blessings.

She slid the clippings back into the envelope, careful to keep them neat and orderly. His notes had revealed many clues to his identity. She knew that the train brought his mail into town, so he lived near a railroad line. She knew the approximate date his town had been founded. He owned and operated a new resort built from logs and located on a lake. He was unmarried, which she could only hope proved true, forty years old, clean living, and exceptionally well educated.

A lifetime habit of prayer prompted her to whisper, "Dear God, I know I shouldn't have started this mess in the first place, but please help me to find him."

Yet even as she spoke the words, a conflict rose within her. In the vast Northwoods of Wisconsin, locating one man who did not wish to be located would be nothing short of miraculous. Why should she expect God to bless her rebellion? If He had provided her with a suitable husband in the first place, she wouldn't have been tempted to advertise for a man. But then again, God knew she would advertise before she ever picked up the pen to write that first inquiry, so why shouldn't He bless her feeble efforts to force His hand?

∽∾∽

Monte strolled along the train platform, his gaze scanning the sky until he found a circling pair of eagles—two dots against the blue. A gentle breeze rippled the lake, scattering the reflected trees. A horse's snort gave him an inward start, and he realized how tense he had become. This would never do.

He swung his arms back and forth and rolled his head from side to side until his neck crackled. He sucked in a deep breath and exhaled noisily, attempting a grin.

It was no good. Nothing could lure his thoughts away from the approaching confrontation. For weeks, doubts and speculations had milled within the enclosure of his mind like corralled mustangs, determined to break free. No matter how diligently he reinforced the fences with known facts, those wild-eyed doubts kicked and pushed and jostled until the facts splintered and fell. Wriggling through the gaps, the ugly worries stampeded his composure.

He wanted a drink. More than once he cast a glance along Front Street toward St. Elmo's Saloon. It had been years. Many long years. Surely one drink to bolster his nerves wouldn't offend the Almighty.

To distract himself, he returned to check the lineup of Lakeland Lodge wagons waiting near the depot amid vehicles from other hotels and lodges. Petunia and Buzz nickered at the sight of him, and he placed his hands on their faces for comfort. His own comfort.

Forty-two guests would soon arrive. Not his first large party; he'd had several. His drivers would competently convey the tourists and their luggage to Lakeland Lodge, where uniformed staff would direct them to their rooms or cabins. His cook and kitchen crew were even now preparing a divine repast for the evening meal. A small fleet of boats awaited the arrival of eager fishermen.

He felt confident of his lodge and its staff. They could not fail to please. No doubts on that score rankled his mind.

"Monte," one of the drivers, who was also his friend and business partner, called out. "I see smoke away down the line. Train's coming."

He waved acknowledgment. "Thanks, Hardy."

Selling a half interest in the business had allowed Monte more free time to continue his writing. Harding "Hardy" Stowell was a good businessman and a brother in the Lord.

His worries whipped back like a compass needle returning to NORTH. How long had it been since he last saw Myles? Eighteen years? Nineteen? What if he didn't recognize his own brother? What if, when he revealed his identity, Myles hopped back on the train and took his family with him? What if. . . ? What if. . . ?

Rising panic finally drove him to pray. "Lord," he muttered through his teeth, "help me face him. Give me strength to admit how weak I've been." Imagining a look of disappointment and condemnation on his brother's face, he grimaced. "I don't have any idea what to say. I should never have done this."

A distant train whistle brought his head up. Black smoke drifted above the treetops across the lake. Monte returned to the platform. His leg bones must have liquefied. Bile rose in his throat. He swallowed hard and felt nauseous.

The locomotive's brakes started screeching while it was still on the trestle.

Its deep *chuff, chuff* slowed, and the great billowing monster finally halted with its passenger cars beside the platform. Steam hissed in a white plume from its side.

He could hardly bear to watch the passengers disembark. The sun's heat became unendurable. His mouth was parched.

Laughing, talking people descended the steps, gathered on the platform, and stared at their surroundings with evident interest. Children ducked and scrambled amid the legs and skirts. One man made a grab at a young boy, catching him by the back of his jacket.

It was Myles.

Chapter 2

Fear thou not; for I am with thee: be not dismayed;
for I am thy God: I will strengthen thee; yea, I will help thee;
yea, I will uphold thee with the right hand of my righteousness.
ISAIAH 41:10

Monte recognized his younger brother instantly, not by his appearance—which had changed over the years—but by his graceful movements and an indefinable quality in his bearing.

"Myles," he whispered the name.

"Mr. Stowell?"

A tall, burly man with graying blond hair had approached Monte unnoticed.

"Uh, no. Mr. Stowell is over there." He nearly introduced himself, but indecision tied his tongue in a knot. Hardy had handled all reservations and business with this group from Longtree.

"But you're with Lakeland Lodge, aren't you?"

Monte nodded.

"David Schoengard here. I'm a minister." Rev. Schoengard smiled and shook Monte's hand. "It was a long ride, but we're here at last."

"Welcome to Minocqua. The town isn't much to look at, but wait until you see the lodge." To his surprise, his voice sounded normal.

Only dimly aware of his actions and praying in his heart, he supervised the loading of luggage, including fishing poles and tackle. "You people are serious about your fishing," he said to a bearded old gentleman waiting near the wagon hitched to Petunia and Buzz.

"That we are, sir." Anticipation gleamed in the man's faded blue eyes. "Are you our driver?"

"I am." Monte climbed into the wagon bed, slid a valise beneath one of the bench seats, and arranged fishing poles along a side panel. "You've never had better fishing than you'll find around here."

"This is a lifetime opportunity. I've read the advertisements for this lodge in our local newspaper these past many months and dreamed about landing one of those record muskellunge."

Monte climbed down and gripped the man's surprisingly powerful hand. "I sincerely hope your dreams will come true, Mr. . . . ?"

"Obermeier. Gustaf Obermeier, sir. And this is my wife, Elsa, and our

274

daughter. . . . Ah, well, she's here somewhere."

"She's helping Beulah with the children," Mrs. Obermeier said. "What is your name, sir?"

"Just call me Monte." He tipped his head toward the wagon. "Your luggage is loaded. I imagine you're eager to reach the lodge and start fishing."

Mrs. Obermeier chuckled. "Please don't tempt him, Mr. Monte. Morning will be soon enough for that, I should think."

He took the woman's elbow to assist her into the wagon.

"Mother!" Rapid footsteps clopped on the platform.

Mrs. Obermeier turned back. "There you are, dear. Are you riding with us or with the Van Huysens?"

Hearing that name gave Monte a jolt.

"Beulah asked me to ride with them—the children are nearly beside themselves with excitement. I'll rejoin you at the lodge." The younger woman spoke rapidly. She had a rich-sounding voice. Monte wondered which man in the party claimed her as his wife. That ash-blond hair of hers would catch any man's attention.

As she walked away, more guests climbed into Monte's wagon: a young couple who behaved like newlyweds and a family of four whose names he missed. While Monte clucked up the horses, his passengers launched into happy discussion of the coming weeks. They mentioned names he found vaguely familiar, probably from seeing them in news articles.

At times he glimpsed Hardy's wagon ahead on the road. Myles and his family were in that wagon, he knew. Sunlight glinted off the lake alongside the Minocqua and Woodruff Road. In summer there could be no cutting across the lakes to shorten the trip home, but the local roads were in decent-enough repair. "What lake is this, Mr. Monte?" one of the women asked.

"Just Monte, ma'am; no 'mister,' please. It's called Kawaguesaga Lake. Up ahead here the road splits off, and we'll head west toward the Lac du Flambeau reservation." He jiggled Petunia's reins to wake her up.

"Will we see any Indians while we're here?"

"You're likely to, ma'am."

"Are they friendly?" Mr. Obermeier asked.

"Mostly." He shrugged. "They're like any people—some are friendly; some are not. One of the lodge's fishing guides is Ojibwa. We call him Ben. If he can't find you a big fish, no one can."

They again conversed among themselves, leaving Monte to his thoughts. When would be the best time to approach Myles? Probably not tonight, while the children were overtired and ornery. In the morning, perhaps? But he could never wait that long! Somehow he had pictured himself walking up to Myles on the station platform to reveal his identity, but that idea had fizzled. Myles and his wife had been far too preoccupied with controlling their numerous offspring even to notice his presence.

The lead wagons turned off the main road. "Are we nearly there?" asked one of the men.

"I'm sorry, but the lodge is a good distance off yet," Monte said.

"No need to apologize, Monte." Mr. Obermeier sounded tired but cheery. "We all hoped for adventure in the wilderness."

Monte smiled back over his shoulder. The old man had pluck.

When the lodge appeared between the trees, along with the glimmer of the lake beyond, a chorus of appreciative gasps and exclamations lifted Monte's spirits. "Is this the same lake that surrounds the town of Minocqua?" Mr. Obermeier asked.

"Yes and no. This lake is linked to that one by a channel. However, both parts of the lake chain are called Lake Kawaguesaga at present. It gets confusing."

"The lodge is magnificent," the little bride said in evident satisfaction. "George, I'm so glad now that we came here for our honeymoon and not Niagara Falls. You were right."

Monte left his wagon for the hired men to unload and escorted his party of guests into the large foyer. A quick glance around for Myles left him frustrated once again. He checked the register to remind himself which cabin his brother's family had reserved. Number Five. The largest. If he'd been thinking clearly, he would have guessed as much.

"After you register, head into the dining room where supper is presently being served. Your luggage will be delivered to your rooms or cabins."

The little group of guests thanked him and moved on about their business.

It might be kinder to wait until Myles and his wife had time to settle their children for the night, but this protracted delay was destroying his nerves. Taking a deep breath, he gazed around the crowded lobby. The staff worked smoothly and efficiently. He felt a moment's pride; the lodge was everything he had envisioned, thanks in large part to Hardy Stowell's business expertise.

If all went as he hoped and planned, Monte would be able to relax and enjoy this next month.

That was a mighty big *if*.

⌘

"Miss Obermeier, I hope and pray your visit here at Lakeland Lodge will be some of the best days of your life."

Marva watched Mr. Harding Stowell twist his hat between his hands and took pleasure in his evident admiration. "Thank you, sir."

"If you need anything—anything at all—just send word."

"I'll do that, Mr. Stowell."

He finally clapped his hat back on his head and walked down the cabin's steps. Marva watched him for a moment, smiling to herself. He was about the right age, single, a Christian man, well educated. . .and rather endearingly socially inept. Although she couldn't be certain he was "Lucky," her suspicion had strong grounds.

She might have wished for a bit more physical appeal in a potential husband, but she supposed his looks would grow on her as she learned to love the man within. He couldn't help his plain features.

Yet it seemed too coincidental that her correspondent beau should be the first man she encountered in Minocqua, the owner of Lakeland Lodge. Not that God couldn't do miracles, but... Well, time would tell.

At Beulah's request, the lodge kitchen staff brought food to the Van Huysens' cabin for the exhausted children and parents. Marva helped feed the hungry brood, told stories and sang songs to Cyrus, Jerry, and Joey, and tucked the three middle boys into bed. When she finally left the darkened bunkroom, leaving the door slightly ajar, her body and head ached.

Beulah and Myles sat in matched rocking chairs near the stone fireplace. Ginny snuggled against her mother's shoulder, her eyes half-closed. Trixie clung to her father and wailed, her face pink and damp. Both parents gave Marva apologetic looks.

"What would we have done without you today?" Beulah sighed. "Are they asleep?"

"Very nearly." Marva glanced around. "Where's Tim?"

Myles tipped his chin and his gaze upward. "In the loft. He's claimed it as his hideout."

Trixie's crying increased in volume. "Stubborn little creature," her father said in evident frustration. "She's been crying for three hours now."

"I'll put Ginny down and take Beatrix for a while so you can unpack your things," Beulah said, rising slowly.

Rap, rap, rap at the cabin door.

The three adults exchanged glances. "I'll get it," Marva offered.

A man stood on the porch, lantern in hand. "Uh, is this the Van Huysens' cabin?" He removed his hat.

Marva recognized him but couldn't place his identity. "Yes, it is. How may I help you?"

"I need to talk to Myles Van Huysen." The man's eyes had a desperate look. Uncertain, Marva glanced back at Myles for direction.

"I'll talk to him." Myles spoke over Trixie's wails and stood up.

Marva turned back. "You may come in, but please be quiet, sir. We're just now getting the children to sleep." She pushed at the screen door. He opened it and stepped inside, then stood there shuffling his hat between his hands. Marva's curiosity rose.

Myles stepped forward and extended his hand from beneath his daughter's trailing nightgown. "Good evening, sir. Is there a problem?"

The man opened his mouth, closed it, and took Myles's hand. Sweat gleamed on his forehead, though the night air was cool. "I—I—Hello, little brother."

Utterly confused, Marva stared back and forth between their rigid faces.

Trixie flailed in her father's arms, but Myles seemed oblivious even when her arm struck his jaw. The color drained from his ruddy face.

"Monte?" he whispered.

Marva backed toward the kitchen area, feeling entirely out of place during this family moment. To her relief, Beulah emerged from the bedroom, studied the two men, and then approached to stand beside her husband. Trixie climbed into her mother's arms. Myles let her go, his gaze still locked with the stranger's.

Then the two men embraced, both speaking at once in choked-sounding voices.

"You were dead!"

"I'm so sorry!"

"How can this be?"

"I wanted to see you—"

Beulah looked at Marva, then back at the men, her eyes full of questions. Trixie's cries rose in volume, as she jounced in Beulah's arms.

"I'll take her so you can talk," Marva said. "We'll go out on the porch." She took the thrashing toddler from Beulah and stepped outside.

To her surprise, Trixie fell silent and clung to her, shivering with sobs. A breeze rippled off the lake and whispered through the trees. Trixie sighed and wiped her slimy face on Marva's shoulder.

"It's so beautiful here, baby girl."

Marva heard voices rise and fall from inside the cabin. Chairs scraped on the floor and cupboard doors closed. Beulah must be preparing coffee or tea.

Little brother. Marva dredged up memories from the distant past and vaguely recalled Myles talking about a long-lost brother. How very strange that they would meet here and now! Nothing about this felt real. The entire day seemed like a mis-shapen dream. She shook her head, wondering if she might wake up soon.

Chapter 3

Confess your faults one to another,
and pray one for another, that ye may be healed.
The effectual fervent prayer of a righteous man availeth much.
JAMES 5:16

Monte sat across the table from his brother and sister-in-law and prayed for courage. Their pale faces increased his sense of guilt. They were so tired, and now this. How could he ever make them understand? Especially when he didn't understand his own behavior or motives.

"You have a fine family." The comment sounded flat even though he meant it sincerely.

"Thank you. You've never married?" Myles, too, seemed awkward.

"No." Monte turned his coffee cup between his hands.

"Where have you been all these years? How did—?" Myles shook his head and held up both his hands in entreaty and bewilderment. "How did this happen? You here, meeting us?"

Monte pinched the bridge of his nose, still praying. "Is this a good time to tell the story? You both must be weary to death."

His brother snorted. "I'll not sleep after this. You might as well tell us."

Beulah nodded in agreement, her dark eyes wide.

"What about—? I mean, the lady outside and your little girl. . ."

"They'll be fine. Marva is almost like family," Beulah said.

He took a deep breath for fortification. "Where shall I begin?"

"I saw you get shot out of the saddle and fall into a stampede of cattle," Myles said. "All these years I thought I had watched my brother die." His voice held a hint of accusation and a world of curiosity.

Die? Monte flashed him a quick look but saw only truth in his brother's face. After taking a few deep breaths and a swig of coffee, he cleared his throat and launched into his story-telling mode of address.

"I knew Jeb Kirkpatrick was after my hide," he began. "I had owed him a bundle of money for months, and he knew I didn't have the cash. . . ."

◦◦◦◦

Hugging the tiny girl close, Marva hummed softly. Her back and arms ached. How long had she been out here—an hour? Every once in a while, she overheard a word or a sentence of the conversation inside the cabin. Caught between curiosity and guilt, she closed her eyes, as if that would make a difference. Sometimes the brothers raised their voices. Other times everything went so quiet that she wondered if they were all asleep.

Were they going to talk all night? Surely some of their catching up could wait for morning. She sat down on the top step, adjusted Trixie in her arms, and leaned her head against the railing. Sleep weighted her eyelids.

Some thing, or things, rustled in the shrubs near the edge of the porch.

Marva's eyes opened wide.

A shadow slipped from the shrubbery and moved along the cabin wall toward her. Glittering eyes reflected the porch lamp. Another something burst out of the bushes and tumbled across the grass, squealing, grunting, and chattering.

Marva scrambled to her feet and rushed for the door, imagining teeth sinking into her legs at any moment.

<hr />

"I ended up working as a hunting guide at a Wyoming ranch that catered to rich city men with dreams of trophies hanging on their den walls. Some wanted a bear, some a bison, some an elk," Monte said. "The hardest to bring back were the bighorn sheep. Those critters are wily, nimble, and difficult to track. I befriended some members of the local Indian tribes, too."

Beulah yawned and patted her mouth. "Oh, I'm sorry!"

"I ought to let you two get some sleep." He'd been running off at the mouth like he often did when nervous.

Feet pounded on the porch, the door flew open, and the blond woman burst into the room with the tiny girl limp in her arms.

Monte and Myles both jumped to their feet.

She stopped short and returned their startled stares. "I'm sorry. I—I—Um, it was dark. . . ." She glanced down at the sleeping child. Firelight glinted on her pale hair. "Trixie is—Where do you want me to put her down?"

"There's a cot beside our bed in that room." Beulah pointed. "Marva, did something frighten you?"

"There was. . .I mean. . ." She glanced back over one shoulder. "I heard something." Her voice sounded tiny. "I saw some kind of creatures out there."

Monte quickly stepped outside to the dark porch. Moonlight sparkled on the lake's rippled surface. Small shadows waddled across the lawn area between cabins, chattering and bickering softly. *Raccoons.* A smile spread across his face as he rested his hands on the railing.

That Marva woman was really attractive. He'd heard nothing yet about a husband. . .but women that handsome didn't stay single into their thirties, which age he estimated she must be. She might be widowed. Lifting his brows, he looked back over his shoulder at the cabin door and pursed his lips in contemplation.

<hr />

Marva's entire face burned. "These creatures with glowing eyes came rushing at me, making strange noises. I thought of bears or. . ." She handed Trixie into Beulah's outstretched arms and covered her hot cheeks with her cold hands. "I'm sorry I interrupted. I'll leave now."

"No, you won't," Beulah said firmly. "Not until Monte can escort you to the lodge. You think we're going to let you walk back alone and be attacked by a bear? Have a cup of coffee and sit with us. You're family. You might as well hear the story." She disappeared into the cabin's bedroom.

Myles gave her a tired smile and poured a cup of coffee from the pot on the back of the stove. "It's still plenty hot."

"Are you sure?" she asked. "I mean, about my intruding on your family time."

"Yes. Why not?" He offered her sugar.

A deep voice spoke behind her. "There should be milk in the icebox." The cabin door closed.

Myles's gaze flicked past Marva. "Really? Thanks."

Reluctantly she turned to face the stranger. "I suppose there was nothing out there."

"Nothing dangerous." He smiled slowly until his white teeth showed beneath his mustache. "You'll get used to the darkness. But from now on, you'd probably best not be alone outside at night. There *are* bears in these woods, but I'll protect you."

Marva tried to smile in response to his teasing grin. This man was too ruggedly handsome, too confident, too. . .something. She glanced back and forth between the brothers and saw the resemblance. Monte was taller and broader than Myles, with brown hair instead of red. Myles's voice held a musical quality that Monte's lacked. The likeness lay in their facial features and mannerisms.

Myles placed Marva's coffee and a jug of milk on the table. "I should introduce you. Marva, this is my brother, Montague Van Huysen. Monte, this is Miss Marva Obermeier, our long-time friend."

Marva extended her hand. Monte clasped it in a warm grasp and bowed slightly. "I am honored, Miss Obermeier. I believe I met your parents earlier."

Why was he still holding her hand? She tugged it away and tried not to let her discomposure show. "Oh. Really?"

He still gazed steadily at her face. She tried to meet his eyes but felt her throat tighten. "This is the first travel vacation they have ever taken."

That charming smile spread across his face again. "I'm glad they chose Lakeland Lodge."

Of course, his simple statement meant nothing more than the obvious.

Beulah joined them. "Thank you, Marva. She's sound asleep. I doubt cannon fire could waken her after all that crying." She turned to Monte. "I told Marva to stay until you can walk her back to the lodge."

He looked pleased. "Certainly. Are you in a hurry, Miss Obermeier?"

"No, sir."

"I haven't much more to tell, if you don't mind listening." He pulled out her chair in invitation.

"If you don't mind my hearing it, I don't mind," she said and sat down. He scooted her chair forward, then seated himself beside her, across from Myles and Beulah.

"So go on," Myles urged.

He took a deep breath and released it slowly. "Okay, the last few years in a nutshell. One night, after a particularly exciting hunting adventure, I started writing down the day's events so I wouldn't forget. That story turned into my first published magazine article."

"You always did like to write," Myles said.

"Using my experiences, I began writing for magazines, serial stories that were later printed as books. Western novels. I write under the name 'Dutch Montana.' Somebody called me that once, and I thought it made a good pen name."

Dutch Montana? The name rang a bell inside Marva's head, but why?

Something thumped on the ceiling. The adults glanced up in time to see a pair of bare legs swing onto the loft ladder. Tim Van Huysen descended rapidly, his breathing audible in the sudden quiet.

"Tim, have you been eavesdropping?" Beulah sounded shocked.

"I couldn't help overhearing, Ma. I can't believe it! I've got a new uncle, and he's *Dutch Montana!*" The boy, still fully clothed, approached Monte boldly. His dark hair stood on end, and he clutched his pant legs at his sides.

"Howdy, Tim." Monte grinned at his nephew and shook his hand. "I'm honored that you read my books."

Tim gaped up at his uncle's face. "The fellers back home won't believe this! Would you sign my books? I brought a bundle of them."

"Sure."

"Books. That figures. No wonder your bag was so heavy," Myles said in amusement. "Well, sit down and join us, why don't you?"

Marva blinked as realization struck her. Papa had been reading one of Tim's Dutch Montana books on the train—that's why the name had seemed familiar to her. She felt a sudden urge to giggle over the coincidence but restrained it. No sense in advertising her overtired condition.

Monte didn't continue his tale until the boy squeezed a chair in between his parents and nestled against Myles's shoulder. "A few years back, I traveled to New York on publishing business and tried to look up the family. The prodigal returned, and all that. Problem was the fatted calf and sundry had disappeared in the meantime. I went to the old family offices and discovered that the Van Huysen Soap Company went out of business long ago, which came as a shock. After much fruitless searching, I thought of looking up Gram's old attorney. He told me to ask Mr. Poole, the detective, about you, and Poole gave me your location—in strictest confidence."

"Why all the secrecy? Why didn't you come see us then? Gram spoke of you on her deathbed." Myles's voice held an accusing note.

Monte flinched. Trying to respect his feelings, Marva kept her gaze averted and sipped her coffee. She really should have insisted on walking back to the lodge alone.

Monte took a breath and opened his mouth as if to speak but closed it again. After a long moment he tried again. "I was afraid."

"Afraid of Gram? Monte, you were the light of her eyes!"

Marva glanced over in time to see him shake his bowed head.

After a strained silence, Beulah spoke softly, "We're thankful to find you now, Monte. I imagine your grandmother is looking down from heaven and smiling to see her boys together again. She prayed faithfully for you all those years. For you and Myles both. She knew you had given your life to the Lord, Monte, and that knowledge sustained her."

He nodded. Was he crying? Marva wanted to put her hand on his arm and try to comfort him. Shocked at the very idea, she sat still and watched her own fingers trace circles on her coffee cup.

Tim rubbed at his eyes and yawned noisily.

Monte sat up straight and forged on. "I heard about land available in the Northwoods and traveled up here soon after the railroad stopped in Minocqua. I've kept track of your family from a distance these three years."

How? Marva wondered but didn't dare ask the question. She glanced up in time to see Monte cast a brotherly look at Beulah. "By the way, little brother, I must say you've found yourself a peach of a wife."

"God has blessed me, for certain."

Monte drew a deep breath, then asked, "So, Myles, what were you doing all those years after Texas? I'm pleased beyond measure to discover that God finally got through your thick skull."

"That He did, though it took years for me to pay attention. After your death—as I thought then—I drifted about, taking jobs at cattle ranches, until a great man named Obadiah "Buck" Watson hired me on to work his farm. Buck is the man whose testimony God used to change my life. Then Buck's stepdaughter stole my heart." Myles reached his arm around Tim's nodding head to touch Beulah's shoulder.

"You've made better use of your time than I have. Regrets are sorry companions, Myles. If I had been responsible all those years ago, the Van Huysen Soap Company might still be—if you'll pardon the expression—afloat, and your children would have an inheritance."

Myles shook his head. His expression seemed to blend emotional strain with spiritual peace. "Water under the bridge, Monte. You can't undo past mistakes, and blaming yourself does no one any good. The Lord had other plans for all of us. I, for one, do not regret the loss of the business, unless it was for

Gram's sake. But she lived out her final years in great joy, surrounded by her great-grandchildren."

Silence fell, broken only by Tim's soft snore.

"Guess I'd better escort this young lady back to her parents," Monte said softly, scooting back his chair.

Young? Marva gave him a sharp look, suspecting the flattering remark, but he appeared unaware of having said anything questionable.

Beulah took Tim into her arms, freeing Myles to escort his brother to the door. "Good night, Monte, and welcome back to the family. Marva. . ." She paused. "Thank you."

Marva slipped around the table to give her friend a kiss on the top of her head. "You try to get some sleep, darlin'. I'm glad I could help."

Monte and Myles shook hands, then gave each other an awkward embrace. "We'll talk more tomorrow," Myles said. "Too many years to catch up on in one evening."

Monte nodded and offered Marva his arm. "Miss Obermeier?"

Chapter 4

Trust in the LORD with all thine heart;
and lean not unto thine own understanding.
PROVERBS 3:5

Moonlight scattered shadows in confusing patterns across the path as wind rustled in the trees. A loon's haunting cry floated through the night. In spite of herself, Marva shivered. Monte pressed his elbow and her hand close against his side, as if to assure her of his protection, and set a slow walking pace.

"So you're an author," she said to make conversation. That feeling of being protected was too pleasant for her emotional comfort.

"Some people think so. Others would dispute that title," he said with an undertone of amusement. "I don't claim to write great literature, by any means."

"When do you find time to write? I assume you work here at the lodge. Are you a hunting and fishing guide?"

A short pause, then he said, "I do some guiding, yes. I do most of my writing during the evenings and in winter. What do you do with your time, Miss Obermeier?"

"Mostly I help my father run the farm and help my mother run the household."

"Who's running the farm and household while you're all away?" he asked.

"My father hired a man to look after the farm, a Mr. Parker, who—*Aaack!*"

A huge, panting creature emerged from the darkness and leaped upon Monte's chest, knocking him back a step. Just as Marva drew breath for another shriek, Monte clapped his hand over her mouth, holding the back of her head with his other hand. "Hush!" he said, his voice full of laughter. "You'll have every guest in the place panicked! It's just my dog, Ralph."

She looked up at him and caught the glint of moonlight in his eyes. Humiliation rolled over her like a wave. He must think her an utter fool.

"Calm now? No more screams?"

She nodded, and he released her head. "I'm sorry I grabbed you that way. All I could think of was our sleeping guests. It's late, you know."

The dog panted and huffed around their feet, sniffed at a nearby tree, and then plunged down the slope toward the lake. "He probably caught scent of the raccoons that frightened you earlier," Monte said.

Marva's overtired brain projected images of her being clasped against this man's broad chest, his hand stroking her hair. She drew a deep breath and forged ahead on the dark trail.

He caught up with her in a few strides. "Are you all right? Miss Obermeier, I'm sorry Ralph startled you."

"I am very tired, Mr. Van Huysen."

"Call me Monte, please. Are you angry?" He seemed genuinely concerned, watching her face as he kept pace at her side. Large lanterns framing the lodge doorway guided her steps.

"I'm not angry; I'm exhausted, Mr. Van Huysen. If I awakened any of your guests, I am truly sorry. A good night's sleep should restore my good sense, but. . . how do I locate my parents' room?"

"You haven't been to your room yet?"

"No, I was helping Beulah and Myles with the children."

"We'll check at the desk." When she tripped over something on the path, he said, "Won't you please take my arm again? I know this path like I know my own face. Too many roots and rocks lying in wait to trip you up in the dark."

She laid her hand on his forearm and sensed his satisfaction. She would have to guard her heart closely against this charmer. He was nothing like serious Myles, she realized. And she liked the differences.

While Monte scanned the lodge ledger for her parents' room number, Marva studied the expansive foyer built entirely of polished logs. The antlered head of a huge deer surmounted a rock fireplace, and a standing black bear waited in the dining room doorway, its mouth open in a snarl. Thick rugs lay scattered about on the gleaming hardwood floor. Oil chandeliers made from deer antlers hung from the square-beamed ceiling, casting a romantic glow over the room. Birch boughs lined the arched doorway into what might be the dining hall. A grandfather clock located between two doors indicated ten minutes past eleven.

"The halls should be lit, but you might need a lamp once you get into your room. Wait a moment and I'll find one for you." He tapped her elbow.

She nodded. From any other man she would have resented this frequent touching, but somehow from him it seemed appropriate. She gave her head a little shake. As if rules of propriety should not apply equally to every man.

He disappeared through a door behind the desk. She suddenly felt very alone in this strange place and rubbed her arms.

"Cold?" He reappeared, a glowing lamp in hand. "I imagine it's cooler here than in your part of the state. Wish I had a jacket to offer."

"I'll be fine, thank you." Was he this solicitous of every female guest? She could imagine women of all ages swooning over his chivalrous manners.

He offered his arm again. She looked from it to his face. "I'm sure I can find my way if you give me directions."

"Why take chances?" He opened one of the doors near the clock and indicated that she should enter first. "Quietly, please." As soon as the door closed behind him, he set the lamp on the floor, took her hand and tucked it through the crook of his elbow, and then retrieved the lamp.

Oil sconces turned low lined the hallway. "Your room is near the end on the left," he said softly.

Marva nodded and followed his lead.

Outside room 21, he stopped and turned to face her. "Take the lamp now, and keep it as long as you like. I'll see you in the morning, Miss Obermeier."

Did she imagine anticipation and warmth in his voice and eyes? He certainly had an enthusiastic personality.

"Good night, and thank you, Mr. Van Huysen." He reached behind her to open the door, and she stepped inside. After the door closed with a soft clank of the latch, she heard his footsteps fade away along the hall.

As he left the lodge, Monte found himself grinning uncontrollably. What luck! No, not luck. What a blessing! Unless he was greatly mistaken, Marva Obermeier was his Lonely in Longtree. She must be! How many Christian women of her age lived alone with elderly parents and ran a farm? Well, probably hundreds did, but how many in Longtree, Wisconsin? That she and her parents should be not only acquainted but close friends with his long-lost brother defied probability. That Miss Obermeier was strikingly attractive? This fact utterly boggled his mind. Only God could arrange things so well.

Ralph approached at a gallop, panting noisily. Remembering Marva's squeals at the dog's "attack" provoked a chuckle. "Tonight you were a bear or wolf, old man," he told the dog. "Come." He slapped his leg, and Ralph heeled.

Light glowed in the window of Myles and Beulah's cabin. He looked forward to becoming acquainted with his brother's large family. Myles was a blessed man. A busy man, for certain. Six children! Monte laughed softly. If all six children proved to be as charming as young Tim, these next few weeks promised to be pleasantly entertaining.

Myles and Beulah were most likely discussing the day's surprising revelations. Remembering the friendly warmth in Beulah's eyes, Monte felt reassured. And Myles had seemed pleased, though also decidedly stunned and disturbed. How would he feel about the situation, about his brother, once he'd had time to fully consider facts? Monte knew he had plenty more explaining to do. He felt his smile change to a frown at the worry that twisted his gut.

All this time, he had thought Myles was ashamed to acknowledge him, while in truth, Myles had thought him dead. Had he known that Myles had reconciled with God, he might have attempted a reunion sooner. But who could tell?

He entered his own cabin and flopped into his favorite chair, staring into the darkness. Ralph dropped to the floor nearby, heaving a contented sigh.

"If I had really trusted You, God, I would have approached Myles years ago," he prayed aloud.

Ralph rose and shoved his muzzle into Monte's hand. He petted the dog absently, lost in regret. All those years he might have spent with his brother—forever lost. And never again would he see dear old Gram alive on earth.

He leaned forward in the chair, elbows on his knees, and rubbed his face with both hands. So many empty years of aimless wandering. Sure, he'd been serving God here and there, spreading the gospel message, writing his books, befriending needy people. But the longing for home and family had driven him on, never entirely at peace with himself, never satisfied.

"I suppose it could be worse, God. I could have waited until Myles and I were both doddering old codgers." He grimaced. If the church group from Longtree had not conveniently decided to vacation at his lodge, he might have waited yet another twenty years for the "right time." Shame weighted his heart.

The dog laid his head and one large paw on Monte's knee. "I'm a coward, Ralph." He gently pulled the dog's soft ears, letting them slide through his fingers. "You've got a yellow-bellied marmot for a master." Ralph's tail whacked the footstool on one side and thumped the table leg on the other.

"No more."

Ralph pricked his ears at the harsh tone of his master's voice.

"No more cowardice. I've let fear rob me of love and family. I'm forty years old and going gray, Ralph. I don't want to live out my days alone. There's a woman who might consider marrying me if I'm ever brave enough to ask. If she's the woman I think she is. . ." Sudden doubt made him falter. "I'd better make sure before I stick my neck out too far."

Even if Marva Obermeier did turn out to be his newspaper sweetheart, what if she turned up her nose at the thought of. . .of his past? Had she been able to overhear his confession from her position on the cabin porch? Her manner had been reserved rather than friendly.

He had better advance cautiously.

⁂

"Push me, Miss Marba." Trixie kicked her dangling legs, red curls in chaos around her shoulders, little hands clutching the swing's ropes.

"Say please," Marva reminded.

"Pwease."

While hitching baby Ginny higher on her hip, Marva gently pushed the swing suspended from a sturdy oak branch. Trixie laughed in excitement, although she swung back and forth a total of only three feet. Watching the child's joy, Marva smiled. It took so little to please these small ones. . .yet they constantly demanded attention.

Joey played with a friend in the sandbox, content to dig and dump. The three older Van Huysen boys were off playing with friends, exploring the grounds, with strict orders from their fathers not to stray into the surrounding forest or venture into the lake. Judging by the *clank* of horseshoes and the ripples of laughter from the clearing, the other young people were finding ways to amuse themselves. The lodge seemed to be nearly filled with guests. Where had they all come from?

A breeze rustled through branches overhead—Marva was learning to love that restful sound. Blue sky and puffy clouds played backdrop to the dancing oak and maple leaves. The vivid colors nearly took Marva's breath away whenever she sneaked a glance upward. And the lake! She loved its every mood—serene, playful, agitated, intent—always in shades of blue and gray.

Myles, Beulah, and Monte were somewhere, not too far away, catching up on the past.

Again.

Still.

Twenty years was a long time, but in how much detail must it be recounted? *That Monte is a talker, for sure.* A smile twitched her lips at the thought. But then, of all people to criticize... She had once been notorious for being able to talk the hind legs off a donkey.

Age had brought with it an awareness of how ridiculous she'd often made herself in the sight of her friends. More than one man she had frightened away with her wagging tongue and almost frenetic energy. Not that men found her any more attractive since she withdrew into herself.

Except for Mr. Stowell, who was even now strolling down the path from the lodge. As she caught his eye, a wide smile brightened the lodge owner's face. "Miss Obermeier, how good to see you. You're looking lovely, as always."

"Good afternoon, Mr. Stowell. Finished in the office for the afternoon?"

"I wish it were so. I'm looking for Monte—Mr. Van Huysen. Have you seen him?" He paused before her. Although his words were businesslike, his eyes roved her face with an almost-rapt expression.

Was Monte in trouble with the boss for neglecting his work?

"I believe he and the other Van Huysens are down by the lake."

"Thank you. I—I hope to see you later." Mr. Stowell's face turned pink. "At supper. Perhaps you... Might you have time for a stroll this evening?"

"I might." It would be a good opportunity to sound him out concerning the *Longtree Enquirer*. But then again, Beulah might need help with the children.

Mr. Stowell beamed. "Thank you." He started to say something else, stopped, and repeated, "Thank you," before moving on toward the shore.

At last, the prospect of a social moment for herself. Not that Mr. Stowell was her ideal man, but he seemed steady and pleasant, and he owned the lodge. If he did turn out to be "Lucky," he would probably make her a good, dependable husband.

A loon warbled out on the lake. Shading her eyes, Marva sought a glimpse of the bird—it sounded nearby.

Two men in a fishing boat rowed toward the shore. Her father's white beard was unmistakable. The man with him was most likely Rev. Schoengard, another devoted fisherman. She wondered if they had caught anything, but she didn't dare leave the children long enough to find out. They tied the boat to the wooden dock and hoisted their poles and tackle ashore.

Mother was probably napping in the shade with her friends. Unlike Marva, she had time to socialize with other women her age.

Self-pity crept into Marva's thoughts. After all, she had been brought along on this trip for purely practical purposes, namely as a child minder to keep the little ones from disturbing anyone else's peace. Her parents were caught up in their own activities. Marva had known this would happen when she agreed to come, but she had expected to chat with Beulah while they watched the children together.

Monte Van Huysen's presence had thrown a wrench into the clockwork, in more ways than one. Beulah told her that Monte had never married, which Marva found difficult to believe. He was far from shy, successful in his field, and appealing to the female eye. Why was he single at age forty? Probably because, Christian man though he claimed to be, he had no desire to settle down with only one woman.

She wrinkled her nose, determined to remain focused on her goal of locating and identifying Lucky in Lakeland. If only she knew a few more details about Lucky's life and his person aside from his age and his business. He seemed a serious-minded individual, articulate and responsible. Most of their conversations had centered on topics such as religion, hobbies, future plans, and dreams—topics that could freely be discussed in the open forum of a newspaper.

Lucky had claimed to enjoy fishing. She would have to ask Mr. Stowell if he pursued that hobby. Lucky had also expressed a desire to mentor young Christian men and encourage them in the faith. The memory of that particular letter started a warm glow around her heart. She could easily imagine an earnest, devout expression on Mr. Stowell's face as he expressed such a desire.

But what if she learned that Harding Stowell never read the *Longtree Enquirer*?

Chapter 5

Let your conversation be without covetousness;
and be content with such things as ye have:
for he hath said, I will never leave thee, nor forsake thee.
HEBREWS 13:5

Trixie suddenly thrashed her legs in an effort to hop out of the swing. "Dog!" she cried in excitement.

A large brindle-and-white hound sniffed at a nearby tree. Marva recognized it as Monte's pet. "I'm not sure if it's friendly, Trixie. Better just talk to it from here."

But the little girl touched her feet to the ground and started running. "Trixie!" Marva trotted after her with Ginny bouncing on her shoulder.

A throng of children, including Joey, had already gathered around the dog. Its tail whipped their legs as it tried to lick every face. When Trixie approached, the dog gave her a slurp from chin to forehead, and she sat down abruptly, knocked off balance. Marva expected her to cry, but instead she laughed in delight.

Although the dog seemed friendly enough, its increasing excitement worried Marva. It could unintentionally knock a small child flat. She bent over to catch Trixie's arm and pull her to a safe distance. The dog gave a little hop, and its warm tongue slopped over Marva's lips and cheek.

"Eeww! Eeww! Oh bleah!" She staggered back, wiping her sleeve across her face. The children laughed, entirely unsympathetic, and continued to pat the dog.

A shrill whistle split the air. The dog's ears pricked; its head cocked. An instant later it vaulted Trixie in one bound and swished past Marva's skirts.

She spun around to see Monte, Myles, and Beulah approaching, all three wearing wide smiles. The dog capered around Monte's feet, tongue lolling.

"Mama!" Trixie scrambled up and ran to greet Beulah, who scooped up her disheveled child.

"Are you hungry, sweetie pie? It's nearly time for supper."

"I hungry." Trixie pointed at the dog. "Dog."

"Yes, dear, it certainly is a dog. A rambunctious dog."

"Ralph loves children," Monte said quickly. "And pretty women." He met Marva's gaze, and she saw a twinkle in his eyes. He had definitely witnessed Ralph's display of affection.

"We'll have to clean up all these children before supper, but we'll meet you in the dining room," Myles told his brother. The two men thumped each other on the shoulders and parted ways. Monte and his dog headed toward the shore.

"I can't thank you enough for this, Marva," Beulah said as Myles took the fussing Ginny from Marva's arms. Joey clung to his father's leg and jabbered about dogs. Myles smoothed his son's sand-crusted forehead and smiled absently at his talk.

"Did you have a good talk with. . .with your brother?" She wasn't sure what to call him, though in her thoughts he was Monte.

"Very good," Myles said. "He's an amazing man. What a blessing to see the changes God has made in his life! And he's just as startled by the changes God has worked in me. The last he knew me, I was a bitter young man."

"How nice." Marva's arm felt weak and light, empty of Ginny's weight. A damp spot where the baby drooled on her shoulder felt cold. "I believe I'll go freshen up, too. See you at dinner."

What kind of friend was she to begrudge Myles and Beulah this special time with Monte? The children were not particularly difficult to watch.

To her surprise, Monte joined her on the path to the lodge. "I know Myles and Beulah have thanked you for watching their children these past few days, but I want to add my own thanks. You're a generous woman to give of your time for our benefit."

More guilt heaped on her conscience. "I'm glad I could help."

He held the door open for her. "Thank you," Marva said. In Monte Van Huysen's dark eyes, she read admiration, gratitude, and. . .something more?

"I'll see you at supper, Miss Obermeier."

An idea took shape in her mind. If she was ever to find Lucky, she needed to visit other lodges in the area. Members of the Lakeland Lodge staff must travel into town occasionally for supplies, mail, and news. Monte was a member of the staff. He probably ran errands for the lodge along with his guide duties. She could ask him for a ride and. . . Dreams of Monte's attentive company blotted thoughts of the elusive Lucky from her head.

In the hall outside her room, she stopped cold and clapped one hand over her face. *No! I am here in search of Lucky in Lakeland, and I must not allow myself to be distracted. I am through forever with chasing after men or even thinking about chasing after men! If Monte Van Huysen wants to be with me, he will have to do the chasing.*

~∞~

"Monte, have you got a minute?" Hardy Stowell burst into Monte's office, nearly colliding with him in the doorway. His wispy hair stood on end like a wavering halo of gold around his head.

"Sure. What's wrong? Sit down before you collapse." Monte caught his friend by the shoulders and pushed him into a chair.

"Nothing is wrong! I wanted to tell you earlier, but your family was there. . . ."

Hardy fanned his face with an envelope and rubbed his head. "She said she might walk with me after supper—Miss Obermeier did." His electrified hair sprang back out as soon as his hand passed over it.

"Oh. Really." Monte realized how flat his response sounded and tried again. "That's nice."

Hardy gave a little laugh.

"Don't get your hopes up too high," Monte warned in mild concern and a flash of jealousy.

Hardy shook his head and stood up. "I know. A woman like her wouldn't look twice at a fellow like me. I can't help wondering why she's never married. Bad disposition? Hard to believe with that angel face of hers. Domineering parents? Disappointment in her youth?"

"Hard to say," Monte responded after an empty pause. "I suppose you could ask her."

Hardy smiled, and his pale eyes shimmered. "If I have the courage."

After his partner left the office, Monte flopped into his desk chair and glared at the opposite wall.

⁓⊗⁓

Everyone gathered in the lodge dining room for supper that evening, a fish fry of walleye and bluegill. Marva sat at her parents' table, enjoying her first quiet meal. George and Dorothy Hilbert, the newlyweds, joined them, chatting happily about their hiking excursion into the local woods. Above the murmur of conversation, Marva heard Trixie Van Huysen scream in garbled protest about something. She ate slightly faster in case Beulah might need her help.

Sensing a presence at her elbow, she looked up to meet Mr. Stowell's hopeful gaze. "Miss Obermeier?"

While chewing and swallowing a mouthful of fish, she patted her lips with her napkin and laid it on her plate. "Yes, sir?"

"I see you're not yet finished. I trust you still have the time and inclination to honor me with your presence this evening? To take a walk?"

"Oh." She glanced around at the Van Huysen table. Trixie perched on her uncle Monte's knee, playing with his string tie. The children appeared to be cheerful and cooperative. "Yes, I believe so. That would be nice, Mr. Stowell." Sensing his impatience, she decided to forgo dessert.

"There is no hurry. You may enjoy your meal while I visit other guests. Simply let me know when you're ready."

"Very well."

Mr. Stowell shook her father's hand and greeted her mother, then nodded to the Hilberts. The man had good manners; that was certain.

When Marva rose and brushed off her skirt, Mr. Stowell hurried across the room to join her. Everyone at the lodge must know by now that she had agreed to walk with him. With one hand at the back of her waist, he escorted her from the dining room. As they passed the Van Huysens' table, Beulah looked up and gave her a knowing smile. Monte remained focused on his nieces and nephews.

Evening light lingered over the lake. "Shall we stroll down to the shore, or would you prefer an actual walk?" Mr. Stowell asked. "The dragonflies are out in vast numbers tonight to protect us from mosquitoes."

"How thoughtful of them," Marva said with a smile. "I think I should like to take some exercise after that meal."

"As you wish." He offered his arm, and Marva looped her hand through the crook of his elbow. They fell into step, following the wagon track away from the lake.

"Tell me about yourself, Miss Obermeier. Why has such a lovely woman never married? Or am I too bold?" His voice sounded tight with nerves.

"The answer is simple enough. The right man has never asked me." Marva felt calm and composed. "Why are you unmarried, Mr. Stowell?"

"I was married once."

"Did your wife pass?"

A pause. "Yes, she is dead." His tone discouraged further questions, which seemed unfair to Marva.

"I'm sorry. How long has it been?" Hearing a high-pitched whine, she waved at her ear.

"A few years. Do you wish to marry, Miss Obermeier, or do you intend to remain single?"

Irritation prickled. "I would marry if the right opportunity arose." She gazed up at his taut profile. "Do you ever read the *Longtree Enquirer*, Mr. Stowell?"

He gave her a puzzled look. "The what?"

"It is our local newspaper. Your lodge advertises in it, which is how our group came to be here. I merely wondered if you ever read the paper." Now a fly buzzed into her face; she swatted it away.

He looked thoughtful. "Now that you mention it, yes, I believe I have seen a copy lying around the lodge upon occasion."

She decided to take the plunge. "Have you ever written a personal note to the *Longtree Enquirer*, sir? In answer to an advertisement or some such thing?"

"I have not." He licked his lips and looked uncomfortable. "Might I inquire as to where these questions lead, Miss Obermeier?"

"I wish to locate a person who has been communicating with me through the newspaper; that is all. It is unimportant, Mr. Stowell."

Now that she knew he bore no connection to "Lucky in Lakeland," Marva was eager to return to the lodge and escape his company. "Ooh, the insects are dreadful this evening." She slapped her arm, and her hand felt sticky with her own blood. "I do not think the dragonflies are doing their job properly after all."

"Perhaps if we strolled down beside the water where there is a breeze—"

"I think we had better take cover, Mr. Stowell, but thank you anyway." Her pace nearly doubled on the way back.

His face revealed disappointment when she bade him farewell at the lodge's front door. "Such a pleasant stroll. Thank you again."

Once back in the small suite she shared with her parents, she picked up a certain book from her father's bedside table and found her place. The lurid cover art no longer amused her; she was entirely engrossed in the adventurous, slightly romantic tale of the Wild West. She read the book only when her parents were not around. There was no point in advertising her foolish interest in its author.

Sometime later, a loon's call startled her back to reality. The bird sounded close. Although she knew quite well that she would not see it from the window, she rose to pull aside the curtain.

A moonlit path shimmered on the lake, so lovely that tears pooled in Marva's eyes at the sight. Such a night was meant for lovers. But God had given it to her, as well, and she would not let His gift go to waste.

⌘

Monte scribbled out a new scene while listening for his partner's return, but his gaze kept returning to the clock. Focusing with an effort, he shuffled through his pages. His fictional hero seemed to him hapless and idiotic: The Sioux braves who had trapped the "idiot" alone in a gully behaved more like children than like genuine warriors, the "idiot's" romance with the widow of a settler had fizzled with no conceivable hope of renewal, and even the "idiot's" mustang behaved like an oversized hound dog. Who would want to read such twaddle? Monte jabbed his pen into its holder and shoved back his chair.

Rising, he paced across his office and stared out the dark window. Moonlight glittered on the lake. Were Hardy and Marva enjoying the sight together? Could a beautiful woman like Miss Obermeier find a man like Hardy appealing? Stranger things had happened. After all, Hardy was a good fellow in his way. It may be that he and Marva had discovered soul mates in each other. They might talk for hours and never run out of topics. They might enjoy a comfortable silence and drink in the beauty of the night, arm in arm. Even hand in hand, if the romance progressed rapidly.

No, surely not. Marva seemed too reserved for that kind of familiarity. But maybe she was only reserved with Monte. Maybe with other men she could relax and laugh. Beulah had said something once about Marva's reputation for talking nonstop. Why did she seem constrained and uncomfortable in Monte's presence? Was it because he talked too much and overwhelmed her? Was it because she sensed his physical attraction to her?

He pulled out his watch and glared at its face. The burning heaviness in his chest revealed more about his feelings than he wanted to know. *Lord, when will I learn to be content with reality?*

Just when he thought he had finally outgrown his weaknesses, just when he was ready to settle down in a prosaic marriage with a desperate-yet-steady spinster, just then, Miss Marva Obermeier stepped off the train and knocked him emotionally sprawling. Here he was, forty years of age yet still easy prey to temptations of the flesh and the heart. Who would have thought that his steady, godly, mature correspondent would turn out to be the kind of woman he had always dreamed about?

But then. . .what if he was wrong about Miss Obermeier being his newspaper lady? He was 98 percent sure, but that remaining 2 percent loomed large in his mind despite his attempts to ignore it.

Real life never resembled fiction. . .did it?

Chapter 6

The heavens declare the glory of God;
and the firmament sheweth his handywork.
Day unto day uttereth speech, and night unto night sheweth knowledge.
PSALM 19:1–2

Monte shoved the watch back into his pocket and leaned on the windowsill. His eyes opened wide; then he jutted his chin forward and squinted in disbelief. Was he seeing things?

Silvery moonlight gleamed on the pale hair of a lone figure seated on the end of the dock. Monte saw no one else nearby, although a person could be hidden from his view by intervening trees. Squinting and trying to peer around these brushy obstacles, he searched for. . . For what? His rival? Why was he behaving like a jealous schoolboy?

The sound of a familiar, hacking cough almost stopped his heart. Immediately he stepped across the hall and knocked on the door of the office that connected to Hardy's sleeping quarters. No answer. He knocked harder.

"What is it?" Hardy growled. "I'm in bed. Go away."

"When did you get back? I've been waiting to talk to you."

More coughing. "I got back before you did. Can't it wait until morning? I'm tired."

He was heartless, no doubt, to feel cheered by the depressed tone of his friend's voice, but Monte couldn't stop his reaction. "All right. See you then."

He quickly closed up his office and left the lodge. A few guests lingered in rocking chairs on the long veranda facing the lake. He returned their greetings and hurried on toward the lakeshore.

His steps slowed gradually, and his breathing became short. There she was, still perched on the end of the dock. With hair like spun starlight, it could be no one but Marva Obermeier. He heard water splashing as she swung her feet.

As soon as his boots touched the dock, she turned her head to look at him.

"Mind if I join you?" he asked softly. "It's a perfect night."

She faced back toward the lake, her shoulders stiff. "I have no claim on the dock, Mr. Van Huysen." Her shoes made a dark mound on the boards behind her.

"No, but you do have a say about whether or not a man sits beside you. I promise to be quiet if you're craving peace." He proceeded to the end of the dock.

She braced her palms on either side of herself but made no move to rise. He sat nearby yet not too close. "Is the water warm?"

"It's nice." Her voice was so quiet he had to strain to hear.

"I'd take off my boots and dangle my feet, except I'm afraid the stink of my feet would chase you away."

She laughed, a quick snort and chuckle. "I'm not that sensitive, Mr. Van Huysen. My papa keeps pigs. I doubt your feet could smell worse than their sty on a summer night."

"You might be surprised."

Monte untied his boots and removed them and his socks, one after another. The cool water gave his feet a shock at first, but within moments, he scarcely felt the chill. Happiness filled him so full that some of it had to escape in a deep sigh.

"A busy day?" she asked, back to that polite and formal tone.

"No busier than usual. Tomorrow I've got to make a run into town."

She looked at him with evident interest. "May I come along? I have. . .inquiries to make."

Inquiries? His thoughts raced ahead. "If it's not impertinent to ask, what kind of inquiries must you make? Perhaps I might be of assistance."

She clasped her hands in her lap and studied them. Monte simply watched her, enjoying the view.

"I need to find out about resort lodges in the area. I need to. . .to meet their owners."

Monte rubbed his hand over his mouth to hide his smile. "You're dissatisfied with Lakeland Lodge?"

She shook her head. "Not at all. This is another matter. A private matter. I spoke with Mr. Stowell today, and he told me that several local lodges are owned by unmarried gentlemen."

"I can think of a few. Why must the owners be unmarried?"

"That is not your business, Mr. Van Huysen."

He turned his face away until he could keep amusement out of his voice. "Tell you what: After I pick up the mail and supplies, I'll drive you around to some local lodges. We'll make up a list, and you tell me which ones you want to visit."

When she turned to look at him, her face was in shadow. "Do you really have time for that?"

"It would be my pleasure, Miss Obermeier. At Lakeland Lodge, guests always come first." He gave a little seated bow. "If you don't object to a personal observation, I'd say that you need a break from my nieces and nephews for at least one day."

When she said nothing, he continued. "I admire how you help Beulah with her children. She can't praise you highly enough, to my way of thinking."

"They're dear children."

"I agree, yet even the dearest children get tiring. You must have patience beyond the lot of mortals. From the Lord, that is."

She laughed again. "I get wearier and crankier than anyone knows, because if I expressed my frustration, everyone would know the real me—and I can't let that happen!"

Although she spoke in jest, he heard the note of truth in her words. "Aren't we all that way—hiding our real selves from the world? But the good thing about it is that we can sympathize with one another. I still admire the fact that you keep up a cheery front—put on a brave face."

She gazed out across the lake, moonlight turning her features to marble. "If I were truly brave and cheery, it wouldn't have to be a front. I know I should trust God and be grateful for the life He has given me, but instead of being content, I doubt His wisdom and try to force change into my life."

Startled by this sudden glimpse into her soul, he pondered an equally honest reply. "My method of doubting Him is more along the lines of being afraid to attempt changes."

Silence fell between them. Monte could think of nothing more to say, yet he wanted to prolong the moment.

She turned around and picked up her shoes. "What time do you plan to leave for town in the morning, Mr. Van Huysen?"

"Not till after breakfast." He rose and helped her up. Her hand felt cool and strong in his. "I'll bring the wagon around in front of the lodge."

"Then I'll see you in the morning." She smiled briefly at him and walked toward the shore, her footsteps nearly silent on the dock. He hoped her bare feet wouldn't pick up splinters.

⚬⚬⚬

"But Marva, I don't understand why you feel this need to go into town. I disapprove of an unmarried woman riding around this wilderness land with an unmarried man, even if he is Myles's brother."

Marva tucked a wisp of hair back into her bun and picked at her breakfast pancakes with a fork. "I simply wish to make a few inquiries around town, Mother, and there is nothing indiscreet about sitting beside a man in an open wagon."

Papa cleared his throat. His beard bobbled back and forth as he chewed. He swallowed and said, "I believe your mother is asking what kind of inquiries you intend to make. I confess a curiosity along those lines myself."

Marva met his direct gaze and acknowledged herself defeated. "Never mind. It isn't important anyway. But I do believe I am old enough to travel about unescorted without setting too many tongues wagging."

"Not with a handsome man like Monte Van Huysen, you're not," Mother said with uncharacteristic shortness. Marva sensed her parents' displeasure at her refusal to explain, but she wasn't about to deceive them, and neither would she tell them the truth.

Now that she thought the matter over objectively, she realized how awkward it would be to interview lodge owners with Monte Van Huysen hovering in the background, possibly nosing into her personal business. And if she were to find Lucky, he might well object to her coming to meet him in the company of another eligible bachelor. Her parents' objection was probably for the best.

She asked for Monte at the front desk but was told that he had already left his office. "You might find him at the stables, ma'am."

"And the stables are. . . ?"

The grizzled desk clerk pointed straight at the door, then jerked his finger to one side. "Quickest way is out the lodge door, turn left, and follow the path until you see the stables."

After hurrying back to the dining room to tell her parents where she was going, she started her quest. The lodge grounds were quiet at this hour. A doe and her spotted twin fawns crossed the path ahead of her, stopped to stare, and then trotted on into the underbrush. A woodpecker hammered somewhere overhead, but Marva couldn't spot it.

She soon saw weathered buildings in a clearing. From the confines of a large corral, a mule and several horses observed her approach with mild interest. The distinctive odors of horse and hay mingled with the scent of pine.

As she rounded a bend, she saw Monte Van Huysen in front of a carriage house, harnessing a horse. The animal pricked its ears and snuffled at her approach, and Monte turned to follow its gaze. Seeing her, he straightened and brushed off his hands. "Miss Obermeier."

"Good morning, Mr. Van Huysen. I came to tell you that I will not be able to go to town with you today after all." She couldn't help but be pleased to see his evident disappointment. "My parents disapprove of the idea. Mother thinks it unseemly for me to ride alone with you into town, which I think is ridiculous, but I cannot change her mind."

"They're welcome to come along with us."

She shook her head. "That wouldn't work, but thank you anyway."

"Maybe another day?"

"I—I don't think so."

He sighed. "All the anticipation just drained out of this day, Petunia, old girl." He addressed the words to his horse. Marva smiled in amusement.

"Do you enjoy fishing?" he asked, giving her a look from the corner of his eye.

"Sometimes. I used to enjoy it anyway."

He took a step closer. "I'm taking your father out tomorrow morning. You could come along. . .if you wanted to. You haven't truly experienced the Northwoods until you've been out on the lake early on a summer morning."

"I might just do that. Thank you. Have a good trip today, Mr. Van Huysen."

She felt his gaze follow as she walked away, head high, shoulders back.

But finding Lucky should be her focus. Frustration with her own weakness for a handsome man increased her determination. Somehow, one way or another, she must visit neighboring lodges. Time was slipping past, and soon her chance would be gone. If she did not make an opportunity, no one would.

Mr. Stowell rose politely and smiled when she entered his office.

"Please, Mr. Stowell, could you arrange for me to borrow a horse and cart?"

He gripped the back of his office chair. Standing with his shoulders against the wall, he seemed to use his desk like a shield against her influence. "I would be pleased to drive you anywhere you wish to go."

"Thank you kindly, but no, I would not feel right about dragging you away from your work. I am an able driver."

She at last wangled a promise from him that she might have use of a horse and dogcart Thursday morning. He still seemed uneasy, but he did agree.

"Thank you ever so much! I appreciate this more than you can know, Mr. Stowell. You are a gem and a true friend."

"Am I?" His face flushed.

"I can harness and hitch a horse by myself," she offered.

"That won't be necessary. Our boys will ready one for you. At nine o'clock?"

"Ideal! I shall be there. Oh! One more thing—do you have a map of the area, and might you be willing to mark on it the locations of the nearest vacation lodges?"

He appeared bewildered. "A map? I don't know the area all that well. Mr. Van Huysen would be better able to assist you in that way."

"Mr. Van Huysen? I would prefer he not know about my venture. I wish you would please do it." She used her most persuasive tone and blinked sweetly.

"I'll—Well, I'll try."

Something in his tone informed her that he remained wary.

Chapter 7

Not by works of righteousness which we have done,
but according to his mercy he saved us,
by the washing of regeneration, and renewing of the Holy Ghost;
which he shed on us abundantly through Jesus Christ our Saviour.
TITUS 3:5–6

Take my hand—careful now." Marva gripped Monte's hand and stepped cautiously into the small fishing boat. Papa took her other hand and helped guide her to the small bench set in the bow. She turned in time to see Monte release her skirt from a splinter on the gunwale while Papa rescued a bucket of bait from overturning.

"I'm sorry. I hope this wasn't a bad idea, my coming along today." She knew she had made them get a late start. The rosy pink in the eastern sky was already fading to silver blue, and sunlight peeked through the treetops across the lake.

Papa made a noncommittal little grunt. Monte loaded a tackle box, untied the boat from the dock, and hopped in. Just before he started rowing, he glanced back at Marva over one shoulder and winked. "A woman aboard ship may be bad luck, but we'll take the risk." He turned to her father. "Would you please shove us off?"

Marva turned forward, letting the moist morning air brush her face. No breeze disturbed the lake's mirror surface. With each stroke of the oars, the little boat surged forward. Just beneath the water's green surface she saw the tops of water weeds and an occasional fish.

"Right around here is where the reverend and I caught those walleye the other day," Papa said from his seat in the boat's stern after Monte had rowed a good distance.

"This is a good spot," Monte said. "Want to drop anchor here and give it a try?"

"Why not?"

Marva heard him ship oars as quietly as possible. The anchor made a little splash when he slipped it over the side. She tipped her head over the bow and stared down into the dark water, straining her eyes to glimpse a fish.

"You'll catch more fish with a pole and some bait, Marva-girl," Papa said in mild reproof. She turned with a smile and had to shade her eyes. Morning sun reflected off the water with almost unbearable brilliance.

"Good thing you wore that sun hat. It's going to be a hot day," Monte remarked.

Marva adjusted her hat's broad brim. "I do burn easily. You don't share your brother's complexion, I notice."

"I was lucky. Our mother was a redhead like Myles. I got my hair and complexion from our father, though I burn more easily than he did." He adjusted his cap. "Still need a hat on a day like this, though. No sense in taking chances."

The two men were already baiting hooks and adjusting their lines. Marva disliked impaling minnows or worms; she preferred artificial bait even if nothing bit at it. Smoothing her skirt, she allowed herself to watch Monte. So active and strong. Gray sprinkled the hair at his temples, and his face was lined from squinting into the sun. . .or maybe from smiling. This evidence of age was comforting rather than repelling, since her own face and form were beginning to show signs of wear.

He turned to straddle his bench and gave her a sideways look. "I dug beetle grubs out of a rotted log last night. Sometimes I have luck with them. Want me to bait your line?"

She nodded. "Thank you."

"Always tried to break the girl of squeamishness," her father said regretfully. "Never could get her to bait her own hooks."

Monte chuckled. "Gives us men a purpose—hook baiters." He handed her the pole with the squirming grub swinging from the end of its line. "Know how to cast?"

She nodded and concentrated on taking the pole without hitting herself or anyone else in the face with the grub. Monte slowly released his hold and sat back to watch her cast. The grub sailed smoothly through the air and hit the water's surface with a tiny *plop* a good distance away.

"Nice cast."

"Thank you." Marva returned his smile.

Soon the three of them sat and watched their bobbers. A bald eagle soared near the shore and landed in a dead tree, studying them with its head turned to one side. Marva could see its yellow beak and ruffled feathers.

Monte sat with his feet propped on the edge of the boat, leaning his elbows on his knees. She heard him humming softly but couldn't catch the tune. He reeled in his line, grumbled over stolen bait, and cast again.

"Look over there."

Marva followed Monte's pointing finger and saw a V-shaped ripple moving near the shore. "What is it?"

"I'd guess it's a muskrat. We had a family of minks nesting on our shore two years back. They cleaned out all the muskrats and chipmunks. But then the minks moved on, so the little critters are coming back."

Papa caught a small bass, too small to keep. He baited his hook with a minnow and tried again on the other side of the boat.

The sun's heat began to penetrate Marva's hat and her blue cotton gown. She shifted uncomfortably and thought about taking off her shoes. *Oh, to be a carefree child again!*

A breeze sent ripples over the lake's surface, making the boat gently rock and spin in a lazy circle around its anchor chain. Marva leaned her arm on the side of the boat and rested her head on it. Sunlight trickled through the weave of her hat. She closed her eyes, waving off a fly.

Sometime later she stirred, dimly realizing that she had dozed off. Something brushed against her side, and she started up. "Oh!"

Monte was kneeling on the floorboards beside her seat, holding her wildly bending and pulling fishing pole. He glanced down and saw that she was awake. "You got one, Marva! Hurry up, take the pole and reel it in!" He grabbed her hand and shoved the pole into her nerveless fingers. Still dazed, she couldn't seem to grasp it properly, so he helped her, his hand over hers on the reel, his other arm reaching around her to steady the pole. His touch served only to increase her ineptitude. "There he is! We've got him now!" The fish's silvery sides flashed in the sunlight as it made a wild leap into the air.

Monte half stood in the teetering rowboat, his chest pressed against the back of Marva's head, his hands reaching for the line. "Get the net, Mr. Obermeier! Hurry!"

Papa scrambled to hand him the net and moved Monte's pole out of the way.

Leaning far over the side of the boat, Monte reached for the fish as it dangled from the end of the line. Water sloshed into the bottom of the boat. Marva tried to hold the pole steady, but the fish flipped and struggled.

"Easy! Reel him in a bit farther."

"I'm trying to. He's heavy!" Finally the netted fish lay in the bottom of the boat.

"A magnificent walleye! What a fish! Congratulations, Miss Obermeier, you are the fisherwoman of the day!" He sat beside her on the narrow bench and gave her shoulders a squeeze. The walleye lay on the floorboards, gasping for breath. Marva felt like gasping for breath, too.

"Isn't he a pretty fish?" A brainless comment, yet she didn't know what else to say or do. Did Monte know what he was doing to her?

Papa seemed entirely unaware of his daughter's reactions. He and Monte both crowed over the fish and praised Marva to the skies.

On the pretext of examining her catch more closely, Marva bent over, out of Monte's casual grasp, and reached out to touch the fish's slimy side. It gave a final, violent flop. Startled and nervous, she sat up with a jerk, coming halfway to her feet just as Monte started to rise. Her head connected solidly with his jaw.

"Ow!" His cry blended with hers. Grabbing the top of her head, she sat down hard, nearly missing the bench. The boat rocked wildly. Amid scrabbling thumps and startled exclamations from both men, a bait bucket turned over and doused Marva's feet with flopping minnows and smelly water. Squealing, she jumped up again, lost her balance, and dropped back to her seat.

Splash! Water cascaded into the pitching boat as Monte back flopped over the side. Marva and her father stared, openmouthed, Marva clutching the top of her head. Her hat dangled over her shoulder. Minnows skittered around her feet in a good inch of lake water.

Monte surfaced, wiped water from his face, and wiggled his jaw back and forth. "All these years as a fishing guide, and this is the first time I took a plunge."

"Are you all right, Mr. Van Huysen? I'm terribly sorry!"

"Nothing permanently damaged—except my pride. Balance the boat, please. I'm coming aboard." He pulled himself over the side, dumping another wave into the bottom of the boat in the process.

"We've taken on water," Papa said in vast understatement. "Better do some bailing out." He used a tin cup as a scoop.

"We're starting our own onboard aquarium," Marva observed, watching minnows dart around her feet. Even her walleye looked somewhat encouraged by the rising water level. She started scooping water over the side with her cupped hands.

Meanwhile, Monte hauled off his boots and emptied them over the side. His socks were holey, Marva noticed. Using one of the oars, he fished his floating hat from the water and plopped it on the bench.

He met Marva's gaze and began to chuckle. She smiled but felt dangerously close to tears.

He reached out one big, wet hand to squeeze her arm and gave her a wink. "Guess I needed cooling off anyway."

Did he intend some double meaning? He laughed again, pushing his dripping hair straight back from his forehead. Taking another cup, he helped bail, rounding up minnows and returning them to their bucket. With all of them working, the water level inside the boat eventually dropped.

She tried not to grimace while Monte strung a line through her walleye's gills and lowered it over the side. "I always feel so sorry for the poor fish once they're caught."

"Nonsense," Monte said. "He'll be delicious once he's fried."

At that moment, Marva's father gave his pole a jerk and eagerly started reeling in another fish. Monte hurried to assist him, just as he had helped Marva. She wanted to kick herself for being so stupid, so susceptible, overreacting to Monte's touch the way she had. He must find her amusing in a pathetic sort of way.

To Marva's relief, the men decided to end the outing early, since sitting around in soggy clothes wasn't Monte's idea of a good time. He rowed them back to the landing and helped Marva climb ashore before he unloaded any of the gear. "Wait," he said, clambering up after her. "Miss Obermeier, please don't feel bad about my. . .uh. . .swim today. It wasn't your fault. I was hovering too close and got what I had coming." He dropped his gaze, then grinned up at her with his chin still lowered. "I've never been fishing guide to a beautiful woman before. Guess I found out what not to do."

Ralph came rushing to meet Monte halfway to his cabin. Tongue lolling, the dog frisked about, stopped to sniff his master's wet trousers, and then burst back into wild frolicking. Monte watched Ralph's antics with a fond smile. "Oh, to have such energy and enthusiasm again."

He was hoping to escape observance and comment by avoiding the main path, but no such luck. "Mr. Van Huysen, what happened to you?" a female voice called.

He turned to see a cluster of women on the trail up to the lodge. Every eye was turned upon him. He recognized Marva's mother in the mix.

"I fell into the lake," he said with a wave of his limp hat. "Have a nice luncheon, ladies." Before they could question him further, he hurried off, shivering.

"Foolishness," he muttered while standing on the uneven floorboards in the middle of the cabin's main room, stripping off his wet garments. "I acted like a fool kid. She probably thinks. . . No telling what she thinks. I'm too old for such foolishness."

Grimacing and growling, he continued to berate himself while donning fresh garments and hanging the wet ones over his clothesline hung between two pines. The daunting prospect of facing curious people in the lodge dining room prompted him to rummage through his own poorly stocked cupboards. A can of pork and beans made an unappetizing meal, but at least it stopped his stomach from growling.

He stepped out on the porch with Ralph at his heels, leaned on the railing, and stared through intervening branches at the glittering lake. After a moment's thought, he shook his head and closed his eyes, wanting to pray but unable to put a request into words.

What to do? Thinking back over the morning, he could make nothing of Mr. Obermeier's comments and reactions from the day's adventure. Was the old man aware of Monte's attraction to his daughter? Did he approve or disapprove? That bland German face of his revealed nothing except good humor. Monte thumped his palm on the railing.

And Mrs. Obermeier was no easier to read. Mild and friendly, she seemed sweetly oblivious to any emotional undercurrents.

But then, how did he want them to react? What would he do if Mr. Obermeier came calling to inquire about Monte's intentions toward Marva? If she were eighteen and he were twenty-one, that might be the natural course of events. But now? He had much to offer a woman as far as material possessions were concerned, and all honestly gained.

If only he had not made such a hash of his life back in those early days. A woman like Marva would recoil from him if she knew his past. How could she not? But for God's grace, he would be long since dead, a dried-up corpse hanging from a cottonwood tree on the plains of Texas.

But for God's grace. Because of Christ's cleansing blood, he was no longer a hopeless sinner. When God looked at Montague Van Huysen, He saw a man clothed in His Son's righteousness, sanctified and holy.

God looks on the heart. However, man looks on the outward appearance, and a man's past had a way of haunting him throughout life on this earth.

Again Monte shook his head and sighed. Yet even while he headed to his office to catch up on paperwork, part of his mind calculated where Marva might be at this hour.

❦

"Certainly, Hardy." Monte leaned back in his chair and peered over the tops of his reading glasses. "Are you planning to spy on our competition?"

Hardy frowned. "No. This is for a lodger who requested a map of the area."

"For what purpose?"

"I was not informed. Does it matter?"

Monte lifted his brows and tapped the map with his knuckles. "It might. Although we warn our guests about the hazards of wandering unescorted in these woods, there are always some who scoff at danger."

"The main roads are safe in daylight hours."

"That depends on which roads, which hours, and which traveler, I should say. Hardy, is this map intended for Miss Obermeier?"

His partner's blush was answer enough.

"I see. And you intend to accompany her?"

"She turned down my escort. I promised her the dogcart," Hardy mumbled under his breath and fidgeted.

"All right. I'll take care of it."

"But she's expecting me to provide the map. She. . .uh. . . didn't want you to know about it."

"You will provide the map, and for all she knows, I remain in ignorance. As soon as I finish marking it, I'll leave it on your desk. What time did you order the dogcart?"

"For 9:00 a.m. tomorrow."

Monte bent over the map. "Very well. I'll be running errands myself tomorrow, so I'll do what I can to make sure Miss Obermeier comes to no grief."

Hardy's worried expression vanished. "Good. I didn't want to have to follow her around. At least now I know why she never married. She may be beautiful, but she's far too bossy."

After his office door closed behind Hardy's back, Monte chuckled, quieted and thought a moment, and then laughed aloud.

Chapter 8

Boast not thyself of to morrow;
for thou knowest not what a day may bring forth.
PROVERBS 27:1

Morning sunlight dappled the road and the horse and Marva's hands on the reins. She gazed up, way up, at shimmering golden green leaves arching over her like the high roof of a cathedral. Blending with the *squeak* of leather, the *clank* and *whir* of metal, and the *clip-clop* of hooves was the clamor of birdsong from every side. A flock of some kind of chirping bird must have settled in this particular patch of trees, for their chatter was nearly deafening.

Her horse, a wiry brown gelding with a sour expression, answered to the name of Buzz according to the stable boy. So far his nature seemed sweeter than his looks indicated, for he trotted along willingly enough.

Marva studied her map, frowning. It was difficult to judge how far she had traveled along the dotted line indicating Lakeland Lodge's driveway, but the main east-west highway, Lac du Flambeau Road, should appear ahead soon. According to Hardy Stowell, the drive to Johnson Lake would take little more than an hour. From there she intended to drive over to another lodge on Brandy Lake, then head home. Taken at an easy pace, the outing should take no more than five or six hours, depending on how much time she spent at each lodge.

Should she locate Lucky in Lakeland. . . Well, in that case, her calculations might fall through. She drew a deep breath and wriggled her shoulders in an attempt to relax.

Somehow, when she had pictured coming north to search the area for Lucky, her mind had failed to grasp the enormity and the wildness of this lake country. Interviewing local lodge owners had seemed like a straightforward proposition back then. Perhaps if she were a man and acquainted with the lay of the land, she might have visited every lodge in five counties within three weeks. Ha! Maybe not.

She had also failed to consider how awkward it would be to ask about unmarried lodge owners. Why did people have to be so nosy?

But perseverance and ingenuity had paid off. She hoped. Her parents had plans for the day; if all went smoothly, she should be back before they so much as noticed her absence.

Yet, even after all this effort, she still might find no sign of Lucky.

Actually, in all likelihood, her efforts would come to naught.

"Lord," she prayed aloud, "I know I'm bullheaded as can be, but You've opened this door for me, so I'm asking You to bless my efforts. Please let me find Lucky today and bring some answers to my questions! If he is not the man You want me to marry, then I guess You'll say no, but I would really appreciate knowing Your reasons why or why not."

The forest suddenly opened up onto a road still shadowed by trees. Buzz turned right without any command from Marva and picked up his pace. A fresh breeze cooled her face until she shivered slightly. Trying to hold her map still, she checked her next turn.

A small bridge ahead spanned a stream or small river. Buzz laid back his ears when his feet hit its echoing timbers, and when the cart's wheels rumbled, he bolted into a canter; but Marva quickly brought him back into control. With the bridge behind, he settled back into his quick trot, ears twitching.

"Testing me, were you?" she commented.

He snorted, appearing to ignore her.

A doe and her fawn grazed on the roadside ahead. Heads lifted, ears pricked, they watched the horse and cart approaching. Turning his head in their direction, Buzz looked at them and whinnied. Immediately their tails lifted and they bounded into the trees.

"I think you've been rejected, Buzz," Marva commented.

A wagon appeared on the road ahead, tiny in the distance. At the sight, Marva's heart picked up its pace. Of course, she could be in no real danger; this was settled country, after all.

Two Indian men, one young, one with gray hair, occupied the approaching wagon. They studied Marva with impassive stares, returned her polite nod as the vehicles passed on the road, and traveled on west. She heaved a sigh of relief, waving dust away from her face.

The road ahead forked. "Whoa." Buzz stopped, champing at his bit and snorting softly. A hand-painted signpost with three branches read WOODRUFF, SQUIRREL LAKE RD., and MERRILL. The tilted post indicated points midway between the three roads. She wanted Trout Lake Road. Confusion formed a lump in her chest. She looked from her map to the roads but saw no correlation. Had she somehow managed to miss the highway? Was she at some crossroads not even located on her map?

At last she decided to take the right fork, which seemed to lead straight ahead. If only she were a better judge of direction. . .

Within fifteen minutes she knew she had made the wrong choice. Or had she? A lake appeared on her right, but it appeared to be small, nothing like the large lake on her map. At last she reined in Buzz and sat staring straight ahead. "I'm lost." There was nothing to do but go back, which meant turning her horse around. Rather than attempt turning Buzz on the narrow road, she climbed down and went to his head. He allowed her to turn him until the dogcart faced back along the road she had just traveled, but as soon as she let go of his bridle, he trotted quickly away. "Whoa!" In a panic, she chased the cart along the road, but the horse rapidly outdistanced her. Would he run all the way back to the lodge?

Monte saw Buzz and the empty dogcart approaching at a rapid clip. Marva must have realized her mistake and tried to turn around, and Buzz had played a prank on her. Stupid horse.

He turned Petunia sideways to block the road and called softly to the runaway. "Whoa, Buzzard Bait, you rotten beast, you." The gelding pricked his ears, slowed, and turned off to graze on the verge as if he had never intended to run home. Monte dismounted, watching the back trail for signs of Marva. If possible, he preferred to keep her unaware of his presence, since she was certain to resent it. He decided to wait in hiding on the assumption that she was unhurt. Buzz was not a vicious beast, just ornery at times.

He had to admit: *Like his owner.*

Flies bombarded Marva whenever she stopped to pant, so she pressed on until a stitch developed in her side and sweat dampened her shirtwaist. A brisk walk while wearing a corset was pure misery, and the thought of the miles of road between her and the lodge deepened her woe. She removed her stylish suit jacket and felt slightly cooler, but she still could not draw a full breath. She must have been out of her mind to attempt this trek on her own in a strange place.

But then, rounding the road's slight bend to the right, she saw Buzz ahead, grazing contentedly at the side of the road. He lifted his head and pricked his ears in her direction, gave a derisive little snort, and then ripped up another mouthful of grass. She approached the horse cautiously, talking in her calmest tone and hoping he wouldn't sense her anxiety.

He allowed her to catch him and lead him back to the road, and he stood quietly while she climbed into the dogcart. Relieved, she thanked God for His intervention on her behalf.

Soon she once again headed east, having lost nearly an hour from her time schedule. An unmarked track on her left caused her to stop and study her map again. Surely that could not be the road she wanted. . .or could it? Taking her chances, she forged on ahead. As she passed lakes not marked on her map, fear built in her chest. *Where am I? Lord, please help me!* A crossroad appeared ahead. This might be Trout Lake Road, although it did not look the way it was marked on her map. She turned left.

The forest on either side of the road gave way to clear-cut spaces and farms, resembling farmlands much farther south, although the houses and barns looked quite new. At another fork in the road, she saw a sign for the town of Woodruff. Stopping Buzz once more, she studied her map and realized that she had traveled far out of the way.

However, if she turned left here and passed through Woodruff, she could turn left again just north of town and reconnect with the road she had missed, making her way to the lodge on Johnson Lake. The knot inside her chest eased slightly. At least she now had some idea where she was.

Woodruff resembled Minocqua in its rough-hewn timber construction and appeared to be a thriving town. New construction met her gaze on all sides. Several horsemen and a few buggies and wagons occupied the streets. She saw only two women and a few children, but many men of all ages. Her passage through town garnered more interest than she desired. One man whooped out a comment, which she mercifully could not decipher.

Once more, she seriously doubted the wisdom of this solo endeavor. But then again, whom could she have brought along? Not either of her parents, certainly. And Beulah was far too busy with her children.

The road crossed railroad tracks, then turned left, which would be west, she figured. Hardy had drawn a dotted line indicating a turnoff to the—she squinted at the map—Northwoods Oasis, owned and operated by Mel Hendricks of Milwaukee.

Buzz's trot had slowed. She clucked and jiggled the reins. He laid back his ears but picked up his pace again. Buildings became scattered, and fences marked pastureland and fields. Did crops grow well here? The growing season must be short this far north.

Where was that lake? Stumps dotting many of the surrounding fields indicated that the area had been clear-cut for lumber. Marva had expected more shade during this drive. Her wide-brimmed hat kept direct sunlight off her head. She had decided against wearing driving gloves because they stung her hands, which had sunburned slightly on the lake the day before. A poor choice, she realized now that it was too late. The tops of her hands were mottled red and white and felt like fire.

Sweat trickled down her temples and between her shoulder blades. Who would have thought it would be so hot and humid today? She slipped one hand beneath her hat. Her hair was nearly hot enough to scorch her fingers.

She shaded the map with her hat and looked again for directions. The images blurred before her eyes. She fanned herself with the map and hunted for her canteen. Where was it? Had it fallen from the cart? Had she even put it into the cart that morning? Of all things to lose! But never mind. Once she arrived at the Northwoods Oasis lodge, she would surely be offered a cool drink and a chair in the shade.

Buzz must be suffering from the heat, too. Sweat foamed between his hind legs and darkened his shoulders. She should have stopped to get him a drink when they passed through Woodruff. If not for all those staring men, she might have thought of it.

According to Hardy's map, the turnoff should be someplace along here. She watched for a wagon track, for a post—anything to mark the place. At last she saw a track—shade at last! This area had retained most of its trees, probably for the sake of the resort.

Buzz shook his head as she asked him to turn, and he dropped to a walk; but he willingly stepped from the main road onto the shady, bumpy track. When a lake appeared ahead, the horse seemed to gaze at it longingly and snorted. "I'm sure you must be very thirsty, Buzz, and though I'm terribly sorry, we can't leave the track to get you a drink. Be patient a few minutes more, and we'll be at the lodge."

The horse walked on, his head bobbing with each stride. Once he turned his head to look back over one shoulder and neighed. Marva thought she heard a horse neigh in reply, but when she turned around, she saw nothing. The forest had closed in behind them.

At last a house came into view. If it could be called a house. Marva frowned and looked back at her map. This couldn't be a resort—it was a mere hovel built of unpeeled logs—and yet the track ended here.

A dog barked savagely from the end of its chain. The cabin door opened, and a hulking, unshaven man stepped outside with a rifle gripped in his hands. "Lady, you don't belong here."

"I'm looking for the Northwoods Oasis," she said.

"This ain't it."

"Oh. I'm sorry to have bothered you." She urged Buzz to turn. He bent his neck around and took a few steps. She clucked and snapped the reins, and he took one more step. "Buzz, please," she begged. "C'mon, boy, just turn around, and I promise we'll stop soon."

The stranger stepped outside and approached her horse. "Give me your whip. I'll get him moving for you."

"That won't be necessary, but thank you." Marva snapped the reins harder and tried to cluck, but her mouth had suddenly gone dry. "Buzz, walk on."

Buzz took one more step, champing at his bit and showing the whites of his eyes. The chained dog continued to bark, lunging and snarling and clawing at the ground with its front paws. Its owner ignored the clamor.

The strange man took hold of Buzz's bridle and led the horse around to face the track. But instead of letting go, he held on and appraised Marva with red-rimmed eyes. Grime streaked his throat, and the stench of him hung in the air.

"Your horse is tired. Why not step down and set a spell? You look like you could use a drink."

"Oh no, I'm expected at the lodge." Not at the Northwoods Oasis, but certainly she was expected back at Lakeland Lodge, so it wasn't a complete fabrication.

He smiled, showing blackened stumps of teeth. Approaching the cart, he took hold of the reins just in front of Marva's hand and jerked them from her grasp. His hand, easily the size of a baseball mitt, closed over her elbow. "Come on. I'll help you down."

Incoherent prayers flashed through Marva's mind as a wave of dizziness struck her.

Thudding hoofbeats approached on the track, and a rider came into Marva's view. "Monte!" she whispered.

The stranger turned around at the approach of his new visitor, releasing his grasp on Marva's arm.

Monte trotted up on his bay mare. "Here you are. We were about to send out a search party, Miss Obermeier." He gave her a smile and a wink. "Sorry about the intrusion, Blanchard. This young lady has a talent for heading off on rabbit trails."

"Why are you out this way?" Blanchard growled.

"Following my guest, here. May we water our horses before we move on?"

Blanchard gave a sniff. "Help yourself." He lumbered back toward the house.

Monte dismounted, pumped fresh water into an algae-filled trough beside a broken hitching rail, and let both horses drink sparingly. "Take it slow, Buzz ol' boy." The horse rubbed his sweaty ears on Monte's shoulder. Marva watched them from her seat with a strange sense of detachment. She kept seeing black spots that wouldn't blink away.

Taking hold of Buzz's bridle, Monte led both horses along the track until they were out of sight of Blanchard's cabin. Then he led his mare to the back of the dogcart and tied her to a metal ring on the tailgate. Standing beside the cart, he handed Marva a canteen. "Scoot over. I'll drive."

Marva made room for him on the seat and handed over the reins. Relief flowed through her, and she took a long, shuddering breath. The black spots nearly filled her vision, and her head swam.

"Are you sure you still want to visit the Northwoods Oasis? Not to be unkind, but your face is red as a beet, and you look about ready to drop."

Great sobs suddenly shook her, and the canteen slipped from her limp fingers. Everything seemed confused after that.

Chapter 9

Therefore shall a man leave his father and his mother,
and shall cleave unto his wife: and they shall be one flesh.
GENESIS 2:24

M iss Obermeier? Marva!" Monte caught the canteen, then grabbed Marva's arm before she could fall out of the dogcart. But she flopped forward and would have smashed her face on the dashboard if he hadn't caught her. "Marva!" Clutching her with both hands, he glanced around, trying to decide on his next move.

"Stand, Buzz," he told the horse. Holding Marva on the seat, Monte climbed down, then hefted her into his arms. She moaned softly and lifted one hand to her face.

He laid her on a bed of pine needles beneath a tree and removed her hat, then shrugged out of his coat and made it into a pad for her head. Next thing was to cool her off. He opened his canteen, lifted her head, and held the bottle to her dry lips. She drank a little, coughed, and tried to sit up. "No, just lie still. See if you can drink a few more swallows."

After taking another sip, she squinted up at him, her brow furrowed. "I feel awful."

"I think you've had too much sun. Just a minute." Pulling his handkerchief from his vest pocket, he hurried down to the lakeshore. He dunked the cloth and wrung it out, then returned to Marva's side.

Her eyes flew open when he laid the folded handkerchief on her forehead. Instead of leaving it there, he patted it over her cheeks and temples. "That's nice. Thank you," she murmured, her eyes drifting shut again.

He took the opportunity to study her attire. A high-necked white shirtwaist and a skirt of some stiff, shiny blue fabric flattered her coloring and figure. However, such a trim and immobile waistline suggested stays, which would also explain her rapid, shallow breathing. But a gentleman could hardly suggest that she loosen her undergarments. "You might unbutton your collar," he suggested.

She gave him a shocked stare.

"I could toss you in the lake instead, I suppose. I've tried that method of cooling off, and I know it works." He grinned, and her lips twitched in response.

"Very well." When she reached for her collar, Monte turned away and loosened his own tie. He felt much better himself without that wool coat.

Picking his way back down to the lake's edge, he dipped his handkerchief in the water again to freshen it. "You'd best relax and rest here awhile longer. Then I think I'll take you to the Oasis and send for a doctor. We're not heading back to Lakeland Lodge until late afternoon. No more sun for you today, my lady."

She blinked up at him as he approached. Her flushed face made her eyes seem bluer than ever. "How did you come to be here?"

"I followed you," he admitted and knelt beside her. "Had to make sure you came to no harm. These Northwoods are not as domesticated as people like to think. Too many uncivilized loggers and drifters in the area."

"Mr. Stowell told you?"

"Told me that the map was for you? I already knew you wanted to visit other lodges, so guessing didn't require great powers of deduction. I'm also guessing that you didn't request my escort for the day because your parents would disapprove." Monte talked while smoothing Marva's damp hair away from her face with his handkerchief. "What did they think of your taking this jaunt alone?"

She closed her eyes. "I didn't tell them."

"I see." He studied her tightly closed mouth and the flare of her nostrils. Aside from a few faint lines at the corners of her eyes and mouth, her skin was still nearly flawless. Even while damp and sweaty, her hair was fascinating. Such a handsome woman was seldom seen on the streets of Woodruff; he could scarcely blame other men for staring. Good women were still rare in these parts.

He slowly stroked the handkerchief down her cheek, letting his thumb slide over her skin. She gave a little gasp and held her breath. Her lashes fluttered, though her eyes remained shut. The wild thought struck him that he would like to kiss her. Startled, he scooted around to sit with his back against the pine's trunk, squeezing the handkerchief in his tight fist. The lake's color and sparkle resembled Marva's eyes.

A laugh rose in his throat, but he turned it into a cough. Obviously he had not been writing enough fiction lately, since his cowboy hero's poetic musings were starting to replace his own rational thoughts. Marva had made it clear way back in her first letter that she desired a marriage conducted like a mutually beneficial business partnership. *I neither expect nor desire romantic overtures.* She meant during courtship, surely. Or did she?

Tugging at his collar as if it choked him, he gave her a quick sideward glance and shook his head. Unless she married a man already on his deathbed, a platonic marriage would never work. And it *shouldn't* work. God had not ordained marriage to be a platonic relationship. From Monte's observations of Marva, admittedly limited, he suspected she wanted more from a marriage than her letters indicated, whether she realized it or not.

He would allow her to rest and recover for a few more minutes. They would have to return to the main road whether he took her to the lodge or back into Woodruff, and he wasn't eager to expose her to more afternoon sun.

"I hope that awful man doesn't come this way or release his dog," she said into a long silence. "I can't tell you how relieved I was to see you. I felt as if I might faint both from heat and from fear, and then what might have happened? God sent you. I know He did."

Monte couldn't honestly say that Blanchard would not have harmed her. "I know little about him, actually. Blanchard, I mean." He laced his hands around one upraised knee and pondered how to phrase his next statement. "I don't blame you for wanting a few hours to yourself, for wanting some privacy and independence, but it's just not safe for a woman to drive out alone around here."

Now would be the time to indicate that he knew why she wanted to interview local lodge owners, but he couldn't find the words. Come to think of it, why didn't she connect *him* with Lucky in Lakeland? He obviously fit the role. Her attitude was confusing, almost as if she hoped anyone besides Monte would prove to be her correspondent. It was slightly insulting, if he were entirely honest with himself.

She rolled to her side and sat up, leaning on one hand and rubbing her temple with the other. "I'm no longer overheated, but my head aches terribly." A thick lock of hair studded with two hairpins dipped over her shoulder.

"Drink more water." He shifted closer to her and held out the canteen.

She scooted over a little and accepted it, and for a moment, their eyes met. Tipping back her head, she drank. A little water dribbled down her chin and dripped on her blouse. She lowered the canteen and wiped the back of her hand over her lips. "Thank you."

He took it back and drank a few swallows himself. Anything to keep occupied. While screwing the lid back on, he considered his next move. "I want you to see a doctor. Sunstroke can be dangerous."

"I don't think I'm that ill. Mostly I just want to lie down in a cool, dark room and sleep. I feel. . .weak." Tears suddenly brimmed in her eyes. "And stupid."

"You're not stupid. Far from it." The tears were his undoing. He scooted just a little closer and put his arm around her shoulders, hoping she might see it as a fatherly move and allow the familiarity this once. His actual motivation was anything but paternal. To his surprise and delight, she laid her head on his chest and let her shoulder touch his side.

An unfamiliar blend of passion and protective tenderness whipped through his veins, making him feel twenty years younger. He rubbed her arm and tightened his grip, realizing in a flash that he was unprepared to handle this onslaught of temptation. A quick plea for strength gave him just enough willpower to sit upright and try to brush the moment aside. "We'd better get to the Oasis quickly. You can interview Hendricks while we wait for the doctor, if you feel well enough, that is."

☙❧

Marva sat upright. Monte's abrupt withdrawal stung her pride. She had sought only consolation and a safe haven. Did he imagine she'd been craving romance? Utterly ludicrous! Tears burned her cheeks until she wiped them away.

He brushed off his trousers and offered her a hand up. She thought about ignoring his offer but reconsidered. Her head still swam, and she still felt sick. After shifting to a position from which she could rise, she gripped his hand. It felt warm and rough with calluses.

He pulled her up, but her legs refused to cooperate. Again he caught her before she could pitch forward on her face, quickly shifting his grip to her shoulders. The world spun around her, and her stomach roiled.

"Marva, can you walk, or should I carry you?"

"I can walk," she tried to say, but it came out sounding more like a breathy wail ending in a sob.

He put one arm behind her shoulders and the other behind her knees and scooped her off the ground. She felt him stagger to regain his balance, but otherwise he didn't seem overly strained by her weight. Wrapping her arms around his neck, she hid her face in his shoulder and tried to pretend he was someone else. Anyone else.

He gently deposited her on the seat of the dogcart, waited to make sure she could sit upright unattended, and then went back to retrieve her hat and his coat. Marva's vision narrowed to a small tunnel of reality; everything else was black. Yet when she closed her eyes, she was fully aware of her surroundings. She felt the cart tip to one side when Monte climbed in beside her; she felt his shoulder bump hers, then the comforting warmth of his arm sliding around her and pressing her toward him. She heard him exhale a deep breath just above her head. Her position was awkward, yet she knew it enabled him both to drive and to make sure she didn't fall out of the cart.

Monte shook the reins and clucked. Marva heard the creak of harness and the clop of Buzz's hooves, and the cart lurched forward. Light flickered over her eyelids, and motion freshened the air on her face. She drew a deep, shaky breath and let it out in a sigh.

How would he treat her during the remaining days of her vacation at the lodge? She couldn't help but wonder why he had chosen to follow her. What if Harding Stowell had come to her rescue? How very different she would feel about resting against *his* shoulder! Monte Van Huysen was easily the most attractive man of her acquaintance, married or single. Why couldn't he have been her newspaper correspondent?

If she had waited for God's timing and not attempted to find herself a husband, she would have met Monte without her head full of plots to hunt down a certain lodge owner, and maybe, just maybe, something might have developed between them. It might still. After all, he might come to Longtree to visit his brother's family sometime. And if he did, she might encounter him at church or in town. . . .

Marva had little experience interpreting the behavior of men, and though she was probably ridiculously mistaken, her heart conceived the tiniest hope that Monte found her attractive. Not in her current sunburned, bedraggled condition, of course, but maybe at her best, she might catch his eye. Just maybe. Any hope at all was better than none.

If only her head would stop spinning.

Chapter 10

Wherefore be ye not unwise,
but understanding what the will of the Lord is.
EPHESIANS 5:17

The sun had dropped behind the tallest trees before Marva succeeded in convincing Mel Hendricks, owner of the Northwoods Oasis, that she felt well enough for Monte to drive her home that evening. Monte wrapped his arm around her shoulders with a proprietary air as he escorted her out to the waiting dogcart.

Seeing his rifle on the floorboards as she climbed to her seat, Marva looked up at him, wide-eyed.

He climbed in beside her. "Just in case. I don't expect trouble, but it's best to be prepared."

After a quick wave at Hendricks, he clucked up Buzz and headed home. Petunia, tied to the cart, trotted behind.

Although dark circles underlined her eyes, Marva sat upright on the seat beside Monte, chin up, shoulders back, hands folded in her lap. She wore her jacket again now that the temperature had cooled, and he once again wore his sack coat, conforming to propriety.

"Mr. Hendricks was kind to send for the doctor, but it was unnecessary," she said into a peaceful silence. "I simply had too much sun."

"Better to be safe." He clucked Buzz into a faster jog. "I hope your parents aren't worried."

"I do, too."

A flock of ducks flew overhead, quacking, headed toward Johnson Lake.

"Did you have a chance to interview Mr. Hendricks?"

"No, but it doesn't matter. I've abandoned the idea."

"What idea?"

As he expected, she didn't answer the question.

"We should be home within the hour, before dark. The drive home should be faster than your drive out, since I don't reckon on taking the scenic route like you did. I lit the side lamps just in case we don't beat the dark, but we shouldn't need them."

"I'm not very good with maps." Her voice sounded humble. "You also carry the gun 'just in case.' What kind of 'trouble' might we encounter?"

He rolled his shoulders and heard his spine crackle. He gave her a quick glance, hoping she hadn't noticed. "Oh, maybe a bear. Maybe a drunken drifter. You never know in these parts. The rifle wouldn't do us much good if I left it in the scabbard on Petunia's saddle."

"Have you shot a bear before?"

"Sure. Out in Wyoming, that was. Nothing but blackies around here, but we used to shoot grizzlies out West. Big, mean bears."

"Myles got attacked by a grizzly bear back home."

"Huh, not in southern Wisconsin, he didn't. He must have been pulling your leg."

"No, it was a grizzly bear. It escaped from a circus."

Monte thought about that one. "If you say so."

She chuckled. "You don't believe me."

"I didn't say that."

"You didn't have to say it. Ask Myles when we get home. He'll tell you. It stole a steer from Obadiah Watson—he's Beulah's stepfather—and when the men hunted it down, it nearly killed Myles. That was right around the time he committed his life to God."

"Really? He didn't tell me that story. I'll have to pound it out of him."

"Spoken like a true big brother."

He smiled at her, then couldn't look away.

"What?" she inquired, looking self-conscious yet pleased.

"Smile again."

She smiled readily but covered her cheek with one hand. He pulled her hand down.

"You have a dimple in your right cheek. I noticed before but didn't really notice."

She turned her face away.

"Why have you never married, Marva? You're a lovely woman, sweet, able—I don't understand it."

She touched her cheek again but kept her face averted. "The right man never came along. I waited patiently for God's timing, but it never happened."

He recognized sadness and a hint of bitterness in her voice. "You could still marry now." Realizing how that comment might be construed, he faced forward and studied Buzz's hindquarters. The horse had dropped to a walk without his noticing.

"The right man would have to ask." Her voice trembled as if with restrained tears. "I spent years being angry with God because He never gave me the husband I wanted. All those years gone, wasted! I should have enjoyed each day as it came and recognized that if I remained single it was because God knew singleness was best for me."

Had she married years ago, she would likely not be available to marry Monte now. This fact occurred to him while she spoke. But should he be so arrogant as to imagine that God had reserved such a woman and set her aside to be his bride?

"Why have you never married?" She returned the question.

"I've never asked a woman to marry me."

"But why not? Surely you have met many attractive women during your travels." Although she spoke lightly, he sensed heaviness underlying the questions.

"None that I wanted to share my life with."

She turned on the seat and fixed him with a quizzical stare from beneath her hat's brim. "But why ever not? Are you so difficult to please? Or do you conceal some dark secret in your past?"

That last question struck home. She obviously did not know—Beulah must not have told her—or she would never have spoken so lightly.

"I never stay in one place long enough to suit a woman," he improvised. "Some men aren't cut out for marriage."

"But you—" She fell silent.

"But I what?"

"Never mind."

A mosquito whined in Monte's ear. He smacked himself on the side of the head and knocked his hat askew. "Bugs are bad tonight."

"They seem to be bad most every night."

The first stars glimmered in the steel gray sky above. "It won't be long now. I hope they saved us some supper."

"I'm not hungry, but for your sake, I hope so, too."

Before he turned off the main road into his long driveway, the last glimmers of twilight had faded and stars filled the night sky. The bobbing lanterns threw small puddles of light that scarcely reached the nearest trees. One of the dog-cart's wheels bumped into a pothole, and Marva bumped into Monte's shoulder. "Sorry about that," he said teasingly.

"I shall try to forgive you," she retorted calmly.

He grinned, and a sudden wave of affection for her rolled over him. Driving along with this woman at his side felt right somehow. He could easily imagine spending the rest of his life in her company, and the thought started a longing ache in his soul.

As they approached the lodge grounds, a bonfire's glow appeared between the trees. Hardy must have lit it for the guests, who sat on the log benches around the fire pit, singing hymns. He slowed his horse, thinking Marva might like to join her companions, but she laid her hand on his forearm. "Please don't stop. I need to go to my room."

Without a word, he drove the dogcart to the lodge steps, secured the reins, and came around to help Marva alight.

Lanterns burned dimly on either side of the main door. No one sat on the porch tonight; the lodgers must all be down by the bonfire. Marva reached out to take his hand. Her grip felt uncertain. Courage and determination must be keeping her upright. He sensed that she was ready to collapse. Releasing her hand, he reached for her waist to lift her down. She murmured a token protest. He set her on her feet, facing him, but did not let go. "Can you walk?"

Her head bobbed. "I think so."

"I don't." For the third time that day, he hefted her into his arms then mounted the porch steps and fumbled for the latch. She simply let her head bob against his shoulder.

Once inside, he carried her across the foyer. No one was behind the desk. He entered the hall, trying to avoid bashing her head or feet on anything, then walked its length and stopped at the door to her room. It was unlocked, so he pushed it open and carried her inside. Guessing which bed was hers, he laid her on it. "Marva, are you all right?" he said, trying to stop gasping for breath. His heart raced, mostly from exertion.

"I'm. . .terribly. . .sleepy," she mumbled as if drugged.

He untied her hat and tugged it off her head. Her forehead was warm but not feverish. He gripped her hand and considered what to do next. Feeling around at the foot of the bed, he located a wool blanket, which he spread over her. He would have liked to remove her shoes, but that seemed too personal.

"I'll let you rest now," he said, reluctant to leave her alone. Deep, steady breathing was her only reply. He smiled. Once more he touched her forehead then bent way over and kissed her soft cheek. "Good night, my dear."

☙❧

"Marva! Marva. . .why, you slept in your clothes! Whatever possessed you to do that? Where were you all day yesterday? Your father and I began to worry when you didn't show up at the bonfire."

They hadn't worried until then? Marva sighed and reached up to push tickling hair from her face. She groaned. Every muscle ached, and her head still felt heavy.

"I went for a drive and got lost. Mr. Van Huysen found me and drove me back home. I had too much sun." She shifted her legs over the side of the bed and watched listlessly as the blanket slithered to the floor.

"You'll have to repeat that, since not one word of it was clear." Mother sounded irritable. Mother was never irritable.

Marva straightened her shoulders and groaned again. "I hurt everywhere."

"Now that I understood."

Mother stood beside the bed in her faded lavender dressing gown, her silver braid hanging over one shoulder. Her normally serene face was creased with frown lines.

Slowly Marva repeated her explanation, holding out her blistered hands for her mother's inspection.

"I should say you did have too much sun! Child, will you never develop good sense? Why did you drive out alone, and without gloves, and on such a hot day? We can be grateful that Mr. Van Huysen found you, or you might have become hopelessly lost in these dreadful woods!" She suddenly clasped Marva in a tight hug. "The Lord watched over you, for certain. Had I known all this before I went to bed last night, I'm sure I wouldn't have slept a wink! We saw you sleeping when we came in after the bonfire last night, but I never dreamed. . ."

"I'm fine, Mother, only rather tired and blistered."

"Marva, is there anything you want to tell—"

A knock at the door brought her mother upright in an instant. "Now who could that be? Your papa went fishing." She hurried to remove the chain lock.

"Ma'am." Marva heard a woman's voice say. "Miss Obermeier's bath is ready in the washroom across the hall. We left extra rinse water."

Mother paused then said, "Thank you very much. I'll tell her." Closing the door, she regarded her daughter in surprise. "You ordered a bath?"

Marva blinked in confusion. "There must be some mistake."

Her mother's head tilted. "Actually, you could use one. Why not take it, since it's already prepared for you?"

Reaching one hand up to her hair, which was stiff with sweat and road dust, Marva nodded. A bath sounded like heaven.

Minutes later, she soaked in steaming, rose-scented water in a huge aluminum tub. Her hair floated around her shoulders. Her sunburned hands stung in the water, but her aching muscles began to relax.

She remembered Monte carrying her into the lodge the night before. Or at least she had vague but lovely memories of his comforting arms and gentle voice, the scratchiness of his coat against her cheek, the bump of her foot against a doorpost, and his apology. He had laid her on the bed. She knew that much but recalled nothing afterward.

Tightness built in her throat. He was so dear! So kind and considerate and gentlemanly! Why had such a man never come into her life before now?

Hot tears blended with the water while she rinsed soap from her hair. Yet a faint hope grew within her that maybe, just maybe, *now* was God's perfect timing.

Chapter 11

Every way of a man is right in his own eyes:
but the LORD pondereth the hearts.
PROVERBS 21:2

Watch me, Ma!"

Jerry Van Huysen jumped off the swim platform with a modest splash. When he surfaced, Beulah and Marva applauded and exclaimed to the boy's satisfaction. Myles treaded water nearby, watching over the flock of young swimmers.

Listening with one ear to Beulah's chatter, Marva tried to soak in the beauty of her surroundings, to store it up for memories. This picnic was the last event of the Longtree vacationers' holiday at the lodge. Tomorrow they would load back on the train and head south. Somewhere behind her she heard Monte's deep chuckle. He must be talking with one of the other families. Would he come and sit with his brother's family to eat his meal?

An ache rose inside her chest. The idea of leaving, of never seeing this beautiful place again—of never seeing Monte again—did not bear contemplation.

"Funniest story you ever heard. . ." he was saying. His voice faded for several beats, then she heard ". . .still doesn't know the truth." Laughter followed.

Hearing Beulah speak Monte's name, Marva refocused on the current conversation. ". . .come back anytime we want to. You know, he insisted that we pay nothing for our lodging, but of course it would be best if that news didn't spread since he and Mr. Stowell can hardly afford to lodge our entire group for free."

"He and Mr. Stowell?"

Beulah spooned applesauce into Ginny's waiting mouth. "Yes. They're partners, you know. Mr. Stowell bought half ownership of the lodge last winter. He runs most of the business end of things. That way Monte has time for his writing again. I thought you knew all this."

Marva tried not to let her face reveal her confusion. "I probably heard it at one time but forgot. You're saying that Lakeland Lodge originally belonged entirely to your husband's brother? He owns the lodge?"

Beulah nodded. "Monte's been keeping track of our family for years, mostly by reading our town newspaper. He got the idea of advertising his lodge in the *Longtree Enquirer,* and of course it worked. We came without any idea that Myles's brother lived here. All our arrangements were made through Mr. Stowell."

324

"Oh." Without any idea—she could relate to that part.

"I thought you knew all this, Marva," Beulah said again. "You were at our house that first night when Monte explained everything."

"I must have been outside with Trixie during that part of the story." Marva's heart pounded so hard that she felt dizzy. All this time she had assumed Monte merely worked at the lodge as fishing and hunting guide. Remembering his air of command, his office inside the lodge, and the respect shown him by staff members, she suddenly felt stupid. How blind could a woman be?

She rested her forehead on her open hand. "But why the secrecy? Why didn't he come to Longtree to visit his brother? I don't understand."

Beulah sat up straight, a spoonful of applesauce poised in midair. "If you didn't hear him tell his story, I really don't think it's my place to pass it on to you. He had his reasons, Marva. Maybe you should ask him yourself."

Ginny voiced a protest, and the applesauce quickly entered her mouth.

Marva tried to laugh, but it sounded strangled. "I hardly know him well enough for that, Beulah. You're right—it's not my business to know his motivations."

A step sounded behind her, and Monte himself settled beside Marva on the quilt, folding his long legs awkwardly. "Hello, ladies. I hope you're enjoying this fine day. I ordered it for your pleasure."

"So thoughtful of you, brother," Beulah said with a smile. "I also appreciate your getting the applesauce for Ginny. She was too hungry to wait."

Ginny crawled across the quilt and climbed into her uncle's lap, smiling from ear to ear. Monte appeared startled yet pleased.

"Oh, let me clean her up," Marva offered. "She'll get applesauce all over you."

The baby protested, but Monte held her still so Marva could wipe her chubby face.

"Thank you." His eyes twinkled. "I hope you're all as hungry as Ginny. The kitchen crew prepared a feast. They'll be setting up on the outdoor tables soon."

"My tribe is working up an appetite." Beulah indicated Myles and the swimming boys. "Some of the men are fishing—their last opportunity to catch that monster fish."

"My father never caught a muskie, but he can't say enough about his half-dozen nice walleye and that big bass he pulled in last week," Marva said.

"And Myles and the boys must have nearly emptied this side of the lake of bluegill and perch." Beulah chuckled. "Monte, this has been the most wonderful, relaxing holiday! We can never thank you enough."

He focused on Ginny, who had pulled out his tie to chew on. "Don't try. These have been some of the best days of my life, too."

Marva caught his glance in her direction. What, exactly, was he implying? A trickle of doubt entered her turbulent pool of thought. Was he playing a joke on her? Had he written notes under the name of "Lucky in Lakeland" to build up a lonely woman's dreams only as an amusing diversion?

Had he known all the time that her search for an unmarried lodge owner was actually a search for him? If so, and she began to suspect that this was the case, he had a cruel sense of humor and was not the man she had believed him to be.

He had attended the church meetings Rev. Schoengard held on Sundays and entered into the worship with apparent sincerity. Was it all an act?

Or had his letters been sincere? Beulah's intimation of some secret in Monte's past made her think. Hadn't Myles mentioned something years ago about his deceased brother's scandalous past? But she couldn't recall the details. Maybe Monte feared rejection. Could her own self-doubt and insecurity cause her to misjudge the intentions of a good man? How could she learn the truth?

"I invited some local acquaintances to the picnic," Monte said. "They should arrive soon. Two of the local vacation lodge owners. You'll remember Mr. Hendricks, Miss Obermeier. He is eager to see you again."

His sidelong glance held a glimmer of mischief, and Marva's suspicions strengthened. He was laughing at her!

Trixie suddenly tripped on the edge of the quilt and crash-landed beside Marva, bringing with her an abundance of sand. An instant later, a very wet and sand-encrusted hound vaulted the toddler and sprawled in the middle of the quilt, tail lashing.

"Ralph! Off," Monte shouted. "Bad dog."

By the time the quilt had been shaken out, sand brushed from the toddler, and the dog tied up at Monte's cabin, the lodge staff had finished setting out a picnic luncheon on tables in the open area near the playground. Myles took the boys up to their cabin to change out of their swimming costumes while Beulah and Marva prepared plates for them.

As the children distracted his relatives, Monte pulled Marva aside for a moment. "Would you like me to bring them to you here, or shall I introduce you later?"

"Of whom are you speaking?"

"Mr. Hendricks and Mr. DeSamprio."

"Why did you invite them here?" Anger sharpened her voice.

"To help you out, of course. I know you never got the chance to interview Hendricks the other day."

Hot blood rushed into her face. She could think of nothing, absolutely nothing, to say. Did he know? He must know! And if he knew, he *must* be. . . Anger and humiliation fomented in her belly until she felt ill. Rather than spew out questions and accusations, she jerked her arm from his grasp and returned to Beulah, who was, thankfully, too distracted by her children's disputes and scuffles to notice Marva's agitation.

⌘

Monte had a sudden impulse to go beat his head against a tree. *Idiot!*

Startling revelations raced through his head. Rather than think through his jumbled motivations, he hurried away to find Pete DeSamprio and Mel Hendricks, the two lodge owners he had invited to join the picnic. Their company might serve to distract him from guilty thoughts and convictions.

Neither of the visitors had any idea why he had invited them to join his lodge picnic, but they dug into the spread of food without reservation. "Good chow, Van Huysen," DeSamprio said, shifting a mouthful into one cheek. "Great view. You ask us here to rub our noses in it, or what?"

Monte tried to smile. "Maybe we can get tips and ideas from each other and band together to bring more business north. This group read about my lodge in their local newspaper. We offered reduced rates for a large party."

At that moment, the minister requested silence for a blessing on the food. DeSamprio and Hendricks followed Monte's lead by removing their hats and bowing their heads. Rev. Schoengard gave thanks for the luncheon, requesting God's blessing on those who had prepared it and asking for safety during tomorrow's journey home. As soon as the pastor said, "Amen," the men resumed eating.

Monte brightened, seeing Hardy strolling in their direction with a loaded plate in hand. He waved his partner over. "Join us." Within minutes, Hardy had the two men discussing advertising and profit margins, and Monte could let his attention wander.

Casually he scanned the grounds for Marva. To his surprise, she was seated at the next picnic table with her parents and the Schoengards. He rested his elbow on the tabletop and his chin on his palm and let his eyes drink her in. With her white skin and that stunning hair against the backdrop of the deep blue lake, she made a striking picture.

She glanced up and caught his gaze but immediately looked away. He watched her try but fail to finish her luncheon. Folding her napkin, she laid it on her plate and glanced once more at Monte. He smiled and nodded. A little frown line appeared between her brows, and she quickly stood up.

Monte rose to intercept her as she left the table. "Leave your plate on the table. The staff will clean up."

She set down her plate. "Do you have something of importance to say, Mr. Van Huysen?"

"You don't wish to talk to Mr. DeSamprio and Mr. Hendricks?"

"I do not." She propped her fists on her hips and looked him in the eye. "If you have nothing further to say, I believe I shall go inside and begin packing."

"You look lovely today, Miss Obermeier. Like. . .like summertime."

She bobbed a curtsy. "Why, thank you, kind sir. Good day." And she walked away.

He winced behind her back.

Jealous of his own pseudonym, that's what he was. Why couldn't Marva forget her newspaper beau and love *him*—just plain Monte Van Huysen? Did she find him irritating in person? Maybe he smelled bad or had some annoying habit of which he was unaware.

Hardy approached him and clapped him on the shoulder. "I know just how you feel. That is one peculiar woman. I imagine she's mentioned to you a man who communicated with her through a newspaper."

"I know something about it."

Hardy chuckled without mirth. "I figured she asked you to invite Pete and Mel here. Did she ever talk to them?"

"No."

"Can't say I'm surprised. I'm thinking she's the type who likes a man in theory better than a man in the flesh. Try not to break your heart over her pretty face, partner. You won't be the first or the last, I'd guess. Oh look—there goes Mel after her."

Sure enough, Mel Hendricks followed Marva toward the lodge. Monte barely restrained a groan.

❧

Marva gritted her teeth to keep back tears. She had to force a smile at Dorothy Hilbert when she passed her on the path to the lodge; almost everyone else must be down at the shore. She could only hope her parents would linger and talk for at least another hour, giving her time to control her overwrought emotions.

That man! That beast! She wanted to kick him in the shins. She would love to give his mustache a sharp tug and smack the smile off his face. How dare he mock her openly! How dare he bring those men to meet her!

"Miss Obermeier!"

At the sound of this hail, she turned on the path. Mr. Hendricks approached, his smile revealing a gold tooth. "I trust you're fully recovered? Mr. Van Huysen told me the other day that you'd attempted to drive to my lodge to interview me. Do you write for a Milwaukee paper?"

"No sir, I don't." Heat rolled up Marva's throat and flooded her cheeks. "I simply wished to. . . Oh, never mind. The reason no longer exists. I'm ever so sorry you came all this way to no purpose."

Puzzlement spread over his pleasant face. "It was no trouble, I assure you. Mr. Stowell told me you especially wished to interview unmarried lodge owners in the Northwoods. I'm a widower. Does that count?"

She shook her head. "The man I'm looking for has never married. Thank you anyway, Mr. Hendricks."

She turned and rushed up the lodge steps before he could say another word. Once inside, she ran to her empty room and started packing. Anger flowed through her every movement, and she had to refold several items before she could pack them.

I don't care if I ever see that man again!

Was he really a jokester without a sensible thought in his head? No, that was too harsh a judgment. Myles and Beulah esteemed him highly, and the children adored their uncle. He had befriended most of the men in the party while guiding them to the best fishing spots on the lake.

And Marva would never forget his gentle strength and thoughtfulness the day she went looking for Lucky and got lost. That day, he had been a true hero.

Marva was uncertain what her parents thought of him, beyond his abilities with the lodge.

Tired of packing, she sat on the side of her bed and let her thoughts drift. How smug he had looked at the picnic, staring openly at her with that silly smile on his face! Why did he have to be so handsome? It would be much easier to dislike him if she could only find him physically disgusting.

She bent over and pulled her packet of newspaper clippings from the drawer of her bedside table. Leafing through the few papers, she read over Lucky's words—Monte's words?—and wondered again if Monte Van Huysen concealed a sensitive, serious heart behind his charming manner.

❧

"You're not coming to supper?" Mother repeated with concern in her voice. "But it's our last night here, Marva. Everyone will miss you."

"I have a headache," Marva answered truthfully. "Please make my excuses, Mother. I'm truly not up to socializing this evening."

She felt her mother's cool hand on her forehead, then her cheeks. "Too much sun again, maybe. Is there anything you wish to tell me, dear one? I saw you talking with Mr. Van Huysen at the picnic, and then you disappeared. He seemed quieter than usual all afternoon."

"Don't read too much into that," Papa said. "A man can have many reasons for being thoughtful that have nothing to do with a woman, difficult though that may be for you to believe." He gave his wife a wink and squeezed her shoulder.

Mother looked chagrined. "I do tend to imagine too much at times, and I know my speculations have caused you hurt in the past, Marva dear."

Marva knew her mother referred not only to the long-ago misunderstanding with Myles, but also to imaginary interest from dozens of other eligible men over the years. She reached up to take her mother's hand. "It's not your fault. I do the same thing—read too much into people's emotional states and assume they all relate somehow to me." Hearing a betraying quiver in her voice, she smiled and fell silent.

Her mother's eyes held sympathetic understanding. "Tomorrow will be a long day. You just rest. I'll see if we can't bring you a little something to eat."

Chapter 12

*Now the God of hope fill you with all joy and peace in believing,
that ye may abound in hope, through the power of the Holy Ghost.*
ROMANS 15:13

Marva busied herself with arranging her bags in the overhead compartments, trying not to eavesdrop on the farewells between Monte and his relatives, yet at the same time straining to catch each word he spoke. Would he take time to bid her an individual farewell? There would be no privacy in this crowded train car, and she had no reason to return to the platform...not that privacy could be found there either.

Her hatbox kept popping out of position and threatening to drop on the head of the passenger seated beneath it, who happened to be Caroline Schoengard, the minister's wife. "Excuse me—I'm so sorry—" Marva reached over the other woman's head one more time to shove the box back in place. Caroline claimed not to mind, but Marva sensed her irritation. Everyone was tired and edgy, dreading the long train ride home.

"Here, let me." Monte reached around Marva to rearrange the boxes. Grateful and shaking in every limb, she stood back to watch. "There. That should stay put." He lowered his arms.

"Thank you."

"Yes, thank you," Mrs. Schoengard added. "Now I don't have to worry about something dropping on my head at any moment."

Monte smiled briefly at her, then focused on Marva. "Was that your last box?"

She nodded.

"Where are you sitting?"

She pointed to the row. "With my parents, for now."

"Until Beulah needs you," he added.

The train blasted a long whistle. People raised their voices above the clamor. The cacophony bombarded Marva's ears, and fear blocked her throat. Desperately she wanted to ask the question—this might be her last opportunity ever!—but how could she ask it amid all this confusion?

Someone bumped into her from behind. Monte quickly placed his hand on the small of her back in a protective gesture. A party of strangers had entered at the front of the car and appeared determined to make their way to the rear, shuffling everyone in the aisle aside or ahead. A carpetbag struck Marva between the shoulder blades; angry voices protested on all sides.

Monte guided her to the back of the train carriage. A lady climbed the steps and pushed past them. This time Monte bracketed Marva with his arms, protecting her from wayward luggage. He looked down into her face, shook his head, and smiled briefly. "I don't believe we're going to find a more private place than this to say our good-byes. I hope you'll forgive me for staring at you yesterday. It was rude, I know."

"Certainly," she said, brushing that awkward request aside, "and thank you for a lovely vacation, Mr. Van Huysen. You did so much for my parents and for all our friends. I imagine you'll be visiting your brother and his family sometime." Formality was difficult to maintain while he stood so close.

He suddenly gripped her hand and looked down at it, then up into her eyes, and then down at her hand again. His fingers pressed hers, his thumb rumpled her glove, and then he took a step back without meeting her gaze and breathed as if he'd sprinted to catch the train.

Marva waited, expecting him to make some declaration or comment. He seemed to be deadly earnest. In fact, he behaved almost like a man in love. . .but then, how would she know how a man in love behaves? Actually, he looked more like a man in pain.

"Mr. Van Huysen, are you well?"

The conductor bellowed his last boarding call. Monte jerked as if he'd been struck. "I—I'll be visiting sometime. Like you said." He squeezed his eyes shut and heaved a sigh. "Thank you. Meeting you was—I hope we meet again. Sometime. I—" The train gave a lurch, and his eyes popped wide.

"Marva."

"Yes?"

"Good-bye." He released her hand, bolted down the steps, and disappeared.

Marva caught herself as the train gave another jolt and straining metal screamed in protest. Using the seat backs for leverage, she staggered up the aisle and slipped into the vacant seat beside her mother.

"Mr. Van Huysen is waving to us from the platform, Marva. You should wave at him." Her mother sounded pleased. "I do hope he comes to visit Myles and Beulah. I hope you don't mind my saying this, but I think he admired you, dear."

Marva caught a glimpse of Monte and Hardy Stowell standing side by side, waving. Monte held his hat over his heart with a funereal air. Pulling a handkerchief from her pocketbook, she waved it at him. As the train gained momentum, the buildings along Front Street slipped out of view; as the train cars moved onto the trestle, the clacking changed in tone.

Would she ever see this little town again? Sparkling sunlight on the lake's brilliant blue surface brought tears to her eyes. Was that a loon's white breast in the distance? An open window brought a whiff of water and pine. The breeze felt cool against her damp cheeks. Why was she crying?

She lowered her handkerchief and wiped her eyes and nose. Depression weighted her chest like a stone. How she longed for privacy, the chance to release her emotions in a storm of tears!

"Marva?"

She looked up. Myles wore an apologetic expression. "Beulah is hoping you'll help us with the children. Trixie is nearly frantic, and the baby needs to be fed."

She nodded and rose. It was good to be needed.

∽⊗∾

Monte watched the train cars slip past. Once he took a step forward, determined to catch hold and climb aboard one of the passing coaches. It wasn't too late! He could still grab on. . . .

The last car rattled past, and the train slid over the trestle, its noise gradually fading in the distance. He found himself breathing in deep gasps. Why? Why hadn't he told her? The words were simple enough: "I am Lucky in Lakeland. I love you. Please marry me."

But no, it wasn't that simple. Marriage involved much, much more.

He would see her again. Myles had demanded a visit from him before the end of the year. This wasn't his last chance. He could work up a plan, a perfect way to propose marriage and sweep her off her feet. Heavenly visions of a future with Marva drifted through his imagination.

But between him and that idyllic future loomed his past.

It would be so much easier to pretend he had never met Marva Obermeier and simply resume his undemanding bachelor lifestyle. With luck, he could avoid mentioning his unsavory past to anyone ever again. It was nobody's business anyway. He'd made no promises; Marva would expect nothing from him. If Lucky in Lakeland never placed another ad in the paper, she might be disappointed, but she would soon forget and move on with her life. A woman that wonderful wouldn't remain single forever. It was nothing short of a miracle that she had remained unmarried this long.

"Monte, are you gonna stand here all day?"

He turned to stare at Hardy's sweaty pink face. "No."

His voice sounded so weak that Hardy's brows lifted in evident surprise.

Monte pulled himself together and said more firmly, "No. Just admiring the view."

"Really? Whatever you say."

He followed Hardy's glance toward the train yard, weedy, grimy, and strewed with refuse. "No, the lake." He waved his arm. "Out there. It's a gorgeous day. Blue sky, blue lake."

His partner's lopsided smile told Monte he was getting nowhere. "You head back, Hardy. I've got to stop for mail and supplies."

"Right." Hardy gave him an ironical salute and walked away, shaking his head.

Monte could ignore the heaviness in his spirit as long as he kept working, but the long, solitary drive home allowed far too much thinking time. Propping his elbows on his knees, he bowed his head over the reins clutched in his hands. Shoulders hunched, he let the regret flood over him.

"Coward," he muttered. Then louder, "Coward!"

Buzz and Petunia flicked their ears back as if to listen and tossed their heads in seeming uncertainty. "Do you hear?" he said in a calmer tone. "Your master is an idiot and a coward."

He tipped his head back and sighed deeply. "I did it again, God. When will I learn?" Tension stabbed at his temples and tightened his shoulders. "I'm still afraid. What if she rejects me when she knows?" The perfect weather seemed to mock his misery. How could skies be blue while storms raged in his heart?

For over twenty years, he had carried around the wreckage caused by sin. Sure, God had forgiven him—his eternity in heaven was guaranteed through Christ's cleansing blood. But here on earth, he still dragged a burden of guilt behind him wherever he went.

"Why, God? I want to be free!"

Trust Me.

The words came into his head, not as a voice but as a clear message.

Blinking, he looked up as if expecting to see God in the sky.

❦

That evening Monte still wrestled with his questions and argued with God's clear request. After tossing on his bed for hours, he finally lit a lamp and opened his Bible. Turning to the place marked by a ribbon, the passage in Matthew where he had left off reading that morning, he glared at the page. "If You have something to tell me, I'm looking. I've got to have peace, God. If You don't give it to me, I don't know where to turn."

This disrespectful prayer was the best he could manage at the moment. Hopefully God would bear with him. At least he was turning to the Bible instead of a bottle.

He let his tired eyes drift down the page. Chapter 7. Jesus was talking about beams and hypocrites. Pearls and swine. He sniffed and, with one finger, rubbed his mustache.

Then verse 7 caught his attention. " 'Ask, and it shall be given you. . . .'" He read through the section. " 'Or what man is there of you, whom if his son ask bread, will he give him a stone? . . . If ye then, being evil, know how to give good gifts unto your children, how much more shall your Father which is in heaven give good things to them that ask him?'"

Monte sat up, swung his legs over the side of his bed, and rested his forehead on his clenched fists. "But, God, if I ask for Marva, what if You say, 'No'? Surely You don't mean that I'm supposed to ask for something specific, just for my own pleasure. Do You?"

No matter how he might beat around the bush when he prayed, requesting peace, asking for love, begging for a wife, one obvious fact remained: Both he and God knew that Marva and none other was on his mind. He might as well be honest.

"Dear God." He paused and then amended, "Dear Lord God, You know my heart's desire. You know I want Marva Obermeier as my wife. Please, Lord, I want her to love me! I know You don't force people to love each other, but I don't know how else to ask this. I'm a miserable beast and entirely unworthy of a woman like her. I feel like an idiot for even asking this. . .but You tell me over and over again to trust You, so I'm trying my best."

Chapter 13

Thou wilt keep him in perfect peace,
whose mind is stayed on thee: because he trusteth in thee.
ISAIAH 26:3

Marva put one hand to the small of her back and rubbed, leaning on the top rail of the pigpen. The pigs snorted and squabbled over their slop, ears flopping, snouts wriggling. The shoats had grown and fattened nicely over the summer and would provide some good eating over winter. Papa intended to sell several of them, but others would soon hang in pieces in the smokehouse.

J. D. Parker, the hired man, sauntered past her and tipped his hat. Marva merely nodded. Although she usually appreciated good manners, his behavior—or maybe it was his expression—seemed too familiar for their degree of acquaintance.

The hog stench finally got to be too much. She entered the barn and climbed the ladder to the hayloft—her first time up there in many years. The rich hay aroma, the golden motes of dust revealed by sunlight slipping through cracks in the barn walls, and the mounds of hay stored for winter feed all created a sense of nostalgia, of slipping back through time. Seating herself near the loft door, her back against a prickly wall of hay, she gazed out across the Wisconsin countryside and felt like a child again. A lonely, listless child in a middle-aged woman's body.

Late summer sunshine flowed over the fields of corn and wheat. A breeze made ripples across the expanse like waves on a huge, golden lake. Her mind instantly pictured a sun-flecked blue surface with reflections of silver-birch trunks against the dark, upside-down images of pines. She heard again the slap of water against the shore and the quacking of ducks. The wind against her face brought back the sigh of pines and the rustle of oak and maple leaves instead of cornstalks.

This ache in her soul—how could she bear it?

"Marva?" her father called from below.

She was tempted to remain quiet and preserve her peace. "In the loft, Papa." She heard his boots on the ladder rungs.

"What are you doing up here?" His head rose through the trapdoor, bits of hay dangling from hair and beard.

"Nothing much."

"Your mother's been looking for you." He rested his forearms on the loft floor, still standing on the ladder. "I've been meaning to tell you that I'm gonna hire J. D. Parker on full-time. He kept the place up well while we were away last month, and I like the way he tends to things as if this place were his own. I disapprove of the way he frequents local taverns, but since the drink doesn't interfere with his work, I can't complain."

Marva nodded. "I'm sorry I can't help you more."

He snorted. "A farm needs a man to work it. You've done more'n your share around this place since you were a little thing. It's time to face facts. I'm too old to keep it up."

Gazing at her father's weathered face and stooping shoulders, Marva knew he was right. "Are you planning to sell the farm?"

He climbed all the way up, brushed off his trousers, and then sat beside her and chewed on a straw. "I'd always thought to hand it on to you, once you married, but I don't see that plan coming about unless you suddenly take a shine to Parker." He gave her a teasing wink. "I know you love the place, but your heart isn't fastened to it. To be honest, I ain't so dead set on living out my days here as I used to be."

Marva pondered this in silence, doubting his words. Papa's roots were deeply planted in the soil of his farm. "Where would we go?"

"I'm consulting the Lord on that matter, as is your mother. You might try asking Him for suggestions yourself, daughter." He gave her a sidelong glance. "Anything on your mind these days?"

She studied her clasped hands, noting a torn fingernail. "Nothing I can talk about right now."

He sighed softly. "Well, when you're ready to talk, I'm ready to listen." He reached out to pat her cheek with his callused hand. "The Lord has a plan."

Instead of watching him leave, Marva gazed across the fields once more.

⁓⊚⁓

That evening, after cleaning up the kitchen and after her parents had gone to bed, she sat down at the table and opened the newspaper. There had been no letters from Lucky since well before her trip up north. Her mind told her to stop looking, since finding nothing brought only hurt and frustration, yet her fingers turned the pages anyway.

The ad caught her eye almost instantly:

Dear Lonely in Longtree, This is a difficult letter to write, which is why I've been silent so long. I told you once before that God changed me, but you need to know how and why. As a young man, I fell into wild ways. Needing money to pay gambling debts, I stole cattle. By God's grace, I was not hanged for my crimes. I have paid my debts, but the stigma of prison will always be with me. If, after reading this, you still wish to correspond, I shall be forever grateful. If not, may the Lord's peace and blessings rest upon you. Ever yours, Lucky in Lakeland.

Marva read the note three times. Cattle rustling. A prison sentence. A vivid picture of a cold-eyed villain with a pockmarked face, an evil sneer, and prison pallor flashed through her thoughts. Lucky could look exactly like that Blanchard man at the cabin near Brandy Lake. He could smell even worse. He had never described his physical appearance, and she had never given hers.

A woman simply did not rush into marriage with a former convict. Even though the Lord had forgiven him, even though he was now a respected businessman—or so he said—he still might not make a good husband. Not for any woman. Particularly not for her.

What would her parents say? Papa was generally a kindhearted man, but he had a tendency to be suspicious of former sinners. To his way of thinking, such men could never completely change. This viewpoint put man-made limits on God's powers of redemption and sanctification, which was entirely wrong, yet could anyone convince Papa of this? Not as yet. Not to Marva's knowledge.

Mother was more likely to think the best of people, yet she would follow her husband's lead. Much though she wanted her daughter to be happily married, she would no doubt blanch at the thought of a former convict for a son-in-law.

This knowledge gave Marva a measure of comfort. Parents were provided by God as sources of wisdom and protection from foolish choices. The very over-protectiveness she had disparaged for years might now prove useful.

Folding up the paper, she sat for a moment longer, her thoughts scattered. *Lucky. Prison. Monte?* No matter how often she tried to dispel the notion of Monte being Lucky as impossible, it kept returning.

With her thumb and forefinger, she tugged at her lower lip, struggling to remember. Hadn't Myles said something, years ago, about his older brother? Or had it been Virginia Van Huysen, Myles and Monte's grandmother? The dear old lady had loved to reminisce about her elder grandson to anyone who would listen, and Marva had often sat beside her in a rocking chair on Beulah's porch of a summer evening. But no, Virginia wouldn't have mentioned Monte's flaws; she had tended to dwell on the fact that he'd committed his life to the Lord before he died. That was understandable.

Pressing two fingers against her lips, Marva leaned back in her chair and stared out the kitchen window. Myles had run away from his grandmother's home to join the circus. Mrs. Van Huysen had sent Monte to find and bring back his little brother; he hadn't been involved in Myles's circus-performing days. From the circus, Myles had run out West. That ugly gray horse he used to ride, the one named after a cactus, had it come from Texas? She couldn't recall. Wherever it was, Monte had followed Myles someplace out West, and supposedly he had died in a cattle stampede.

Marva shook her head and dropped her fisted hands to her lap. This was no good. If Myles had ever mentioned Monte in connection with cattle rustling, she couldn't recall. She could ride over and visit Beulah tomorrow. . .but no. At the lodge, Beulah had refused to discuss Monte's past.

Leaving the newspaper behind, Marva slowly rose and climbed the steep stairs to her tiny bedroom above the kitchen. Through her open windows flowed the familiar chorus of crickets, but tonight's show featured a solo performer—a lone cricket chirped from somewhere inside the room. It fell silent when she searched for it, naturally.

Two cats curled atop her coverlet. "What good are you?" she asked, smoothing the calico's soft fur. "Sleeping while a cricket roams the house." The cat rolled over and stretched without opening her eyes. Marva stroked the other cat's striped back and gently squeezed one white paw, but it never acknowledged her.

Her candle's light flickered over the sampler hanging above the head of her bed. Amid a field of faded flowers, crooked words stitched thirty years ago by her own hands proclaimed truth from Isaiah: "Thou wilt keep him in perfect peace, whose mind is stayed on thee: because he trusteth in thee."

Marva set her candleholder on the side table. "Peace," she whispered. Her eyes slowly closed. Sinking to her knees beside the bed, she flung her arms above her head and buried her face in her quilted coverlet. "I have no peace, Lord! I have no peace because I haven't trusted Thee. What shall I do? Oh, whatever shall I do!"

After the storm of emotion cleared, her knees began to ache. She sat back on her heels, then turned to sit with her back against the bed frame, rubbing her raised knees with both hands.

The cricket began to chirp again. The sound seemed to come from behind her dressing table.

"Lord God, I have no idea what to do next. I should answer Lucky's letter. . .but how? I cannot tell him that I'll marry him no matter what, because I don't even know if I want to marry him."

The truth rose in her thoughts, but she tried to squelch it. "I know I should never have advertised for a husband. I don't know what I was think—Well, yes, actually I guess I do know. Rebellious thoughts, that's what I was thinking. I wanted to force Your hand. And now look what a mess I've made of things!"

She scrubbed her hands over her face. "The only man I want to marry is Monte Van Huysen. If he won't have me, I'll simply live out my days as a spinster. Maybe I'll find a widow or another spinster to set up housekeeping with me, and we'll be eccentric together and keep dozens of cats."

Her back began to ache. She climbed up on her bed, blew out her candle, pulled the striped cat into her lap, and stared out into darkness. As her eyes adjusted, the moonlit farmyard transformed into a magical world of shadows and light. An owl glided silently past the house and disappeared into a clump of trees.

"If Monte really is Lucky in Lakeland, then I do want to marry him, no matter if he does have a prison record in his past. I'll admit that much. I don't know if my parents will approve the match, but I know my own heart on that score, at least." She rubbed the cat around its ears and chin until a rumbling purr rewarded her efforts.

Did she truly know her own heart? A few weeks' acquaintance at a vacation lodge had provided sufficient time for her to develop a powerful attraction to the man, but did she know him well enough to pledge her love and fidelity for life? At times she thought she had glimpsed a depth of character behind his charming smile, but at other times he had seemed shallow. Physical attraction gave a relationship zest, for certain, yet a lifetime relationship required much more.

Remembering the solid strength of his arms, the warmth of his gaze, his gentle touch on her cheek. . .she lifted her hand to touch her face where he had once touched it. Disregarding the sleeping calico kitty, she flopped back against her feather bolster and tried to remember how it felt to rest against Monte's shoulder.

Love always involved risk. To love was to open one's heart to pain—the pain of loss, of rejection, of death. Was Monte Van Huysen worth such risk?

And what if all this speculation were baseless? What if Monte had never so much as seen her advertisement for a husband?

How can I know? How can I find out? I can scarcely ask Lucky in a public newspaper ad if he is Monte Van Huysen.

But to write a letter to Monte at the lodge. . . She dared not take so great a risk as that.

The calico cat, irritated by Marva's unrest, hopped off the bed.

"Lord God, please help me resolve this situation in a way that causes the least pain or embarrassment to everyone involved."

The cricket chirped.

Thump!

Marva's eyes opened wide.

Silence, then *crunch, crunch, crunch.*

Marva grimaced. "I did ask for that, didn't I? Thank you for doing your job, Patches." Still wrinkling her nose, she slid off the bed to change into her nightdress.

Chapter 14

Yea, all of you be subject one to another,
and be clothed with humility: for God resisteth the proud,
and giveth grace to the humble.
I PETER 5:5

Crown Him with many crowns, the Lamb upon His throne." Marva sang along with the rest of the congregation while her fingers played the closing hymn. As soon as it ended, she picked up her book and her heavy shawl.

"You played the piano beautifully today, Marva. Thank you, as always, for serving so willingly. My hands are too stiff these days for me to do much playing, and Beulah and Myles have no time."

Marva looked into Violet Watson's smiling blue eyes and felt cheered. "I enjoy it, although I sometimes feel self-conscious. Myles plays so much better than I do."

Beulah's mother brushed that aside. "You do very well at accompanying while the congregation sings. Myles plays better than any of us, but if we depended on him for our music these days, we'd be in trouble. Beulah needs him to keep those boys in line during church services." Violet shook her head in mock despair, though evidently proud of her grandchildren.

Marva could think of nothing more to say. At one time she would have babbled on without thinking, but more often these days she found herself withdrawing into silence. She simply smiled and fell into step with the older woman as they exited the small church building.

Violet Fairfield Watson had remarried after her first husband's death, providing her three children, Beulah, Eunice, and Sam, with a loving stepfather. Obadiah and Violet Watson now had three sons of their own, all named for Old Testament prophets. Marva could never keep their names straight.

Obadiah Watson had served a long prison term for bank robbery, Marva recalled. But he had since been cleared of the crime, and the true criminal's identity had been discovered. Lucky, on the other hand, admitted that he had deserved *worse* than a prison sentence for his crimes.

Violet touched her arm. "Are you coming to Beulah's house for fellowship supper today? The pastor's family is joining us."

"Yes, I believe we're planning to come."

340

The crowd at the Van Huysen farmhouse included the Spinellis, an Italian family who owned and operated the town's bakery, and the pastor and his large family. Children of all ages and sizes swarmed the premises inside and out, frequently slamming doors.

Beulah had baked a ham, and all the guests had brought food to share. The children filled their plates and sat outside on the porch chairs and steps. The adults clustered inside to partake of their meal, laughing and chatting.

Marva decided to fill her usual role and keep an eye on the children.

"Do you mind if I join you out here?" Caroline Schoengard let the screen door close behind herself.

"Please do. There's plenty of room." Marva smiled at the older woman.

Caroline pulled up another rocking chair beside her. "Since my incorrigible twins tend to start the most conflicts, I figure I'd better be responsible and prevent serious injuries, if possible."

"Are all of your children here today?"

"No, Scott, our oldest, is visiting his young lady friend over in Bolger."

Caroline nibbled at her food, but Marva sensed a question building. Sure enough, after setting down her fork, the pastor's wife asked, "So, did you enjoy our holiday in the Northwoods?"

"Yes, very much. I know my parents did as well. How about your family?"

"They all had the time of their lives. Even the girls enjoyed themselves. I believe we will attempt to make the trip again next year. I know it did my husband good to relax for a time. I worry about his health. His heart troubles him, you know."

"I hadn't realized that. I'm sorry to hear it," Marva said. "It is difficult for me to imagine Rev. Schoengard ill. He is always so vigorous."

"Well, we're all getting on in years."

Several of the larger boys started tossing a ball around and arguing among themselves. The little ones ran off behind the house to play. Two girls ran toward the barns, probably in search of kittens.

Marva pushed with her toes to rock her chair and enjoyed the temporary peace. It was a fine day with the crisp edge of autumn adding spice to the air. Some of the maples along the drive held touches of red.

The football game broke into shouting and accusations. Caroline rose and approached the porch rail. Cupping her hands around her mouth, she shouted for the boys to quiet down and behave like humans instead of beasts.

All those big boys wilted into submission, and their game resumed peacefully.

Caroline sat back down and gave Marva a self-conscious smile. "I know I'm loud, but I've had to learn to project my voice to make myself heard."

"I'm impressed. All those large beings intimidate me," Marva confessed. "But I suppose a mother can't let herself be intimidated by her own sons."

Caroline laughed. Sobering, she gave Marva another sidelong glance. A nosy question was coming, and soon. What it would be, Marva could only guess.

"May I ask you a rather personal question?" Caroline asked. "I've been longing to ask it for a long time now. You'll probably think I'm silly, but. . .well, I'm not the only person who has wondered. Gossip is a sin, so I thought I would rather ask you directly than discuss the matter with anyone else."

"What is it?"

"You'll probably think I'm silly to ask, but. . ." Caroline sucked in a quick breath and let it out in a gust. "Awhile back—oh, many months ago—I saw an ad in the paper."

Oh, no.

Caroline chuckled and shook her head. "At first I thought it was a sales gimmick—you know how newspapers can be. But then. . .well. . . Oh, I'm messing this all up. You see, it was an advertisement from a single woman looking for a husband. My husband laughed about it at the time and teased that his daughters might try the same thing someday if it worked for this woman. None of us thought anything would come of it, but then there came an answer from a man."

She suddenly stopped and gave Marva a close look. "Have you seen the letters? Do you know what I'm talking about?"

"Yes, I've seen them."

"Oh, good. I thought you must have. People have talked about it off and on for a long time, but now more than ever. Have you seen the latest letter?"

"The one in which the man confesses his past? The prison sentence and all?"

Caroline nodded. "Isn't that heartrending? I've seen no answer from the woman yet. All of us are afraid she will turn him away now. One can hardly blame her, but still. . ."

Marva merely nodded. "What was it you wished to ask me?"

Caroline met her gaze for an instant, then laughed and shook her head. "You must think I'm crazy, but. . .many people in town believe that you are the woman who writes those letters. You're a Christian woman, and you live with your elderly parents on a farm—you fit her description exactly!"

Marva lowered her chin. "I can think of several other women who fit that description. Two or three even at our church."

"You're right, of course. . .but, oh well, it would have been so romantic! You're beautiful, so everyone immediately thought of how blessed that poor, lonely man would be to marry a woman like you. I mean, most of the other spinsters in this area aren't. . .well, they just aren't like you."

"Thank you. I had no idea. . . ."

Caroline chuckled. "You look years younger than any other woman your age, married or single. I think half the married women in the church are jealous of you. I know I am sometimes. By the time I was your age, I had lost my figure and my complexion."

"You were married with several children. That makes a difference."

"Perhaps. No one can understand why you've never married, Marva. Most people think you're too particular, but I disagree. Better for a woman to remain single than to marry in haste. The apostle Paul would uphold your position. I'll confess that David and I thought you and Monte Van Huysen made a striking couple, while we were up north, you know."

"Did you?" Marva smiled, hoping to appear amused by the notion.

"And when that most recent note appeared in the paper. . .well, one can't help adding two and two. Everyone acquainted with the Van Huysens knows the tragic story of Virginia's lost grandson, the prodigal who never got the chance to return. My fertile imagination immediately sprouted the notion that Monte must be Lucky in Lakeland. He's the right age, he owns a lodge on a lake, and the letters sound like him."

Caroline's anxious eyes studied Marva's face. "You undoubtedly think I'm crazy, coming up with this incredible romance for you. Once again, I appear to have added two and two incorrectly. Dave constantly tells me I must stop speculating about people and their business. I know he's right, but I can't seem to help myself."

Marva tried to end the conversation on a noncommittal note, but Caroline's words haunted her.

Saturday night, Marva examined her reflection in her dressing table mirror, seeing the fine lines around her eyes and mouth, noting the deeper lines in her white neck. Silver blended almost unnoticeably with the gold of her hair. Deep blue eyes were her best feature by far. Although she had always worked to protect her complexion from the hot sun, her hands showed definite signs of wear and tear. Her figure, though far from ideal, was better now than it had been fifteen years earlier, since she no longer baked and ate many pastries and cakes, having long since given up on capturing a man with her cooking skills.

Would a man truly feel blessed to have her as his wife? Why now, and not twenty years ago? Gazing into her reflected eyes, she recognized the changes God had worked on her heart over the past few months. Bitterness no longer lingered at the corners of her lips. Her expression held sorrow, mostly over the tangled results of her own headstrong behavior, yet hope brightened her eyes.

After church the next morning, she cornered the pastor's busy wife. "Caroline, you should be a sleuth," she said quietly.

Caroline stared at her blankly for a moment—then comprehension dawned. She clapped one hand over her mouth. Her shoulders began to shake. Giving up, she threw back her head and laughed heartily. "And you should be an actress! Marva Obermeier, you had me entirely convinced that I'd dived down the wrong rabbit hole." Eyes glowing, she gripped Marva's arm and whispered, "How right was I? Did you write those letters? Is Monte the man?"

"I wrote the Lonely letters, but I'm not sure about Monte. I need to answer Lucky's letter in a way only Monte could understand. I've been trying to work up enough courage. I've been thinking how to do it. Caroline, does everyone think I'm crazy? I'm so ashamed, so embarrassed for ever writing that first ad!"

"Nonsense." Caroline patted Marva's arm. "Everyone I've heard talking about the matter thinks it's the most romantic story they've ever heard. And if it should turn out to be Monte. . . Even Dave noticed the way Monte watched you while we were at his lodge. The entire company was buzzing about it."

"Buzzing." Marva repeated the word, her hands trembling. "Oh, Caroline, please pray for me. I don't want to do anything foolish again, trying to force God's hand."

"No one can force God's hand," Caroline said firmly. "Be honest and true, and let Him handle the consequences." Her eyes began to twinkle again. "And tell me *every detail*!"

⟡

Monte awaited his turn in the barber shop, listening with part of his brain to the other men discuss fishing and hunting successes and failures, but mostly pondering the fact that Lonely in Longtree had not yet replied to his confession.

In all his consideration of her possible responses, it had never entered his mind that she would refuse to answer at all. He wanted to believe that she was simply taking great pains with her response. But, then again, her taking such great pains would indicate a kind yet negative response. He sighed and folded his arms over his chest.

Whenever he worked up enough courage to pick up his mail today, he would probably find the latest edition of the Longtree paper. It might contain Marva's reply; it might not. Dread of yet another disappointment caused him to procrastinate.

He had promised Myles a visit during the autumn or early winter. A visit to Myles would entail attendance at his church, where an encounter with Marva was nearly inevitable.

If Marva turned him down, if she could not bear the shame of his past, he would prefer never to see her again, rather than torture himself with the unattainable. He might be obliged to explain this fact to his little brother, rather than risk wounding Myles and Beulah by breaking his promise with no explanation.

"Van Huysen, you're next." The barber waved him over.

⟡

A short time later, Monte rode Petunia north on the Woodruff Road, his sober gaze fixed on nothingness. His saddlebags contained the day's mail, including a newspaper that he had not yet opened. He sensed it there behind him, waiting.

The autumn days were growing short and cold. Wind rippled Petunia's mane

LONELY IN LONGTREE

and tried to steal Monte's hat. He clapped it down more firmly on his head, then wriggled his fingers in his thick gloves. He and Hardy and the lodge staff had been busily storing boats and equipment for the long winter, sealing up the cabins and the lodge, and otherwise preparing for hibernation. Although Monte looked forward to free time for his writing, he dreaded months of loneliness.

"This is stupid," he told Petunia. "I'm putting myself through torture." He stopped the mare right there on the road, dismounted, and unpacked the newspaper from his saddlebag. He was obliged to remove one of his gloves in order to turn the pages.

Petunia turned to *whiffle* softly at the fluttering pages, then closed her eyes as if awaiting her master's pleasure.

Fighting the wind, squinting to read the newsprint by fading twilight, Monte scanned the page of ads. Then his entire body jerked. There it was, her reply. He looked away for a moment, almost unconsciously praying for strength.

Dear Lucky in Lakeland, Thank you for your honesty. Now that you have bared your soul, it seems only fair that I confess weaknesses of my own. I am overly sensitive to the sun's heat and to the ridicule of other people. I have a dread of unscheduled detours, yet I appreciate shadows of substance. If you can endure these peculiarities, perhaps we should plan to meet. Do you care for petunias? Lonely in Longtree.

Monte crammed the unfolded paper into his saddlebag, wrapped his arms around Petunia's neck, and buried his face in her mane. A few minutes later, he spun around and whooped.

Calming and catching his startled horse consumed a few extra minutes of his time, but he was too happily distracted to care.

345

Chapter 15

If any of you lack wisdom, let him ask of God,
that giveth to all men liberally, and upbraideth not;
and it shall be given him.
JAMES 1:5

Marva stepped out of the chicken pen and latched its gate. The basket on her arm held few eggs. This cold weather discouraged the hens from laying, even though they were snug inside the barn.

One of the cows lowed plaintively. The farm always seemed quiet and peaceful as autumn advanced toward winter. Last week had been hectic, what with slaughtering the pigs and all the work involved in that unpleasant chore. No matter how much she enjoyed eating sausages, Marva intensely disliked making them.

"Miss Marva?"

She tried not to reveal her surprise. J. D. Parker had a way of appearing out of nowhere. The hired man approached her from the stanchions where the milk cows licked up the last of their evening feed.

"Yes, Mr. Parker?" She smiled. J. D. was stocky in build, nearly bald, yet rather nice looking.

He twisted his cap between his large hands, and his face turned an unbecoming red. "I know this is bold of me, but I've discussed it with your father, and he's agreeable if you are. I'd like to marry you, ma'am. It would be a good thing for everyone involved. Your parents could stay on with us in the house as long as they live. You and I would make a good partnership."

Marva felt as if she were watching the little scene from somewhere far away. She stared at Parker's earnest face until he looked away in confusion. "Meaning no insult, ma'am. I thought—I hoped—you might approve the idea."

With an effort, she gathered her senses. "I am not insulted, Mr. Parker. I simply. . .I had never considered such a thing. You say my parents have approved?"

He nodded, his gray eyes lighting up. "I'll not press you for an answer, Miss Marva. We've time to consider." He bobbed an awkward little bow and made his escape.

Marva returned to the house as if in a trance. Marry J. D. Parker? Her parents wanted her to marry him?

While she prepared the evening meal, Marva pondered this unexpected turn of events. Her parents chatted comfortably to each other, apparently unaware of their daughter's inner turmoil. During supper she picked at her food, feeling J. D.'s frequent glances from across the table. As soon as he finished eating, he excused himself and stepped outside. He never stayed for Papa's nightly Bible reading.

Thinking of J. D.'s proposal, of all that marriage to him would certainly entail, gave her an inward shudder. Nice man though he was, she had no interest whatsoever in giving herself to him as a wife. At one time she might have snapped up his offer, considering it the best chance she was likely to receive. At one time she had been foolish.

But then again, had she ever actually been that foolish? Over the years she had discouraged the attentions of many would-be swains. Always her heart had continued to hope that somewhere out there in the great world existed at least one man whom she could respect and love without reserve.

Was she being unfair to J. D.? Although he attended church regularly, she had no idea what he believed about God and salvation. He was also rough with the animals at times, demonstrating a lack of patience and kindness.

Papa closed his Bible, and Marva realized she had not listened to one word. While he led in prayer, she closed her eyes and had her own private conversation with the Lord.

Please guide me, Lord. I am terribly confused! I have pleaded with Thee for wisdom and guidance, but I've heard no answer. I don't know what to do!

Papa shoved back his chair and patted his stomach. "Another excellent meal, daughter. Nothing like fresh pork chops." Something crackled in the bib of his overall. He paused and reached into the pocket, pulling out a folded, crumpled letter. "Ah, forgot about this."

She reached to take the letter he held out to her.

"It came the other day, and I plumb forgot about it. I ask your pardon for an old man's faulty memory."

Marva glanced up from her perusal of the unfamiliar handwriting on the envelope long enough to smile at her father. "Of course, Papa. I'm just as forgetful as you are."

"Who is it from, Marva?" Mother asked.

"I'm not sure. I'll read it after I clean up the kitchen." She had no desire to read her unexpected letter under her parents' curious eyes.

Although she didn't like to suspect them of inordinate curiosity, Papa and Mother did seem to stay up past their usual bedtime hour. Once, while she swept the kitchen floor, she caught her mother watching her with an expectant look. "What's the matter?" Marva paused to ask.

Mother waffled for a moment, then said in carefully casual tones, "I was simply wondering when you planned to read your letter."

"Probably after I go upstairs." Hearing a *meow*, she opened the outer door to let in two waiting cats. They rubbed about her ankles while she hung up the dish towels to dry over the stove. After giving each one a small plate of minced pork chop, she squatted down to pet her kitties while they ate.

Before she headed upstairs, she kissed her parents good night. Her mother wore a fixed expression as if trying to appear unconcerned. "Good night, dear." Even her voice sounded restrained.

Marva caught her father giving her mother a warning look, but he instantly switched it to a fond smile as she bent over him. "Good night, Papa."

"Good night, my Marva."

The cats followed her upstairs and laid claim to the bed. Her bedchamber was cold. She probably should have brought up a hot brick for her feet, but she hadn't thought ahead to warm one. Shivering, she set her candle and the letter on her bedside table and deliberately prepared for bed. She took down her hair, brushed it, braided it, and tucked it beneath her nightcap. Wearing woolen socks with her flannel nightgown, she slipped beneath her coverlet and two quilts. The cats immediately curled up at her sides like two purring hot-water bottles.

At last she reached for her letter and tore open the envelope. Rising to lean on one elbow, she tilted the page so that the candlelight fell upon it.

Dear Marva,

I hope I do not offend by addressing you so, but in truth, you are inestimably dear to me. Your recent letter in the Enquirer *with its clever allusions to our adventures together fills me with hope that my suit is not entirely abhorrent to you. Can you truly forgive and forget my wicked past and accept me as a new man in Jesus Christ? I would have spoken many times while you graced my lodge with your lovely presence, and I would have revealed my identity as your newsprint admirer—had not fear held me in its grip—fear of your rejection if you knew me for what I am. I do not know how long ago you guessed my identity as your devoted Lucky in Lakeland. I guessed—I hoped—you might prove to be my Lonely in Long-tree that first evening when I met you at my brother's cabin.*

Already I was fond of you in print. Never had I imagined that my hoped-for bride would be as beautiful as a man's daydreams! How often have I invented for my fictional heroes lovely heroines whose descriptions closely match yours. I laugh to think of it. How well God knows my heart!

Does your letter indicate that you forgive my cowardice, my foolish attempt at deception? Is it possible that you return my regard? Is it possible, dare I dream, that your parents might accept one such as I as their son-in-law? I can hardly eat or sleep for mixed dread and urgency to learn your reply.

I could write paeans to your beauty and grace—in fact, I have written them, and they lay crumpled around my feet. Lest I annoy you with rapturous expressions of devotion, I herein attempt to be sparing of words and simply ask the questions that weight my soul.

Soon I shall travel to your town to visit my brother and his family. Although I eagerly anticipate my visit with them, my true heart's desire is to be with you again, to deepen our acquaintance into friendship and more—much more. I demand nothing of you, beloved; I have no right. I simply lay my heart at your feet and humbly implore you to take me as your husband.

Yours always,
Montague Van Huysen

PS I am extraordinarily fond of one particular Petunia.

Marva read the letter through several times. It was true! Her fondest dream was actually true! How could this be? Dare she believe that all these years her heart had waited for this one man to enter her life? That God had caused her to wait in solitude while He prepared Monte Van Huysen to become her husband?

But this was not the time for deep introspection; this was the time to revel in his admiration and love. And his beautiful writing! How many men of her acquaintance could express their feelings with such poetic grace?

None other. Not even one.

Monte wants to marry me! He thinks I'm beautiful!

Smiling, laughing, and crying, she hugged her cats and gave whispered thanks to the Lord. Long into the night she lay awake, thinking and dreaming and wondering. What would he do? When would he come? Would he insist upon a proper courtship, or would he ask for a quick wedding? Which would be better?

But when morning dawned, doubts and indecision crept back into her heart. The main question was the one Monte had asked: Would her parents accept him? They had seemed to like him well enough at the lodge, but Monte as expert fishing guide and genial host was a vastly different proposition from Monte the ex-convict as a prospective son-in-law.

She did her morning chores distractedly, sometimes drifting off in thought until a protesting *moo* or a lashing tail brought her back to reality. While watching her chapped hands draw milk from a cow's pendulous udder, she recognized the irony of her current dilemma.

J. D. Parker offered exactly the kind of marriage she had decided to settle for back when she wrote that original ad—a loveless business partnership designed to keep the farm in Marva's family. But she no longer desired that kind of marriage. How had she ever imagined that such an arrangement would satisfy her needs? Blind stubbornness and disrespect for God had brought her to make such foolish choices.

Although Parker had worked around the farm since early summer, she scarcely knew the man and felt no attachment to him whatsoever. As far as she could tell, he had no feelings for her either. His interest lay entirely in the farm; proposing marriage to Marva was simply a necessary step in obtaining possession of her family's property.

Hearing a *mew*, she turned to see Patches and Tigress watching her hopefully. With a smile, she squirted a little milk in their direction and watched the cats lick it from each other's fur. Funny creatures.

Rising, she patted Annabelle's bony hip and lifted the full pail. The elderly shorthorn still produced a fine calf every year, and her milk production rivaled that of younger cows. "Good ol' girl."

Marva lugged the pail toward the milk room, where sloshing noises indicated that J. D. Parker was hard at work. The cats followed at her heels, cleaning up any involuntary spills.

The top of Mr. Parker's head reflected lamplight as he bent over a milk can. He looked up at Marva's approach and set down an empty bucket.

"Here, let me take that."

Marva handed over her full pail and watched J. D. empty it into the can. Patches hurried to lick up a puddle near the can, but J. D. shoved the cat away with his boot. "Git."

Marva scooped up her insulted kitty for a cuddle. What would it harm to let the cats clean up spills? They earned their keep on the farm by keeping rodent populations down.

Most of the birds and beasts raised on a farm would someday be killed for food, yet Papa treated his animals with kindness as long as they lived. Whenever he was obliged to slaughter a beast, he always dispatched it as quickly and painlessly as possible. Although Parker was never cruel to the animals, he showed little regard for their comfort or feelings.

A sudden memory of Monte's mare resting her head on his shoulder while he rubbed her ears and murmured nonsensical sweet talk brought a smile to her face. Monte would appreciate her cats, she felt certain, and they would like him.

Was she making excuses for her possibly selfish decision to choose Monte over Mr. Parker? Emotions could easily blind a woman's heart to wisdom. She needed wise and objective counsel, but where could she find such a thing?

Holding his carpetbag in one hand, Monte stepped onto the crowded station platform. The little town of Longtree was busier than he had expected. No one greeted him at the station, since he had sent Myles no definite date of arrival. Rather than crowd into his brother's house, he had decided to lodge in town.

Stopping a gentleman on the street, he inquired, "Can you recommend a hotel or boardinghouse?"

"Certainly, sir. Amelia Martin runs the best place in town."

Monte followed the stranger's directions and soon found himself at a neat establishment located on a side street. The proprietress, an angular, gray-haired woman wearing a stiffly starched apron over a baggy gown, showed him to a small but immaculate bedchamber. "Dinner is served at six in the dining room." Her voice was incongruously deep. "Don't be late if you want to eat."

After the door closed behind her with a sharp click, Monte unpacked his bag and hung his clothes on wall hooks. Kicking off his shoes, he stretched out on the bed, folded his hands behind his head, and regarded the ceiling. Although no coherent requests passed through his mind, let alone his lips, a constant prayer rose from the depths of his spirit.

When he arrived downstairs at precisely six, men of varied descriptions filled the dining room with rumbling voices and nearly overpowering body odor. Most of these diners would not be residents of the boardinghouse, he deduced. Women were noticeably absent from their number. He pulled out a chair between a natty salesman-looking type and a sweat-stained laborer with shaggy hair and beard.

Mrs. Martin and an elderly man called Boz waited on the table. Boz had full use of only one arm, yet he managed to carry platters and bowls of food, pour drinks, and otherwise satisfy his customers. Monte soon guessed that Boz was husband to Mrs. Martin.

The food was excellent, and the dinner conversation offered nearly as much information as a scan of the weekly newspaper. Monte heard many familiar names, including his brother's, during the course of the meal.

"Listen up! I got news."

Everyone, including Monte, gazed toward the far end of the table, where a man with a large red nose tapped on his glass with his spoon. "I just come from the Shamrock, where J. D. Parker bought drinks all around 'cuz he's fixin' to get married."

The man seated next to him shook his head. "I heard that tale, too, but the fact is, she ain't given J. D. no answer yet. Ask me, and I'd say he's counting his chickens too soon."

"Who's the woman?" another man called from Monte's end of the table.

"Marva Obermeier," answered Red Nose.

Monte's fork stopped halfway to his open mouth.

"Eh, he's good as married. That woman's been desperate to catch a man for twenty years." Bitterness laced the speaker's voice.

"If that's so, why'd she turn you down, Nugget?" someone else shouted, earning raucous and mocking laughter.

Recovering his poise, Monte laid down his fork and took a sip of water.

"And you, Buff. I hear you proposed to her once."

"That was ten years ago. I reckon most of us have made a try for her and her farm at some time or other," the burly farmhand at Monte's left admitted.

"I heard tell she advertised for a husband in the paper."

"That was a sales gimmick," another voice said in scoffing tones. "Face it, Marva could take her pick of us if she weren't so particular. If J. D. wins her, he's one lucky fellow."

Amelia Martin burst into the room, leaned over, and smacked a platter of bread on the table. "Enough of your gossip," she snapped. "And they say women talk too much!"

Monte took a bite of buttered bread but found it difficult to swallow.

Chapter 16

*And this I pray, that your love may abound yet more
and more in knowledge and in all judgment.*

PHILIPPIANS 1:9

Mr. Parker, may I have a word with you?" Marva hoped he would attribute the quiver in her voice to the morning chill. Hands clutching at her shawl, she watched him load a full milk can into the wagon.

He immediately hopped down and faced her, rubbing his gloved hands on his thighs. His quick breath steamed from his smiling mouth. "Anytime." Bold admiration glistened in his pale eyes.

"This will take only a moment of your time, actually." She squared her shoulders and forged ahead. "After much prayer and consideration, I have determined that I must refuse your flattering offer of marriage."

He stared at her without blinking. She saw his hands close into fists. "Why?"

"I have already given my heart to another man. If he will not marry me, I shall remain single."

Tight lips and an angry glare revealed the man's feelings. "Who?" he finally asked through clenched teeth.

"I cannot see how that information is your concern, sir. I appreciate the honor you gave me by requesting my hand in marriage, but such an arrangement would never work." With a quick nod, she turned back toward the house.

His hand closed over her upper arm, stopping her short. Sensing his vastly superior strength, she turned to stare at him, her throat closing in fear.

"I'll not stay on this farm as a hired hand. Tell your father either you marry me or he sells the place to me or I leave." Anger glittered in Parker's red-rimmed eyes.

Marva nodded.

He released her and turned away.

⟨⟨⟩⟩

Tension stretched a long silence to the snapping point. Marva chewed a tiny bite of chicken and had to wash it down with a quick gulp of milk. Parker's sullen stare from across the supper table made her flesh creep. No matter what her parents might say, she did not regret refusing his proposal.

At last Papa laid his napkin across his plate and reached back to pull the

Bible from its shelf. Before he could open it, Parker pushed back his chair and spoke.

"Unless you'll sell this place to me, Obermeier, I'll be pulling out in the next few days."

Papa laid the Bible on the table and folded his hands atop it. "I see no reason why we cannot discuss terms of sale. Shall we set up a time to meet tomorrow at the bank?" He spoke with unaccustomed formality.

Parker's aggressive manner dissolved into pleased surprise. "Yes, sir, that would be right fine with me."

"After dinner, shall we say?"

"After dinner," Parker agreed. "You are serious? You'll consider selling out?"

"I'll certainly consider your offer, Mr. Parker."

Smiling, the hired man rose and excused himself. To Marva's relief, he did not glance her way. "I'll check the stock once more before I head to town."

"You have always been dependable and hardworking, Parker. Thank you." Papa rose to shake Parker's hand before the hired man departed.

As soon as the door closed behind him, Mother let out her breath in a long and noisy sigh. "Oh, Gustaf, how marvelous! Thank the Lord!" She suddenly covered her face with a handkerchief.

Marva stared in startled consternation. "Mother?"

Her mother lowered the handkerchief to reveal her smiling face. "Such a relief! Oh, thank God! I was so afraid you would agree to marry that man, Marva. He asked your father's permission to propose marriage to you, and we feared you would accept him out of desperation. How I have prayed that you would be wise!"

Papa snorted softly. "I told you to have faith in our daughter's good sense. Parker is not a bad man, but why should Marva marry him?"

Mother leaned forward, her intense gaze holding Marva captive. "Years ago, Papa and I promised each other never again to interfere in your matters of the heart, but I never expected to find it so difficult to keep that promise! When you advertised for a husband in the newspaper, I thought I should die of shock."

"You knew?"

"Not at first," Papa answered. "But over time we figured it out."

"Always we hoped you would confide in us," Mother said, her tone reproachful. "We might have helped in your search for Lucky while we stayed at the lodge."

"Although, as it turns out, we found him for you on our first attempt," Papa added with a grin. "I suspected he might advertise his lodge in our newspaper for a reason. Never guessed about his being Myles's lost brother, of course. To be honest, I thought Mr. Stowell was the man at first. I didn't know about his partner."

"Dearest, why are you tormenting that man?" Mother asked. "Have you answered his letter? His past is disgraceful, to be sure, but the Lord has changed him into a man whom any woman should be justly proud to wed."

Marva could hardly speak. "How long have you known?"

"We figured things out sooner than you did," Mother said, reaching across the table to pat Marva's hand. "Probably because we could observe the matter more objectively. Both Mr. Stowell and Mr. Van Huysen admired you from the first, but Mr. Van Huysen had an air of purpose about him."

"Purpose mixed with fear." Papa frowned. "I didn't understand the fear until I read his confession in the newspaper."

"You know he is truly a man of God now, don't you, Papa?" Marva asked.

"Had I not come to know and respect him prior to his confession, I would have been reluctant to admit such a change would be possible. This old man has learned a lesson about God's redemptive power. It galls me to marry my only daughter to an ex-convict, yet at the same time, I am proud to marry my only daughter to a godly man and famous author. I believe he will make you happy."

Mother smiled and shook her head. "Happy is too weak a word. Such joy I found in seeing a fine man look upon our daughter with love and devotion in his eyes! And to know that she returns his love!" She heaved another ecstatic sigh. "God's ways are always best."

"But now what shall we do?" Marva asked. "I have not yet answered his letter because I did not know what to say. Yes, I love him and wish to marry him, but I cannot simply hop on a train and travel north."

Papa nodded decidedly. "Leave that to me, child. I'll write to inform Mr. Van Huysen of our plans to sell the farm and move north."

"You plan to move north, too?"

Her parents appeared surprised by her question. "But of course," Papa said. "We have been discussing this for months—ever since our summer vacation. The winters up north might be harsher than winters here, but there we might remain indoors in a luxurious lodge, read, and visit with our daughter and her husband. What more could a lazy old couple like us desire?"

"We shall come with you and accept your Mr. Van Huysen's proposal. I've been sorting through possessions these past months, preparing for a move," Mother said in her practical way.

Marva's gaze shifted back and forth between their beloved faces as her thoughts scrambled to catch up. Laughter built inside her until it spilled out in a hearty peal. "You darlings! How sneaky you are!"

∽⊗∾

"We're home!"

Marva hurried to the door to greet her parents. "How did the meeting go?"

"Quite well," Papa said, letting her take his muffler and hang it on a wall hook.

Before he could say another word, Mother inserted, "Marva, guess who we saw in town—Monte Van Huysen!"

Marva paused with her mouth ajar, then gathered her thoughts enough to respond, "Oh."

"He apparently arrived the day before yesterday, and of course he's been at his brother's house to visit, although he is staying at the Martins' boardinghouse." Mother's eyes snapped with excitement. "He stopped your father and—" Her flow of words cut off suddenly, and she gave her husband an apologetic glance. "But Papa can tell you. . . ."

Papa finished hanging up his coat and Mother's. Then, placing his arm around Marva's shoulders, he walked beside her into the kitchen. "He asked if he might call on us this afternoon."

"Today?" Marva's throat nearly closed with a combination of panic and joy.

"You'd best tidy yourself before he arrives," Mother suggested. "The bread smells wonderful, and you baked apple kuchen as well, did you not?"

"I'll brew fresh coffee," Papa volunteered.

Marva changed into her blue dimity frock, the most becoming of her gowns, though rather light for the season. Seated at her dressing table, she fussed with her hair, pulling wisps down to wave in front of her ears. Her cheeks were rosy, her eyes bright.

Could a woman die of love? For the first time, she believed it possible.

※

The sheen of frost coated grass and trees. Monte's breath froze on his scarf, and his hired horse's breath beaded its whiskers. *Clop, clop, clop.* It trotted along a country road, carrying him ever closer to Marva, ever closer to his future.

The Obermeier farm looked much like every other farm in southern Wisconsin. The barn was in need of repair, and the paint on the house's porch had peeled off in strips; yet overall the place wore an air of comfort. His horse whinnied, and a cart horse in the corral answered.

Smoke trickled from the chimney. Although the farmyard appeared deserted, he knew Marva and her parents were at home. He dismounted and wrapped his mount's reins around a post.

His boots clunked on the steps, and his own breathing seemed noisy. Now that the moment had arrived, his brain felt wooden.

After closing his eyes to pray silently for strength, he knocked on the door.

He heard footsteps inside. A bolt slid back, and the door opened to reveal Mr. Obermeier. "Come in, Mr. Van Huysen, and welcome. Hang your hat and coat on these hooks. My wife will be grateful if you will scrape your boots."

The greeting seemed restrained. Monte could read nothing in the older man's expression. At their meeting in town that afternoon and always during his stay at the lodge, Mr. Obermeier had seemed friendly. Now he exuded dignity and detachment.

Delightful aromas of cinnamon, yeast, and coffee wafted through the house. Mrs. Obermeier appeared from the kitchen. "We're so thankful you found time to visit us, Mr. Van Huysen. Our Marva has baked *apfel* kuchen, and we've prepared fresh coffee. I hope you can stay for supper as well."

If his plans went smoothly, he shared that hope. If not. . .

"Come on into the kitchen where it's warm." Mrs. Obermeier beckoned him forward. Her manner, at least, was reassuringly unchanged.

As he entered the room, Marva straightened and turned to place a steaming loaf on a wire rack. "Good evening, Mr. Van Huysen."

"Good evening, Miss Obermeier."

After giving him a shy smile, she draped the dish towels she had used to protect her hands over a bar on the oven door and removed her apron.

"Please be seated. I'll pour the coffee and serve up the apple cake."

The minutes seemed to drag. Monte did his best to engage in small talk with her parents, mostly about his relatives, yet he felt acutely aware of Marva's presence. "Ginny took her first steps the other day. Beulah tried to make her walk to me, but she would only walk away from me to her mother."

"How quickly these children grow!" Mrs. Obermeier observed, giving her own daughter a fond glance, as if Marva were taking her first steps. Monte found this glimpse of maternal affection both amusing and appealing.

Once Marva had served coffee and cake to everyone, she took her seat across the table from him. He found himself caught between the desire to watch her, to drink in her beauty, and the need to conceal his fascination from her parents. The small talk continued while they ate. Monte burned his tongue on his coffee. Marva crumbled her cake with her fork and ate little of it.

Mr. Obermeier cleared his throat. "As we informed you earlier, Mr. Van Huysen, my wife and I were at the bank today to discuss the impending sale of our farm. Our hired man has offered to buy it."

"J. D. Parker?"

"Why, yes. How do you know his name?" Mr. Obermeier lifted one bushy white brow.

"Talk around the table at the boardinghouse the other night concerned his plans to marry into the Obermeier family."

"Well, of all the nerve!" Marva snapped.

Monte met her irate gaze, trying not to smile in relief. "One can hardly blame a man for trying."

She huffed, but he saw her lips twitch. "He proposed, but I turned him down. He told me my parents wanted me to marry him, which not only confused me but was also false. I could never have married him under any circumstances."

He studied her guileless blue eyes. "I'm glad to hear it."

Her cheeks flushed, and she looked away.

Mr. Obermeier linked his hands together and set them before him on the table with an air of importance. "Our daughter tells us you have made her a proposal of marriage as well."

Monte's throat tightened again. "Yes, sir, I have."

"We are also aware of the newspaper correspondence you have pursued these past two years. In your most recent post, you mentioned a prison sentence in your past. Before I give a yea or nay to your proposal, I would hear your story."

Monte saw Marva give her father a startled glance, and his hopes took a downturn. He cleared his throat and shifted on his chair. "It is not a pleasant story, sir, and I take no pleasure in repeating it."

"Perhaps this will be the last time repetition will prove needful," Mr. Obermeier said, his pale eyes offering neither reprieve nor condemnation.

"Myles and I both worked for a cattle outfit owned by Cass Murdoch in Texas. It was hard work with decent pay and lots of adventure. But I—I fell into bad company. Very bad company. I did things I don't ever want to think about."

He could not look up from his coffee cup. Shame burned his face. These inescapable memories galled him always; to relate them to Marva and her parents was more painful than he had imagined.

"God listened to my grandmother's prayers. He gave me no peace. I was miserable all the time. Nothing gave me pleasure. Finally, I attended a camp meeting in the next town and heard an evangelist preach about Christ's death on the cross and His resurrection. I'd heard the story all my life, knew it by heart, yet that time God skewered me with it. I walked up the aisle and prayed with the minister. I can't describe the relief I felt when I handed my worthless life over to God."

Chapter 17

Monte's voice broke. Mrs. Obermeier pressed a handkerchief into his hand, but he blinked hard and controlled his emotions.

"At first I didn't know what to do. I told Myles what God had done for me; I gave him a Bible so he could read for himself, but at the time he wasn't grateful. I know he was ashamed to call me his brother, and he had every reason to feel that way.

"A no-good gambler named Jeb Kirkpatrick was after my hide. I had owed him a bundle of money for months, and he knew I didn't have the cash. Always before when I got into gambling debt, I'd rustle a few head of beef. But since I gave my life to God, I knew stealing wasn't the answer to my problem. I kept praying, asking the Lord to show me what to do, and all the time, Jeb kept getting madder and more insistent that I pay up.

"One night, I was riding watch over the herd, all the while fighting my green-broke mustang. Jeb and his gang came riding up and demanded the cash. I told him I would have to make payments to him out of my salary. His antipathy to the plan was evidenced by the way he hauled out a gun and shot me. I'd be dead right now if my horse hadn't reared up and dropped me off. The cattle stampeded. I got stepped on at least once before I rolled into a ravine and hid."

Marva reached across the table and took his hand. "Myles thought you were dead," she said.

He nodded. "I didn't know it at the time, but Myles saw the scene from a distance. After the stampede, he came looking for me, didn't find me, and thought I'd been trampled to dust, I guess. He thought I was dead. I thought he left Texas because he never wanted to see me again. It took us twenty years and more to get our stories straight."

"What a shame!" said Mrs. Obermeier. "But how did you keep alive?"

"The next thing I remember is waking up in an Indian's house. Not a tepee, but a house made of bricks. It was a family of Apaches—a man, his wife, two small children, and an old woman."

"Surely not Apaches," Mr. Obermeier interrupted. "They're the most savage of all Indian tribes. At least, so I've read. . . ."

"In Dutch Montana's books," Marva finished his sentence.

"And other places," her father defended himself.

Monte suddenly felt more relaxed. "They were Apaches right enough, and some of the most Christlike people I've met in all my days. The man spoke English and could read. A missionary had given him a Bible. He shared it with me while I stayed with them.

"I did some deep thinking while my wounds were healing. God started nagging me about all the stealing I had done. I read in the Bible where God wanted thieves to pay back what they had stolen—to make restitution. So as soon as I was back on my feet, I returned to Murdoch, my boss, and confessed. It wasn't an easy thing to do, but it was the right thing. Since I owned up, Murdoch was merciful. I spent two years locked up."

"How awful for you!" Marva said just above a whisper. "Yet it was the right thing to do."

Monte nodded. "While I was behind bars, Jeb Kirkpatrick and his gang were caught rustling, and some vigilantes lynched them on the spot."

"Lynched?" Mrs. Obermeier inquired.

"It means a hanging without a trial," her husband said, his tone grim.

"Had I been caught rustling, I would have been strung up alongside the others."

"God's plans for your life helped put a stop to your wild ways just in time." Marva's gentle squeeze of his hand lifted his spirits.

"Did you ever make restitution to your boss?" Mr. Obermeier asked.

"As soon as I got out of jail, I started working off my debt. It took more than two years to pay for the cattle I'd helped steal, and then Murdoch kept me on for another year after that. I talked with him a lot about God, and he started attending church with me. His wife and daughter became believers, and then the boss did, too. Not long afterwards, I cut loose and headed north."

"Leaving all your friends behind?" Marva asked.

"It was time. I thought of hunting for Myles but hadn't a clue where to start looking. No one knew where he'd headed. I thought of returning to New York, but I wanted to wait until. . .well, until I had made something of myself. I was too proud to go back with my pockets empty. Stupid, I know, but that's how I felt."

"And that was when you went to Wyoming and became a hunting guide and then started writing books?"

Monte nodded, grateful for Marva's conclusion to his tale.

A short silence fell. Monte studied Marva's strong, white fingers wrapped around his. The connection gave him comfort.

Her father cleared his throat. "Well, well. Thank you, Mr. Van Huysen, for sharing your story. I am certain it was not easy for you, but I believe the truth needed airing. To be sure, if anyone but you had told me such a drastic change in a man's life was possible, I would have scoffed. So often I have witnessed these dramatic conversions that later come to naught. . . . But yours is obviously genuine."

Monte did not know how to respond to this. He simply nodded, holding the old man's gaze.

"Since your present reputation is built upon twenty years of honest living and hard work, Mrs. Obermeier and I give our approval to your suit. Why don't you two go on into the parlor where you can propose in private? We'll stay here." Just as Monte and Marva started to rise, he added, "However, we believe a proper engagement period should be observed, since you've spent little time together in person."

"Yes, sir." Stepping to the end of the table, Monte gripped his future father-in-law's hand. "And thank you, sir."

Mrs. Obermeier pulled Monte's head down and kissed his cheek. "She'll make you happy, Monte."

He returned her teary-eyed smile. "And I'll do my best to make her happy, ma'am."

Carrying a lamp, Marva led the way to the parlor as if walking in a dream. A rush of cold air met them as Monte reached around her to push open the door. She stepped inside and set the lamp on one of her mother's hand-carved walnut tables.

"This room isn't very comfortable," she said in apology.

"We shouldn't need to stay long." He caught her shoulders and turned her to face him. "I've got to do this thing right." He lowered himself to one knee and took her hand. "Marva Obermeier, my dear Lonely in Longtree, will you marry me and allow me to end your loneliness?"

Clutching his hand with both of hers, she laughed with a catch in her voice. "Yes, oh yes!"

"Then I shall truly be Lucky in Lakeland." Using the sofa for support, he climbed back to his feet. "That going down on one knee is not as easy as it should be." He took both her hands in his and turned her so the candlelight revealed her features. Gently he caressed the line of her jaw. "You are so lovely. I cannot tell you how grateful I am to the Lord for keeping you for me, for only me!"

Joy filled Marva's heart so full that she could not speak.

"May I kiss you?" he asked in a whisper.

She nodded. Her legs shook until she feared they would give way beneath her.

Slowly he leaned forward. His mustache brushed her cheek, and then his lips touched hers in a chaste kiss. Marva looked up into his dark eyes, wanting another kiss but too shy to ask. His hands slid up her arms to grip her shoulders, and he kissed her cheek, then her temple. With a little groan, he wrapped his arms around her shoulders and pulled her against him. "Marva, I love you so very much."

Growing bolder, Marva slipped her hands around his waist and listened to his heart beating against her ear. "I love you, Monte." Being in his arms felt so strange, yet so right.

He swallowed hard. "How—how long is a proper engagement period? Are we talking weeks? Months?"

"I don't know. Shall we ask my father?"

"I don't want to head back north without you, but I can't leave Hardy with all the work for too long." He pressed his cheek to the top of her head.

She squeezed his waist. "I don't want to be left behind."

They held each other for another minute or two before he admitted, "I can hardly bear to let go of you."

"I know." With her face against his chest, she nodded, smiling yet serious.

"We'd better go talk to your parents before they come looking for us." He took her by the hand, gazing once more into her eyes, then picked up the candle and led her from the room.

Marva's parents turned expectant faces their way as they entered the kitchen. "Your daughter has just promised to marry me," Monte said, his voice hoarse. He had to clear his throat.

"Then we can start making plans," Papa said, sounding nearly as gruff. "What do you say to marrying in December? Can you stay in the area that long?"

Monte's grip on Marva's hand tightened. "Yes, sir, I can make that work."

"Good. That gives us plenty of time to sell this place and pack up to move north. I am assuming your offer of a home for your wife's parents still stands? I seem to recall such an offer early on in your newspaper correspondence with our daughter." Papa's eyes held a subtle twinkle.

Monte grinned weakly. "It still stands, sir. She told you about that, eh?"

"Marva didn't have to tell us," Mother said quickly. "We figured it out. I cannot tell you how hard it was to keep my mouth shut while we were in Minocqua! You two and your secrets." She sniffed, but her smile took any sting from her words.

⁓

"You are so lovely, my dear." Mother smoothed Marva's hair over her ear and stepped back to admire. "That deep blue brings out your eyes."

"I hope Mr. Van Huysen approves of my appearance." Marva felt suddenly shy and uncertain.

"I am certain he will approve. If he does not, he knows nothing of fashion." Mother touched the piped trim at Marva's wrist and nodded in satisfaction. "Men seldom notice a woman's attire anyway. He will focus on your face. Smile, child. You've caught yourself a fine man."

Marva bridled. "I did not catch him, Mother. I wrote the first letter, but ever since then, he has pursued me. I was careful to leave matters entirely in his hands."

Mother patted her hand. "Calm yourself; it is merely an expression. I am well aware that you have learned to put such matters into the Lord's keeping, since I have been learning the same lesson. I always longed for my daughter to experience happiness with the right man, but only because I love you so dearly."

Relaxing, Marva tried to smile. "I know, Mother. Had I met Mr. Van Huysen twenty years ago, he would have broken my heart. The Lord's timing is perfect."

"Amen."

Marva turned at the sound of her father's voice. "Papa, you look so handsome in your best suit." It was slightly threadbare at the cuffs, but no one would notice.

"*Hmph.* Are you ready? The others are waiting."

"I am ready, Papa."

Her parents escorted her into the magistrate's office, where Monte waited along with Myles and Beulah. "Marva, you are so beautiful!" Beulah exclaimed, embracing her friend.

As Monte stepped forward to greet his bride, Papa removed her hand from his arm and placed it within Monte's grasp. "She is yours now, son." His voice cracked, and he tried to cover it with a *harrumph.*

Marva listened closely as Monte repeated his vows to her, hoping she would always remember his tender tone as he promised to love, honor, and cherish her as his own flesh. His brown eyes glistened with unshed tears as he placed the ring on her finger.

To her surprise, her own voice sounded clear and steady as she pledged to love and obey this wonderful man for as long as they both should live. After the judge pronounced them husband and wife, Myles clapped his brother on the back. Marva found herself lost in a flurry of hugs and congratulations.

More friends attended the wedding dinner, held at Boz and Amelia Martin's boardinghouse. Marva chatted with friends of all ages, seeing their faces through a happy blur. Monte remained close beside her, yet the two of them could seldom exchange a word. Once, while Myles proposed a toast and the attention of others was distracted, Monte caught his wife's hand and lifted it to his lips. Marva returned his smile and felt an immediate renewal of her spirit.

When the celebration ended and the guests finally departed, Marva followed her husband upstairs. But instead of entering their room, he continued on to the back steps. "Where are we going?" she asked in surprise.

He put his finger to his lips. "To the stables. We're driving to the next town to stay the night, then taking a train north in the morning. Don't worry; I worked it all out with your father."

Understanding dawned. "To avoid a shivaree?"

He nodded. "I have no desire to be kidnapped or paraded through town in my nightshirt."

"But would they really do that to you? You're practically a stranger in town."

"I'm taking no chances. Rumors have reached my ears, and your father suggested this plan. Watch your step and hang onto my arm while we cross the yard.

It started snowing while we ate."

Monte located their bags in the loft of the Martins' stables and loaded them into a buggy. The horse waited, already harnessed, where Marva's father had left it. "What if they come searching for us?" she asked.

He helped her into the buggy and covered her with rugs. "We run that risk, but at least this way we have a chance." He climbed to his seat and clucked to the horse. "Let's just hope nobody sees us leaving town. Myles promised to provide a distraction. I think he's playing the piano and singing."

"I'm sorry to miss that, but I'd be sorrier to get shivareed." Snowflakes swirled around the side lamps like tiny moths. Marva buried her face in Monte's shoulder, yet she could hear the horse's hooves thudding in mud and spattering in puddles.

Once they were safely out of town and on the road to Bolger, she felt her husband relax. Marva sat upright. "I used to think a shivaree was funny, but now that I'm the bride, I don't care for the idea one bit." Snowflakes found their way beneath the buggy top to chill her cheeks.

"It's a crude and disrespectful custom, in my opinion," Monte said. "We can't drive faster than a walk because of ice, but I'm hoping the cold will discourage anyone from trying to follow."

"Maybe someday we'll travel to Niagara Falls, but Minocqua will be honeymoon paradise enough for me." Marva spoke with certainty.

Monte chuckled. "Don't expect it to look like it did last summer, sweetheart. We've had little snow here as yet, but I imagine we'll find plenty of it farther north."

"I don't mind. Being snowed in with you will be exciting." She hugged his arm, and he reached over to pat her mittened hands.

"Thank you." His voice held a wealth of love.

Epilogue

D id you hear that?" Marva sat bolt upright, lowering her book.
  Monte loaded another log on the fire, set the screen back in place, and straightened. "No, I was making too much noise. What did you hear?"

"I think I heard a loon." Marva dumped Patches the cat from her lap, rushed to the cabin door, and stepped out on the porch. Ice still clung to the far shore, but the lodge side of the lake was open. Moonlight sparkled on its surface. How delightful was the splash of water on the shore after months of frozen silence!

Monte followed her outside. Ralph pattered down the steps and rushed toward the lake. A flock of ducks took off with a clamor of quacking and flapping wings.

"It's early yet, but you might have heard one. The lake ice is slow to break up this year." Monte wrapped his arm around his wife's waist, rested his other hand on the rail, and listened with her.

Marva shivered and hugged herself, leaning into his solid warmth. "Maybe I imagined it."

"I don't think so. Let's wait a minute more and see if it will call again. It might have been flying overhead when it called, you know." He let go of the rail and held her with both arms.

Marva could not imagine greater happiness than she had known since her marriage to Monte. The two of them clashed at times, yet they resolved their differences without acrimony; their brief periods of discord seemed only to emphasize the general felicity of the match. Monte wrote during the day while Marva was busy with chores and projects. Every evening they spent together, reading beside the fire or simply talking. Often they planned travel vacations, perhaps to Florida or even to Europe, yet neither cared if anything actually came of their plans. For now, it was enough to be together.

Marva's parents had chosen to live inside the main lodge, where they seldom needed to step outside during winter months. Papa, however, engaged in ice fishing whenever his rheumatism would allow it. Mother kept busy sewing for the needy in the community and organizing a Concerned Women of Minocqua club.

Myles and Beulah, who was expecting again, planned to travel north and visit for an entire month during the summer, and Beulah's parents also planned to holiday at the lodge that year with their children.

Ralph trotted back to the cabin, a dark shadow with a wagging tail. Panting, he collapsed on the porch with a rattle of his bony legs against the floorboards.

Marva smiled at the familiar sound. Her two cats despised the good-natured but clumsy dog. Tigress had moved into the lodge with Marva's parents. There she earned her keep by cleaning out an invasion of deer mice. But to Marva's relief, Patches had seemed to declare and maintain an armed truce with Ralph throughout the winter. Now that the hound could spend more of his time outside, the calico cat would undoubtedly be happier in the cabin. Marva's pets could never again roam outside, since too many Northwoods beasts and birds viewed a cat as a tasty snack.

A piercing, warbling cry drifted across the waters, repeating again and again as if two birds called to each other. Monte and Marva remained quiet until the echoes died away. "A mating pair, do you think?" she asked.

"Most likely the same pair that raised two chicks down that way last summer." He pointed to his right across the lake.

"Now I can believe that spring is here," Marva said, nestling close to his chest. "Now that the loons are back."

He quoted softly, " 'For, lo, the winter is past, the rain is over and gone; the flowers appear on the earth; the time of the singing of birds is come, and the voice of the turtle is heard in our land.'"

He paused. "That works if you substitute *snow* for *rain* and *loons* for *turtles*."

"It means turtledoves."

"I always thought it meant snapping turtles."

Marva laughed and tried to push away. "I was savoring your sweet quote, and then you go and spoil it with snapping turtles. Have you no romance in your soul?"

"I have," he protested, drawing her back. "As you know very well, woman."

Again the loon's call echoed across the lake.

A Letter to Our Readers

Dear Readers:

In order that we might better contribute to your reading enjoyment, we would appreciate your taking a few minutes to respond to the following questions. When completed, please return to the following: Fiction Editor, Barbour Publishing, Inc., P.O. Box 719, Uhrichsville, OH 44683.

1. Did you enjoy reading *Wisconsin Brides*?
   ❑ Very much—I would like to see more books like this.
   ❑ Moderately—I would have enjoyed it more if _____

_____

_____

2. What influenced your decision to purchase this book?
   (Check those that apply.)
   ❑ Cover   ❑ Back cover copy   ❑ Title   ❑ Price
   ❑ Friends   ❑ Publicity   ❑ Other

3. Which story was your favorite?
   ❑ *Time for a Miracle*   ❑ *Lonely in Longtree*
   ❑ *Myles from Anywhere*

4. Please check your age range:
   ❑ Under 18   ❑ 18–24   ❑ 25–34
   ❑ 35–45   ❑ 46–55   ❑ Over 55

5. How many hours per week do you read? _____

Name _____

Occupation _____

Address _____

City_____ State_____ Zip_____

E-mail_____